THE
GREAT
BIG ONE

J. C. GEIGER

LITTLE, BROWN AND COMPANY
New York   Boston

Copyright © 2021 by J. C. Geiger

Cover art © 2021 by Dana Ledl. Cover design by Angelie Yap. Cover copyright © 2021 by Hachette Book Group, Inc.

Little, Brown and Company
Hachette Book Group
1290 Avenue of the Americas, New York, NY 10104

Visit us at LBYR.com
First Edition: July 2021

Little, Brown and Company is a division of Hachette Book Group, Inc. The Little, Brown name and logo are trademarks of Hachette Book Group, Inc.

The publisher is not responsible for websites (or their content) that are not owned by the publisher.

Additional copyright/credits information is on page 379.

Library of Congress Cataloging-in-Publication Data
Names: Geiger, J. C. (Jeffrey Clayton), 1979– author.
Title: The great big one / by J. C. Geiger.
Description: First edition. | New York ; Boston : Little, Brown and Company, 2021. | Audience: Ages 14 & up. | Summary: Seventeen-year-old Griff has grown up in the shadow of his twin brother, Leo, and their prepper community, but hearing a radio broadcast of strange, beautiful music compels Griff to decide if surviving is truly living.
Identifiers: LCCN 2020041108 | ISBN 9780759555396 (hardcover) | ISBN 9780759555389 (ebook) | ISBN 9780759555372 (ebook other)
Subjects: CYAC: Survivalism—Fiction. | Brothers—Fiction. | Twins—Fiction. | Bands (Music)—Fiction. | Dating (Social customs)—Fiction. | High schools—Fiction. | Schools—Fiction.
Classification: LCC PZ7.1.G448 Gre 2021 | DDC [Fic]—dc23
LC record available at https://lccn.loc.gov/2020041108

ISBNs: 978-0-7595-5539-6 (hardcover), 978-0-7595-5538-9 (ebook)

Printed in the United States of America

LSC-C

Printing 1, 2021

• • •

For Emily,
who lights the lamp
and weathers the storms

OVERTURE

For all at last return to the sea—
to Oceanus, the ocean river, like
the ever-flowing stream of time,
the beginning and the end.

—RACHEL CARSON, *The Sea Around Us*

They're playing our song.
Can you see the lights?
Can you hear the hum?

—ISRAEL NEBEKER, "3 Rounds and a Sound"

ONE

THE OCEAN SENT MIXED SIGNALS.

It loved your precious heart; it meant to kill you.

The Pacific had given Clade City a gorgeous scribble of a white-sand beach, a lighthouse fine enough to stop your breath, and waves that drummed the shore like the world's oldest song. The town clung to the sea the way a barnacle cleaves to a humpback's belly, hanging windswept on the western edge of America with fisheries, state-of-the-art research facilities, and seaside tourist shops. Their town existed because of the ocean; the ocean would destroy them.

Every child in Clade City by about the age of six—old enough to read past the silent *T* in *tsunami* and pronounce *evacuation*—knew their days were numbered.

It was the only reason Griffin Tripp agreed to hang the siren.

"It's beautiful," his brother, Leo, said. "Just wait until you see it."

A siren was not the music Griff wanted to bring to his hometown. The ocean's song was reminder enough. The distant tide sang through the brothers' open bedroom window in brief, foggy summers, and raged on the battered jetties in winter. It whispered in the hollow mouths of shells in their mother's Main Street collectibles shop, which, at dusk, reflected the lighthouse in its tall windows. The beam seemed to grow solid in the low drizzle and swung like a ghost ship's golden boom, tacking in the wind.

WHOOMP!

When he'd been a boy of nine, music already deep in his bones, Griffin had imagined a sound to go along with the light. He'd lie in bed, watch the golden splash on his window, and whisper, puffing his lips—

Whoomp, whoomp—

The lighthouse was Griff's favorite part of Clade City. It felt safe.

The ocean was tricky. Romantic. You could harness it with a surfboard. It sang and dropped gifts at your feet, some all the way from Japan—license plates, fishing floats like opaque crystal balls. The gifts were stolen. It sank ships and ate their treasure. And just as tourists harvested shells, the ocean harvested tourists. Plucked them from rocky outcroppings like grapes. Put them in the headlines, never returned the bodies.

Dogs, children. It didn't matter.

In bed at night, Griff listened to the ocean's heartbeat, watched the lighthouse flash. It needed a sound.

Whoomp, Griff exhaled.

Leo, across the room, would say:

"Stop talking to yourself."

It was hard to explain he wasn't talking to himself. He was vocalizing for the lighthouse. That sounded strange. It's hard to keep secrets in a shared bedroom. Harder if you're a twin. A twin who shares your full biological curvature, slim eyebrows, fingernail moons, wide lips, angular chin. Same distance from nape of neck to shoulder blade.

Also, a mirrored internal circuitry. A twin innately knew the profane sewers and dreamy air ducts of your mind. Possessed the same map and skeleton key to every secret desire and absurd belief. Like the day in their father's truck, listening to the radio stations, when Leo said:

"Dad, can you tell Griff the music doesn't come from the lighthouse?"

They were eleven then.

Griff's cheeks burned because he had assumed something that—once brought into the daylight of rational conversation—made no sense whatsoever. A collection of old radios and tape decks once glimpsed in the lighthouse keeper's quarters had conjured a belief, planted a childish seed that, untended, had developed into a full-bloomed thought system Leo had somehow been able to see and expose. It was likely Leo had just—a moment before—confronted this same false belief in his own mind, and thus felt qualified to expose Griff to their father.

"No one broadcasts from the lighthouse," their dad said. "That's just old equipment."

"I know that," Griff said, staring at his feet.

The trouble with being born second.

Leo had maneuvered himself—in utero, likely with elbows and illegal kicks and eye-gouges—to the front of the birth order, saw the light three minutes earlier, and had seemed to be ahead ever since. When Griff turned seventeen, Leo was already seventeen and three minutes.

The first morning of their junior year, in their father's truck and on the way to K-NOW Radio, Leo was in the front seat as always. He was wearing the camouflage coat their father had given them to share and which Griff had worn exactly once. Leo was talking to their father about who would hang the siren.

"I'm happy to go up and rig it," Leo said.

He glanced back at Griff, like he was sniffing for competition.

Griff tried to want very few things.

He'd learned to keep his sparse wants behind a set of

imaginary white bricks in his mind, which he morticed into a barrier late at night, lying and waiting for sleep, sometimes still giving his breath permission to *whoomp, whoomp, whoomp*. Currently, two wants behind the wall. A late-night radio show, and the desire to know her better.

Would not name her, even in his mind. Not with Leo here.

Leo would intercept the thought like a rogue signal on their dad's transistor. Her name, so energetically palpable and electric in his mind—Griff suddenly became aware of how badly he wanted those two small things, so that the police lights flashing near the station seemed to be for him—a thought crime, all this wanting.

K-NOW 1590 AM Disaster Preparedness Radio stood at the western edge of downtown, a small glass box of a building on wooden stilts. Out in the front lot, leaning on his cruiser, Officer Dunbar. The man was white, stout, and hairless as a bar of soap. Full uniform, face splashed in emergency colors.

"What's with the lights?" Griff said.

"Look at him," Leo said. "The star of his own tiny crime drama."

Griff laughed.

"The story of one bald man," Griff said, doing a voice-over.

"On a quest for purpose," Leo said. "Searching for a killer. Or a friend."

"Be kind," their father said. "Think charitable thoughts."

Charitable! Of all the words. *Charity, Charity, Charity*— Griff gripped the seat, put the word out of his mind. Could his father see behind the wall?

They got out of the truck.

Dunbar and his father met with an elbow bump. The pandemic had erased handshakes from the Lost Coast Preppers. Nearly the whole Junior Prepper crew was there, in the parking lot. Dunbar's son, Jonesy, wore a camo hoodie and sunglasses, chewing and spitting sunflower seeds. Beside him, Slim. Also just starting their eleventh-grade year.

"Where's the gear?" Slim asked.

He was summer-tanned, rubber-banded together with nervous energy. Without tools to cling to, Slim's hands fussed and pinched and rubbed at the air. Dunbar pointed at the battered brown pickup, boils of saltwater rust over the wheel wells. In the bed, blue tarp lashed down and cinched tight. A tiny blade of yellow, shining from inside.

That was it.

"Scruggs is already on-air," Dunbar said. "Where's your boy?"

He was asking about Thomas. When they all turned to look at Griff, he felt a jolt of otherness. He was out of uniform. The lone jeans. Them: camo and Carhartts. Their haircuts, defined by clipper guards: Leo a number 6, Jonesy and Slim a number 3, Dunbar was a zero—the inevitable endgame of the clipper countdown. All but Griff wearing bulky paracord bracelets around their right wrists, just in case they suddenly needed an emergency bow-stringer, tourniquet, or horse halter.

Griff shrugged. Cotton jeans growing heavy in the drizzle.

The group perked up, attuned to the approaching sound.

Cherrrreeeeeereeeeup—che—che—che

"Here he comes," Jonesy said.

The ThunderChicken—a powder-blue Thunderbird renamed for its preternatural fan belt squeal—came screeching past their mother's shop, Shoreline Gifts, and blasting past the so-called Barmuda Triangle: the Drift Inn, the Sea Shanty, the Longhorn Pub—

CHEEREEREEREREREEEEP!

The Thunderbird bounced into the station's parking lot. Music spilling from the windows. AC/DC's "Thunderstruck."

Thomas belted the chorus, beat on the wheel. Smiled up at them. He'd timed that. He hand-cranked up his window and stepped out in full camouflage. Boots, shirt, pants, belt. Griff laughed.

God—were those camo *socks*? It was impossible to know if Thomas had done this ironically.

"Good morning, Thomas," Dunbar said.

"Good rising, Officer," Thomas said, squaring up with him. "No mourning here. We're saving lives. So how about 'good rising'?"

They did an elbow bump.

"I'll consider it," Dunbar said.

Thomas got away with more. He'd designed their famous Early Alert Response System (EARS) for the Great Cascadia Earthquake. It had taken months in his basement workshop. When Thomas committed, he was in it down to the socks.

"Let's get it done," Leo said. "Who's going up?"

Dunbar pulled around the bucket truck. One of those long-necked service vehicles recruited to repair snapped power lines and rescue treed cats.

"How about Mr. Blue Jeans?" Dunbar said, looking at Griff. This was dreadful.

At a workshop over the summer, Griff had successfully tied all twelve knots in a survival knot workshop and earned the unfortunate reputation of being *good with his hands*.

"He's good with his hands," Dunbar confided.

"They can both go," their father said.

Leo shot Griff a look, like it was Griff's fault. A sharp, snapping sound. In the pickup, the blue tarp sheeted up in the wind, a great glistening sail as Slim and Thomas pried off straps and bungees.

"Look at this sweet beauty!" Thomas said.

Big. The siren filled the truck bed. Screaming yellow. When

they stood it up, it was taller than his father. Cubed stump of a base, skinny neck. The mouth of the siren was square and toothless and wide enough to swallow a boy whole.

It took five of them to carry it to the bucket truck.

"Thing's heavier than our piano," Leo said. "Goddamn."

"Oops!" Dunbar said. Dunbar did not take the Lord's name in vain.

Dunbar, Griff, Leo, and Slim squeezed themselves into the bucket, which was like a high-walled white garbage can.

"Couldn't we have gotten a crane?" Slim asked.

"The crane's down at the deuce," Dunbar said.

Highway 2 carved delicate switchbacks eastbound through the Coast Range—the only way out of town. For years, it had been shedding pavement the way a dying glacier calves ice, losing great chunks of itself in flash floods and mudslides—described in Clade City parlance as "dropping a deuce."

The bucket truck jerked as it rose, wobbling, into the air. The siren slipped in Griff's hands. Top-heavy. Griff and Leo shouted, pulling it back upright.

"Why are we doing this?" Griff said. "On the first day of school?"

"That's why," Dunbar said.

He pointed south down the coast, to the Ruins. Though the ocean took regular nibbles of beaches and tourists—that was the time it took a bite. In 1964, the most devastating tsunami in US history made landfall in Clade City. Ocean waves got to 150 feet. Over a dozen people died.

That had been nothing. The big one, they'd been told, would knock San Francisco's bridges into the sea. Make Seattle skyscraper stew. Claw every small, scrappy town from the Pacific Coast. Flick Clade City from the map like a crumb hanging on the corner of God's Mouth.

"Get her up, boys!"

Without a crane, they had to lean way out. The slipping center of gravity made the bucket tip. Griff's stomach sloshed, flipped. He stepped wrong. His foot screamed under the weight, slipped with a squeal, and the whole yellow monster canted left, numb fingers screaming on the brittle housing.

"Damn it, Griff," Leo said.

As a group, they gathered their footing. They slipped the Thunderbolt's base over the pole. It slid home with the metallic scrape of a blade.

Back on the ground, Griff looked up. They'd stapled the bright yellow siren to Clade City's skyline.

"Are we going to give it a spin?" Leo asked.

"Of course," their father said, walking toward the ladder. "Griff? You're staying down here?"

Griff nodded. He just wanted to get to school.

The rest of them climbed the rungs to the radio tower. With Leo far away, behind glass, he allowed himself to want.

He closed his eyes in the drizzle. Wet, cold.

Charity Simms. A person who understood music.

He pictured their drive home, after the show in July. She'd asked him to ride home with her. Him, specifically, when she could've asked Leo or Thomas. Windows down, ringing ears. Wind whipping their hair like a wild storm. Her smile made something warm bloom in his chest when she lifted her gaze from the road and put it on him. The Martian-green glow of the dashboard, counting mile markers and willing them to freeze, asking that winding highway to please spool out and become a runway to the whole big world she talked about finding—

The siren shook him.

rrrrrrREEEEERERREREEEEEEEEEE

The brutal sound shaped the air, made his shirt hum on his damp skin. It was a soft noise, at first. Like an old door opening on rusty hinges. As it grew louder, the inner parts of his ears itched. He pictured the siren like a flood. Rushing through streets. Dripping from the eaves. It washed over the lighthouse, threatening to topple it.

Griff's breath caught.

What if the siren stopped it? Shattered the old Fresnel lens, the way a sudden jolt can shock an old heart to stillness.

Flash again, he thought. Flash one more time and I'll get to see her again.

Wanting something badly made death seem imminent. The disaster would surely happen now. The ground would choose this moment to shake and liquify and swallow him whole.

The lighthouse flashed.

Griff whispered to himself—

"Whoomp."

It felt like a prayer.

TWO

GRIFF CAUGHT A GLIMPSE OF CHARITY AT LUNCH—IN THE CAFETE-ria's long, tray-clattering line—white skirt, black top, and hair in loose, dark ringlets. Brown skin. Tall. It was her. Real. She looked better than he remembered, which he'd hoped would not be the case.

It made it less likely she'd sit with them.

"Think she'll come?" Thomas asked.

In a slight smile, Thomas revealed that he knew everything. If Thomas knew, Leo knew. Griff's cheeks burned; he had no chocolate. Chocolate helped sometimes, with a sudden rush of nausea and anxiety. The bite into a stiff, bitter bar of 70 per-cent dark could provide momentary reprieve, but all he had on his tray was a floury, floppy rectangle of cafeteria pizza. His existence seemed to coalesce there—hopeless, limp.

"Charity!"

His voice. Like the thought had gone bolting out of his own mouth—but it was Leo speaking. His brother stood, waving her over.

And she was coming.

Charity left a table of empirically more attractive people. Surfers, and others with unquestionable athletic gifts. She came to their table.

"My concert people!" she said.

Her posture, shoulders back, arms out. A hug, already? Leo

stepped up first. When it was Griff's turn—ah, the smell of her! It whipped up warm like July, turned the blank sky to a bowl of stars and campfire ash, ringing ears, and the buzzing didn't stop when Charity sat. They put words to the feeling, patching memories together, reconjuring the night of the show.

"—the path, coming out like, how does this barn even exist!"

"—that was just the opening set—"

"—I can't even talk about the encore," Charity said. "It might be too soon."

"Double encore," Griff said.

Leo sang a few bars from the final song—

I can't see what it will be—

"Stop now," Charity said. "You are dismantling me on the first day of school. I cried for like three weeks. I almost didn't go to that show."

She'd come alone.

Griff and Leo had spent a significant amount of time investigating the universe's mysteries. This was one of the greatest.

Charity Simms, a girl apparently dripping with friends, invitations, opportunities, had driven two hours to a show by herself. Griff had spotted her, studying the tour art pinned to the barn's exterior wall. Out of context—she'd looked like a familiar stranger. Someone he'd once met in a dream.

Thomas said it first:

"That's Charity Simms."

She'd been in Clade City since eighth grade. Griff remembered her arrival. The glittery, shooting-star popularity of the new kid—rocketing through the collective imagination of the school—*maybe she'll be my best friend, maybe we'll fall in love*—and of course Charity had found a superior group, some thrilling lover. Griff had stopped paying attention. It was as if she had vanished, and reappeared that night at the show. It killed him, knowing the months and years they'd been sharing classrooms and hallways.

"How are you, Griff?" she asked him.

Griff looked up at her.

"We hung the siren," Leo said, cutting him off. "Did you hear it?"

"You hung that horrible thing?" Charity asked. "I hate it."

"It's not supposed to sound good," Leo said. "It's supposed to keep us alive."

"They actually got it from right here," Thomas said. "Down in the boiler room. They had that sucker rigged up during the Cold War for duck-and-cover Tuesdays. My dad still remembers crawling under his desk and cursing the Russians."

"What's it for now?" Charity asked. "Like an air-raid siren?"

"The earthquake, mostly," Griff said.

"And here we thought fear was a thing of the past!" Thomas said. He did a great Mid-Atlantic accent, like a black-and-white-TV news anchor.

"That camo, Thomas. I didn't know you guys were so serious," Charity said.

"I'm in it for the radio show," Griff said.

"Yo," Thomas said.

Griff and Thomas high-fived.

"You're getting a radio show?" She smiled. "On the disaster channel?"

"Yep," Thomas said. "K-NOW Disaster Radio, late night. Griff and I will rock this sleepy little town to its core."

Thomas clenched his fist as if crushing an aluminum can.

"Really?" Leo said. "That's the secret plan? A graveyard radio show no one listens to?"

"I'll listen," Charity said.

"Our fans don't even know they're fans yet," Thomas said.

"Speaking of the siren," Leo said, "you know Thomas invented EARS."

"Thomas invented ears?" Charity said, pinching her lobes. Unattached.

"The Early Alert Response System," Leo said. She stared back. "EARS. For the Juan de Fuca Plate?"

Charity shrugged.

"Oh man." Thomas palmed his forehead. "What's the musical equivalent? That's like—you don't know the Beatles. Paul McWho?"

"The Cascadia Quake?" Leo said. "The big one?"

"The Rolling Whatsits?" Thomas said.

"I know about the impending tsunami," Charity said. "I just forgot the fault line's special name. I'm reminded regularly—I didn't grow up here."

Charity was looking at them differently. Whatever spider thread of a miracle had pulled her softly to their table was fraying. Griff could feel her about to stand up and float away.

"Did you see our water balloons?" Thomas asked. "The ones that said *Don't Turn Your Back on the Ocean*. My idea."

Not helpful.

"It's real," Leo said. "The quake is going to happen."

Charity looked across the cafeteria.

Past dozens of tables, buzzing conversations, two people alone.

Slim and Jonesy. She nodded toward them.

"True. But also—with every piece of camo, every hung siren and awareness campaign, you're all drifting closer to the Lonesome Table of Scary White Boys."

They assessed their fate in silence.

Jonesy ate his pizza with a stabbing motion, like it wasn't dead yet.

Slim was doing what? Stroking or—whittling, of all things. Whittling wood in front of God and everybody. Griff could attest that Slim was an artful whittler, cute animals and such, but did not think his repertoire would impact Charity's opinion.

"And poor Thomas in camo socks. You boys might already be too far gone," Charity said.

"I may be invisible," Thomas said, "but I can still hear you."

"It's just a phase," Griff said. "Remember in eighth grade, how he wore suits and carried a pocket watch?"

Charity squinted.

"Ohh," Charity said. "That was you, Thomas?"

"The Amazing Thomas to you," he said.

"And the semester he made balloon animals and dressed like a clown?"

"Wow," Charity said. "When I moved here I thought the town was full of weirdos. It was just Thomas in different costumes."

Griff laughed.

"So, Charity," Leo said. "How was the rest of summer? Still making music?"

Just like that, Leo cut in. Dropped the survival talk. Quick pivots. A master of the jibe—moving to catch someone's full interest, to get himself, eventually, where he wanted to be.

Charity shrugged.

"I had a few projects fall through," she said. "People flake. Stunning how folks cannot follow through. Do you have this problem? That's why I drove to the show by myself. I was like—to hell with those who cannot execute a plan."

"I follow through," Leo said.

"We do," Griff said. "Maybe we should see more shows together."

"Maybe we should have a band," Charity said.

"Us?" Thomas asked.

Charity shrugged.

"Y'all play piano," she said to Leo and Griff. "You're good. I can sing. Thomas, what can you do?"

"Make balloon animals and drop sick beats."

She laughed.

Thomas covered his mouth, made a few bass thumps, worked his hand like a DJ.

"That's terrifying," Charity said.

"He's got great recording gear," Leo said.

Charity raised an eyebrow. "Is that so?"

"Yeah," Griff said. "Like a total recording studio down in the Rat's Nest."

"In the what?" Charity asked.

"Very exclusive," Thomas said. "I'll see if I can get you in."

"He's good with sound," Leo said.

"Well, I'm serious," Charity said. "What else is there to do? We live in Clade City."

"Okay," Leo said. "We're now a band. The four of us."

Leo stood and high-fived each in turn, pinning them down into the plan like spokes in a wheel he'd built. But it still felt good. He was a master of certainty. Always the one to harvest wisps of late-night dream talk and bring the idea into daylight. Leo could turn a fantasy into a list and draw the map to get there.

So he led the conversation. Set their first date for a practice.

Here was the problem: Griff had dared to want something.

When they left the lunch table, Charity was walking with Leo.

THREE

B<small>ACK HOME THAT NIGHT, GRIFF WAS IN THE BATHROOM. LEO WAS</small> summoning him to practice.

Da dun!

C-sharps. The call from the Knabe piano. Another gauntlet. Another contest. Griff had just finished showering. He could hear the key-strikes through the drywall. Leo must've heard the water turn off. He went to the mirror, thinking of Charity. How she'd walked off with Leo.

Griff wiped the condensation from the mirror and relaxed his features.

Let his brow drop. Lips fall naturally.

When he looked at himself this way—straight-on—he saw Leo.

It was a habit, making himself ugly. Griff sucked in his chin. Puckered his lips. Showed imperfect bottom teeth and a whale of a tongue, crinkled his nose until the reflection fit.

Da dun!

The sharps struck the door like thrown knives.

It was from one of the pieces they were meant to learn for the winter concert. Hungarian Rhapsody No. 2. Strikingly beautiful, playful, and equally challenging to play with four hands as with two. An extremely popular piece. So much so that at a four-hand-piano music camp, players summoned one another to the bench by playing the opening two C-sharps. Leo had grabbed right on to that.

Da dun!

There was no avoiding it.

The French doors to the piano room were open. Their instrument was a thing of beauty. An 1887 Knabe, chestnut wood, meticulously cared for, with lush golden pedals and a soundboard that made every note ring full and soulful.

Leo rose from the bench. Stepped back.

"Glad you could make it," he said. "Ready?" They always played piano four hands. Their thing. Twenty fingers and eighty-eight keys. Their next show was incredibly ambitious. Stravinsky and Liszt. The Liszt should have been committed to minds and hands by August. Delayed due to a three-day survival camp in the Coastal Range, two bunker meetings per week, the Jams & Jellies Preservation Party, all Lost Coast Prepper commitments Leo attended with increasing frequency.

Together, they approached the bench. "I thought you didn't have time for music," Griff said. "Now you want to start a band?"

"I'll start a band with Charity," Leo said.

"You like Charity?" Griff asked.

"Who doesn't?" Leo asked. "Have you heard her sing?"

Why would this be any different than Milena in eighth grade? Why any different than the mysterious Australian girl, Rhiannon, on the beach last summer?

Leo had the bench too close. Griff jerked it backward.

Bench position was incredibly important. Distance from arms to elbows to wrists to fingers to keys was a game of inches, and it started with the bench. Leo looked down, scooted the bench forward. Leaned on it, like he was trying to burrow a hole in the carpet.

"It goes there," Leo said.

A famous family story: Once, on a family kayaking trip to Alaska, the burly guide had asked their mother and father if they wanted individual kayaks or a two-person model. When they picked the two-person, he shouted into the storage shed—One divorce boat!

Two people, one instrument—the same:

Divorce Piano.

Leo sat, so the bench couldn't be moved. "Let's play."

The first piece in the winter show would be a piano adaptation of Stravinsky's Symphony in Three Movements. With a full orchestra, the overture came barreling at you with blood-rushing theatrics, a giant swell of fearsome sound that felt more like climax than introduction—to Griff, it sounded thin on a solo piano, but Leo had chosen the work for its wild, virtuosic key-slides, flying fingers, and elbow-jerking theatrics.

All the best pyrotechnics on the bass clef.

Griff was left dangling on the treble, pecking out notes here and there, filling in. He got to shine in the second movement—andante. Slower. Deeper. The part in the show when Grandpa fell asleep and people went home.

When Griff brought up the Sleepy Grandpa Issue, Leo reassured him:

"The scherzo, bro! We've got to make them earn it!"

The final act. The Italians call it scherzo—(pronounced *scared-so*): the joke, the dance. Here, the twins would trade sides on the bench, leapfrogging fluttering hands to pound octaves on opposite sides of the imaginary-mirror line that split them, giving the audience thrilling, if slightly contrived, twin-bending thrills!

Griff loved playing this way with his brother. Leo was fun, but lately, he'd worked only on the overture. A gnawing suspicion that Leo would never play the scherzo with him. Maybe he only intended to play the first movement, win Charity's heart, and leave Griff dribbling out with his tinkle-tinkle andante. Even now, as Griff took his turn with a slow, measured section, Leo took one hand off his side of the piano and checked his phone.

"Seriously?" Griff said.

"Sorry!"

"Skip it," Griff said. "Let's do the scherzo. Or Liszt."

"Let's go rock star," Leo said, confirming Griff's suspicion about the scherzo.

Leo meant Franz Liszt—composer, pianist, the first rock star in the world. The man who pioneered playing in profile to the audience. Stunning hair. Jawline suitable for a minted coin. Apparently, women would pelt Liszt with medieval undergarments. Griff wondered if he'd been knocked over by ancient underwear—industrial belts, buckles, steel hoops.

"Just one bra," Leo had said, choosing the piece. "That's all I ask for."

Again, Leo played the opening C-sharps:

Da dun!

This was the hardest possible engraving of the piece. Between bunker meetings and survival camps, Griff had spent comparatively more time on the keys. Secret practices. His goal, to leave Leo gobsmacked at the cadenza. They played slowly. Then faster. Their first time in over a week.

The piano bench shook beneath their weight.

Four-hands playing was like call-and-response:

Are you there, brother?

Right here, Leo.

Can you keep up, brother?

Damn right.

"Been playing a lot?" Leo asked, breathing hard.

"Maybe," Griff said. He turned the page.

The stand, thick with duets—page turning was his job. Griff, who had the song committed to memory. And when he turned the page, Leo often whispered—*good*. That little breath. Infuriating.

"Good," Leo said. "Slower."

Not tonight. Leo pounded harder, trying to compensate for Griff's superior finger-rolls. For once, Griff was playing better. They hadn't even reached the cadenza—the optional improvisation *at liberty, as you desire*—which Griff had drilled for hours. Hands flying, pounding, Griff hit his hardest arpeggio, fingers blasting to the key block and back—Leo grabbed his wrist.

"Where's your bracelet?" he asked.

"Hey!" Griff said, shaking free. "What was that? Let go!"

Griff leapt up from the bench.

"I can't believe you grabbed me."

"Sorry, I just noticed," Leo said. "You should never take that off. That's life or death."

"Life or death at the piano?" Griff said.

"You never know when it's coming."

The bracelet was a gift from their father. Twin paracords. One white, one black. Woven in a clever way that mimicked piano keys.

"Plus, we should match," Leo said.

Griff stared at Leo. Was this asshole serious?

Griff had learned he could not win a direct argument with Leo. He must be like water. Absorb impact. Flow away from conflict. Drip down through floorboard cracks in the sacred crawl space even Leo couldn't see. There, Griff buried his minor, essential pieces of resistance.

He told himself: I will never wear that bracelet, brother.

Griff thought it deep into the dirt.

Leo looked at him, prying with his eyes.

"Dinner!" their mother called. "Special Corn."

"Where have you been practicing?" Leo asked, standing.

"Your mom's house," Griff said, slapping him on the back of the head.

Leo punched him and then they crashed into the wall, headlocked—but the fight had somewhere to go. An old, ingrained tradition to race like human bumper cars to the table when there was Special Corn involved, pinging off the hallway walls as they raced to get there first.

So that's what they did.

FOUR

THE NEXT DAY—THEIR FIRST FULL DAY OF CLASSES—A SIXTH-
period miracle.

Charity was in Griff's study hall.

There she was. Sitting at a four-person table in the library.

Never once had Griff received a gift from the Scheduling Gods. Forever separated from Thomas. Every potential crush had landed in the wrong homeroom, the opposite table group—but this made up for everything.

Griff cupped his face. He breathed deeply.

"Thank you," he whispered.

A square of light fell from a high window and came to rest on her lower neck—a miraculous clavicle—glowing as if spotlit by museum directors. He walked in and promptly ignored her.

Turned toward books.

He took a breath. He must sit far away. He could in no possible way picture himself walking up to the table, saying hello, sitting down.

"Hey," she said.

Looking at him.

Hey—the same way Griff's father said it when he didn't know which son.

"Griff," Griff said.

He pointed to himself when he said it. Like a caveman—oh man.

"I know." She smiled. "You have homework yet?"

"Syllabus week," Griff said.

"Right?" She laughed. "Killing time. Do you like puzzles?"

Sure, he could like puzzles. They went over to the pile of games. Being the beginning of the year, everything was neatly stacked and ready. She went straight for the jigsaws.

"I don't mess with any less than five hundred pieces," she said.

"You're into puzzles."

"Just like you guys," Charity said. "My life is mostly about survival. When you spend your life in church basements, you do what you have to. Let's do a big bad one."

"Well," Griff said. "This is the stupidest one."

"Oh yeah," she said. "Love it."

The puzzle, *Open Water*, was based on an award-winning painting in Grand Rapids. A thousand pieces cast in subtle shades of blue and white. They tipped the puzzle onto the table. The water was almost as inscrutable as the brown cardboard backing.

"I feel absolutely destined for failure," Griff said.

She looked at him.

"C'mon now. Apply some strategy. Edges. Corners. Look for anything that stands out. Right there. Little piece of sunlight."

Near the center, a bright sunburst struck the water. They searched for it, flipping pieces. Griff couldn't think of a single word to float over to her. Head full of stupid synonyms— *turquoise, aqua, periwinkle, azure, cerulean*, another word for *blue*.

"What did you do all summer?" Griff asked, finally.

Brilliant query, Inquisitor!

"Went to LA," she said. "Caught up with friends."

"The ones who flaked on you?"

He bit the inside of his cheek.

"Some," she said. He had her eyes now. Soft, golden. "I miss them. No one here makes me laugh like them. You know, when you just have that flow with people?"

"I do. Thomas makes me laugh harder than anyone."

"Yeah," she said. "I'm looking forward to laughing with you and Thomas."

What did he say now? Griff reached into his backpack. Endorphins needed. Snapped off a piece of chocolate and placed it under his tongue. Good stuff. Melted slow with notes of berry and plum and what tree bark would taste like in heaven.

She smiled at him. Confidence and chocolate surged in the blood.

"You really want to be in a band with us?" Griff asked.

"Do you always carry around chocolate?"

He snapped her off a piece.

"Mmm," she said, closing her eyes. "That is good. I think yes."

"Who do you usually hang out with?" Griff asked.

Charity stared at him. "Want to know a secret?"

She motioned him in.

"Nobody," she whispered.

"Really?"

"Yeah," she said. "I've been keeping that secret since I moved here."

"You always seem to be with people."

"When your secret is being lonely, sometimes you need people to help you keep it."

Her honesty pulled like a draft through an open door. He could fall straight in.

"You're lonely?" Griff asked. How, then, could there be hope for anyone? "Will you go back to LA after next year?"

She shrugged, ran a hand through her long black curls.

"I think—it's like we talked about after the show. I'm following the music. Wherever it goes. It's a big world out there."

It's a big world out there.

The words rang a bell in his chest.

"Well," Griff said. "Now we have a band."

"Yeah," she said. "I need it bad after this summer. Mother Simms's Crazy Carnival of Church Camps. Catholic Ladies' Camp. Lady Rangers Camp. Touchdown Jesus Camp."

"Touchdown Jesus?" Griff said.

"In Colorado," she said. "Jesus stands on a hill like this."

Charity held her hands in the air. Griff laughed.

"Do you like it?"

Her eyes went still, looking into last summer.

"Parts of it," she said.

"What was the best part?"

He offered her more chocolate.

She smiled. "You want the truth?"

"Let's be real," Griff said. "We could die tomorrow."

"Skinny-dipping," she said.

Griff made sure the words he heard matched her lips. Ran them over in his head.

"You swam naked?" he asked.

"Shhh," she said. "Don't boys always do that?"

"Always?" Griff said. Where had she gotten her information about boys? "Have you been in the ocean here? I wouldn't find my testicles until next July."

He was chocolate-drunk. She laughed.

"So you've never?" she asked.

"I'd be terrified."

"Ha! The survivalist!" she said. "What's terrifying? It's just you out there."

"What's more terrifying than that?"

"Vale la pena," she said, then looked at him. "Worth the risk."

"Spanish?"

"It comes out in the summer," she said. "My dad's Dominican."

It was the first time she'd mentioned her father. They'd talked for hours on the way home from the Collection show, but almost all about music. First the show itself—then the life-altering power of a song. How the right one at the right time could sear itself into a season. Pull you apart, put you together. It was then he'd decided to get the radio show. He wanted to be on-air, playing the perfect song for whoever was listening.

"Hey," Charity said. "Where do you go when you do that, with the glassy eyes?"

His throat tightened. He'd gotten lost behind his brick wall of wanting.

"You want the truth?" he said.

"Yep," she said. "We're dead tomorrow."

"Sometimes I'm thinking about what I want," Griff said. "Sometimes I'm trying to figure out the secrets of the universe."

"Ooo," she said. "Tell me more."

"There's this box in our bedroom."

"You share a room?" Her nose scrunched up. "That's cute."

He bit his cheek.

"Anyhow, there's this mailbox—"

"The TOE Box!" Charity said.

He stared—did others keep TOE Boxes?

"Leo was telling me about your files," she said. "Tell me more."

Leo. Pilfering all their best idiosyncrasies for his own

endearing purposes. Asshole! What could Griff tell her to appear more fascinating? Political coincidences? Astrological observations?

"So Einstein said 'God does not play dice with the universe.' It means, everything fits together somehow. From the stars to subatomic particles. It's all part of the same story."

"Like what?" Charity asked.

"Take the moon," Griff said. "The moon's polar circumference is 27.3 percent of the Earth's circumference, and the moon orbits the Earth every 27.3 days. Also, the Earth turns 366 times each orbit of the sun. And the moon orbits the Earth 366 times every 10,000 days."

"What's that mean?" she asked.

"Who knows?" Griff said. "But it feels like a plan. A secret map in the stars. Hidden in white noise. If you listen hard enough, it's almost like a voice trying to whisper something."

Charity leaned over the puzzle. Whispered:

"What's the voice say?"

He smiled.

"Have you ever heard of the Skip?"

"No."

She didn't know!

"Oh my god," Griff said. "This is like—I get to give you a gift. The Skip is about radio waves. The way they behave, but only at night."

"Only at night?"

A warm memory—the evening in their father's workshop when Griff learned how to catch a song. He and Leo, taking turns, exploring the AM radio band. He could tell her everything. And then Charity was looking up.

Leo.

Impossible, but Leo was now walking into the library. That

way he walked at things, like he was chasing something to wrestle it to the ground.

"Study hall together?" he said. "That's lucky."

"Where are you supposed to be?" Griff asked.

"Wherever I want," Leo said. "Independent study."

Leo was supposed to be playing piano.

"Griff was telling me about the Skip," Charity said.

Leo raised his eyebrows. "Where's your teacher?"

Griff and Charity looked. Mr. Michaelson was nowhere in sight. When they looked back at Leo, he was smiling like he'd gotten away with something. Please, no, Griff thought—what's his plan? Please don't let him transfer into this study hall.

"Friday," Leo said. "Band practice. Thomas's place."

"I'll see what the Warden says," Charity said.

"We can always sneak you out," Leo said.

He winked. Leo could wink with impunity. Perform shoulder touches. If it was Leo at this table, he and Charity would've stripped down to nothing and gone swimming naked in the puzzle.

"Tell me more," Charity asked when Leo finally left.

The bell made Griff jump in his seat.

Time had run out.

FIVE

Wednesday evening, blindfolded in the backseat of his father's truck, Griff considered Charity's comment.

You boys might already be too far gone.

Griff was blindfolded because he was not yet in the inner circle. If you had a bunker, you didn't tell anyone. Passcodes and encrypted maps. Acronyms like SHTF and TEOTWAWKI, because when Shit Hit The Fan and it was The End Of The World As We Know It, there would only be so much to go around.

Griff jolted in the truck, teeth clicking.

Something about blindfolds made him feel like he had a rag stuffed in his mouth. Like it was hard to breathe. The truck bent left, floating around a hairpin turn. He focused on the rise and fall of his chest. Facts.

This was okay. Not terribly strange.

Thousands of backyard bunkers in the US. There were Raven Rock and Mount Weather for government employees. Rising S, named after the Rising Son Jesus Christ, which offered basic backyard models and UnderEarth Luxury Condos. Underground dog parks, movie theaters, saunas, in-ground pools. Bunkers were the United States of America's new gated communities.

The truck stopped, engine ticking.

"Clear," his father said.

Griff removed his blindfold and squinted, sweat chilling the creases of his eyes. They were parked on Highway 2. At the cusp of the redwood forests, the air hung heavy, chilled with mist. They walked into a grove of ash trees, each an identical height and wingspan. It tickled the primal brain with a flutter of panic—trees don't grow up naturally together and all at once unless something bad happened.

They walked into the woods. Sky darkened.

Leo and their father walked up ahead, talking too low to hear. They used to walk all together. Mosquitos here, notoriously small and quick, drawn to the damp corners of your eyes. A whine in Griff's left ear. He slapped at it. Jammed a finger in. Nothing. You couldn't catch them.

They walked for half an hour.

In a nondescript clearing, they stopped at a concrete plug in the earth. Their father got on his knees and showed his face to the camera. The bunker plug made a deep-throated click. Griff was last inside the vertical tunnel. Welded rungs bubbled up where they met concrete. The powdery dry-goods scent made his throat constrict. In a town where the greatest threat was a tsunami, it seemed unwise to descend into an airless cement egg in the ground.

Someone belched in the main room. You could smell every bodily thing.

Griff followed Leo and his father past a sign printed on typing paper in bold font, duct-taped at the corners:

COMMUNITY ROOM

The space was roughly the size of a small classroom. Bricked in by neatly packed Rubbermaids, stackable blue bricks of purified water, and sealed #10 cans that held the provisions for a survival force of twelve:

4800 pounds of hard white grains
360 pounds of powdered milk and canned cheese
720 pounds of sugar
72 pounds of powdered eggs and baking powder
72 pounds of salt
360 pounds of fat
720 pounds of beans and lentils

Survival had a powdery taste.

Griff looked into the room at the other Preppers bleached white by LED lights. He felt the gravity of Scruggs's approaching beard before he saw him. Even post-pandemic, the Senior Prepper was a hugger.

"Hey, buddy!" Scruggs said.

Griff's vision was eclipsed by the man's wreath of facial hair, squeezed by strong arms and a broad chest. Griff couldn't fathom why someone so genuinely joyful could live by himself, have so little to do. Aside from the radio station, a beard was the closest thing Scruggs had to a hobby.

"Missed seeing you at the Hanging," Scruggs said. He chewed his lip, like something was wrong. "You and Thomas still planning to do a late-night show?"

"Oh yeah," Griff said. "If you've still got space."

"All we got is space and time," Scruggs said. "Let's get you trained up. Thomas, you still in?"

"Rock and roll!" Thomas called from across the room.

It felt good. Something he could do that Leo couldn't touch.

Dunbar used a bike bell to bring them to order.

Each member took a seat in a stackable green chair: Jonesy, Slim, Dunbar, Thomas, their father. Jonesy took a Bug Detector from the shelf and scanned the room. Griff tapped his own pocket. He'd remembered this time.

"Scruggs," Jonesy said.

"Oops, dangit," Scruggs said. He took his phone from his pocket and removed the battery. Standard security protocol.

The first item of business was the Board—a ten-foot magnetic spreadsheet with DISASTER TYPE (Y-axis) vs. THREAT LEVEL (X-axis). Current potential disasters included:

Mudslide
Forest Fire
Terrorism
EMPs
Solar Flares
Global Pandemic
The Great Big One
Nuclear Strike
Dirty Bomb

Threat levels: MILD, MODERATE, SEVERE, IMPENDING, INEVITABLE. Being September, forest fires dialed back from Severe to Moderate. Pandemic moved from Moderate to Severe. The Great Big One never budged from Impending, and the most robust conversation happened around Nuclear Strike. Dunbar perseverated on the likelihood of being nuked, maybe because that was the only scenario in which the bunker made sense.

Griff had initially found these conversations fascinating. Terrifying, even.

They'd watched videos of nuclear tests. Like God breathing fire. Nevada palms turned to feather dusters, then dust. The nuclear flash burned shadows into permanent ink stains and turned sand to melted glass. Kilotons, megatons. The bunker felt like the most thrilling backyard fort a boy could dream up and a man could build.

Now Griff mainly dwelled on the shrinking chance of losing his virginity before the apocalypse.

"We've got intel on twenty-three new missing warheads—" Dunbar said.

Sitting up in his green plastic chair, Griff contemplated never having laid his hands on an actual set of breasts. The mechanics of clasps and the one-handed bra removal trick Leo had bragged about. Despite his ability to tie knots. One simple clasp. Griff's fingers fidgeted, imagining. Clasp, release.

"—a single activated warhead can deploy a cluster of thirty-six devastating explosions, and I don't need to remind you that this will make Hiroshima look like a game of patty-cake—"

Griff sized up his fellow Preppers. Fairly certain all of them, even Jonesy, had probably been with a girl or at least made out for a satisfactory amount of time. He felt a sudden surge of jealousy. It seemed impossible anyone would let these boys' tongues, willingly, into their mouths. And here he was, thoughtful. Cared about music. Played piano. Yet something was apparently wrong with him—

"—the fires would be worse than the bombs, we'd get swallowed—"

Griff paid attention to his mouth. Ran his tongue along his teeth. Licked his lips. Could he do it properly? What if the Thunderbolt 1000T went off—could he kiss and be kissed? He retreated to the fantasy scenario in which the school reacted to news of impending doom by flying into unbridled, erotic abandon. Couples shoving up against lockers, on the floor, shutting themselves into supply closets, whipping off clothes as sirens wailed and the impending apocalypse counted down to zero—

The conversation moved to the lighthouse.

Griff perked up. This was important.

Dunbar had continued to repeat his idea, steady as war drums.

"We need to deal with the lighthouse."

Meaning: convert it from a lighthouse to a military-style outpost. A long-simmering idea among the Preppers. Remove the only Fresnel light on this stretch of the coast. A two-ton, steel-and-glass miracle of engineering. Hundreds of concentric rings in a bull's-eye pattern, visible for over 20 miles. They wanted to replace it with equipment to monitor incoming warheads, sea levels, the unsubstantiated threat of patrolling Russian submarines.

"Not like a lighthouse is useful," Jonesy said.

"Not for the last few decades," Dunbar said, agreeing with his son.

"It's good for tourism dollars," Griff's father said. Smart. He knew the word *dollars* would find purchase somewhere in the slick interior of Dunbar's mind.

"Then who is on SubWatch this week?" Dunbar asked.

Griff let his eyes go blank. Imagined little glass plates in front of them. SubWatch, as a duty, was the Prepper equivalent of scrubbing toilets. Outside in waders. Holding a giant copper receiver. Listening to the wordless thrum of low-frequency broadcasts until you prayed for someone to please just bomb the coast already.

"See?" Dunbar said. "Everyone wants to save the lighthouse, but no one wants to work!" Jonesy finally volunteered, and they moved on to assigning the three available alert tones for the Thunderbolt 1000T siren. Tone one would signify a warning for the Cascadia Subduction Earthquake. Tone two: Nuclear Attack. After a debate on wildfires vs. mudslides vs. terrorist incursion, they agreed the most practical use for tone three would be to announce monthly city council meetings, as tardiness had become an issue.

Dunbar played the three tones on his bunker stereo. Tone one. Tone two. Tone three. He played them again. Everyone leaned forward, squinting. Griff could not tell the difference between the tones. Leo and he exchanged a look like, *what the hell?*

"They all sound the same," Griff said.

"They do not," Dunbar said. "What do you think, Leo?"

"More or less," Leo said. "Like any three AC/DC songs."

"Oooo," Jonesy said. The whole room looked at Thomas.

"That comment has been logged for future retribution," Thomas said.

"That's kind of a problem," Griff said.

"Yes," Griff's dad said. "We don't want people to mishear. They could show up for a meeting on proper land use development and get vaporized by a Russian nuke."

"Or pancaked by a Pacific Goddammit," Thomas said, smiling. Thomas had a number of them—Pacific Goddammit, the Cascadia ComeGetcha, the Juan DeFucYou.

"Oops!" Dunbar said.

Conversation drifted to a better siren, problems with mounting, and Dunbar's mind rolled back downhill on one of the few paths available and landed back at the lighthouse.

"That darn lighthouse is the pretty little albatross around our neck," Dunbar said.

Griff's mind could not ride these rails anymore. He reached for his chocolate bar, which had become an empty wrapper. He slapped his crinkling pocket.

Never mind one had to kill an albatross before having it tied around one's neck—that being the *point* of the albatross-around-the-neck—he would not win this fight with a demand for accurate metaphors. How had the search for truth led him to this bunker?

Nights, once spent digging through their grandfather's

Mysteries of the Unknown books, up late on the computer, piecing together the riddles of the world—Catatumbo lightning, the secret language of trees, riddles of the afterlife—the feeling that you could lie on your back in the lawn and fall up into the stars and never stop—how *enormous* it felt. Secrets so important they needed to be guarded like treasure.

They'd found the old federal mailbox outside Downtown Depot. Abandoned. Waiting for them like another sharp corner of the universe's puzzle. They'd hauled it home four awful blocks with one broken flip-flop and a bloody toe and they'd painted it black and decorated it with TOE, their first secret acronym—the TOE Box—out of reverence for Griff's poor toe, but the letters stood for the Theory Of Everything, because anything less than the perfect intersection of science, and magic, and love was beneath them. Just two years ago, they'd both known what Charity still knew—it was a great big world out there.

Life had gotten small.

Small chairs. A small room. Scruggs took out a small flask and tipped it into his beard. Jonesy and Slim spat small black seeds into their small cups. Even Jonesy used to talk about extraterrestrial life and watch the sky for UFOs. What happened here?

"Well, okay," Dunbar said. "Done."

Dunbar rang the bike bell.

They stood for the postmeeting Hangout. Slim, Jonesy, Thomas, Dunbar, Leo, and their dad stood in a circle. Each man roughly the same distance from the next. Like mutually repellent magnets. Drinking. Spitting seeds. This was the Hangout.

"Given any thought to the Gap?" Dunbar asked Griff.

The Gap was the one-year program after high school based in Arizona, meant to give graduating seniors a year of practical survival experience instead of college. He had no desire to go.

— 38 —

"I've given it some thought," Griff said. He tried to breathe. The bunker air felt sandy.

Mouth on autopilot. Saying whatever slippery thing could get him out of the conversation. Slim brought in the indestructible yellow DeWalt stereo. Griff's father poured brown whisky for the adults. Griff felt like a candle being snuffed. Flickering for lack of oxygen.

He walked quickly through the group, toward the ladder, praying the concrete plug would open, praying the whole big impossible world was still up there where he'd left it.

● ● ●

At home, Griff and Leo lay in bed. The lighthouse flashed on the window. Waves drummed.

"Bro?" Leo asked. "What happened down there?"

"Whoomp," Griff whispered.

"You kind of lost it."

Griff stared at his brother. A smudge in dim light, propped on his elbow. They used to talk for hours this way.

"Do you ever still have night terrors?" Griff asked.

For years, Leo used to wake up thrashing. Screaming with his eyes open. Gasping, he clawed up through the air like a desperate swimmer. Griff would try to shake him awake. One night, his father had lifted his flailing son into the shower with ice-cold water and Leo had shrieked as if being stabbed. That's how they learned not to wake him. During night terrors, the victim must wake themselves.

"Not for a long time," Leo said softly.

"What stopped them?"

He was quiet.

"Maybe the range," Leo said.

"C'mon."

"Shooting is meditative," Leo said. "It's about breathing. You should try it. You know, you might want to get more involved. We've actually got a good crew down there."

"Jonesy?" Griff said.

"So you want to be outcasts again?" his brother asked. "Go back to the Tripp Me Twins?"

Griff held his breath. Leo's words conjured the horrors of middle school hallways.

"We finally belong, bro," Leo whispered.

No, Griff thought. For the guys in the bunker, music was a light switch. Something you turned on or off. And they liked pieces of Griff. His accuracy with a nail gun. Occasional jokes. Knots he tied. Small features of his personality, sorted and lifeless as equipment on a table. This group of friends reflected him like a warped mirror. After too long, he'd start to resemble the reflection.

"I just feel like there's more out there," Griff said.

When the lighthouse flashed, it limned their window in white light.

"There is," Leo said softly. "There's Charity."

SIX

THE MORTIMER ESTATE STOOD PROMINENTLY AT THE CORNER OF Fifth and Price, blue, three stories high, and shaped like a pretentious high-backed sofa. Griff, Leo, Thomas, and Charity assembled on the front patio and Thomas gave them a warning.

"I'm not trying to scare you," Thomas said. "But my parents should be avoided at all costs."

"I'm already scared," Charity said.

Leo giggled. He was always giddy at the start of a new plan. A band! With Charity on Thomas's front patio, everything felt brand-new.

"My father, Halford Mortimer, roams the house like a Dickensian ghost," Thomas said. "His soul has been vacuumed up by endless stock trading. If he looks you directly in the eye, you will be transformed into a large pile of numbers."

Charity laughed.

"My mother, at this ripe old hour of seven, has likely transformed from a kindly homemaker into the Shambling Gin-Breathed Zombie." He pointed. "Avoid the CigBiz."

"CigBiz?" Charity asked.

"S, G, B, Z," Griff said. "CigBiz."

"I see," Charity said.

"Okay, team. Shoes off."

Charity removed her shoes. Fashionable canvas shoes with cool frayed laces. Bare feet slipped out. Toes!

They entered the house. An ocean of white carpet lay between them and the basement steps. To the right, a room arranged like a furniture showroom, mirrors glinting in curio cabinets. Thomas stepped as if probing a frozen pond for cracks. Leo used the fox-walk stalking technique—heel first, rolling his foot. Soundless.

A creak. They jolted.

A figure suddenly rounded the corner by the stairway. A tall, pale man—chinless as a pencil. They froze, staring at him like a deer they'd chanced upon in a misty clearing.

"Hal?" a voice called from deep in the house.

Mr. Mortimer gave them an understanding nod, then vanished up the steps. The group crossed the room, bursting into giggles as they ricocheted down into the basement, past wood-paneled walls to the workshop door:

A wooden sign above the entrance marked with Sharpie:

THE RAT'S NEST

The name originated with Mrs. Mortimer, who, when agitated, would rail about Thomas *ratholing* himself in the basement for hours, *ratholing* their family's community property, *ratholing* visitors and guests.

"*Ratholing*," Thomas concluded, "is a great word."

And here was Charity. At the Rat's Nest. Such a strange feeling, to be near her, living and breathing—

Thomas opened the door.

A vast space, largely unfinished, with an odor like a wood-chip playground and old books. Exposed pipes. Small ribboned flags crisscrossed the ceiling, pegboards outlined in marker. Distantly, floor-length tapestries carved the space into mysterious enclosures. And in the center—the workbench. It exerted its own gravity, drew them close.

"My god," Charity said. "What a lair."

On the bench, three opaque spheres roughly the size of tennis balls. Around them, a confetti of circuitry.

"EARS," Thomas said.

"Thomas invented ears," Charity said matter-of-factly.

"See," he said, "there are fifty-two of these submerged up and down the Pacific Coast. Temperature sensors. Electromagnetic detectors. Pinhole cameras."

"Can I touch one?" Charity asked.

She reached out for an orb, the size of a Christmas ornament. Translucent, squishy like a rubber ball. Inside, a soldered nest of circuits and wires. Twinkling solar panels. Thomas unrolled a bag of tortilla chips.

"Amazing," she said.

"If it works," Thomas said, "it buys us seven to ten minutes advance notice."

"That's it?" she asked.

"Every second counts," he said.

Thomas ate chips by placing them in his flat palm, then forcing his palm against his mouth like a sucker fish that had never discovered fingers. Charity stepped back from falling chips. Looked at the ground. Froze.

"What's that?" she asked. "Cat?"

Thomas shook his head.

Charity stared at her bare feet.

"Rat?" Charity asked.

"Shit, Thomas," Griff said. Leo and Griff exchanged a look. They were going to lose her.

"It's just Neapolitan."

Thomas crouched and made a chirping sound in the back of his throat. The rat was in Thomas's hands now. White fur with chocolate-colored splotches. Pink eyes and claws. All the colors of Neapolitan ice cream.

"Cute," Charity said. "Why a rat?"

"It's my first disaster alert system," Thomas said. He extended his hand. The rat moved from his palm to Charity's. She gasped.

"Oh my gosh," she said.

Neapolitan turned, exposing her long, earthworm tail.

"Uuff," Charity said. "That tail, though."

"I know," Thomas said. "If people could cope with rat tails we'd save thousands of lives."

"Hey, all," Leo said with his best smile. "Should we start practicing? You should see this gear, Charity."

"What do you mean, Thomas?" Charity asked.

"My original plan for an alert system was the Clade City Promise! Everyone gets 10 acres and a free rat."

"Are you kidding?"

"He's not," Griff said.

"Look," Thomas said. "Rats know before people do. Helice, Greece, 300 BC, rats poured onto the roads and climbed the hill to Corinth five days before the earthquake hit. Five days! Same thing in Haicheng, China, rats and toads and snakes came out of hibernation and in Thailand, in 2004, it was fla-mingos and rats and elephants—"

When Thomas got really excited about a concept, sometimes spit formed at the corners of his mouth, and Griff was getting nervous about how long he would talk when Leo called—

"C'mon, guys!"

"Maybe we should go play," Griff said.

"Okay," Charity said. "Fascinating, Thomas."

Neapolitan squirreled around in her palm. Leapt onto the floor.

The practice space was framed by hanging curtains C-clamped and clothespinned to exposed floor joists and cables—very cool. A keyboard. Guitar in a cradle. Drum kit and serious audio decks. Six different pedals plugged into a sound-mixing nerve center. Four microphones.

"Wow," Charity said. "What a playground. You gonna drop some sick beats, Thomas?"

And then something happened. Surrounded by instruments and colorful tapestries, sealed off in the basement, Griff stopped thinking she'd run. It felt like they belonged just where they were.

Thomas dropped some beats. A low bass pulse in his throat, hissing through his teeth like a hi-hat cymbal. Funny, but good. Griff played a few major chord progressions on the keyboard and a song whipped up out of nothing.

"Keep it going," Charity said. She came over to Thomas's microphone.

"My name is Thomas Mortimer," he sang, spitting words like a drumbeat.

"—and he's got ratssssss," Charity sang.

"You need evacuation routes, and I got maps—"

"You need a couple bug-out bags, I'll show you where they at—"

Griff played a solo—bright, funky thing—then Leo jumped in. They kept it rolling. Not like a practice room, or a concert. They were just playing together.

"Okay," Leo said when the energy finally calmed. "Should we practice for real?"

"That felt like practice," Charity said. "It was fun."

"I thought we'd pull together an actual song," Leo said.

"What's that look like to you?" she asked.

"I've been working on a few things," he said.

Leo pulled out a binder.

Suddenly it became Leo's practice. The room seemed to shrink around him. Leo's first song, "Old Country Bridge," relied heavily on imagery of dry riverbeds and the brightest stars he'd ever seen. He sang the first chorus alone. The second time through, wordless sounds joined with the music, perfect pitch. Griff mistook it for one of Thomas's sound board miracles—it was Charity.

Her eyes closed, lips near the microphone. Humming. A crooning sound, from some deep, hidden place. Her voice cast a spell. Like striking a match in darkness and seeing, briefly, the flash of a cathedral.

Leo stopped.

"Could you put words to that?" he asked.

"Hmm?" Charity asked, seeming to come out of a trance.

"Maybe echo my lyrics back?" Leo asked. "Could we try that?"

Charity did what he asked. Leo had plenty of corrections. As minutes passed, her voice crawled from her chest to her throat and then lived mostly in her mouth. After an hour, Leo announced:

"I think we have a song!"

"I think we've got a band!" Thomas said. Practice was over.

Griff was still puzzling through it—the feel of Charity's voice, the unexpected magic of their first song—and then Leo, ahead of the game with a binder, a stack of songs, and now, again, Griff moving too slowly through the mud of thinking to recognize Leo had already leapt ahead into the most important race of the night:

The Walk to the Big Blue Chair. Big enough for two.

Griff had learned that the making of a couple often happened with the same split-second thunder of a hawk snatching up a vole. On the California beach, with the sweet Australian girl, Rhiannon, she and Griff had laughed more and talked longer. Built a sand castle together, with a far superior moat. But when they all stood to see the sunset, Leo grabbed her hand first. Just like that.

Rhiannon and Leo walked. Talked. Kissed. Griff watched their silhouettes dance off down the sand and wondered what he'd done wrong. He went alone into the ocean. Held his breath until his lungs screamed and wondered if that was how it would feel to drown.

Hard to breathe now, watching Leo and Charity walk toward the chair.

Leo had likely diagrammed the route with tactical discipline. Timing his stride and shoulder position with the precision of a fox-walker. He angled his body and Charity sat in the blue chair. Room for one more. The space beside her pulled like the whooshing force of an airplane window blown out at 30,000 feet. Lights flickering. Passengers screaming.

Griff's blood jumped and—

Leo pivoted and sprang into the blue chair like a ruthless cuddle cheetah. Charity, not a vole, could throw an elbow, one "no" was all she needed—but what was this?

Mmmmmm.

Air conditioner kicking on? Ice machine?

Purring? She relaxed into him. Smiled. Leo smiled back.

After all those corrections? After the binder and the song about a dry river? Goddamn then, let the earth shake. Let the ocean rear up and knock it down to nothing. Drop the bombs. Roll the credits.

World, do your worst.

SEVEN

AS WOULD LATER BE RECORDED IN TOWN RECORDS:

Clade City's evacuation siren went off at 2:27 AM.

The sound came pulsing through the mists of sleep and soft sheets of coastal drizzle. Griff bolted up.

BADADADABADeeeeeeeEEEEEEEE

Leo fumbled for his phone.

"Not a mistake," Leo said.

In the house, a banging door. Slamming cupboards.

A light pulsed in the hallway. The cadence of his father's voice through drywall. Griff fumbled on the bedside table. Flipped on the radio. The prerecorded message:

THIS IS NOT A DRILL. PLEASE EVACUATE TO HIGHER GROUND—

"Shit," Leo said.

For a moment, Leo looked ten years old.

"Ready?" their father filled their doorway. Already dressed somehow. Black pants. Tactical vest. As if he'd slid down a Batman fire pole directly into his disaster gear.

"Remember the drills," their dad said. "You're doing great."

"Tsunami?" Griff asked.

Their father listened to another rotation of the siren.

BADADADABADeeeeeeeEEEEEEEE

"Yes," he said. "Yes. See you outside."

Griff stood. He flexed toes into carpet, trying to anchor

himself. Trainings, mixed up. Neat kits of knowledge dumped in the same toy box. Tsunami vs. nuclear bomb vs. home intruder and acronyms went soupy in his head, grabbing his EDC (Every Day Carry), his BOB (Bug Out Bag), and his INCH (I'm Never Coming Home) sack from their dedicated spaces in the closet. The boys laced their boots tight. Looked around the room.

The last time they'd see it.

"TOE Box," Griff said. He put a hand on it. Leo put a hand on Griff's hand. Griff flinched. Leo hadn't done that in years.

"Goodbye," Leo said. He nodded. It was time.

In the hallway, the French doors to the piano room were open. Their beautiful Knabe.

Gone.

"Remember your doors!" their father shouted.

Doors. They each had to knock at three homes, part of the plan. Their mother stood dazed in the kitchen as if beamed down from a distant planet. Gold hair frizzed in the overhead light. She looked at the doorway to her studio, where she made sculptures, jewelry, custom greeting cards.

"Mom," Griff said. "Can we help you with some stuff?"

"It's all ocean things," she said.

Two minutes had passed. The water was coming.

Time crawled in a nightmare way, carpet turning to marshmallow, air thickening, and they could not seem to get to the garage, to get outside, to finally get to the truck, which was running, facing forward down the driveway. Their father ran south.

"You're that way?" Leo asked, pointing north.

"Yeah, bro."

They split, and Griff's assignments were already moving. One couple, one family, one single woman, all with lights on.

Garage doors flung up. The siren was working. Maybe they'd saved some lives.

Their father stood in the driveway calling for Leo.

"Leo! C'mon! Leo!"

In the passenger window, Griff's mother stared ahead. She exhaled, breath trembling through her chest. When would the shaking start?

"Leo!" Griff shouted.

Now?

Leo tore around the corner, piled into the truck.

"Cranzlers were dead asleep," he said. "They flopped around like they were getting ready for a garage sale or some shit."

Griff laughed.

"I'm serious. They were like 'We'd better pack up, baby.'"

"Here we go," their dad said.

They pulled out. Raced to the corner. The truck lurched to a stop. Anticipation stretched like a wire coiling around his chest.

"Do we really have to stop, Dad?" Leo asked. "We're at four-forty."

"Keep your belts tight," he said.

When the shaking started, the town's whole infrastructure would spring like an ambush. Power lines would snap and spit sparks. Roads, cratered to pits. Treefalls. Mudslides. Their whole neighborhood was awake and moving, outside on driveways like a spontaneous late-night block party they'd never had.

Never would.

And Charity. Was she awake? He texted her without thinking.

NOT A DRILL. BE SAFE.

They passed the first TSUNAMI EVACUATION sign.

His father clutched the wheel with both hands, heading toward town, Emergency Route #4. The radio tower looked precarious in the dark sky. A glass piñata. Downtown Clade City hung out like an empty pocket. Doors open, lights on. The soft din of shouts and a small swarm outside the Drift Inn. They passed Shoreline Gifts.

Their mother watched her shop pass, lips pulled tight as a stitch.

The truck swallowed more blacktop. Leaving it all behind.

"Seven minutes," Leo said. "Wow."

Thomas would be proud. The system had worked. Griff texted Thomas:

YOU OKAY?

His dad turned on K-NOW. Dead air.

"Strange," he said.

Two more evacuation signs flashed in the headlights, then they were deep into the night, NOW EXITING TSUNAMI EVACUATION ZONE. High enough to avoid water, still in critical danger of mudslides, towering trees, boulders balanced on fragile slopes—

"Why is Dad pulling over?" Griff asked Leo.

A narrow gravel shoulder just before the road split.

"Just quick," their father said, eyes eager, "I want to show you where we're going."

Leo and Griff exchanged a look.

Their father had his explorer shine—the firm-set jaw and eager eyes of the man who had taught them to surf, led them through bushwhacking adventures in Alaska, brought them safely to the lighthouse. He pulled a pamphlet from the glove box with the flourish of a bouquet.

"Kissimmee!" he said, grinning. Leaning toward her.

"What?"

"Don't worry. We've got a place," he said. He unfolded the pamphlet for their mother. Griff and Leo crowded up to see. A galley kitchen. Balcony. Communal pool.

"What's this?"

"Plan B," he said.

"What? Where?" their mother asked.

"Kissimmee!" he said again. Griff suddenly feared their family's future had been written primarily for a romantic punchline in his dad's private evacuation fantasy. Knowing his father, it was possible. His mother sighed and lifted her phone.

"Dad," Leo said, "can you drive?"

"KISSIMMEE," his father's phone boomed. "LET'S GO!"

Only his phone was enthusiastic about Florida.

"Kissimmee is landlocked," their mother said.

"Well, maybe that's better," their dad said. "All things considered."

"My business is coastal treasures," she said.

He sighed. "Shoreline Gifts? C'mon, Angie."

A bad c'mon. Mean. No one was going to Kissi-him.

"Dad," Leo said.

A snapping sound. The brothers jolted. Their mom, grabbing the door handle.

"Let me out," she said.

"Baby."

"Want to be open and honest? Let's be open and honest."

She got out of the car. Rummaged in her bag. Lipstick? The tip glowed blue. A pipe. She walked to the edge of the headlights, exhaling smoke.

"Mom smokes pot!" Griff said.

Leo laughed. "Holy shit."

"Language," their dad said. "Stop!"

"Stop what?" Griff asked.

"Stop watching her!"

Griff's phone buzzed. He pulled it from his pocket. Up front, their father's phone made a soft *ding*. All their faces illuminated by a new green glow.

"Oh," their dad said. He tapped his phone like a broken speaker.

FALSE ALARM. PLEASE RETURN HOME.

"Oh no," Griff said.

"We are so dead," Leo said.

He meant, the town would kill them.

Maybe they could keep driving. Make a clean break for Florida.

Their father wasn't speaking. He poked his phone, as if trying to wake it up.

Griff remembered once, years ago, their parents had pulled the car over like this to dance on the shoulder of the road. Now their mother stood outside, alone in the hot lamplight of the truck. She didn't know yet that it was fake. A plume of smoke escaped her lips and gave him a strange, dislocated feeling. Like whether the tsunami came or not, the life they'd left behind was gone.

EIGHT

CLADE CITY DID THE FALSE ALARM WALK OF SHAME.

It had happened before. Not like they were the first idiots in the world. Hawaii, for North Korean nukes that never came. Huntington Beach, for an imaginary tsunami.

Traffic was a mess. Middle of the night, no one knowing where to go. Blown stop signs, horns. About 4 AM, the news finally settled into the town's bones. The Tripp family reentered their neighborhood as part of the slow, sad parade.

No thanks be to God. No grateful twirling of domestic partners, kissing of lawns.

It was a funeral procession.

Everyone returned to what they'd left behind.

His own house looked smaller. Frowned at them from the lawn. Going in felt like trespassing. Like being a ghost. Open cupboards stared back with forsaken dry goods, quietly accusatory. In their bedroom, the TOE Box huddled like a sad pet. When was the last time he'd gone through the files, or showed it any attention? He put a hand on the box, like patting a shoulder.

He remembered the sweetness of Leo's hand on his.

He wondered how many decisions had been made in thirty minutes of desperate confusion. How many hands touched? How many Floridas disclosed? He lay in bed and shut his eyes, just on the brink of dawn. Trying to untangle his own knots.

When he'd thought it was all over for Clade City, he'd felt—how?

Scared. Regretful, maybe. For not having lived a better life. Something else. Deeper, buried, pulsing magma-hot.

A thrill.

The end of this place, this life. Hunger for the whole big world.

Leo was afraid of what the town would do to them. They wouldn't have to worry about the people who wanted to stay. The trouble would be the ones who didn't want to come back.

NINE

LATER THAT MORNING, THE FAMILY BREAKFAST EXPERIENCE sloped into an uncanny valley between Life As They Knew It and Something New and Strange. They sat together at the kitchen table. Eggs and toast. Half their mother's office was unboxed in the living room—shell necklaces, silk screens, stamps, drawers of loose agates. Dry goods from the basement cluttered the counter: hard white wheat, survival stew.

Leo asked: "Do we really have to go to school?"

No one had slept much. But the bizarre ritual continued. Griff looked carefully at his mother and father, his surroundings. Everything felt a few inches off.

"Want some juice?" their mother asked their father.

"Sure," he said. She poured him a bright, brimming glass. All the way to the uncomfortable tip-top.

"Florida quality," she said.

"Does it have cannabis in it?" he asked.

Their father drove them to school.

"It's already started," Leo said.

Leo looked at his phone. Griff had turned his off. Memes. Texts. Angry videos, circulating. The hallways would not be gentle.

"Good luck out there," their father said. He meant it.

They climbed out and Leo walked ahead. Good combat technique. Spread out. Minimize casualties.

Walking, Griff felt as if he had a giant, unsteady stone balanced across his shoulders. He just had to make it to tonight. His radio show, still on. He'd been working on his playlist for weeks. Charity would be listening. Near the front doors, someone kicked the back of his right foot into his left leg—*Tripp twin!*

He breathed and let the boys pass. Weight on his shoulders. He didn't drop it.

You've done this before, he told himself. Tonight, you've got a show. Charity, listening.

Just make it through the day.

● ● ●

When Thomas and Griff arrived at the station, the Thunderbolt hung still and quiet at the top of K-NOW tower. Clouds, the bruised shade of dusk. Griff eyed the siren as if it might pounce.

They climbed steel rungs to the small catwalk and the narrow green door.

The sea breeze slashed through the control room, ruffling pamphlets on the wire rack. Triple-thick windows stretched from waist height to ceiling, giving a crow's-nest view of the wild Pacific, the lighthouse, the desolate streets of the Ruins. On the walls bumper stickers, patches, flyers:

DON'T TURN YOUR BACK ON THE OCEAN!

SEE SOMETHING, SAY SOMETHING!

THE DAY AFTER THE DISASTER IS TOO LATE!

Scruggs was alone in the studio. He looked unsettled.

"Glad it's you boys. When y'all pulled up I almost dropped my Pop-Tarts."

"Why?" Griff said. "What's going on?"

Scruggs looked down at the parking lot.

"A number of our fellow villagers have given me the privilege of their opinion on our alert system." He went quiet. "Just curious, Thomas. Have you—"

"Looking into it," Thomas said.

EARS might have triggered the false response, or maybe a software bug. Thomas looked like an essential space behind his eyes had been hollowed out. Like the seventh-grade talent show, when he'd failed to pull the rabbit out of the hat. He'd stayed home the rest of the week.

"Well," Scruggs said. "You're all familiar with the control tower."

He led them to the desk, three computer monitors. Quartered screens. Scrolling information on weather patterns, alerts from the National Oceanic and Atmospheric Administration, EARS data.

"Just keep your eyes open," he said. "With our luck the damn thing hits tonight."

Crossing the room, Scruggs went to the studio equipment.

"Now I'm going to tell you everything I know about running a radio program," he said. "Should take about two minutes."

Something exploded into the window.

A crashing, percussive pop that sent Scruggs lurching to the right. Thomas covered his neck and Griff flattened to the floor. On the east-facing window, something rubbery clung.

Again—*POW!*

"What the hell!" Thomas shouted.

Scruggs crawled toward the opposite side of the room, toward the gun safe.

"Call 911," Scruggs said.

Muffled shouts outside. They saw the next one coming. The

slow, loping arc of a blue bauble—*POP!*—a water balloon. Scruggs moved with surprising dexterity, flung open the door.

"Knock it off!" he screamed.

"Fuck you!" the person screamed back, giving a middle finger. They wore a black ski mask. Climbed into the cab of a white truck.

The truck pulled away. Duct tape over their license plate.

"Davis, you fool," Scruggs said. "Everyone knows that truck."

Griff peeled a puckered balloon remnant from the window.

"Our balloons," Griff said.

DON'T TURN YOUR BACK ON THE OCEAN

"That's a nice touch," Scruggs said.

Scruggs locked the door. He taught them how to cue up public service announcements, set and execute a playlist, proper microphone distance, the hazard of popping *P*s, monitor levels, phone calls.

"Do people call?" Thomas asked.

"Most of the time this tower just howls like a ghost," Scruggs said. "But people are listening. You'll just never know who."

"I feel ready," Thomas said.

Seeing the microphones, Griff felt a sudden prickling on his back. Tongue drying up.

"I appreciate you boys taking over," Scruggs said. "I've been working too many late nights. My little kitties were about to lose it."

"Scruggs," Thomas said, "how many cats do you have?"

"Don't ask a lonely person how many cats they have," Scruggs said. "That's like asking a lady her age."

Scruggs gathered up his rucksack and floppy, wide-brimmed hat, his jacket, and what looked to be a half-eaten can of emergency survival stew. Scruggs must've cracked it the moment the siren blew.

"Oh," Scruggs said. "Two things. One: Remember the police reports."

Officer Dunbar's prerecorded reports. On-air, he always pronounced it *pleece reports*. Like, rhymes with *fleece reports*.

"Two: Stick to the playlist," Scruggs said.

"Sir yes sir," Thomas said, giving him a stiff salute.

"Be safe." Scruggs left the tower. Outside, his truck started. Taillights vanished around the corner.

Alone, radio controls glimmered like the handles and levers of a rocket ship. Who might be out there, waiting for the perfect song?

"What was that about a playlist?" Griff asked.

"Oh," Thomas said. "Just the songs we're allowed to play."

Thomas unsnapped the teeth of a white three-ring binder, peeled off a laminated sheet of paper. About a hundred songs.

"You're kidding, right?"

"No," Thomas said. "We have a limited license agreement. There's good stuff, though."

Five AC/DC songs. Aerosmith. Everly Brothers. Garth Brooks. The Eagles.

"Sadly, no 'Thunderstruck,' " Thomas said.

"No," Griff whispered.

"Can you imagine a better evacuation song?" Thomas said, perking up for the first time. "If I was sitting up here when the missiles came screaming in, I'd cue that motherfucker up for sure. Thun-der. THUN-DER!"

He spread his fingers out like imaginary vapor trails, raked them across the sky.

"Ne-ne-ne-ne-ne-ne-ne—" He attempted the solo with his mouth.

— 60 —

"You didn't tell me there was a playlist," Griff said, standing. Griff's chair tipped back, hit the floor. He clutched the sheet.

"Whoa," Thomas said.

"Why would I do all this for a fucking classic rock playlist? Hanging the siren? Hanging out with goddamn Slim and Jonesy? Canning parties? For a radio show where I can't even play any real music! You know how much time I spent picking our songs!"

Griff threw the sheet as hard as he could. It took a soft glide path in the space between them. Landed with a whisper on the floor.

"I don't know," Thomas said. "I thought maybe you wanted some quality time."

"With you?"

Thomas shrugged, looked to the side.

"Hey, hey. I do. Thomas. Buddy. I'm sorry."

Thomas looked around the station. Hollow look, creeping in.

"I would've missed you if it was real," Thomas said. "And Leo. My parents had this whole plan. I don't know if I ever would've seen you again."

"Yeah," Griff said.

"But still. It felt like—I don't know. An adventure."

Thomas looked down at the town. Three lit blocks. And darkness.

"Feels small, doesn't it?" Thomas said.

The sea washed in, high tide. Yes, the town looked small. The ocean did not. Between them and the whole world—the most refractive, musical thing on earth. Water bounced radio waves the way a mirror bounces light. And in the thrum of the ocean, Griff understood how to win Charity's heart. He hadn't been thinking big enough.

"It feels small," Griff said. "But it's not."

TEN

THE NEXT MORNING, GRIFF WOKE TO FIND THE CONTENTS OF THE TOE Box spread over the floor—file folders, note cards, maps, diagrams.

"Just doing a little research," Leo said at breakfast.

Such a lie.

Griff did not need to ask Leo what he was doing—his brother was somehow trying to impress Charity. Griff had looked over the small, neat stacks—EVPs, intergalactic visitors, time travel. What was Leo's angle?

Sometimes on a family hike, Leo would duck off onto a side trail—claim to be exploring, *picking thimbleberries*—then around the next switchback, there was Leo, 20 feet ahead, arms raised in a V for Victory.

It couldn't happen again.

Griff decided right there, eating an over-easy egg between toast, the only way to win was to be better at absolutely everything.

Now that Leo was back into music for Charity's sake—Griff heard him constantly hammering on the Knabe, sometimes taunting him with the C-sharp summons—*Da dun!*—often playing when Griff was busy, sneaking practices. Leo practiced during their study hall, which Charity had skipped for days—doing independent work for student government. Their puzzle sat in disarray on a table Griff had begged the teacher to keep safe. He was losing the game of time with Charity. He was losing at piano.

He arranged to have his own after-school practice that Monday.

In the music room, their teacher, Mr. Jung, was delighted.

"Of course!" He peered up from his tiny round glasses, sitting at his desk. "Just you?"

Griff nodded.

"I can't wait to see what you and your brother have on offer this winter. May I ask, will it still be Liszt?"

"And Stravinsky. Symphony in Three Movements."

"Ooo. Delightful."

Mr. Jung unlocked the small room, and Griff was alone. Inside, buzzing fluorescents and the plink-plink upright. A soundproof door and a tiny window. No audience. He did not want to be watched. No one could see his hands or face.

It took a few minutes to adjust to the instrument.

A loose pedal. The action on the whole right side was off, the sticky B-flat, but there was something good about this little wood shanty of a piano in practice room 5.

It had heart.

When Griff was alone, it only took a few minutes to calibrate to the piano. For the keys to sink into dreamspace. The bench, untethered from the room. Fluent, unburdened.

—gone—

A slim crack in the world, and he slipped inside. Like a river. Like water. He found himself in a section of Hungarian Rhapsody No. 2. Deep in the heartbeat of the piece, chasing the flow toward the cadenza. He did not know how badly he wanted to play until he was playing *at liberty, as you desire*—

In the background, words fluttered, trying to describe:

Forget words.

Let him be a vessel. Let him be pen and ink but never words.

He played two pieces. Three. Four. He'd play forever. More than an hour later, something flickered in the room's small window. Mr. Jung's wide eyes. An O of a mouth, gaping like a fleshy bowling ball. Griff's fingers fumbled to a stop.

Mr. Jung ducked out of the window.

But the spell was broken. Griff placed his hands on the keys. Just hands again.

Plink-plink.

Outside, beyond the school's front lawn, everything popped. Autumn light draped the maples in warm velvet. His body buzzed from the playing. A warm, pleasant exhaustion, like having spent the afternoon in a sunny river.

And Charity. Right there.

Standing on a curb. The practice had sharpened his eyes, dialed up his sensitivity. She leapt from the backdrop of the world, like she'd been cut in from a different movie. Higher definition, sharper colors.

She was staring at him. He knew the look. Which twin?

"Griff! What are you doing here?"

He walked to her but it was unclear where to stop, how close to get.

"Practicing."

"Practicing what?"

The music had turned his sensations fluid, everything spilling over and unable to fit in the boxy containers of words. He wanted—what? To hold her. He imagined the feel of rocking in her arms. A perfect harbor. To hold her would be like lying stretched in the well of a wood-bottomed boat, turning in a stone bowl.

"Piano," he exhaled.

Door 5 clapped shut in the parking lot. Two strong engines.

One white truck with an American flag. Tires squealed. One guy yelled something out the window. At them, maybe. Like— *Have a good time, hope y'all get something.* Both trucks blasted out of the parking lot, blaring the same song.

New Country AM.

They turned the corner, chirping their tires.

"Do you like living here?" Charity asked.

"Sometimes," he said. "You?"

"No," she said. "It's like a tiny American diorama. This town is a shoe box."

"So, hey," Griff said. "I had this idea, during our radio show."

"Your show!" She shoved his shoulder. "What happened? I was listening for the Collection. Some beats. It sounded like the soundtrack to an old white guy's garage."

Griff pinched the flesh on his wrist. She'd actually listened.

"There's a stupid playlist," he said.

"Of course!" she said. "Always. That's why we're trapped in a Radio Bermuda Triangle with the same hundred songs, all fenced in by old people. You know people over thirty mostly stop discovering new music? At all? Can you believe these people are making decisions about radio stations or politics or the environment? How can they think differently listening to the same music?"

He laughed.

"Nailed it," he said. "The problem with humanity."

"Humanity," she said. "Society. Let's solve it all, Griff. Make a playlist to save the world."

They talked for an hour. About music. About the Collection. Rhiannon Giddens and the New Basement Tapes and Donald Glover and their band. Talking about music widened her eyes, lifted her voice, and runways of conversation shot out into the wider world. She wanted to see France. Brazil. Walk the Camino in Spain.

They talked about the far-off and far-away. They stood closer together.

Standing on the curb in the circle drive, balancing on one foot, then the other, they wove something in a slow-looping dance. Charity twined with the low thunder of windblown leaves. The mossy smell of wet grass and the moment merged with September the way a good song sinks into an evening and etches itself in memory.

From now on, every September would have her in it.

"I should go," she said. "The mother meltdown is coming."

Talking to her, the concept of time was impossible. In silence, the world cobbled itself back together crudely around them—pale green weeds in the sidewalk, a buzzing streetlight with a hopeless halo of moths, scabby parking lot. The whole sad shoe box.

He wanted to grab her hand, her arm, anything to make her stay. He used words.

"Wait. What are you doing here, anyway?" he asked.

"I didn't tell you? I'm a student leader now. That's why our puzzle is so neglected."

She opened her mouth. Gagging.

"Student leader of a diorama town?" He laughed. "Why?"

"I think melanin," she said. "They were way down. So now they get a Dominican and a Black person. Two for one. Someone actually said that. I told them they're just getting a Black girl. Anything else costs extra."

"Good ol' Clade City," Griff said.

"Yep," she said. "Welcome to Oregon. Where the white people are even whiter."

He laughed. "Weather doesn't help."

"It really doesn't," Charity said. "I don't know what you all did out here to scare summer away. I've been cold since the day I moved."

Griff looked down at his jacket. Not as nice as their dad's.

"Want my coat?"

"Oh," she said. "I'm not ready for camo yet. That's going to be a big step."

Her phone buzzed.

"How does time vanish with you, Tripp?" Charity asked. "Can you figure that out with your crazy TOE Box?"

She nudged his foot with hers and he remembered the way her bare foot had looked that first time, and before he could feel the shiver of that she said—

"See you soon—"

And leapt forward—almost a pounce—and kissed his cheek. His hand went to the warm place she kissed, like something with wings had just landed there.

She laughed. "It's okay. That's how they say goodbye in France."

"Are you—also French?" he asked. She laughed.

"Sure. I'd love to be French for a while. That's a nice thought."

She was walking to her car. One leg at a time. Somehow moving with the same locomotive logic of simple humans. He, however, could fly. He shut his eyes and recalled photos of the Albuquerque Hot Air Balloon Fiesta. Great, bulbous, fire-blown jewels tracing paths over a blue-sands desert.

That was him. A colorful whoosh through the dark sky.

A car honked, but he was aloft.

Honk, fool! I'm flying!

"Griff!"

The voice cut through.

"Griff! Geez, get in."

His father. Griff got in the truck.

"Who was that?" his father asked.

"Who?"

"The Black girl."

"Dad," he said.

"What? African-American?"

"Her father is Dominican. Her mom's Black. Why do you need to know?"

"I want to know what to call her."

"How about Charity," Griff said. "That's her name."

"I see," his father said. "So who is Charity?"

"A friend."

"Yeah?" his father said. "Friend. You know, I once led a workshop on the twenty-seven dead giveaways for habitual liars. Your face is doing seventeen of them right now."

Griff stared back at his father.

"You're lying, Dad."

His father smiled.

"I see you've taken the same workshop."

Griff snuggled in against the truck's warmest vent. He could close his eyes. He didn't want to go home. He wanted his father to vanish and the truck to roll toward the 2. He wanted to sleep and dream until it was all real and he woke up with the sun through the windows and Charity in the driver's seat. She would reach out and take his hand.

"We're here," she would say in the morning, far from this place. "We made it."

ELEVEN

BY PRACTICE THE NEXT NIGHT, GRIFF HAD MENTALLY MAPPED Leo's plan with the band. Step one: Leo gets them a gig to force rehearsals. Step two. Leo cements his role as lead singer. Step three: Names the band something like: Leo Tripp & the Other Guys. Step four: Leo Seduces Charity like a creepy record exec, using promises of power and billboard chart domination.

He did not expect Charity to show up to practice in hiking boots.

"Are you wearing a hiking costume?" Griff asked. She was standing on Thomas's front porch with Leo.

"You didn't tell him?" Charity asked Leo.

Thomas came outside. Also wearing boots, long camo jacket.

"I wanted it to be a surprise," Leo said.

"Are we rehearsing at all?" Thomas said. "Half an hour?"

"What surprise?" Griff asked.

"Let's go," Leo said.

Leo stepped from the front patio. No practice?

The group walked quickly. Leo was carrying their black backpack—the one they kept inside the TOE Box. Charity and Thomas raced ahead. Griff was behind, and had no idea where they were going. They moved west, toward the ocean.

They hustled through neighborhoods. It felt like curfew-busting middle school thrills.

Thomas did tuck-and-rolls on front lawns. Army-crawled. When Leo said *Hide!* they flattened against trees and light posts. Giggling took hold. Thomas discovered and performed his new signature move—a somersault tumble into ornamental shrubbery—and they lost it, howling. The laughing fueled more moves, they crossed the whole town in a wild zigzag.

"I'm glad we skipped practice," Charity said, catching her breath by a tall wooden fence.

"Yeah," Griff said.

Thomas, just ahead, chattered about gradients of twilight: Civil ends at 7:53 PM. Nautical twilight at 8:30 PM. She was breathing beside him. The air had a certain lovely heaviness to it. The still night seemed to hold him in its palm. Charity's clavicle looked slightly sweaty and delicious. He wanted to put his tongue against it. Weirdo.

"Leo didn't tell you anything about this?" Charity asked.

Griff shook his head, trying to erase neck-based thinking.

They ran and caught up with the others in Flagg Park. Overgrown with gone-to-seed wild grass, cathedrals of glistening gorse. They wove to a mammoth grove of Pacific rhododendrons. It shaped itself around the mouth of an aromatic cave bursting with swollen flowers, leaves waxy-sheened and prehistoric looking. Big as kites.

"It's a dream," Charity said.

Her face, dappled in moonlight—this air! You could float, swim, but Thomas had brought a rope ladder.

"We're going to the Ruins," Griff said.

"Bravo," Thomas said. They would descend from Flagg Park. Safer than trying to scale the floodgates, where Dunbar or another bored cop might snap them up.

"Charity," Leo said. "Come here quick."

She went with him, vanishing into a pocket of shadow.

Griff's fingers pinched the skin on his jawbone. He pinched his tongue between front teeth and counted to thirty-seven before they returned—the horrors of what might happen in thirty-seven seconds—but she did not come back flushed or giddy or handholding. Just holding a small red radio. The nicest one their father kept in the basement.

A small trapdoor opened in Griff's stomach, a nauseated rush.

Which shortcut was Leo taking?

She pocketed the radio, and Griff helped tie the ladder to staggered ash trees, then let the roped rungs unspool against the rock like a muffled collapse of dominoes. They peered over the leafy edge into a gaping mouth of darkness.

"I'll go first," Leo said.

They descended through a grove of prickly octopus spruce trees. Clothes caught on stiff-fingered branches, the sharp, enlivening smell of living needles. He took a breath, deep in the lungs of the trees, then his boots touched soft earth.

They'd passed through the barbed canopy into their town's low-lying, forbidden city. A long, soggy park stretched off to their right. A scrap of land in a slow-motion tug-of-war with the ocean, spanning decades. They'd rebuilt the park when they'd planned to reopen the Ruins, before it had been abandoned to an uncertain time in the future, then abandoned altogether—steel floodgates closed and locked.

The historic downtown had been built to mimic the gentle

swoops and bends of a river finding the ocean. The intended effect for a visitor would be a slow, gentle descent through shops and parks to the water.

Having snuck in the back way, they walked the intended route in reverse, passing a phalanx of danger signs.

NO TRESPASSING!

WE PROSECUTE!

They hurried past the signs, quickly surrounded by tall, still structures. Brick buildings, bay windows, clapboard-sided shops. Every shop seemed to be holding its breath.

Underfoot, the concrete wore a patina of sand and crunched like brittle snow. Street posts tapered toward their tips and bloomed into empty lamps that caught the silver halo of the full moon. Storefronts showed real character—no two the same. The New Frontier with sconces like torchlights. The Looking Glass with its bulbous bay windows, driftwood seats, the Gallery Hutch with a hand-carved cornice above the door, depicting a warren of rabbits chasing a man.

It felt like certain remote forests. Sacred groves left untouched.

"Old growth," Leo whispered to Griff.

Yes. The whole place had that subtle mix of magic, where you might just as easily see a towering redwood as a pair of pixies with fluttering wings.

"Can't believe this town keeps a secret this good," Charity said.

She touched a shop door with chipped red paint. Thomas cupped his hands to dark glass and peered inside. They talked in low voices, as if afraid they'd wake something, and finally found themselves at the end of the winding road, standing by the moonstruck steel floodgates.

Shut. Flat, unadorned, pocked with rust.

"End of the road," Thomas said.

"Not for us," Leo said. "What we want is that way."

"We're not going home?" Charity asked.

"We're just getting started," Leo said.

The ocean beat its soft drum. Leo snugged the straps of the black backpack and walked.

They followed Leo back out of town. Buildings broke off to dune grass, parkland, and a generous parking lot.

"Right there," Leo said.

A hulking shape, in the darkness.

"Giant crab," Charity said.

"The half shell," Griff said. He'd seen it in a photo at Shoreline Gifts. A big band on stage. An audience of white and smiling faces.

"Let's get closer," Leo said.

"Across that?" Griffin asked.

Between them and the amphitheater, a moat of industrial wreckage. Broken piles of brick and tile, rusted heaps of rebar. Slick-bellied logs. Plywood split and rotten and fanged with nails.

"Into the Sea of Tetanus, everyone!" Thomas cried.

They took careful steps, checking the grip of their shoes. They followed Leo over the sea of debris to what was now recognizable as a stage, and Charity whispered—

"Wow."

"Hello!" Thomas shouted. His voice hung in the air as if suspended. "Check those acoustics!"

The stage itself was a stew of minnowy cigarette butts, beer can disks, the kind of thick, molten trash that must be cultivated for years.

"Bro. Just look at this venue," Leo said.

Leo's greatest gift. Where Griff saw trash, Leo saw stacked amps and trussed lighting. The adulation of multitudes, crowds stacked back to the low-water mark. This close, the lighthouse beam felt heavy. Shaped by mist, it wheeled through the sky and struck with a palpable force—

WHOOMP!

"We could fix this!" Charity said. Leo's spark had lit a fire in her eyes. "This whole place. Thomas, you've got mad skills. You all do. Imagine if you used your gifts to do something interesting rather than bracing for death?"

Griff and Leo laughed.

Thomas started a song. Laid down a beat. They gathered around. Charity hummed with the sound that rose up from deep in her body and began without words and Griff could hear the musical openings for his own voice. Missed bars slipped past like the open cars of a train he couldn't quite gather the courage to jump. Leo jumped. He sang with a voice Griff had forgotten his brother had.

"Out here on the water," Leo began.

Charity kept her eyes shut, Thomas kept the beat in his throat. Leo sang:

Out here on the water, I sing the ocean song—
Out here on the water, we know we won't be long—

It struck Griff, the truth that his brother was a better musician. No bitterness. The lilt of a pleasant surprise to hear him sing this way. Soft and sweet, like a chorus just short of its final words. They listened, and he stopped.

"Go on," Charity said.

Leo's mouth worked around the next few words. Griff could almost hear them.

"Just messing around," he said.

"C'mon and mess around," Charity said.

"So," Leo asked, voice shifting. "Can we all do a show here? Promise? A great big one?"

"Will you sing the ocean song?" Griff said.

Leo glared. The comment landed wrong, but Griff meant it. He wasn't making fun of Leo. No way to make it right now. Leo would swallow the comment deep down and pretend he didn't care.

"Yes," Griff said. "I promise."

"Hands," Leo said.

"A show," Thomas said. "Right here. Bright lights."

"The best ever," Charity said.

They put their hands in a circle. They all said yes.

"Now," Leo said. "To the beach."

It suddenly made sense.

The missing piece. Griff connected his brother to the clattering in the backpack to the cassette player to the Ruins and the buoyancy in his heart was caving, because Leo had just beaten him to the summit, and Griff knew exactly which secret of the universe he was about to tell.

TWELVE

"WE'RE FISHING?" CHARITY ASKED.

Wind whipped up on the beach.

"Yes," Leo said. "We're going to catch a song."

"You okay?" Thomas asked Griff.

Griff was not okay. He was tender, shaky, listening to Leo give it all away. Griff had a multiweek strategy for the radio conversation he had started with Charity in study hall. Slowly, he'd introduce her to each fascinating aspect of the Skip. Frequencies, and a quick study of the ionosphere. Next, he'd cover the Radio Spectrum Allocation, breadcrumbing knowledge slowly, he'd use the access he'd painstakingly gained at K-NOW to harness the full electric power of the strongest receiver on the coast to do the most romantic thing in the world—musical treasure hunting! Exploring the dark edge of the world together.

Leo was spilling it all, right now.

Like serving a seventeen-course meal all at once by dumping it on the beach.

"Do you ever notice how crazy radio stations get at night?"

Charity nodded.

She pulled out the small red radio. Leo handed Griff and Thomas inferior radios with earbuds. Not even headphones. Charity leaned forward, intent.

"It's because AM radio signals behave differently when the sun goes down. The sun electrifies certain layers in the atmosphere that keep signals close to their source. At night—"

"—astronomical twilight," Thomas said.

"Yes. Radio signals can roam all over the world. Everywhere it's dark. You can hear songs in Russia. Texas. Ecuador. Patagonia. It's a minor miracle."

"Wow," Charity said. "How do I not know this?"

"I was explaining," Griff said. "In study hall."

The words *study hall* landed like a block of wood. Leo plowed ahead.

"It's called surfing the Skip," Leo said. "People do it everywhere. And this is one of the best places in the world. Because of the sea. And the shape of the cliffs."

Leo knew for the same reason Griff knew. Their father, walking them down this stretch of beach. Taking them on low-tide hikes to the lighthouse, explaining the curvature of the treacherous cove at God's Mouth, the ionizing effect of salt in the air, but before Griff could offer information about waves and salt, Thomas was tearing off toward the ocean. Charity ran after him.

Out past dune grass and sand, low-tide mud flats stretched like the malodorous skin of a reptile's back. Wet craters, teeming with life: mollusks seamless as stones, open-throated anemones. Proboscises and pinchers. Thomas crouched near a sand-bound boulder. He popped the stone with a low, sucking sound. Beneath it, a confetti of white-shelled crabs. The simmering reflection like a china-plate moon boiled over, racing off sideways—

"The gift of freedom!" Thomas said. "Run, my crustacean brothers! Do not squander what I have given you!"

Charity was laughing, they were all laughing, and Leo said:

"Please listen."

Everyone had bandwidth assignments. Leo would take 550 to 900. Charity 900 to 1100, Thomas 1100 to 1400, and Griff had the top of the dial, up to 1600 AM.

"What's the goal?" Charity asked. "What are we looking for?"

Leo smiled. "The best song in the world."

Charity took off her shoes. Rolled up her pant legs and cuffed them.

"Put your shoes back a ways," Leo said. "Tide's coming in."

Griff and Charity walked back together. Set their shoes down.

It was a rare night, growing warmer as the evening thickened. Winds laid down calm. Salty breeze just balmy enough to seduce you into the bone-shaking cold of the water. They held still. Griff followed her eyes to the tide line. A blazing white rim at the edge of the world.

"What do you think?" he asked.

"It's the coolest thing I've done since I moved here," she said.

She removed her jacket, revealing her arms, the miracle of flesh between shoulder and wrist. Barefoot, she ran across the flats. Her feet made small, rippling splashes, like skipped stones.

"Charity!" Leo called after her. "We're trying to keep the bandwidths together!"

She banked to the right. Griff followed her.

"I think she's already in the deep end, brother," Griff said, pushing in his earbuds.

"Griff," Leo said. "You, over there."

He pointed a far and lonesome distance from Charity.

Nope, Griff thought.

Leo called after him, then abruptly changed course—chasing something. Griff turned his radio on.

White noise, like his ear hugging a fan blade.

WHUMPWHUMPWHUMPWHUMP

Charity kept going. Did a little leap as a wave knocked into her shins. Adorable. He would just follow her. It was okay to follow her. He walked until the water built to just below his knees. In his ears, a white-noise tumble of voices, notes, a sudden, urgent call—

"Griff!" Leo was screaming at him. "MOVE! OVER THERE!"

Griff raised his hand like a visor, like he couldn't see. Leo was farther off to the left now, too far to stop him. He turned back to Charity. The moon had shed its orange blush and emerged bone white, laying a bright, wobbly carpet across the water. Charity walked the light like a runway and Griff followed—

In his earbuds, the noise changed:

WHUMPSSCCCCCRREEEEEEESKREEEEEE

He fumbled through the noise and into voices—AM talk shows:

—the problem we're dealing with here, we know the problem—

"What have you caught, Griff?" Charity called back to him.

"Scourge of the airwaves," Griff said. "White-Bellied Talk Toads."

She laughed. "Throw them back! Thomas! Hey! What do you got?"

"Raaaaaaaaaack Rooooooock!" he hollered from a distance.

"What?" Charity asked.

"Rack Rock!" Thomas said. "New Country AM. Racks on women, racks on deers, racks of beers, glad I ain't queer—RACK ROCK!"

"Throw them all back!" Charity shouted. Amazing to see her in such joy, leaping the shock of incoming waves, eyes angled on her dial. Determined.

A sudden, thrilling thought.

What if Griff caught the song that changed their lives? Long evenings listening in the basement with their father, they'd hooked wild mariachi bands from Texas and symphonies from New York. They'd found all variety of wild crackpots from late-night basement-style broadcasts, hobbyists, truckers, preppers, floods of fifties/sixties pop, torrents of wordless, ear-tweaking static, and never once landed the big fish.

But tonight!

Griff planted his feet in freezing water, spread his toes for balance, focusing on the tiny notched dial. Numb to the knees, he teased something from the fuzz. A trumpet! Beautiful horn warbling on AM 1550, and he held on as a woman's voice joined, soulful words about a mountain town with one road in—

"Got something," Griff said.

The song sizzled and spat like water on a hot pan.

"What?" Charity asked.

"I'm right around 1520—" he said. "Wait."

Water slapped his knees and his footing shifted, maybe an inch. The song ran. Griff barely touched the dial. Feather strokes.

"C'mon," he said.

White noise thumped, tuneless. Gone. Charity screamed.

She shrieked. "Oh that's cold. Ah, I had drums!"

Tide coming in. Griff's bare feet hunted for his next step, probing for urchins. In the distance, Leo shouted something. Waved his arms. Griff turned up the hiss and Leo's voice dropped away to nothing. That easy.

When he looked back at Charity, she was frozen.

It happened suddenly. Like she'd been stung. Griff's training clicked in. He rushed toward her, long lunging steps, shoving through the water.

"Charity!"

Water lapped at her thighs.

In the moonlight, her face was expressionless. Then her mouth parted with a soft sound. He waded closer, tore out his earbuds. Somehow, over the beat of the water, he heard her radio—

No.

Her voice.

Charity was singing.

The deep, shivery voice she'd summoned in the amphitheater, the one she'd tried out in the Rat's Nest before Leo scared it away. Full of life and sound and wordless. She sang and saw him watching and blinked, as if woken from a dream.

"Song on," she said. "Song on, Griff! Right at 1300—"

He was very close to her now. A wave rocked them toward the shore, pulled them toward the sea. She grabbed his arm. And jolted.

"What?" he asked. "What's wrong?"

She held on to his arm. Pressure of her palm. She clipped the radio onto her belt and she examined her other hand in the moonlight, like she'd just discovered it. She placed her bare hand on Griff's other arm and lit up, more than just touching, there was some secret—

"Find it, Griff."

He turned the wheel, shredding interference, and blew past something like a thick bump in the sound—a crackle of voices, instruments. He wheeled back slowly, and white noise suddenly stopped. The signal deepened like the bold blue water dropping off the far edge of a reef. The silence was profound. Remarkably clear, then he heard them:

A band.

A freezing wave struck his thighs and he was engulfed in strings, bass, percussion—there must've been dozens of them playing—a wild, soulful orchestra. Charity sang along. The music on the airwaves assembled around her voice, like they'd carved out a piece in the beat and melody just for her. She held Griff's arms in a strange embrace, like she might shake some sense into him, or pull him into a ferocious kiss, and she said—

"Touch me, Griff."

"What?"

"Touch and listen."

Griff's arms felt mechanical, devices he no longer knew how to maneuver, fat fingers fumbled the radio into his back pocket, taking care not to touch the dial. Voices coalesced into a chorus—

You've got to find them—

You've got to find them—

"C'mon," she said, eyes hungry.

Griff reached up his left hand and cupped the curve of Charity's bare shoulder. Strings surged. Her skin, conductive. Louder. He touched her bare arm. Horns wailed and she whispered—

"Yes."

He did not know he was pulling her closer until she was coming closer and when her thigh touched his and she shivered he lifted his arms and her body fit just perfectly pressed to his chest and both shaking, sharing the shiver and the song swelled, pulled from the airwaves and into their bodies—

Splashing. Movement—it was Leo.

"What are you two doing?" Leo asked. He looked frantic.

Charity guided his thumb to the song. Then she held his arm to make the music surge.

"Song on," he said. "Thomas!"

Leo's face went slack with wonder.

"Oh my god," he whispered.

Charity touched Griff's neck. Griff touched his brother's arm. Linked, the song swelled larger, and then Thomas joined the huddle, armed draped around the shoulders, swaying with the ocean—SURGE! They laughed and cheered and they were there, at a show together again. Skin to skin and foreheads close. Hard to look in the eyes of someone feeling so much. Sometimes they broke formation, sometimes they looked away, but the music called closer, closer.

Leo looked at Griff. The raw, open eyes of a younger Leo:

"It's the best band I've ever heard."

They'd built the receiver.

Down the coast, God's Mouth said—*HOOM!*

The tide-is-coming sound. The get-to-higher-ground sound.

"Just a little longer," Leo said.

A little longer together in the cold water. We can do it. We can hold on.

THIRTEEN

THE NEXT MORNING—HOW WAS THAT EXACTLY? THE FEELING. THE way Griff's feet fluttered in the bottom of the bed when his eyes opened to the sun and how dust motes twinkled as if on fire. Like being eight years old, the whole world was again a puzzle worth solving.

Questions big enough to nudge him off the comfortable edge of every known map:

Who was that band?

● ● ●

Sitting at the lunch table that afternoon, no one had slept much. Thomas not at all.

"I can't eat," Thomas said, staring at a soggy pile of nachos.

Charity had gotten into a terrible fight with her mother, coming home late and questionably soaking. Leo and Griff had searched for some of the band's lyrics in vain, then fell into a late-night debate on sound propagation, wavelengths, and electromagnetic voice phenomena that caused them—around 4 AM—to crack into the TOE Box together and make the bleary late-night determination that they might have experienced a mass hallucination.

Thomas was taking a more deliberate approach.

"We need to piece together every lyric, every song, every

refrain," he said, "so we have something to search. Then we need a recording."

"I'm an idiot," Leo said.

"Why?" Charity asked.

"I didn't bring a single tape," he said. "We could've recorded the band."

"Ugggh," Charity said, head in hands.

"With a recording," Thomas said, "the world opens up. We can do digital fingerprint scans, acoustic profiles—"

"Okay," Leo said. "So do we go again tonight?"

"I'm grounded until my wedding day," Charity said. "But I've got my radio at home."

"We've got access to the best receiver in the tricounty area," Griff said.

They all looked at him.

"The radio station," Griff said. "Thomas and I will be there tonight."

"It's not as close to the ocean," Leo said. "You won't get the same refraction."

Leo gave him a go-ahead-and-try look, like two middle Cs on the piano.

Da dun!

"Let's make a promise," Charity said. "When we find this band—no matter where they are, how far away, or how expensive, we have to go see them. All of us."

"Obviously," Leo said. Thomas laughed. "We'll open for them."

Hands to the center. It was a deal.

FOURTEEN

"HELLO, LISTENERS," THOMAS SAID. HE TURNED HIS RADIO MONI-
tor up. "You've got K-NOW, AM 550 Disaster Preparedness
Radio, and if you can hear this—you're still alive."

Griff removed the audio gear from his bag: headphone
splitter, cassette tapes harvested from their father's stash. Two
pairs of earbuds. Thomas pressed the ON AIR button, which
dimmed to gray.

"Leo's not coming?" Thomas asked.

"No," Griff said. "He's out with Jonesy, I guess."

"With Jonesy the Troll?"

Griff laughed.

"Bullshit," Thomas said. "After last night? Leo's going to
stand and shiver with Jonesy, looking for Russians? We've got
the best receiver on the West Coast!"

"He's up to something," Griff said.

"Always," Thomas said. "But is it a race to find this band?
Aren't we working together?"

It's always a race, Griff wanted to tell him. We're always
working together.

"Okay," Thomas said. "Fifteen minutes until the *pleece*
reports."

"Great," Griff said. He double-checked the switches—made
sure he was using the monitor, not the broadcast stream.

GO, the switch said on the left. NO GO, to the right.

Griff flipped the switch right and pressed the power, flooding studio-quality headphones with luscious white noise.

"Surf's up," Griff said. This was their chance.

He and Thomas listened, threading swarms of buzzing voices, screeching feedback, trying to match a tone to the memory of last night. Of note: a community baseball game tied at the bottom of the fifth. "Runaround Sue," playing simultaneously on two stations. One particularly abrasive patch of noise—like a metal-toothed toboggan screeching down pavement. After an hour, the throbbing behind Griff's eyes made him pull off the headphones.

"This was a lot more fun last night," Thomas said, "with the touching and the bodies."

"It usually takes time," Griff said.

Last night was exceptional. It could take hours to find anything surprising. Song fishing didn't always benefit from direct attention. The family often surfed the Skip during preserving sessions—out in the garage simmering tomatoes, mashing blackberries through wire mesh, listening to water boil and white noise churn. Already, Thomas was growing irate. Dark lines beneath his eyes, thickening. He pushed the microphone toward Griff.

"Your turn," he said.

"I'm not talking," Griff said.

"Why did you want a show?"

"To play music!"

"Sink or swim," Thomas said. He pushed the microphone toward Griff. In Griff's stomach, a feeling like a quivering hiccup just under the lungs. He smacked his lips, cleared his throat. Thomas punched the button yellow.

ON AIR

"This is Griffin Tripp and you're listening to K-NOW," he

said. He looked over the controls, his mind still as a photograph. Thomas reached over and pressed PLAY. AC/DC's "Back in Black." He released the ON AIR button. Glared at Griff.

"That one sentence really took it out of you, huh?"

"It did," Griff said.

"You straight-up panicked, Tripp," Thomas said. "What would you do in an actual disaster?"

"I'd be great," Griff said. "A total dreamboat."

"Oh shit," Thomas said, jolting.

"Oh shit what?" Griff said.

Thomas pointed at a small, blinking yellow light.

"Is that an alert?" Griff asked.

"Live caller," Thomas said. "Get it."

"Me?" Griff said.

"You were the DJ, so it's your call. That's the rule."

Griff smiled.

"Look at you," Griff said. "You're terrified."

"I just do this because I assume nobody's listening!" Thomas said. "Okay. Press that button. There. Now switch the source."

Griff pressed the receiver to his ear and heard a light breath on the other side.

"K-NOW Radio. Griffin speaking."

"Griffin!" she said. "Ha!"

"Charity?"

"Oh fuck, it's just Charity?" Thomas said.

"I thought you were grounded from your phone," Griff said.

"Landline," she said. "And I've still got my radio, Mr. DJ. Is your knob going to be stuck on AC/DC all night?"

"That's all Thomas," Griff said.

"What?" Thomas said.

"It's nice to hear your radio voice," Charity said.

She said it like a soft growl. Griff's neck hair prickled. Just words, and somewhere in his brain, a dump truck of chemicals crashed into the bloodstream. Itchy, eager, hot.

"Great to hear your voice," he said. He wanted to lean through the phone and fall into her lap.

"Oh, c'mon," Thomas said.

"Where are you calling from?" Griff asked.

"The sex room," Thomas said, tossing a pen in the air.

"My basement," she said. "I'm literally crocheting."

Charity in a basement.

"You crochet?"

"Yes. I'm actually seventy-eight years old, didn't I tell you?"

With studio-quality headphones, Charity's voice sat right in the canal of his ear.

"I want to hear you sing again," he said. "Like you sang last night."

Quiet.

"Okay," she said. "I don't know if I'll be allowed at the Rat's Nest for months."

Griff's mind turned corners, groped for a solution.

"We could get a room, I guess."

"What?" she said. Like she just sat straight up.

"A practice room. Like, a practice room. Choir. Choir practice room," he said. Had he just said *get a room*?

"Fun. Let's do that. Maybe, what day—"

She stopped.

"Charity?" he asked.

"Footsteps. Location compromised. Simms, signing out."

Supposed to be *signing off*. God. That was the cutest.

Griff hung up and Thomas eyed him like a specimen mashed on a slide.

"You, sir, are wearing the idiot goggles. The moron blanket."

Griffin narrowed his eyes. Frowned.

"No use. You still look like you're in love."

Griff let himself smile.

"You're getting a room?" Thomas asked.

"Are you spying on me?" Griff asked.

"I'm a trained spy."

"Just a practice room. Like, for music."

"What's wrong with the Rat's Nest?"

"She's grounded. I thought we might—"

"Wait, wait, wait," Thomas said. "Are you starting a side project with Charity?"

"No."

"Listen," Thomas said. "Side projects kill bands. Like, the Breeders were a side project of the Pixies. And then the Amps were a side project of the Breeders. Members start splitting off like unstable atoms in an uncontrolled environment. Meltdown! Boom!"

"We're just going to try something," Griff said.

"Am I invited?" Thomas asked. "Is Leo invited?"

Griff tilted his head. Then shook it. Thomas laid his hands out flat and seesawed them like a crashing wave. Clenched his fists with a jolt. Preppers sometimes used American Sign Language to communicate in disasters. That was ASL for tsunami, disaster, SHTF, Armageddon.

Thomas pressed the ON AIR button and quietly mouthed the word:

Boom.

FIFTEEN

LEO WAS STILL NOT HOME WHEN GRIFF UNDRESSED AND CLIMBED into bed. He stared at the quiet blue slab of his brother's mattress and wondered about Leo. If Griff had built a wall to disguise his few, limited desires, then Leo—being the better prepper—had probably dug a bunker. Reinforced steel. Large enough for a pool and dog park. The entire state of Florida.

Leo dreamed big. Griff couldn't see his dreams anymore.

Hours later—the peck of a key at the front door, ka-thump of boots, hush of bathroom water, rumple of clothing—it all blended with the routine sounds of nighttime until the door to the TOE Box creaked open. Griff lifted his eyelids to find his brother cross-legged on the floor with his small black backpack.

"It's late," Griff said.

Leo looked up. "Yeah. SubWatch."

Hard to imagine spending hours with Jonesy spitting sunflower seeds, spitting chew, spitting, listening, spitting. Leo was pulling things out of the backpack. Griff scooted to the foot of the bed. Hung his head backward off the mattress and saw his brother upside down. They used to do this together. See who could hang the longest, then whip themselves up for a giant head rush. They'd pretend they could float and walk on the ceiling. Climb over the doorframes. Pebbled paint on bare feet.

"What are you doing?" Leo asked.

Griff whipped his head up. Dizzy. Crawled back to his pillow.

"You should've come to the station," Griff said.

"I've got to get my hours," Leo said.

Leo scribbled something on a wide sheet of paper. He looked hungry in the pale light. Physically hungry. Shaky in the eyes. He rolled the paper like a scroll and placed it in a cardboard tube. Then something else. A flashing silver square. Leo held it, then set it down and climbed into bed.

Griff remained silent.

"Did you see her today?" Leo asked.

His tongue, heavy with sleep. The way they used to talk together in a tent, back when they still shared one.

"No," Griff said.

Maybe it was fatigue, or the upside-down head rush, or the tent-feeling. He wanted to spill a secret. Tell Leo—"Today was a no-circle day." As preppers, they kept paper calendars and recorded events in inscrutable symbols. Dashes. Asterisks. A little black dot stood for Bunker Meeting. The tiny fork meant Radio Station. Griff's used circles for the days he saw Charity. Sometimes he'd touch the circle. Or trace it over and over. Days without them looked empty. Today was a no-circle day. He wanted to tell his brother.

"I hope she doesn't leave the band," Leo said.

Griff propped himself on an elbow. "Why would she leave?"

"Why wouldn't she?" Leo asked.

Griff stared at the ceiling. He thought his brother never doubted anything anymore. If doubt had survived, what else prowled around in his brother's mind when the lights went low? Griff's went still with the sudden weight of it. Leo's voice at the half shell. The way he'd looked hearing the band. Griff missed him so badly. Pressure against the back of his nose, throat, his eyes.

Griff exhaled a shuddering breath.

He wanted to release it all. The whole untamed reservoir. How he wanted out of the Preppers, wanted his own show, wanted to sail on a boat of any proportion into any possible horizon with Charity Simms and—brother, I want you to know how her lips brushing my cheek feel like flying—how mad and out of control I feel now, and how sorry I am for how awkward and how hopeless we've made this, how tired I am of winner and loser and what are you hungry for, brother? Do you love her? Do you feel alone and outside this whole mess of a town like me? Are you lost like me?

The lighthouse flickered in the window.

"Whoomp," Griff breathed.

"What?"

Griff held his breath, and held the words in his mind. *I sing along with the lighthouse.* It struck him—that was the first thing he'd ever hidden from his brother. Griff opened his mouth, tasted the still air. He could say it. Awkward, absurd, and true.

"Stop talking to yourself," Leo said.

Griff pinched his lips shut. Pressed them tightly. Closed his eyes and waited for the pressure to stop. Leo got out of bed. The small silver square, flashing in his hand. He wove it through the eyelet of the TOE Box, seated the hasp with a click. It was a padlock.

SIXTEEN

When the door shut in practice room 5, it was the first time Griff had been sealed in a space alone with Charity Simms, with a door that could close. The primary feeling was a breathless panic, like Thomas's breath puffing—

Boom.

The door clicked shut. Charity's eyes leapt around, the way they had when they'd run to the Ruins. They were getting away with something. Without open space to dilute the electricity, it seemed to tremble in the air. Griff focused on the feeling of his toes mashed in his shoes on the instrument's pedals. Wrists and fingers. He was here to play piano. That's all he was here to do.

He sat at the bench. But, also, he could smell her.

"So what now?" she asked.

Tame the beast, Griff told himself. Lash those hormones with a rope, ride them into significant artistic achievements. It had been done by greater men. Van Gogh. Mozart. He placed his fingers on the keys. Straight lines. Stiff angles. She stood very close to the bench. Her hair bounced, tossing off the sweetest scent, like honey, peaches in the sun, god you wanted to bury your face—

"What kind of singing do you want me to do?" Charity asked.

"Like at the ocean," he said. Words, a challenge.

She nodded.

"How do we start?" she asked.

He hadn't done this before, but maybe like kissing. You lean in, then a little closer, time trembles, slips, and suddenly you're kissing. He released his fingers. The music came slowly, like drawing water from an old well. Creaky pulls at the pump, but it got better. He even played around the edges of the cadenza, and still Charity did not sing.

He looked at her. She flinched.

Was he making a face? He'd seen it in his concert tapes, after Leo mentioned it. Griff's Piano Face. Blank, slack-jawed, fish-lipped. God, he was doing it now.

"Sorry," he said.

"For what?" She smiled. "You're amazing."

"You're not singing."

"It's scary," she said. "You're too good."

"Let's start loose," Griff said. "Okay? Da, da, da, da—"

He sang. She sang back, but her voice was tight. Rubber-banded at the top of her throat. Griff played another riff, teasing her:

"This room is soundproof," he sang.

She laughed.

"C'mon!" he said.

"This room is soundproof—" she sang.

"Griff loves my voice," he sang.

"Griff loves my voice!"

Call-and-response, they sang about their study hall teacher— *Gonna sing it loud, wake Michaelson up from his hundred-year naaaaaaaap*—and when she'd found her deep, glowing sound, he dropped them straight into a song—

"Because we've got to find them," Griff sang, hitting chords he remembered from the broadcast. She sang it back, her own words, new words, and with Charity unleashed, Griff needed more tones. He was still only using half the piano. Her voice crushed the invisible wall. Griff's hands spread out over all the keys and Charity drove the melody. They left the song they'd heard and moved into something new.

Just sounds.

Like they'd both forgotten words and remembered only language.

Chasing Charity's voice, the piece took shape. They kept going. Her eyes closed, riding the current. Lost together, a playful tug-of-war, coming slowly up the underside of a wave and then building, building, crashing down together, sweating, hands trembling, and—was that a sound at the window? A tap at the door?

Griff's hands faltered.

Mr. Jung? Leo? No one, but it couldn't last—a familiar impulse to end it, do it quick before it collapses anyway, before you ruined it all. He played a final flourish and pulled back and Charity was watching him with changed eyes.

Burning. He'd not seen these eyes before. Eyes that could swallow the whole world.

"That's the best music I've ever made," she said.

Griff examined his hands, as if they'd been under the control of someone else.

"Really?"

"Yes," she said, very loud. She laughed. "Yes! Yes! We've got something. Ah, and time again! I have to go."

She smiled.

"You have to?" he said.

"Thank you," she said.

She nodded. Moved closer. She leaned down and kissed one of his cheeks. Her hair brushed his skin—a shivery delight.

"They do that in France," he said.

His jaw could not stop shaking. What if she tried a kiss? On his underpracticed lips, sluggish tongue. Better if she didn't, get out RUN—

"They actually do two kisses in France," Charity said.

She kissed him again, on the other cheek. A long, lingering kiss. He could feel the shape of her lips, the soft sound when they left.

"Three sometimes," he exhaled.

She was breathing like she'd been running a race, his breathing like they'd run it together and she was kissing him a third time. On the first cheek again, and a fourth kiss on his jawline, where her mouth was hot and wet and moving slowly, happy, taking time to his ear and—

Breathe, balance on this bench—

Her tongue merged with his ear like a galactic sensation, a door in his chest opened to a hot breeze and he was nowhere near himself, not in his cage of a body but twirling, shuddering, shivering, and she was again in front of him smiling, breathing the last of the room's air.

"They do that in France?" Griff said.

"Not always," she whispered. She looked at him. Lips close enough to kiss. Hungry eyes. Eyes like *move*, like *kiss me*. Griff looked over his shoulder, and there was no one there.

"Just us," Charity said.

"Okay," he said.

She smiled. Stood up.

"Best practice ever," she said. She walked to the door and turned off the light.

"Hey!" he said.

"*Au revoir,*" she said. And laughed. And left.

SEVENTEEN

CHARITY CAME TO BAND PRACTICE THE NEXT NIGHT, RISKING A lifetime at Christian boarding school. She showed up late, wearing a hoodie. Charity checked the door to the Rat's Nest, checked the clock, looked very nervous until she noticed what Thomas was wearing. She laughed.

"What's up with your shirt, Thomas?"

It was the first time Griff had seen him out of camo in nine months. No paracord. Thomas wore a fitted white T-shirt with a crude depiction of four people with large heads standing in the ocean beneath a swollen moon. The shirt was hand-drawn in black marker. Giant, scrawled letters:

THE BAND

"I made it," Thomas said. "The Band has left me no choice. They have no web presence."

"I keep telling you the Band is already a band," Leo said.

"Oh, who cares," Thomas said. "Now that we're all here, come on over."

Thomas had caught the obsession like a virus. His workbench had transformed from a Prepper Operations Hub to a Missing Persons Command Center—and the missing person was the Band. He led them to a glowing computer tower. On one monitor, a spreadsheet where he'd entered and indexed song lyrics, alternate song lyrics, potential titles. A tab for Persistent Mysteries: How many people in the Band? What genre of music? When and where did they play?

"Amazing," Charity said. "What a mess."

"Oh no. Are those salt and vinegar?" Griff asked, nodding toward crumbs on the floor.

"Not yet," Thomas said. "Charity, you don't have to clean. It's embarrassing."

"It helps when I'm nervous."

She knelt beneath the table, picked up some chip fragments, set them on the table. She made a clicking sound. Neapolitan appeared in her hands. Furry, cute. Giant tail.

She stood with the rat, then screamed.

From deeper in the Rat's Nest, a bright blue pulse reacted to the sound.

"Oh my god," she said, looking at her bare foot. "You have more than one."

"Rats? Oh yeah," Thomas said. "Redundancy measures. That's Pestilence. Got Death. Got Famine. Haven't seen War for days."

"I stand in awe," she said. "Have you found anything on the Band?"

"No. And we didn't hear them last night," Griff said.

Griff looked for his brother, notably absent from the conversation. Slouched in the Big Blue Chair. On his phone.

"I mean, just look at this," Thomas said.

He searched more lyrics. In quotes, out of quotes. Words they'd agreed on.

The rain swirls down, you thirst for the sun—
When you part the curtains, the sun rises still—

"Still nothing," Charity said. "Amazing."

"It was cute, but not cute now," Thomas said. "I'm losing my mind on this."

"At least you're not into the salt and vinegars," Griff said.

"Are we practicing?" Leo hollered.

Again, a blue glow pulsed, throwing stark shadows.

"Did you all see that blue light?" Charity asked. "Or am I losing my mind?"

"C'mon over," Thomas said. He led them deeper into the Rat's Nest. Past the curtained-off practice space to where wooden storage shelves slouched beneath boxes and tubs. The sawdust and urine smell of rodents. On a small workbench, cluttered stacks of transmitters. Mason jars, and a stack of thin steel lids.

In the center, an Early Alert Response System globe. But different.

"Systems update," Thomas said. He clapped his hands. The bauble glowed blue.

"Whoa!" Charity said.

"Sound-sensitive. You can see low-frequency vibrations. If we get these tuned up, we can kiss SubWatch goodbye. And all this lighthouse-repurposing shit. We'll see anything coming. We can light up the whole coast."

"Genius," Griff said.

"Working on tone distinction too," Thomas said.

He whistled. High-pitch. The light got brighter.

"The Amazing Thomas," Charity said. "Is there anything you can't do?"

"Dance on beat," he said.

"Hey!" Leo said. "Bandmates?"

They dragged slowly toward practice. Hard to leave the glowing bauble and spreadsheets and dead-end search results.

Two bright musical passions surged in Griff. The first, they'd all found together, touching skin in the ocean. The other happened in an unlikely practice room with fluorescent lights and a plinking upright where he and Charity had somehow opened the door to God. Now Leo had his binder. Wanted them to sing about star-crossed lovers:

Feeling star-crossed, feeling star-crossed

The song meandered. Bodies anchored to the room, lashed to instruments. Leo scribbled notes, asked them to try different sections. Everyone's mind seemed elsewhere—even Leo's. After an hour, there was a moment of just Thomas looping them together, stitching the tunes together with his sound system. He looked over the group and said:

"Where are you guys?"

"Right here," Leo said. "I feel like no one's trying. This is super serious."

Leo was looking at him. Griff felt his brother's icy fingertips, prying at his Wall of Modest Secrets. And Griff had accumulated certain red-circle treasures behind the wall. Hugs. Secret practices. A tongue in the ear, and he was nervous but giggly, because Thomas was playing Leo's voice back on the loop pedal.

"Super serious. Suuuuuuper seeeeeerious. This is super serious, super serious—"

"Stop!" Leo said. Leo's voice, the way it had been before he'd upended Robbie Anderson's desk in homeroom, for flicking his ear. The room braced for something.

Only Charity seemed unmoved.

"Why is it so serious?" she asked.

"Because I got us a gig," Leo said. "A big one."

Leo had their attention again—but now Leo was leaving. Out through the tapestries, footsteps clipping along the floor, clomping up the steps.

Thomas played the loop again.

Super serious.

"Stop, Thomas," Charity said, pulling on her hoodie.

"We only have a song and a half," Thomas said. "You think we really have a gig?"

"If we don't," Griff said, "we will."

EIGHTEEN

By NEXT WEEK, EVERYONE AT SCHOOL KNEW ABOUT THE GIG.

They'd be playing at the Urchin, of all places—a squat and sprawling windowless bar on South Jetty, tucked behind dock-sale fish shops like a scabby mollusk. Its marquee had read NO SHOW TONIGHT so long Griff wondered if they'd have to pry the salt-encrusted letters off with a crowbar—and what was the name of their band, anyway?

"Lionized," Leo said at the lunch table.

He'd drawn out a poster, enhanced with Thomas's new-found Sharpie design skills. A wild lion with octopus tentacles, clinging to the end of a dock.

"Solid," Charity said. "Retro cool. I mean, I could see this hanging in LA."

She was sitting next to Leo. Charity and his brother had obviously gotten chummy while Griff had been standing in line for a cafeteria cheeseburger. He stared at the thin piece of colorless meat between waxy bread—and it might be for this poor lunch choice that he lost Charity Simms forever. The Cheeseburger to End It All.

"So," Leo said, "we'll work on some vocal arrangements—over the computer if you're grounded—"

Charity nodded.

With the sudden gig, talk of finding the Band receded. Thomas was the only constant reminder—wearing an endless rotation of new T-shirts. This one, a swollen moon above a crooked lighthouse—swimmy words: THE BAND.

"We have two songs, Leo," Thomas said.

"We can do covers," Leo said. "We have almost a month."

"Okay," Thomas said. "A month, okay."

"Let's be bold, people," Charity said.

"You know it," Leo said. They high-fived. That look he'd seen before, excitement in her eyes. A squirmy, sizzling feeling in his stomach. He hated this. Charity's eyes following Leo. Just look at me, just look at me once, please, and Griff walked to the garbage can and dumped his cheeseburger inside and went to study hall early.

He sat at the same table and did not work on the puzzle. It was a stupid puzzle. Exhausting. He wanted to give up. Die maybe.

After school, Charity was with Leo again, and Thomas, bouncing around on the front steps of the school. Desecrating the sacred place where Griff and Charity had once done their soft, slow dance in autumn light. Ruined.

"Hey, Griff!" Leo said. "C'mere. You down to go this afternoon?"

Griff now entered every conversation late, a page behind.

"For what?"

"The Urchin, baby," Thomas said.

Of course. Leo did not incubate and hatch and slowly grow a plan, he unleashed it upon the landscape of your life with the power of a terrible lizard that devoured your daily plans and ate the horizon for dessert.

"Oh boy," Charity said. "A bar."

"C'mon," Leo said, bumping her shoulder like a caveman. "Show some student leadership."

Miraculously, Charity agreed to come.

When they approached the ThunderChicken, Griff was suddenly grateful. Months ago, Leo had claimed Eternal Shotgun like a birthright. There was a spark of recognition in his brother's eyes just before the back doors clapped shut, safely confining Charity and Griff to a single leather bench seat.

"Purr, my sweet chicken of war," Thomas said, patting the steering wheel.

"You could fit a thousand people back here," Charity said, fanning herself out.

"The ceiling sags," Thomas said, pushing up on the fabric. "You have to ride crouched down like this. Low-ride it."

He slouched. Griff and Charity did too. Smiled at each other.

"Hey," she said in a soft voice.

Griff pictured himself, pouncing like a cartoon jungle cat, gliding across the smooth interior. They erupt in a backseat tumble of clouds, emerge with lipstick smears. Griff fastened his seat belt. Windows down, they went whooshing out of the sun-dappled parking lot, Thomas put on Nina Simone's "Feeling Good" and the coastal highway seemed to rise in front of them. Runway for A Brand-New Something. Breakers beat the shoreline, and when Charity's voice twirled with Nina Simone's in the whip of the wind down a coastal highway the feeling just crystallized.

They were a band. Griff smiled. The biggest smile in a month.

Thomas turned onto the South Jetty—

"Do people actually have legitimate businesses out here?" Charity asked.

Griff laughed. "You've never come out here for fish? Anything?"

"This is no-man's-land," Charity said.

The jetty was a wide, crumbling concrete peninsula of shipping containers, a research shack from the university on wooden pilings, and a lawless parking lot that tapered to a clutch of weathered dock-sale fish shops and the Urchin. On the marquee:

NO SHOW TONIGHT

A complete dive. Neon pinks, blues, yellows burned in hollowed-out sections of cinder block, boarded up or painted over. They walked from their distant parking space. The cars—a Buick, a Crown Victoria, three pickups—slouched in the lot. The front door claimed NO MINORS. Black marker said (MINORS BETWEEN 11–7 ONLY). A lottery sign crossed its fingers.

"I should've used the bathroom at school," Charity said.

CLANK. A sour bell as Leo opened the door. The bar exhaled beer breath.

A bank of video lottery machines splashed light in the corners, and a long central bar wrapped around the liquor like an engine belt. Three men on barstools. Two rotated toward them as if attached to the same mechanical arm. Cowboy hat. One in camo. Staring.

Griff heard Charity's breath catch.

She looked back toward the door.

Rab, the owner, came toward them from the end of the bar. Griff knew him from downtown and a few random conversations with their father. Rab the Rambler. He had the weathered, sunburned face of a man too long at sea and walked with a forward lean as if angled against a perpetual headwind. He gave them a warm smile.

"Hello, Leo," he said. He pointed at Griff, Leo, Griff.

"Me," Leo said.

"And you are?"

"Charity," she said.

"A pleasure," he said.

Thomas was already examining the P.A. Leo and Rab talked about the show. The others checked out the stage. Elevated 5 feet. Black curtains. Behind them, a greenroom packed with old instruments, theater props. Burlap sacks. The clinging smell of cigarette smoke, beer. The lingering ghosts of a thousand performances. Behind a heap of clothing and a full-length mirror was a piano.

"All right," Charity said. She leaned over a squat table, tapped the keys. "Is it in tune?"

"No piano is ever in tune," Griff said. "But this one's close enough."

"I'm going to check the circuit breaker," Thomas said.

It was just Griff and Charity. Griff leaned over, snaked his hand through a gap, and played the opening part of Stravinsky. Charity laughed. She was looking at him. A long, steady look.

"What?" Griff asked.

"Nothing," she said. She smiled like she was keeping a secret.

A few minutes later, Leo and Rab shook hands and the bell was clanging them back out the door. The breeze blew hard. Sunlight, diffuse behind gauzy clouds. Charity took a deep breath and spread her arms.

"Free!" she said. "My god, I'm free."

"What did you think?" Leo asked.

"Terrifying," Charity said. "Exciting."

"A few weeks," Leo said. "We've got a lot to do."

As they walked to the ThunderChicken, Leo got tight and close-talking with Charity. Talking about future rehearsals, where they could stand. Never mind he and Leo hadn't practiced piano in days. When they finally reached the car, Leo said:

"Go on, Griff. You can take shotgun."

They were already climbing in back.

Like Rhiannon on the beach. A single car ride could derail everything. So Griff hesitated, then opened the door and climbed in on the other side of the backseat, so Charity was between them.

"Hi," Charity said.

"What are you doing?" Leo asked.

Griff didn't know what he was doing.

"Okay, weirdos," Thomas said. He adjusted the rearview mirror. "I'm not going to chaperone your creepy twin love triangle around. The Chicken has standards."

The three of them looked at one another.

"We're already back here," Griff said.

Griff had never done anything like this. His breath caught in his throat.

Charity was giving him a curious look. He probably looked deranged.

"Not moving," Thomas said, shifting to park.

"Guys," Charity said. "I have to go home. I'll just climb up front."

"Thomas," Leo said. "Just drive. You can play whatever music you want."

"All year," Thomas said without missing a beat.

"All year?!" Leo countered. "This week."

"Month."

"Until Christmas."

Everyone remained silent.

"Fine," Leo said.

"Well then, lovebirds. We begin our drive home with a twelve-hour tribute to Bon Scott—"

"Oh god," Leo said.

"—late lead singer of AC/DC, beginning with *High Voltage* and the Lock Up Your Daughters Tour—"

Charity nudged closer to him. Almost right up against his shoulder. Worth it.

NINETEEN

AFTER THEY LANDED THE GIG, EVERYTHING INTENSIFIED. DRIZZLY days blurred together like wet paint. Whereas September had been a rushing river of endless forks and channels, October somehow hardened to asphalt—inflexible and fixed, tapering the way a road sinks into a forest—no choice but forward.

A busy week. School, homework, bunker meetings, preparing for the winter piano concert. The family together only for dinner. Mom cooking alone most nights, their father on the couch with a glass of wine. Then the bottle, too. Instead of knitting together like flesh and bone, the cracks from the false alarm seemed to widen gradually like the spiderweb fracture in a windshield. Freezing, thawing, and expanding to strange new patterns.

Six no-circle days.

Charity at student government instead of study hall. Still grounded, no phone. In a week, he'd only seen her on a screen—twice in his bedroom, practicing harmonies with Leo. After seeing her on screen, she felt somehow less real. When he found her at their table during sixth period the following Wednesday, he was as shocked as he'd been the first day of school.

"Oh my god," she said. "Is it you?"

"Are you still real?" Griff said.

She gave him a hug. Nice, but brief. She felt like a stranger.

"Did Michaelson save our puzzle?" she asked.

"I asked him to," Griff said. "Do you have time?"

"No," she said. "You?"

"Nope."

"Great," Charity said. "It's better if we're both irresponsible."

They moved a few stacks of books. Two boxes of blank paper. The puzzle was right there where they'd left it. He watched her fingers move.

He'd start with her fingers. Study them until they were real. Thawing her from memory. Slender, quick fingers pushing edges, testing, worrying them with touch the way the mind nudges a question—good, strong, thinking movements, and who could command such fingers? A mystery he followed to her wrists—slender and the long sleek path of an arm, building to the climax of an elbow—

"Hey," she said.

He took a breath.

"Hey," he said.

"There you are," she said. "Are we still on for tomorrow?"

"On for what?"

She frowned.

"Room five."

"Oh," he said. "I guess. Yeah."

She squinted at him. Shook her head.

"What?"

"You forgot," she said.

"No," he said. "We just hadn't talked about it in a while."

"I've got no phone," she said. "And we said same time next week."

"Right," he said.

"I don't feel like..." She sighed, raked a hand through her hair—this was new. "I don't feel like people should have to keep confirming appointments, you know? Like—we make a date, set a time, and that's set. You shouldn't have to keep following up. If it's important, you just do it. You remember."

"I'm sorry," he said.

"Don't be sorry," she said.

How could he tell her? It was entirely shocking every time she wanted to be with him. If he told her that, what else might rush out? How he thought about her face so frequently that sometimes it was terrifying to see her? Would he say there were not enough red circles on the calendar anymore—could he ever tell her about red circles?

"I think we need to bring Leo in on this," she said.

"What?" Griff said. "Into our rehearsals?" His blood went still.

"Not bring him," Charity said. "Tell him. There's nothing wrong with us rehearsing our own songs. And I had an idea this week. I talked to my mom about it."

"What?"

"What if we played at the Urchin? You and me. If we're going to play cover tunes, why not play a couple of our songs?"

"There is a piano," Griff said. His cheeks burned. He sat up straight.

"We can open for ourselves," Charity said. She was giddy, alive with the idea.

"Yes," Griff said. "Of course."

"I'll tell Leo today," Charity said. "Or at practice."

Griff tried not to think about the telling. He tried, for a moment, just to be happy.

TWENTY

"WE'RE STILL WAITING ON LEO AND CHARITY," THOMAS SAID. "But come in. I want to show you something."

While the rest of them had gotten busy, Thomas's obsession with the Band had only intensified. No longer a Missing Persons situation. Now, One Man's Desperate Search for His Daughter's Killer. Computers set in a loose ring. And maps. Big printed sheets of the coast. Northern California to southern Washington tacked to the pegboard, inscribed with notes, the arcing sweep of a compass pencil. Off on a tiny table, a separate computer, isolated from the others. Griff walked toward it.

"Don't touch!" Thomas said, as if Griff were about to grab a snake.

"That one goes to the dark web," Thomas said.

"What are you doing in the dark web?"

"Only 3 percent of the internet is searchable," Thomas said. "They've got to be hiding somewhere." He pulled off his hoodie, tossed it aside. Another custom T-shirt. Ghosts surrounded a condenser microphone, their mouths distended Os.

"Do you have a theory?" Griff asked.

"Yeah," Thomas said. "If they aren't ghosts, or a figment of our collective imagination—they actively don't want to be found."

"So why broadcast the shows?"

"That's the mystery!" Thomas said. He looked crazed. "But if they broadcast once, they'll do it again."

"How can you be sure?"

"Patterns," he said. "Psychology. Geology."

On the pegboard Thomas flipped back large butcher-paper sheets of coastal maps and triangulation. Peeling the onion back into past obsessions. He stopped. This one, Griff recognized. A timeline stretching deep into the geologic Holocene, Pliocene, the murk of the Jurassic, the Cambrian, each punctuated by tall red lines growing like uneven chutes to the present. Each line represented an eruption.

"The Cascadia Quake," Griff said.

That last bright white space—from January 26, 1700, until now. Every 234 years and then—blank. Like the first pause after hours of hiccups.

"I'm familiar," Griff said.

"Okay," Thomas said. "How about this?"

He let the sheets fall. Second from the top, a timeline made with the same compunction for straight lines, right angles, and historic accuracy, but over the last thirty days. The big red spike was the day they'd found the Band. Thomas, being a good prepper, had devised his own code. A series of symbols that consisted of a curly upside-down letter U and lightning bolts. They appeared on simultaneous and alternating dates, snaking up and down the calendar.

"Given the number of people in the Band, and the quality of the broadcast," Thomas said, "my original theory was that they must send the signal daily. Or weekly. Some predictable interval."

Griff smiled, seeing the pattern.

"These are the days at the station," Griff said, touching the lightning bolts. Thomas stared back at him. "So—what are these?"

He touched the horseshoe shapes.

"Another, um—source."

"Who?"

Thomas stared back at him. He pursed his lips and raised his eyebrows like half-moons. The Preppers had not been able to eradicate an ounce of earnestness from Thomas Mortimer. He had all the guile of a tortoise.

"Well," Thomas said, as if to himself, "I didn't tell Leo about your practices with Charity."

"You've been working with Leo on this?"

"Ask Leo," Thomas said.

Thomas was easy to read but impossible to crack. You'd know he had a secret, but he'd bite down on a cyanide pill before he'd turn it over. Griff pored over the maps, tables. They were extraordinary.

Footsteps overhead, soft thunder down the stairs. Leo and Charity entered together. The energy was strange—you could feel the edges of the conversation they'd just snapped off. Thomas and Griff stood at some kind of attention, like they were awaiting orders.

"What?" Charity said.

Leo looked at Griff, then Thomas's maps.

"Nothing," Leo said. "We have a gig next week. Let's practice."

She must've told him about their practices.

The energy improved once they started playing. As it turned out, the potential for public humiliation was galvanizing. Leo and Charity had worked out their sound, Leo in the lead—Charity bolstering his sound like a human repeater. She should've been holding microphone one. Griff kept his eyes on the plastic keys of the plastic keyboard and played the plastic songs and when he looked up Charity was staring at him. Her brow creased, creased harder. She said:

"Hey, all. Can we talk quick?"

"Okay," Leo said. He was chewing his lower lip.

She hadn't told him.

Don't do it, Griff thought. Not now. Wrong time.

"Griff and I have been working on a few songs," she continued. "Leo, I kind of mentioned this to you, the other day."

Leo's face, expressionless.

"Anyway," she said, "Griff, you and I, right, were wondering about opening for Lionized. Fifteen minutes max. We don't really have songs yet, but we've got a great sound."

"How often do you two practice?" Leo asked.

"Just once," Griff said.

"But again tomorrow," Charity said. "And a few times next week, if we need to. Like I said, it's pretty informal. Kind of improv."

Leo looked at Griff.

"So, you have a side project?"

"Oh," Thomas said. "Oooooh."

"It's not a side project," Griff said.

Leo walked straight toward Griff and his muscles tensed. Griff flinched and Leo breezed through the curtains. They opened with a soft flutter, draped themselves shut.

"Let him go," Charity said. But Griff had to follow. It had been a brand-new look from his brother. He'd never seen it before. It scared him.

Griff left Thomas's house and climbed on his bike. The night was humid but cool. The kind of fog that clung to your clothing, made you shiver and sweat at the same time. Griff knew Leo's bike wouldn't be at home, but he checked there first. Then past the McLeans', where Leo had tucked himself behind the hedge after a breakup, past the Marcinis', with the abandoned tree house they'd often infiltrated together.

All the hiding places were old. From the comic-book times. Cards in spokes had not rattled for years and Griff no longer knew where Leo went when he wanted to be hidden.

When Griff came in, dripping, his father was at the kitchen table, surrounded by spreadsheets. No more transistor radio games in the basement, no more big bowls of popcorn. This man owned a condo in Florida. Griff hung up his raincoat.

"Have you seen Leo?" he asked.

"Weren't you both at Thomas's?" his father asked. "Working on EARS updates?"

They hadn't done an EARS update in weeks.

"I thought he was out with Jonesy," Griff said.

"Jonesy!" His dad snorted. "Those two mix like potassium and water."

Potassium exploded in water. These sorts of analogies were part of the problem with making friends and meeting girls. Made you grow up strange. His father looked up.

"Speaking of," his father said. "You're really short on hours for Gap Academy. You haven't been to a rotational meeting in weeks."

"I'm doing radio shifts," Griff said. "I'm not sure about the Gap anyway."

"Well." His father sighed.

Griff edged backward. This was a black-hole conversation. A vortex that would suck him into obligations and sad calendar boxes. Back in his bedroom, the padlock winked from the eyelet hook of the TOE Box, just beside the mirrored closet door. Griff stared at the lock. And the box.

What were he and Thomas doing? Just listening in secret?

Despite their endless contests, Griff had mostly felt lashed to Leo, hip to hip, like joint competitors in a three-legged race. Leo's outside foot always landed first, but they crossed the finish line together. Griff touched the cool lock. Flipped it up so it banged down on painted metal.

TUNG

With Charity, it was different. The feeling hung like hooks in his lungs.

TUNG

Griff chipped off a fleck of black paint. Blue beneath.

He could snap that lock with the torque of twin crescent wrenches. Griff looked up at the mirror and Leo's face was watching him. He turned off the light and lay in bed with his phone.

Finally, he sent a message to his brother:

LEO, WHERE ARE YOU?

● ● ●

After midnight, Leo came in like a cool gust of air. Whistling.

Griff sat up.

"Where have you been?"

Griff was startled by his own voice. He'd been asleep, but sounded wide awake.

Leo kept whistling. The bedroom was cold, like the damp sea air had clung to his clothes and changed the bedroom's weather.

"The lighthouse," Leo said.

"What?"

"Jonesy and I blew it to pieces. Shot it up."

Griff flung off his bedsheets. No light in the window.

Leo took the bag off his shoulder, dug inside. Cassette tapes. Something metal. Cardboard tubes.

Still, no light in the window.

Half tethered to sleep, dreamy images rushed through his mind. Leo, smashing their mother's cream-colored pitcher and bowl set with a hardball after Griff won Best At Bat in fifth grade. His prized snow castle at Hoodoo Mountain, the pains-taking stacking of igloo bricks to achieve the perfect slope, a miraculous window—smashed, battered, caved in with the steel runners of a toboggan because "that's what happens to snow forts," but not exactly. That's what happens when you win.

Leo had the capacity to destroy beautiful things.

Griff raced to the window. Lifted the blinds.

He watched the darkness.

"See?" Leo said.

Thick mist. A blot of white. The lighthouse blinked. Unmis-takable. Griff's shoulders dropped. He didn't mind being lied to, because it was a lie.

"You really believed that?" Leo said. He laughed.

"I don't know what you're doing," Griff said, getting back in his bed. "But I know you've been working with Thomas."

"Not anymore," Leo said.

"I'm sorry about the rehearsals," Griff said. "I should've told you."

"Sure."

Leo shut the door to the box. Reattached the lock.

"Can you tell please me what you're doing?" Griff asked.

"Ask Charity," Leo said. "Tomorrow night, she's coming with me."

TWENTY-ONE

AFTER SCHOOL, CHARITY WAS NOT IN PRACTICE ROOM 5.

When Griff went through the hallways to look for her, he heard his brother's voice down the next hall. When he turned the corner, he saw Leo talking to Charity.

Leo's hands, flashing around. He looked angry.

Griff went back to the practice room and waited five minutes. Ten. He paced the tiny zoo cage of a room. Pulled the skin on his bare wrist. Looked at his phone, looked out the window. His phone again.

When Charity arrived, her face had the flat composure of a smooth stone. Cracks showed around her eyes and mouth. Trembling.

"What?" Griff asked.

"Leo's mad at me."

Another snapped-off conversation, only this time the edges were rougher. For the first time after one of Leo's tantrums, Charity looked rattled.

"What's he want?" Griff asked.

"To go back to the Ruins. I thought it was all of us. But he just wants it to be me."

"Of course," Griff said.

Charity looked at the practice room's small window. No one there. Her eyes looked clouded over. Griff wondered if she looked at him and saw Leo.

"Are you going?" Griff said softly.

"Going alone with Leo anywhere feels like a stupidly complicated choice and all this is already stupid and complicated," she said.

"It doesn't have to be," Griff said.

"Really?" she asked. She looked at him, like she was waiting for an answer.

"Let's play," he said.

It took time to dig out from the mood, smooth the edges. The reservoir of words he was unable to share, he let flow through his fingers instead. A trickle, a torrent, a flood—no more him, no more Leo, barely a room. He let himself be tethered to a bright, humming energy. The sound of Charity's voice.

If he was water tonight, she was the wind.

She chased notes up and down the scales. Her voice shook, wobbled, cracked—broke and put itself together. When Charity sang, it all meant something, and you were part of it, something profound, just past the edge of understanding.

His hands shook. She looked at him.

"You're singing the mysteries of the whole universe," Griff said.

"It's my favorite," she said. "Like my body understands and my mind is trying to catch up. Do you think we have three songs?"

Did they? The music was an exploration. Like a swimmy underwater cave with roundish spaces you might call songs and, in that respect, yes. There were three such spaces.

"Yes. We can play three songs," Griff said.

"Yeah? Still? Thank you."

She came to him, threw her arms around him. Squeezed hard. No kiss.

"Thanks for what?"

"Taking me to a brand-new place," Charity said.

Griff looked at the piano.

"What did Leo want to do at the Ruins?"

Charity shrugged.

"What did he say?"

Charity hesitated, weighing something. She looked at the window, and when she looked back she squinted a moment. Like—*Which twin are you?*

"Leo told me he found the Band."

TWENTY-TWO

CHARITY WASN'T IN STUDY HALL THE NEXT DAY AND SHE DID NOT come to lunch, nor respond to texts. In third period, Griff learned from Thomas that Charity had stayed home sick.

"She seemed fine yesterday," Griff said.

He didn't see his brother all day. And that was the night Leo changed.

He came home later than usual, stinking of the low-tide flats. His energy was all different. Tension in the room, like the suck of breath just before a scream. Griff couldn't stop thinking: Had Charity gone with him after all?

Leo removed his boots. Unlocked the TOE Box.

Movement of materials. The quiet rip of paper. Each cassette, treated like thin glass. Leo pushed the hasp of the lock into the body and jerked once, twice. He went to the shower.

Strange underwater sounds.

You can hear just about anything in running water and a bathroom fan. They provoke auditory hallucinations, the way all types of white noise will. Their father had told them, when they first began song fishing. Given every possible tone, the brain will weave its own thread of meaning—often a repetitive beat, a forgotten jingle, or sometimes your own name being whispered, chanted, screamed.

"You could lose your mind," their father said, "if you're not careful."

Griff listened closely.

He wasn't making it up.

Beneath the water, Leo was singing.

TWENTY-THREE

AFTER THAT NIGHT, THE WORLD REGAINED ITS PROPER EDGES AND corners.

Mostly.

Charity was back at the lunch table. Leo stopped going out late at night. He'd snapped like an overstretched rubber band back into Prepper Life. Running tutorials on his computer—mapmaking, orienteering, survival science. Finding Water. Surviving Thirty Days in the Sand. Maybe he was worried they'd end up in Florida. At night, in bed, Leo listened to music, giant new noise-canceling headphones gulping his ears, head bobbing, feet tapping.

But no commentary. No give this a listen, bro.

On the run-up to show week, Leo worked and reworked the set list of ten songs. Five covers, five originals. He and Thomas made all final decisions. Griff had been cut out, but he'd happily play AC/DC's "Stiff Upper Lip" ten times straight if it meant he got to open with Charity. Their room 5 rehearsals continued to be beautiful, flowing, magic—but no French goodbyes. No ear explorations. The atmosphere with Leo and everyone seemed too tense, too barreling-forward, and any extra thing would be like sticking your arm out the window at 100 miles per hour.

The simmer of excitement in the hallways rose to a boil by midweek. At lunch on Wednesday, Thomas hid in the

ThunderChicken with his PB&J to avoid being asked about the show.

CAN'T HANDLE IT, DUDES, he texted. Sent a picture of himself in the fetal position, curled up in the backseat with sandwich crusts.

Somehow, the show was growing into a Big Deal.

"Break a leg, boys," Slim said Thursday, swinging by their lunch table. He smiled over his tray of two white milks and grilled cheese. He looked earnest. Proud, even.

"Thanks, Slim," Griff said.

"Thanks, buddy," Leo said. "See you there."

"Slim seems sweet," Charity said.

It seemed an okay level of sweet. But the growing excitement gave everything a trembling, up-on-two-wheels feeling. With every backslap, every shout of his name, Griff felt like flinching. Like a shoe would kick into his heel and he'd have to fight to keep on his feet.

Maybe middle school trauma. But maybe something else— like that haunting little animal-brain twitch that shot rats into Grecian streets and drove snakes from their dens in China.

He and Charity had nearly finished *Open Water*. As the week rolled on, it was clear they had an unspoken agreement. They'd finish the puzzle the day of the show.

"You and me, Tripp," Charity said with a smile. "Today's the day."

Griff was suddenly beaming. A dumb puzzle maybe—but it was tied up in everything. Miraculously, he and Charity had been to the Ruins. They'd said big hellos and French goodbyes and somehow his greatest and most secret desire of knowing Charity Simms had come true. More days with red circles than without. And something about locking an impossible puzzle to completion on the day of a first live show was appropriately brilliant. A perfect, if slightly forced, omen. Until Charity's eyes hunted across the table at the handful of pieces, and Griff saw the math on her lips, five, six—

"What?" Griff asked.

Her hands moved quickly, twisting, snapping in. The count-down, palpable. Griff grabbed the box. Opened it, touched the empty corners.

Dropped to the carpet. Hand and knees, fingers combing the tight blue-loop pile. A desert of tiny paper scraps, eraser tailings. Griff and Charity sat and locked eyes over the horizon of the table.

"One piece," Griff said.

They examined the hole. Blank, right where the sunlight should be.

"Close," she said.

Except that piece was the best part. The climax. That little hole—a tiny tear in the picture they'd built. But big enough. If it were real, the water would come gushing through, fill the school like an aquarium, drown the whole town.

Griff didn't have to wonder anymore. The universe had just confirmed it:

Something bad was going to happen.

TWENTY-FOUR

SHOW NIGHT.

"Dude," Thomas said, "Charity's mom is here. Dude—Ms. Simms!"

Leo had already gotten out of the ThunderChicken and was halfway to the front door of the Urchin when the white Bonneville came crackling into the lot. This close to the beach, every car sounded like it was driving on gravel. Griff made himself exit the ThunderChicken.

Brake lights flared. The car stopped. Parked.

Griff's breath hissed through his teeth. Charity's mother. Given her descriptions of this phone-restricting, churchgoing woman, perhaps the door would open with the sweep of a nun's habit and clapping thunder. His mental image did not map onto the woman who climbed out. Young-looking. Energetic. Charity's same springy, dark curls but this woman was very put together. Outfit like interlocking pieces of a fashion set; blue blazer, skirt, and a shirt with swimmy blue and green, like an Impressionist painting. They walked the same. Same determined eyes.

"Hi, boys," she said. Her voice, like a teacher. "Sharon Simms. Pleased to meet you."

"Oof," Charity said.

"You must be the twins I've heard so much about. Are you—"

"That's Griff," Charity said. "The one I've been rehearsing with."

"Oh," her mother said, voice lifting a full octave. "Griff."

What did *oh* mean?

"Lovely to meet you. You too, Leo, Thomas."

But no octave for Leo.

"It's been good for Charity to have a musical outlet," she said.

"Mother," Charity said. "You make me sound like a plug."

Ms. Simms looked at the Urchin. Seeing it beneath her sharp eyes made the space look seedier.

"No drinking," she said. "I'll be back."

"Okay," Charity said. They all nodded.

"I'll smell your breath." She looked pointedly at each of the boys. Walked away. They stood still, as if their commanding officer hadn't released them.

"You can move now," Charity said. "It's okay."

"So serious," Thomas said.

"Always," Charity said.

"Charity, can you give me a hand with the mic setup?" Leo asked. "I'd love to check levels."

"Sure."

They went into the Urchin together, the wraparound bar more full than before. Louder. A Friday-night feeling. Rab came hustling over with his captain-at-sea walk, but frantic now—as if the enemy had pivoted their ship for an eight-cannon broadside.

"Are we good with a three-dollar cover? Or five? People are asking."

"I think three is fine," Leo said.

"And the marquee, son of a bitch."

He set a stack of clattering black letters on the bar.

"I could only find one *I*."

They could be LONIZED or LIONZED or just MUSC TONIGHT? They decided on MUSC TONIGHT and the room seemed to tilt, everything liquid and rushing toward showtime. As with any show, problems multiplied. Cables gained fresh knots, feedback manifested like a poltergeist. Microphone stands had shrunk an inexplicable four inches. Meanwhile, the atonal bell rang in each new guest like an apocalyptic herald.

Here's Don Osterling from geometry—*KA-TUNK*

And Scruggs, done up, beard combed, like a kindly professor; their parents, Dunbar—*TINK, TUNK, TINK*—Mandy Thompson, Chris Adams, Xi Nile—

And Leo constantly demanding:

"Charity, can you help me out with this ladder—"

"Charity, can we run another check—"

"Charity, I think there's one more box in the car, can you give me a hand?"

She went outside with him. There were no windows in the bar, so Griff smiled past some friends, waved to Slim and Jonesy up front, and went out to see what was happening. Why couldn't he help his brother with the box? Charity still needed to change for the show.

Leo and Charity stood by the ThunderChicken.

They were not talking about the box.

Leo looked desperate. Cheeks flushed. Hands flashing back and forth. His words came in bursts and snatches, carried by choppy gusts, *once, can just, why*—and Charity shook her head, twice, three times. Leo popped the trunk. Jerked the box from the back of the Thunderbird. Charity turned toward him and Griff ducked inside.

THUNK—

Swallowed by crowd sounds, the humidity of a full room, bright lights.

Rab called—"Fifteen minutes until show!"

Charity was missing.

He scanned the crowd, which had grown into a strange fever dream—a cobbled-together landscape of foreign and familiar faces, classmates, Preppers, townies—was it possible the music had drawn them? Logging guys burled up to the bar like they'd sprouted there. Surfer Boys, gangly and half bearded, ripping through buckets of Buds on barstools. The Patriots in the wraparound corner booth like a shaky nest of eight balls rattling in the pocket. Cowboy hats. Flannel and Carhartts, and somehow slipping through the room and stepping on stage—Charity Simms.

Her presence put a hush into the crowd, stopped Griff's breathing. Her dress was purple, blue, and dim red, layered like a slow sunset. Her eyes danced. She made the room hum, just holding the silence. Beside her, Leo and Thomas looked like set pieces. Charity was the star.

When Griff finally wove his way up to the stage, she and Leo were talking:

"It's Rab," Leo said.

"Bullshit," Charity said. Griff had never heard her swear.

"What's wrong?" Griff asked.

"Leo suddenly has a problem with our set."

"What's up?" Griff said. "We agreed on three songs, right?"

"It's Rab!" Leo said. "Because we're minors. We can put you guys at the end, if there's time. But it's not fair to the band if we don't get to play our full set."

"Your set," Griff said.

"Hey," Leo said. "Don't worry. We'll work it out."

Leo climbed down. Sitting up front, Slim and Jonesy. The scene at the table looked like a tableau exercise from sophomore-year improv theater. The scene would be called: Jonesy Snuck Something Alcoholic into His Drink. Jonesy clutched his tall cola like it was a pigeon that might fly away. Slim was scooted way over, as if the drink were a bubbling caldron of poison. Jonesy passed the caldron to Leo, who took a sip.

Griff glared at him—before the show? Instinctively, he looked for his parents. Then Charity's mom. She was there—visible in her blazer toward the back.

"What's going on with Leo?" Griff asked Charity quietly.

"I'll tell you after," Charity said. "I should've waited."

"For what?"

She waved him off. They'd arrived at showtime. Rab leapt on stage, taking the microphone and talking too close. Popping *P*s like firecrackers.

"Hello, people! Welcome! Please everyone—"

Although Griff had been privy to every practice, every falling-domino decision that had led explicitly to this moment, it seemed absurd that this show should be permitted to happen at all. He was suspended in the energy of the moment, which carried him to his piano, dropped him onto the bench, and applied his fingers to the keys.

When his hands settled on the instrument, they stopped trembling.

Leo introduced the band. The applause helped. Playing helped even more.

The mechanics of performance crowded out panic. Leo sang and played the few chords he'd learned on guitar. Charity backed him up. Thomas looped their voices and instruments, which doubled and tripled, expanding around them until somehow they'd finished their first original song. More

— 132 —

applause! The next song, Leo and he played together as a duet. "Wildflowers," by Tom Petty. When Leo joined Griff at the piano, the audience cheered before they got started.

"The Tripp Twins!"

Somehow, they were a hit.

The first four songs moved smoothly—better than rehearsal. Thomas and Leo had wisely alternated original music and Americana, an original, then Petty, Ryan Adams, another original—then the fifth song, "Wayfaring Stranger," modeled after a Rhiannon Giddens banjo performance. For this one, Charity owned the microphone completely.

Leo and Griff played understated piano. Charity plucked a ukulele ("Banjo," she had explained, "I have no talent for.") and Thomas worked on atmospherics. When Charity began, the silence turned palpable. At the bar, ice hit glass bottoms like boulders. A lotto machine tweeted obscenely in the back room. A man in a trucker hat stood and found the cord. His shoulder jerked and the machine went black.

I know dark clouds will gather round me, I know the way is rough and steep

Charity cast her spell. Griff's eyes went watery and it wasn't even her best—just halfway to her truest voice. Wild applause snapped the brothers out of it, but they woke from different dreams. Griff was beaming. Leo looked unsettled. It took him a long time to set up the sixth song.

Expectant silence ebbed, gave way to barroom chatter.

"Leo," Thomas said. "What's the holdup?"

"Just wait," Leo said.

Chatter turned to drunken laughter. People shouted requests. Leo took the microphone and switched the set order. Another original. A piece called "Space and Time"—their newest and far from their best, but they followed Leo's lead. Only after the long break, they couldn't quite get the crowd back. After each pause between songs, Leo insisted on tuning, conferencing with Thomas.

"Turn us up," he told Thomas. "More on the mic."

They were sliding backward. Thomas kept turning them up. But volume was not a substitute for attention. Leo started talking more—

"So great to see you all. I'd really like you to listen to this one!"

The crowd was happy, but they were no longer his.

"Here's our last song!" Leo said.

Big cheer. They played their final original, "Wrinkle in the Sky." A strong song, but rather than end with a hard beat, as they'd planned, Leo trailed off into a long rudderless jam. When the song wrapped to modest applause, Griff stood and walked to his brother. "Should I introduce us?"

"What?"

"Charity and me," Griff said.

"Oh," Leo said. "Shoot. I think we might be out of time."

A strong single burst of applause from behind the bar. It was Rab, clapping his meaty hands, approaching the stage.

"Thank you, thank you," he said. "Let's give it up for Lionized!"

The crowd all came back. Shouts and cheers and Griff and Charity smiled, then shared a panicked look, what was happening—

"But don't go!" Rab shouted. "Don't go yet. What did you think of this girl with the golden voice?"

Pounding of the tables. Charity! Go Charity!

"We've still got a headliner for you—"

"Not the headliner," Leo said.

"—what do we call you?" Rab asked Griff and Charity, his eyes bloodshot.

"Just Charity and Griff," Griff said.

"Just Charity and Griff!" Rab shouted.

Charity lowered the microphone. Griff adjusted the bench, moving it where he wanted. Feedback in the monitors. Leo climbed down and joined Jonesy and Slim at their table. Thomas came back to run sound. He turned the lights up, maximum bright.

The crowd went still and in the howling moment of a second, Griff realized his invisible wall had collapsed. Right here, in front of Leo and the whole world, was everything he'd ever wanted.

TWENTY-FIVE

IN THE SPOTLIGHT, CHARITY HAD THE SAME DETERMINED SET TO her jaw Griff had noticed in her mother. She suddenly looked years more experienced, like she'd stepped into a brand-new version of herself, miles ahead of this stage. Griff wondered how long in this short life he'd be lucky enough to know her.

He spread his hands over the keys. He had all eighty-eight.

When Charity began to sing, the audience went still as a held breath. Sometimes in practice, it took her a while to warm up. Not tonight. Charity was fearless—went down deep, pulling up the sweet, clear sound. Her voice flew a four-octave range from a low rumble to a place so high it cracked. In ten seconds, she had the room right where she'd left them after "Wayfaring Stranger."

Griff played his whole heart. Charity was the real thing.

When they finished the first song, the room clapped like their home team had just won in overtime. Like they'd just remembered they were alive. People in Clade City did not stand and cheer for anything without a ball and protective equipment—but some stood now. Griff clapped too, like he hadn't been part of it. The whole place beamed golden light except one quiet cluster up front Griff could feel like a cold pocket in the ocean.

Leo, Jonesy, and Slim.

Leo and Jonesy had fresh drinks poured and sat a distance from Slim. They had a look in their eyes like kids in a parking lot about to throw rocks. Leo found Griff's eyes right away. His face twitched. Puckered lips, bug eyes. Leo was mocking him.

Piano Face.

Hands shaking, Griff put his fingers to the keys and it didn't matter. No one was looking at him anyway.

The second song was their most raw. Slow and challenging for a barroom crowd.

It began to sacred silence. Charity threw her voice up to the top two octaves, where it held on trembling and then broke off. Unlike the first musical exploration, this one came with words—

—*Sometimes you find them, sometimes you won't*—

When she repeated the line, it came with an awful echo. Griff looked at Thomas, on the sound board. Thomas wasn't watching the monitors. He was staring at Leo and Jonesy, who were both laughing. Griff didn't know who had started it, but Leo went next. Griff watched his brother's mouth wrap around Charity's words. Right there at the front of the room, he cawed back at her—

Saaaaawwwwmtimes—

Mocking. Cruel. That face of his.

Him and Jonesy together, the audience quiet enough to hear them. Griff stared at his brother and flubbed the keys. Charity stuttered as if stirring in deep sleep, not quite awake—please don't wake up! She sang, but Leo and Jonesy were contagious. Tables were watching them now, smiling. Shaking heads. Slim watched. He swallowed, like he'd just put down a stone.

Shhhhometimes you dawwwn't—

He saw the understanding land behind Charity's eyes. She'd

heard it. They ended the song early to generous applause, but Charity's voice shook when she said:

"Last song."

In the opening, a wordless melody was meant to imitate the wind. The purposeful shake and crack of her voice—being the most beautiful—lent itself to the most brutal mockery. Leo and Jonesy did it again. Griff tried to keep playing. They'd brought along another table in the cruelty, a voice farther back in the bar.

Aiiiieieiieee—

They squealed as she sang. Laughter. It was a catching thing, mockery. Unlike Charity's music, this was a song the whole town knew. Every time Griff had had his foot kicked into his back leg, every time he'd gotten shoved from behind, they'd been singing it to him:

You don't belong.

This time the song was carried by Leo's voice. They sang backup in the poisoned *hawhawhaw* laughter in the back booths. Smiles stretched to smirks and in the second minute of the song, near the end, people got loud. Griff could see the ugliness swell in them. Hungry eyes, desperate to chew up any beautiful thing they could. Leo had poisoned the room. Charity gave him a quick, trembling look, like someone about to tip backward off the edge of something—and he could not save her.

She climbed down from the stage. She left. Gone.

"Let's give it up for Just Charity and Griff!" Rab howled, hustling toward the stage.

Some people clapped. A sloppy response. Confused chatter.

Griff felt a hot twist in his stomach, an eruption and shouting—his voice. He did not know his voice could sound the way it did, or how fast he could move. How strong he could be. He did not expect the table to flip so easy, the glasses to shatter. The first few sets of arms he shredded like ribbons and aimed for his brother's throat and too many arms, he could not get to Leo so he peeled off and cut through the crowd, moving into the place where Charity's mother had been but was no longer—

Outside.

Mist hung thick in the air and it was warm for October. Two sets of brake lights on opposite sides of the jetty. He ran until his chest throbbed and he tasted iron deep in his throat and the car was gone.

Now, on the edge of the parking lot, the Urchin looked too small to hold such a vast, ugly thing.

He'd let his wall down. He'd let them see. It was his fault, and he'd done nothing.

He tried to outrun the hot, sticky feeling—racing from the pavement to dune grass and onto the slick and stony tidal flats—but the memory filled his lungs and the final look in Charity's eyes cramped in his stomach and beat with the ocean's pulse and the lighthouse swung, oblivious—

WHOOMP!

Stop! He hated it tonight. Wanted to scream, break something.

Griff's foot slipped into a stone tidepool with a deep, throaty glug and he staggered. Freezing water. His sock slurped against his boot's interior. Cold soaked into his toes. The rippling water quieted.

Stale tidepool.

Nothing fine or feathered swam inside. Mussels clung with straw beards. A hermit crab moved with tight, spider jerks, and dozens of prickly black skeletons hunkered in the pool's pocked, moonrock surface. Urchins. Because you had to be barbed and clawed and sealed up tight to survive. What would they all do, now that the music was gone?

He'd listened to enough police reports to know.

What happened next was the Patriots drank until they remembered they hated the Surfer Boys, and the Surfer Boys recalled they never could stand the Lumberjacks, and they'd crash one another's heads in and spill out bloody and broken because the only song left was "You Don't Belong" and the only ones to sing it to were each other.

He could walk back and start a fight. Throw the first bottle.

He turned back and something stopped him. A slap on the rocks, near the ocean. A small silver flash. It landed with a wet, sharp sound, like a piece of meat dropped on a stone countertop. Rockfish. The ones with big, searching eyes. Sad clown lips. They got trapped sometimes, after a full moon tide, and always tried to make it to the water. The rockfish jerked as if electrocuted.

Griff ran. He needed to bring it to the water.

His left foot plunged into another stone bowl freezing and soaked—hold on! Because it would choke on the air. It would starve or split its skull on stone. Get broken by the journey, snatched by a bird, and the whole ocean was so close.

Griff couldn't see it anymore.

You'd find rockfish all the time on the beach, smashed up. Mottled with flies and lifeless and that's how you got broken out here. You made the mistake of thinking you could escape.

TWENTY-SIX

GRIFF SLEPT DOWNSTAIRS WITH THE DRY GOODS, IN A COT between some of his father's salvaged equipment from the '64 tsunami and 200 pounds of rolled oats because they smelled better than most things when they leached through plastic tubs. He woke early to stiff footfalls. Descending steps. Maybe his mother. He was starving. He hadn't eaten since lunch, the day before.

Griff looked up to find Leo staring down at him.

His brother. Griff had not yet entwined the events of last night with the person standing there. The horrific memory didn't seem to fit the familiar body, calm eyes, and measured posture, so it just suffused the air between them—an awful nightmare miasma.

"Hey, brother," Leo said, standing in a shaft of light. Dressed, wearing their dad's camo jacket. He pointed at the basement's only window. "Check it out. Spotlight sun. That maple is The Most Important Tree in the World." An old game they played. Giving names to the things that shone brightest.

Leo was trying to win him over. Hoping the memory of last night would just go whooshing out in the cross-breeze. It would be easier that way.

"Look, I'm sorry," Leo said. He said it like a commandment. Like *Get moving.*

Griff lay and held his breath.

"I didn't—" Leo hushed his voice. "I didn't mean for it to be so loud. It just felt like a joke. I got a little drunk, okay? Jonesy brought whisky. It was stupid."

Griff, in his mind, examined Leo's Standard Relationship Repair Strategies.

Step 1: Optimistic Distraction.

Step 2: Aloof Apology.

Step 3: Embarrassing Admission.

Next, what would it be? An invitation? An us-and-them conspiracy?

"We're all going to the lighthouse tomorrow morning. The whole band. Charity, Thomas. All of us. We want you to come."

"Charity's coming?" Griff asked.

"She said she would."

"After last night?" Griff asked.

"She might come," Leo said. His voice had changed.

Leo's feet clicked up the wooden steps.

Click, click, click, click—

Footsteps stopped. Then returned, growing louder.

Click, click, click.

Griff squeezed his eyes shut. Griff could hear Leo breathing. He looked up. This time he did not know what to expect.

"I shouldn't have done it," Leo said.

This was not on the schematic. Griff sat up. His brother's face, barely visible.

"Why?"

"You know why," Leo said. "I'm tired of always losing."

Griff put his face into the pillow. He was shaking. Eyes squeezed shut. His brother's last words came soft and hollow, like a breath across the neck of an empty bottle:

"You two were glowing up there."

TWENTY-SEVEN

THE NEXT DAY THEY WENT TO THE LIGHTHOUSE.

It was Sunday, October 28.

Griff couldn't remember if he woke with that familiar dread—that something bad was going to happen. Or if it was a day like any other day. Or if those two things had become the same. What he remembered was waking up on the basement cot again to the scent of salt water and old oats and walking up the wooden steps to find Leo already dressed in the kitchen.

He was wearing black pants. White T-shirt. Boots laced up. Their father's camo jacket. Small black backpack.

Griff said, "You always get to wear that jacket."

"Fine. Here. Take it," Leo said. He pulled it off, tossed it across the table.

It made a soft knocking sound—*tok*.

"We're going to the Point?" Griff asked. "Why?"

"There's a plan. You'll love it."

The house had that haunted feeling of parents being gone at odd times. Mom at Shoreline Gifts early to receive a shipment. Dad at a weekend workshop with Dunbar. Dust motes on lazy glide paths. Leo had just eaten a bowl of cereal, a few abandoned flakes swimming in the milk. He was sitting straight-backed in their father's seat like he'd claimed the throne and would be there forever.

"Where are Charity and Thomas?" Griff asked.

"They're meeting us there," Leo said. "I've got the truck."

Had Charity been texting Leo? When she wouldn't respond to him?

Leo stood. He walked past Griff and down the hallway past the rack of hung coats. Never once had their father allowed Griff to drive the truck. Griff looked at Leo. He could leap onto his back and punch hard, screaming—no parents to stop him. Instead, as if pulled by an invisible thread, Griff stood and walked to the door, laced up his boots, taking care to weave all the way up the tongue, catching all the grommets, nice and snug, toe to ankle.

The truck started in the driveway—a bolt of panic—what if Leo left him behind?

Outside, it was surprisingly warm.

Griff took a breath—brief delight at sunshine and rustling leaves. The fresh air blew some of the cobwebs from his thinking. Just a drive to the Point. Charity might be there. It was a beautiful day. He climbed into the truck.

Griff wanted coffee. He would not ask Leo to stop. Refused to give him an opportunity for kindness.

The truck sat up high on the road and Griff rode shotgun. He rolled down the window. The sun lay like a warm glove on his exposed forearm, wrist, hand. The metal body of the truck felt good and strong. Autumn air, cold in his ears, had already grown its winter teeth.

The ThunderChicken was there waiting. Thomas, wearing sunglasses and leaning against his proud vehicle like it was a position he'd been rehearsing for a sunny weekend in October. There were surprisingly few vehicles. Two pickups. One small Geo.

"Where's Charity?" Griff asked.

Leo checked his phone. "Not here yet."

They got out. Leo gave Thomas a backslapping hug.

"Good morning, buddy!"

Griff watched Marine Drive for the flash of an incoming car. In the grassy parking lot peninsula, dead-eyed October sunflowers bobbed their heads as the breeze picked up, carrying a pulse of the Pacific chill, ruffling his hair. Griff grabbed his arms. The coat. He'd left the coat on the kitchen table where Leo had thrown it. They stood around and didn't talk much, waiting for Charity.

They could already hear God's Mouth.

Hoom.

"Did you check the tide tables?" Leo asked.

"Forty-five minutes to low tide," Thomas said.

"We need to go," Leo said. He was right. To make it there and back, you had a window of two hours. They'd lost thirty minutes.

"Without Charity?" Griff asked.

Leo shrugged.

"C'mon," he said. Thomas followed. Griff shook his head, looked back at Marine Drive. He turned and followed his brother. He wondered if Charity had ever agreed to come at all.

The water sounded high.

Some days, it pulsed like a giant lapping tongue. Today, a stone-and-water kick drum. They walked to the west side of the lot, where a small mouth in the canopy widened to a soil-and-sand footpath down through rows of dramatic, wind-whipped lodgepole pines. Twisted by salt and spray, they contorted themselves like a collection of prehistoric insects and wooden giants, needle-hair blown back in great green shocks. Krummholz.

"Walkin' through the crumb holes," Thomas sang. "Stompin' through the crumb holes!"

Charity could've riffed with him. Thomas would've dropped a beat. But no Charity. Without her, they limped along like a three-legged dog. Down at the bottom of the trail, Leo tried to fill the void with enthusiasm. He walked ahead, tossing comments back on the wind—

"—great show overall, though, good turnout—"

"What are we doing, Thomas?" Griff asked quietly.

"Going to the lighthouse," Thomas said. "That's all I know. There's something Leo wants to show us."

"Where's Charity?"

"I don't know," Thomas said. "God that was terrible."

They stepped from loamy, root-bound soil to sand. Flies all over the beach. Big as bumblebees. They clung to long ropy chutes of seaweed. Bullwhip kelp, all over the beach. The smell of vegetable rot, old cabbage. Leo up ahead and crouching over something. His backpack. Riffling through.

"Bro!" Leo yelled back.

"What?"

"Where's the coat?"

"What?"

"Dad's coat!"

"I left it at the house!"

Leo stared at him. Like Griff forgetting the coat had ruined his whole day. Like they might as well turn back because he forgot the stupid coat.

"So what?" Griff screamed into the wind, threw up his arms.

Leo stood up. Paused. Then kept going. Onto the wide mud flats, picking his way through the beached sand dollars. Pulling himself up onto the boulders. Griff hated the way Leo moved. Farther ahead than usual. Was Charity meeting them at the lighthouse?

Griff moved faster. A sand dollar crunched beneath his foot

like a small plate. Alive, now in pieces. Griff walked forward to boulders that rose up from the mud and then he climbed. He should catch up. By the time he reached the trail, Leo was already at the top of the short, steep summit.

He waited for them near the cluster of signs: BEWARE UNSTA-BLE ROCK LEDGES, BEWARE RIP CURRENT, AVOID UNSTABLE LOGS, TSU-NAMI ZONE, BEWARE SNEAKER WAVES. Each depicted its own tragic tableau: a stick figure tumbled from a cliff with small triangular rocks. A stick figure was pulled by an arrow out to sea. A stick figure sequentially murdered by toothy waves, a torrential rainstorm, rolling logs, a falling boulder.

"Clade City," Thomas said. "The most dangerous place in the world to be a stick figure."

They usually paused here, at the top. It was the most sweeping view in Clade City, lighthouse to the right, the Ruins to the left, and nothing but the bold, blue world spread out in front. Griff used to stand in the wind and put his hands to the side of his face like blinders. Erase all signs of civilization, taste the sea, and pretend he was flying, hurtling toward the horizon at unknown speeds.

"There he goes," Thomas said.

Leo hadn't stopped. Already working down the sharp descent and into the canyon toward God's Mouth. The stone path stretched like a catwalk alongside the lip of a turbulent whitewater chute. At high tide, the surf below galloped landward and smashed itself into a cavern you could hear all the way from their bedroom window. Named God's Mouth, because it seemed to speak with each intake of foam.

Shhhhhh or *HOOM!*

The cavern hissed.

"Dragons," Thomas said, clasping Griff's shoulder. "Be careful."

And Leo was already halfway to the crossing. To reach the lighthouse, one had to traverse a stone land bridge 15 feet above the cavern. It was the width of a narrow sidewalk, bald and crumbling on its downward slope. Griff's chest always fluttered, seeing it. The crossing was safe and stable enough. In Clade City, people brought their dogs. Parents took children by the hand. Their father had led them across dozens of times, since elementary school.

"Just don't look down," he'd told them.

The pool at God's Mouth was a violent froth. Churning as if lashed by a submerged propeller. Like it would chop your legs off at the knees. Even in a town with nothing to do but drink and dare each other to go first—nobody went swimming in God's Mouth.

As Leo advanced, a wave came in—high for low tide. It moved like a white horse at a stiff canter and broke itself on the rocks.

HOOM!

Griff sped up. They were supposed to wait before the crossing. Their father had taught them to cross together. Why did Leo have to be so far ahead? Was she really waiting for them at the lighthouse? He moved into a jog. A stone the size of a baseball, underfoot, caught in the arch. Griff stumbled sideways and the stone bounced, clattered down the ragged cliffside, lost to water.

"Careful, bro," Leo said. He looked back and smiled.

That was it. And the lighthouse looked dark. Griff remembered Leo's lie—*Jonesy and I shot it up.* Remembered *Can you tell Griff the music doesn't come from the lighthouse*—Griff slipped on scree then and righted himself on even ground, walking toward his brother.

"Hey—"

Griff came quick.

HOOM!

The sound shook his shirt against his skin. Brine on his lips, rimming his eyes in a saltwater haze, and he'd push through— you could cross the ledge in ten seconds, just hug it close, his father always said, stay on the inside, a tender chunk of rock could come right off under your heel—

"Bro," Leo said, "let me go first. I've got something—"

No. If she was there, Griff would see her first.

Griff pushed past him. Shoved Leo against the cliff wall. A train of blood between his ears, click-clack thunder as he stepped onto the ledge. Griff was ahead and this is when you trip, with everyone watching. He pressed a hand to the brittle cliffside. Cold stone. One foot, the next, count to five and you're halfway—

Deep breath and *HOOM!*

A foamy pop. Water slashed his ankles. Breath trapped in his chest and he spun toward the rock wall, palms on stone. Legs shaking. Don't lean or your boots will shoot out on slick rock and then your stomach drops and you are pedaling air with feet and the shock of water—

"Keep going!" Thomas said.

"It's supposed to be low tide," Leo said.

"Sneaker wave," Thomas said.

"Breathe, bro," Leo said. "Breathe and move."

"I'm fine!" Griff screamed. His words ricocheted against the rock, rang in his ears. Fine. Failure, failing. Leo would help his little brother. Griff seethed, pushing and pulling air through clenched teeth. Cold air, sucking his lips. Chest scraping stone. He sidled over. Almost.

"Just another step," Leo said.

Leo had already started across.

"I've got it," Griff said. "Stop talking!"

Griff crossed. He straightened his feet on the stone saddle where the narrow ledge widened to a broad shelf. Leo was already nearly halfway across, but there was something wrong with the ocean. Drum gone still.

The horizon was off. Too thick and too blue.

Coming fast. Soundless. Griff had never seen a real sneaker wave. Leo did not see it. He was looking at Griff with his mouth parted, a crease between his eyes. Griff knew the look. Leo was worried about him.

Griff did not have time to scream his name.

Leo spun, braced himself against the rock and the wave was too high to pound and break and so it just washed. Like pouring a bowl of water over a baby in the bath. A low wet slosh and no one there now. Puddles, ponds, rivers sluicing down from the ledge, a soft waterfall.

Gone. Rock ledge with Leo. Gone now. The foam in the stone pool was the same, except now Leo was down there. Leo's right down there. His arms and legs and head and chest and voice, down there.

Moving like he never moved.

Loose, jangling. Crumpled and tossed, and Griff grabbed his own wrists. Grabbed bare flesh. He looked down at his brother and back at the ledge and down at the shirt moving in white water and could not see his sweet brother's head. Could not see his brother's face—

"He's, he's, he's—"

A pink bloom in the water. Lips, a bent elbow.

Alive! His small elbow moved in the froth, you could see it move.

HOOM!

Screaming. Who was screaming? He'd jump but boots— boots like stones strapped to your feet and Leo, wearing boots—laces and knots—Thomas with his phone, now crossing the ledge—

"Stop. Griff, STOP!"

Faster! Just jump with boots and now Thomas too close, screaming in his face, screaming NO—LET ME GO LET ME GO—they crashed back against rock—WE'LL ALL DIE, GRIFF WE'LL ALL DIE

Can't paddle foam. Tread foam. Can't tear a wrist and make it a cord. Screaming, grabbing his own shirt because something had to rip and tear, the impulse becoming a plan, something to do—make a line, throw out a line—

MAKE A LINE!

No jacket, no bracelet, no Leo. Thomas tore off his jacket, his shirt, jeans, stood in underwear and Griff was tying square knots strong knots he was good with his hands, denim to cotton to nylon to denim and lying flat, it would reach, because the story is—

HOOM!

—close call, that's the story. Almost happened, the story is wrong and broken otherwise—

Focus.

Griff dangled the shaking line of knotted clothes slapping stone, did it even reach? Can't tell. Water lurching against rock. Foam, no elbow, no lips, no small chin, no eyes no arms no shoulders no legs, hands—

Leo. So strong when his hands grab, it will pull him straight in.

When you grabbed the line you almost pulled me straight in? Leo, remember? Close call.

No hand yet—

Line of limp clothes hanging.

Get up! Rewind, Leo. Put him back. Two minutes please God

if anything my whole life just two minutes and counting—ten seconds okay, you could hold your breath twenty, thirty, sixty scary, getting too long—

—how long until the sirens?

He and Thomas stripped to underwear, shaking and so pale. The sun shone and it was cold.

In the distance, something like a little bell. He couldn't breathe. Yes, like a little bike bell with handlebar streamers on a perfect sunny day. And sirens. A pretty perfect day, then the ledge. A pretty perfect life, now this forever. Wringing shirts and jeans to get them dry, that's how the knots hold better, they hold better when they're dry, so do that, get them dry.

Wringing will split the webbing between thumb and forefinger done long enough, you'll blow your voice out for a week if you scream long enough, so keep wringing those motherfuckers, keep squeezing, hands bleeding on your perfect October day, a day like any other day, or maybe, you just knew deep down and all along that something bad was going to happen.

ANDANTE

The answer is never the answer. . .the need for mystery is greater than the need for an answer.

—KEN KESEY

TWENTY-EIGHT

THE FUNERAL WAS NOT THE HARD PART.

There was no body to stare at. Leo's body was not recovered.

Everyone was dressed in black and you could pour your heartbreak into the empty coffin and the tissues and the hole in the ground, all of which were there, Griff was told, for closure. Food and flowers. Cards and tears, all critical. Given the strong turnout, and abundant food, and weather that was gray but not pouring, there were worse ways to spend an afternoon in Clade City—but where was Leo?

Griff wondered where Leo was for these small white cakes with the cream cheese frosting which Ms. Marizza hadn't made since two Thanksgivings ago. Where was Leo to laugh with when their aunt Christina sneezed on the potato salad point-blank without apology because she was allergic to peppers. Leo, to help count how many drinks the CigBiz had before she moved from the couch to the floor and seemed unable or unwilling to get up for nearly an hour. Leo, to place bets on how many clove cigarettes Uncle Ron would sneak in the garage.

It was Leo's funeral, and he wasn't even here.

Griff was wearing his bracelet, which no one noticed. He wanted to find Leo at the funeral and show him: See, Leo. I remembered. It was the first thing I did when I got home.

Eventually it got dark. People collected their families and

each other. They went with all the same people they came in with. They left the loss behind.

The loss would not be concealed in an empty coffin or shut into a pit in the ground or wrapped in a tissue and thrown away. The loss would be borne. Carried alone. And when there was no longer an accommodating space for loss, it still had to fit somewhere.

Placed in the spaces between notes. In the backseat of Dad's truck. Loss would be the tight and squeezing thing in the toe of your shoes when you walked to school, in your pockets with the jangling keys. The breaths between words.

Mostly in your throat. So you learned to breathe around it.

At school, the day after the funeral, Griff was afraid he'd punch every sad and sorry face, but those faces were helpful. It was better when the whole world carried a piece of it. *When you are sad*, the therapist said, *listen to sad music*. Music should be mood-compatible. At first, the world was mood-compatible. Teachers and parents and relatives and everyone in Clade City played along, except Leo.

How did Leo fit in all this?

Griff wanted to ask his mom: When will Leo be home?

He needed to ask somebody. When he got home from school, he panicked in the room with his brother's empty bed, could not breathe. The question, swelling to block his windpipe. If he didn't get the question out, he would choke on it. "When will Leo be home?"

He made himself say it.

In first grade, Leo always played with the neighbors across the street. They could only have one friend over at a time and had always requested Leo by name. When his brother left, Griff would sit in the window and watch. He couldn't stop asking his mom:

When will Leo be home?

His mother kept the blinds down and curtains drawn. The next day, sometime in the early evening, she came out of her office with bolts of fabric draped across her forearm.

"Magnets?" she asked the room. "Tacks?"

His father stood and went into their bedroom. A few minutes later, something crashed. His father came out with a dustpan full of glass. Light danced on the ceiling, flickered on the walls. His mother followed him and pulled an old burlap coffee sack over the mirror near the front door. Stuck it with pins.

"We're supposed to cover the mirrors," his mother said.

When they could not be covered, mirrors were removed. The interior of the medicine cabinet gaped with metal shelves and Leo's toothbrush. Lotion. Floss. A big plastic jar of vitamin C gummies. In their bedroom, the closet mirror was blocked by a gray tapestry, held with magnets. Leo's clothing hung inside.

Five pairs of shoes, unlaced.

Shoes, waiting. Shirts, waiting. Pants. Plates. Chair and dinner. Hanging keys waiting. Dental floss waiting. Everyone and everything waiting for Leo to come home.

TWENTY-NINE

IT WAS SOME AFTERNOON.

Charity was crying in the hallway.

She was staring at him like someone on TV. He felt trapped behind glass. She was shaking her head:

Why, why, why, why—

Griff was confused, shaking his head too. Charity's hair was shorter. Corkscrews. Her face was different. Not even her. Her eyes were puffy and her cheeks were puffy and she was screaming on the glass screen and saying—

—why won't you just talk to me?

Someone should talk to Charity. She was hurting.

Can't someone do anything?

Griff was crying because she was so sad and—someone do something! He couldn't watch this movie anymore, and thankfully the camera pulled back and Charity grew distant. Her whole walk was different. Like she was wading through something ankle-deep.

Charity exited the frame. Griff was alone in the hallway.

It was him she'd been talking to.

He breathed. Tried to get air over the stone in his throat.

He should message her. Respond in some way. That knowledge

sat like a tiny shiny silver thing at the bottom of a well with a cut rope and broken bucket.

Even if he could fish out that little bit of energy—

Well—

How could he respond?

He couldn't remember a single thing Charity had said.

THIRTY

Sunshine.

Sometime in the spring.

The world was no longer mood-compatible. Springtime. The blooming of sundresses and tans. Smiles and white teeth, hard on the eyes.

Griff and Thomas were standing up front, giving a class presentation on the Cascadia Subduction Zone. Griff looked down. Full camo. Unbelievable. He almost laughed, except he was talking:

"The quake will be a 9.0 at least. We know this because the earthquake has happened every 300 to 500 years since 600 BC. We know it's coming because of the ghost forests left behind, and the stories of native people. Like the Thunderbird and the Whale. How all creation lives on the back of a whale. The Thunderbird picks it up, drops it in the middle of the desert—"

Griff's voice sounded smooth and confident. It reminded him of his brother.

"How likely is this to happen?" asked Mandy Thompson. "Like, in our lifetime?"

"Well," Griff said. He removed a quarter from his pocket. "How rare is it to flip a quarter and have it come up heads twice in a row?"

He flipped the coin. Heads.

"Pretty common," she said.

"It's statistically more likely than that."

These were facts.

People listened to facts. He wondered if it was his words, or the camouflage, or Leo's death. When people looked him in the eyes, they looked compelled and curious but also cautious. They looked into him like he was an abyss. They wanted to know what was down there but were afraid to fall in. Thomas was now talking. This was his part, which played like a campfire ghost story of What Will Happen When It Hits:

"Homes will slide off their slab foundations," he said, doing his most descriptive gestures. "Crumple like paper balls. The land liquefies and gas lines snap and now you've got a 700-mile wall of water—"

Thomas nailed it. Outside, the Thunderbolt screamed. Their weekly drill.

BADADDAADADABRREEEEEEEEEEE!!!!

Half the class jumped. A magician's timing. The only trick Thomas still did.

● ● ●

The wildfires had come.

Now Griff was having dinner with his family. One, two, three. Four chairs again. A big box of red wine. Surgical masks on the table.

"These are the N95s," his father explained.

Green and secured with elastic straps, like something you'd wear in surgery. His father looked so angular. Like his skeleton was swelling, bursting blood vessels in his cheeks. But he was full of energy, talking about these masks. Long fingers dancing on the boxes, prying them open.

"—fine-enough filtration to suspend the particulate matter. Left over from the pandemic. But they need to be secured. Right against the cheeks. Can we try?"

"Now?" his mother asked.

Her hair! So different. Reddish brown with a gray patch on top, splitting like a silver egg yolk over the crown. And her skin. Like she'd taken it off and had it laundered wrong so it came back baggy and stained beneath the eyes and even her teeth looked smaller, like pebbles. My god, what happened to Mom?

Griff could cry, just for Mom.

You are living a nightmare life.

He gripped the table, trying to breathe. The message repeated itself:

You are living a nightmare life.

"There you go," his father said, snugging the mask over his mother's small face. "Feel that? That's perfect. You'll be fine. Griff?"

She sat wearing her green surgical mask. Damp eyes. Griff put his on.

It smelled like hospitals. Breathing in a sauna. Underwater.

No, no.

If he couldn't catch his breath, the table would tilt and he'd spill onto the floor and his parents would fight again. He'd turn them into murmuring, shouting, blubbering whales.

"It's about the cadmium," his father explained, delirious with facts. "The filtration on these respirators at .3 microns can prevent the cadmium—"

Cadmium! That was the thing. Got down into your pink lungs and turned them gray and we don't need to remind anyone here what happens next. Death, followed by endless family dinners. Persistent meatloaf, unbuttered potatoes, corn that tasted like the can it came in.

Would there be Special Corn again?

Had they missed the harvest? Would they even bother to drive to the farm with an empty seat in the pickup? Eat at a table that had an empty fourth chair and then no chair and now, suddenly—a chair again?

"Can I be excused?" Griff heard himself say.

It was happening again. That flutter-eyed feeling.

He blinked his bedroom into focus. Tugged on the bottom of his shirt, which rode too high over his belt, tugged on the ankles of his pants, which rode too high over his feet. Ran a hand through his long hair and looked at the paracord bracelet on his wrist. Pulled it hard.

His desk calendar was full and healthy, dripping with appointments. Hashtags and figure eights and other symbols for Marksmanship Training, Outdoor Survival, Cascadia Subduction Training. Unmanned, the chessboard of his life was still in play. Other people, moving all the pieces around.

He put the calendar on his bed.

He flipped forward all the way to December and saw GAP ACADEMY ORIENTATION. A cold breeze through his chest. Right. That was happening. He flipped back to today and traced the date with his finger. No red circles. It was late June. Summertime. He was no longer a junior.

Oh he could scream.

He could break a window and leap out and run circles or he could just collapse. They don't tell you that you'll still be carrying the loss for months and months after the funeral. Hauling a boulder. That's why you lose weight. Why you cannot sleep or get out of bed. On the days you can get it smaller than your fist, the stone is flat-bellied and sits meditatively on your tongue, soaks up the juice in your mouth and slowly grows big again. If you fell in the water, you'd sink dead to the bottom.

Griff stood. His closet mirror was covered with butcher paper.

Had he done that? What happened to the gray fabric?

TOE Box, still locked. All their notes and files were outdated. Missing the most vital piece to the grand puzzle.

LEO IS DEAD.

Leo's death was part of any universal truth. Part of God, if there was a god. Now, synchronicity and magic and the fabric of existence could not hold together without that tight little stitch—Leo is dead, and you didn't save him.

May as well leave it locked. There's nothing else to know.

THIRTY-ONE

SUMMERTIME.

Jonesy was smoking a cigarette in the front seat, swearing out of the corner of his mouth at every car that failed to do his bidding.

Fuckin' hippie bug. Fuckin' Lexus. Fuckin' Buick.

They were headed to the regional meeting to be honored for the Early Alert Response System, which was now a big deal. There would be over a hundred people there. Jonesy and Slim pronounced *hundred* like *hun-derd*, rhymed with *thundered*, the way *pleece reports* rhymed with *fleece reports*, and *the internet* was *the innernet*, like a tunnel rather than a web.

"Hundred," Griff said to himself. It didn't sound right. Neither way sounded right.

Griff had a binder on his lap. He was presenting on EARS, and bunker construction, and the basics of emergency evacuation protocols because he had just received an early-bird full-ride scholarship to Gap Academy, which would begin directly after his senior year.

"Want a turn, Griff?" Slim asked. He pointed to the radio.

For what? Music. Sweet guy. Slim remembered he liked music.

"It's fine," Griff said.

He didn't even realize anything was on.

THIRTY-TWO

"THERE'S SOMETHING FOR YOU," HIS MOM SAID, "IN THE MAILBOX."

"Why didn't you bring it in?" Griff asked.

"It's fun to get mail yourself. From the big black box. When's the last time you got mail?"

Griff grabbed up his shoes, then felt a strange buzz. Like, he needed to go faster. Whatever was there might dissolve to ashes. He went barefoot and the grass was warm. Squishy dirt. Mud between toes. The earth was still alive. A million blades of grass, still alive. The whole living earth didn't care about Leo or the mail.

Very small card. Maybe half of it had vanished in the time it took to cross the lawn.

Poor-resolution picture of tents. A white statue on a hill. Arms up.

Touchdown Jesus.

On the back, three words: *I miss you.*

THIRTY-THREE

ONE NIGHT IN JUNE, HE WOKE UP.

Something did it. A sound, like a slamming door.

Griff was sitting in the red roller chair at K-NOW. And beside him—Thomas. Still there. Thomas looked okay. Maybe the only one who still looked like himself. It was like time travel, looking at Thomas. A flood of love and relief for his friend. He wanted to scream:

"You're alive!"

That would be strange because they'd ridden to the station together.

Thomas with his hand on the dial, tongue twiddling out from the corner of his mouth. Tuning the radio, navigating through the static, like he'd never stopped.

What had woken him—sound or light? The moon? A full white disk.

WHOOMP!

Yellow light. The lighthouse! Still there.

"What is it?" Thomas asked.

More static. *SHhhhhhhhttttttttttfffffff*

"I think I heard something," Griff said.

Thomas looked at him, startled. As if a statue had spoken. Thomas turned the static up, moved the dial through warbling voices, a baseball game.

"Maybe a little farther," Griff said.

Griff stared at Thomas. Thomas pinched him.

"Ouch!" Griff said.

"Unbelievable," Thomas said. "He speaks! The boy still feels pain."

Thomas reached out to pinch him again and Griff knocked his hand away.

"Don't Tase me, bro," Thomas said.

Griff looked down. On his hip, cradled in a leather pouch. A Taser. A foggy meeting with his father, the sizing of the thing at a gun shop. Griff reached for the knob and Thomas slapped his hand.

"Why do you keep hitting me?" Griff asked.

Thomas stared at him. Jaw trembling.

"Are you back?" Thomas asked.

"Back?" Griff said. "Let's move a little slower with the receiver. I think—"

"I know what I'm doing, Tripp," Thomas said. "Do you even remember? Or realize—"

His voice choked off.

"What?"

"It's been eight months! What do you think I've been doing for the last fucking eight months with you at this radio station? Since the funeral. You're like a goddamn catatonic war vet. Like some mumbling creature I can only soothe with the fucking hiss of the radio or you start wandering around, fucking with the disaster board, interrupting the broadcasts while I'm on-air—"

Thomas's comments, like striking matches in dark corridors of memory, images leaping to life. He was not wrong about any of it.

"Thank you," Griff said. His eyes stung.

"Thank you," Thomas said. "Yeah."

Thomas looked back at the radio monitor. Shook his head. The lighthouse swung.

WHOOMP!

"But," Griff said.

"What?"

"I think I heard something."

"Okay!" Thomas shouted. "Well, strap in, buddy!"

He shoved headphones over Griff's head. Yanked on his own. Blaring static. He turned it up. More. Twisted the dial to maximum, thundering volume, and Griff flung off the headphones.

"Jesus, Thomas!"

"Oops!" Thomas said.

"What's your problem?"

"You want to know what's on the Skip, Griff? And listen closely, because—unlike you—I've been here for the last eight months listening to this shit. Shortwave radio is a bullshitty hobby for old bullshitty people—you know why? There is nothing. West Coast garbage, East Coast horseshit, and miles of Midwestern nightmares. The only thing you discover on AM radio are more ways to hate the people on AM radio, and the people who listen to AM radio, and the people who make you listen to AM radio."

Thomas was shaking. He looked the same but was not the same. His lips trembled.

"What about the Band?" Griff asked.

"The Band," Thomas said immediately. "Didn't happen."

"We were there," Griff said.

"D. H. Rawcliffe," Thomas said, as if reciting Scripture. "Where belief in miracles exists, the belief produces the hallucination, and the hallucination confirms the belief. It was great, Griff, goddammit, holding, all touchy-happy, it was the sweetest fucking night of my life. But I can tell you from the data, from the charts, from months of work, this band is some underbelly of the Amazon, Lost City of Z, Heart of Darkness bullshit and the only thing you will find at the end of that tunnel is madness or death."

Thomas stared at him.

"I think—" Griff said.

"What?"

"Can we go back a few clicks to the left."

"Go ahead!" Thomas threw the headphones at Griff. Walked away. Griff turned down the volume. Easier to search when it was quiet. He threaded back to the short, rumbling gap between the baseball game and a big-band concert, kept going. A deeper pocket of static, something tangled inside.

"Thomas?"

"What!"

"Can you help me clean up the sound?"

"Someone has to run a fucking radio show! This is why we're here! Right?"

Griff watched him, silent. Thomas shook his head. Stood.

"Fine," he said. "Fine! Fine! You want help?"

Thomas went to a stack of programming materials—reports, brochures. He picked them up and flung them against the window. A giant confetti burst of paper. He walked over to Dunbar's neat black plastic pen holder. Smashed it on the ground, ka-rack! Pens leapt, somersaulted, rolled. Chest heaving, he stared at Griff. Walked slowly. Jerked his chair over to the engineer console. Pulled on his headphones.

While Griff moved the dial, Thomas cleaned the sound.

" 'The Boogie Woogie Bugle Boy'?" Thomas asked.

"Just wait," Griff said. He eased the dial, could feel hidden sounds like bumps under a rug. Music receded to the hiss of a record run to dead wax, then something like a propeller churning underwater, wet and warbling *schwooop schwooop*—and—THEN—

"No," Thomas said.

Griff felt it before he heard it. The brain-prickling tingle of a perfect song.

Thomas bucked up from his rolling chair. It hit the ground. He hunched over the mixer, face down close, tweaking dials. He smoothed the sound, set the hook:

In the cold, we hunt the dark, sing on the waves that come at night—

Shiver from shoulder blades to the backs of his legs. New lyrics. New voices, but THEM. Thomas jerked open a drawer, pulled out a cassette tape shrink-wrapped in plastic, he fumbled, cursing—

"Keep them on the line!" Thomas said.

He pulled a knife from his belt, liberated the tape in a crinkling flash of plastic, bolted across the room, snapped it into place, and pressed RECORD. Red light, blinking. His breathing, ragged. Hands clasped as if in prayer, he watched the spools move and Griff looked beyond him, to the town.

Seeing it as if for the first time.

Little windows, tiny headlights, everything dim. Like the ashed-over embers of a burned-down campfire but if you just blew across them—*WHOOMP*—tongues of fire and spark!

Griff looked at the switch.

NO GO. GO.

A one-inch journey, traversable by index finger.

"It's recording," Thomas said. "My god. We have a recording."

Griff turned on the studio monitor. The song flooded the space with strings, percussion, the harmonized vocals—

—*When you told me that, you told it true so tell it again, you—*

"Still think it's a hallucination?" Griff said.

"We won't know till we play the tape back," Thomas said, "if you got sane or I went crazy."

— 171 —

Griff reached for the switch. Thomas laughed, clapped his hands.

"You're are crazy," Thomas said. "You want to play them on the air for these idiots?"

"We promised," Griff said. "If we found them, we'd play them."

Thomas raced to the computer, braced his hands on the keys.

"Armed, captain," Thomas said. "Launch at will."

Griff's finger hovered. He considered Specific Absorption Rate. Measured radiation from radio waves—the way sound actually penetrates your body, down to the cellular level. The whole town would be able to feel it.

"Standing by," Thomas said.

He stared at the ocean. Was anyone listening?

"Now," Griff said. He flipped the switch.

"Kaboom," Thomas said.

The sound filled K-NOW studio—not the auxiliary monitors, the luxurious boom of the ON AIR speakers. Guitar looping in wild, trancey beats, more strings. The Band had gotten better. Thomas came closer to Griff. They stood shoulder to shoulder. The sound blanketed their town. Filled the invisible spaces behind speakers, car stereos, headphones.

"Love you, buddy," Griff said.

He and Thomas hugged. It had been a very long time.

"Caller," Thomas said.

On the board, a single yellow light. Flashing.

"K-NOW Radio," Thomas said. "Hello? Hello?"

He looked at Griff, shrugged.

Outside, lights flashed. The tower walls strobed red and blue. Brighter, flooding the space. Thomas ran to the window.

"Shit," he said. "Dunbarred."

"That was fast," Griff said.

Thomas leapt to the computer and stopped the song dead with a station ID—*You're at the last point of the dial on the Lost Coast of Oregon, K-NOW 1590*—quick, springing footfalls on the ladder as if Dunbar had transformed into a fast-climbing super primate—Thomas ejected the cassette and the door burst open, a quick tunnel of wind, swirling the fallen brochures. Very quiet. Lights flashed.

"You both okay?" Dunbar said.

"What?" Griff asked.

"Your dad had me swing by," Dunbar said. "He's on the way." Dunbar's posture relaxed. He turned his head down, spoke to his shoulder-mounted radio. "Ten twenty-three."

"Is this because of the playlist?" Thomas asked.

"Playlist? Tripp said he was worried," Dunbar said. "Hey. What happened to my pens?" They lay spread across the floor.

"The wind," Thomas said. Dunbar stared at him. "When you opened the door."

Griff's father came fast. He must've driven 60, blown stop signs. Mr. Tripp climbed into the red-and-blue-flashing fun house almost unrecognizable, frantic eyes, crease between the brows hatchet-deep. Like he'd been awake for days.

"All good?" Dunbar asked.

"Yes, thanks," Griff's dad said. "What was that, boys?"

"A band we found," Griff said.

"Right in the middle of a PSA? Not on the playlist?"

His expression became recognizable. Ruddy cheeks. Eyes heating up.

"Sorry," Griff said. "Why is it such a big deal?"

"Because I didn't know what was going on, Griff!" his dad said. "You two up here alone, three stories up, suddenly a strange song cuts in. Thomas, not responding to messages—"

"Sorry, sir," Thomas said.

Griff felt himself dislocating from his body. Drifting toward the dark space outside the window that could swallow him up for months. He fought to stay. Anchored himself, heels to floor. Hands clenched to fists.

"I'm sorry," Thomas said. "I was distracted."

But Griff's dad was already barreling down the road to a consequence in an eighteen-wheeler of parental authority shredding apologies like toothpick roadblocks—"I think Sub-Watch for the next month. Keep your feet on the ground."

"SubWatch?" Thomas said. "Jesus fuck."

"Oops!" Dunbar said. "I'll see if Scruggs can cover their shifts."

"Give us a second, boys," his dad said. "Head out."

Griff and Thomas climbed down the cold, bony rungs. They tucked themselves into the sheltered space beneath the station. Griff looked up, judging the distance. Far enough to break something. Or die. Thomas pulled a small Tupperware container from his pocket, and three emerald gummy bears. He chewed them frantically, like a dog eats bacon.

"Are those drugs?" Griff asked.

"Of course they're drugs," Thomas said. "How do you get through the day?"

Griff looked back up. Remembered his father's face.

"You, I think," Griff said.

Thomas smiled. A genuine smile. Like before October. He took out the cassette tape and held it up to the moonlight.

"Looks like we got about seven minutes of tape."

"I can't wait to listen," Griff said.

"Yeah," Thomas said. "I just hope we hear something."

THIRTY-FOUR

BECAUSE THEY DID NOT RIDE HOME TOGETHER, THEY COULD NOT listen to the tape. Thomas agreed they would listen together at SubWatch, Wednesday night.

He texted Thomas three times Wednesday morning.

TAPE STILL THERE? STILL THERE NOW? ARE YOU SURE?

I SLEPT WITH IT UNDER MY PILLOW, Thomas responded. IT NEVER LEAVES MY POCKET.

KEEP AWAY FROM MAGNETS, Griff reminded him. DON'T FALL ON IT.

SHUT UP, Thomas responded.

Wednesday afternoon, he had a presentation with Slim and Jonesy at the public library. In the Clade City Public Library Community Room, Slim talked about the Knock for a Neighbor program. Jonesy, about the New Duck and Cover. Griff scanned the faces of the crowd. Had anyone heard the song last night? Had life changed for anyone? When they finished the presentation, he exited alone through the front doors and found Charity Simms waiting for him.

Her hair was longer. Between the way it had been before and the way it had been immediately afterward. She had life back in her cheeks and skin—he wanted to apologize. *Sorry* might fit safely through the tight slot of his mouth. Or the levee might break in an endless gush of apologies, sorry for not talking, for Leo, the Urchin, for asking you to be in the band, for—

"You played the Band," she said. "Last night."

"You listened," Griff said.

"I listen every night," she said. "I called, too. Thomas answered. I didn't even know if you were there. You never say anything."

Griff's phone chirped. Slim and Jonesy were looking for him.

"We made a tape," Griff said.

Charity's face fell. The opposite of what he expected.

"What's wrong?" he asked.

"I don't know if you should have a tape," she said. "Have you played it yet?"

"No," he said. "Tonight."

Around the corner, coming through the back entrance, Slim and Jonesy. Both in camo. He'd been with them all day but noticed them now. Sunglasses. Boots. Like a two-person invasion. Charity saw them, turned back.

"Are you still playing piano?"

Sorry for not playing piano—

"No," he said. "Are you singing?"

"Yes."

But he already knew, just by looking at her. What happened with Leo had stripped away a few soft layers—but whatever inner glow Charity had was just closer to the surface now.

"Griffy!" Jonesy called, approaching his truck. "Time to go."

"Hi," Slim said, waving to Charity. The pair got into the truck.

"I want to see you," Charity said.

"Yes," Griff said.

Jonesy honked. Griff found himself saying goodbye, leaving. No hugs, no handshakes—just walking. His body trained to follow Jonesy. Jonesy?! Griffy? Slim opened the truck door and bent the seat forward, reminding Griff where he sat.

On the radio, the same station.

"Can you turn it down?" Griff asked.

"What's up with you and the brown beauty?" Jonesy asked. "I liked the short hair better, personally."

The Urchin snapped right back. The smell of it. Jonesy's sweating glass of Coca-Cola. Jonesy, singing. Screaming that voice at Charity. How had he forgotten? How was he in this truck right now? Griff shifted in his seat. Fire, inside him. He imagined steam in his guts, not venting.

"Heard you pulled SubWatch," Slim said, changing the subject. "Ain't too bad, if you're out with Thomas. If you need help—"

Griff's throat full of smoke, and Jonesy said—

"Remember that night at the bar, though? She sure could sing." Jonesy did the voice.

Reeeemmmwweeeber—

He stopped singing because Griff was crushing his windpipe with his right arm. Jonesy went soundless. He swerved and Griff's head knocked against window glass. The truck fishtailed and rocked and skidded onto the gravel shoulder, where they all opened the doors and got out on the shoulder. Slim stood between them.

"Try it again, you chickenshit," Jonesy said. "Do it—"

Griff charged past Slim. He collided with Jonesy and got his arm back across his throat.

He was doing it again.

Slim broke Griff's hold and yanked him off.

"Calm down, Tripp, okay? Calm on down."

"What the hell is wrong with you?" Jonesy said. "If you want to go off and—"

"Cool it," Slim said, moving between them. "Guy lost his brother, Jonesy."

"Shut up, Slim," Griff said.

"Yeah," Jonesy said. "Shut up, Slim."

Griff stood breathing, deflated. He'd gone from angry god to boneless rag. Jonesy could probably flick him into the ocean.

"You know what we've all done for you?" Jonesy said. "How many meetings?"

Griff had just enough energy to lift one finger.

"Oh is that so?" Jonesy said. "Well, I'm done! Enjoy your walk along the cliffs—Mr. Suicide Watch. Don't get any crazy ideas."

"Jonesy," Slim said, "shut your stupid mouth."

Slim suddenly looked bigger. Ropy muscles taut—like, wow, Slim could thrash a fool. Griff turned to walk. A moment later, footsteps. Quick scuttling behind him and he spun in time to see Jonesy leaping—Griff jerked his arms up, but Jonesy just slapped his backpack and turned tail, running, scuffing up dust on the way to his truck, where he clapped himself inside. Slim called out the window. Looked worried.

"Call if you need anything," he said, giving a small wave.

Jonesy chirped his tires, roared away.

Three-mile walk. The cliffs went straight down with no guardrail and it would only take a second to decide to fall—so Griff walked on the other side with the tall pines, boughs still dripping from the rain, hours ago. Droplets landed like little shivers on the nape of his neck, bringing him back. Here you are, the shivers told him. Still alive.

He took out his phone. Could not process words, notifications, so he just said:

"Call Thomas Mortimer."

The phone rang once. Twice.

"You've reached Thomas Mortimer," Thomas said. "Please speak."

"Hello? Thomas? Are you there?"

A pause.

"Yeah. No one ever calls me. I forgot what I was supposed to say."

"Just hello," Griff said. He looked up at the needles. "Do you still have the tape?"

"Yeah, buddy," Thomas sighed. "I still got it."

THIRTY-FIVE

It was finally time to know if they'd lost their minds.

Down at the slack tide near the southern jetty, Griff and Thomas toted the giant copper poles to the foamy edge of the water and stuck the flat bottoms in the mud. They wore rubber boots, chest-high waders, padded black headphones. Each pole stood around 5 feet high and had a curved shepherd's-crook top. They looked like big, brassy question marks with periscope handles. Hyperconductive copper, designed to intercept the transmissions of hypothetical Russian submarines cruising the Oregon coast.

"Do you have it?" Griff asked. Thomas moved off to the left, headphones already on. Maybe he hadn't heard.

The flats slurped at their boots. Waders did not breathe, already damp at Griff's lower back. Sweat, trickling down his legs. Meanwhile, the whip of cold Pacific wind made his head throb. In this outfit, you are two microclimates. Amazonian swamp below, unsheltered Alpine forest above.

"Right after he comes," Griff shouted. "Right? We can listen?"

Thomas nodded but was quiet.

They tuned in to the 30-kHz band. At that depth of frequency—like in the deepest, blackest part of the ocean—not much survived. The awful trill of navigation signals. Coded transmissions. Hypothetical submarines. The tide pushed and pulled with long slow jerks. You fought to stand still. On the ride home, Griff knew his legs would jitter uncontrollably.

How had Leo done this three nights a week?

"Thomas!" Griff called. Thomas was ignoring him. Maybe too many texts.

Dunbar came during their first hour. Because he did not have his lights and siren blaring, he clearly fancied himself a stealthy little barracuda. After parking, he swept the beach with his searchlight. The beam bleached the sand, fried the landscape hot white and hit Griff's eyes with twinkling blotches. A bull-horn, tin-can voice:

"Keep it up, boys!"

Thomas and Griff blinked at the swarm of lights until they dimmed to taillights, a blinker. Dunbar was gone.

"Okay, we ready?" Griff said.

Thomas shook his head. Griff moved closer.

"Thomas. Do you have the tape?" he asked.

Thomas shook his head.

"You don't?" Griff asked. "Thomas, you don't have it?"

"Charity called," Thomas said. "You saw her?"

"Yeah."

"She told me to wait."

"Fuck!" Griff said. "Why didn't you tell me?"

"I thought you'd skip out on SubWatch."

Water slapped the waders. *Schalop, schalop.*

"Don't worry," Thomas said. "It's safe."

"Where?"

"In the car."

Griff and Thomas looked at the car.

"You don't lock your car," Griff said.

"Who's coming out here?" Thomas asked. Griff looked at Thomas and back at the car. When Thomas's expression changed, Griff ran.

Slow-motion nightmare, running in waders, like up to your

calf in melted marshmallow, and Thomas behind him like a boogeyman. Griff dropped the pole on land and Thomas struck him from behind, a tackle that tipped his balance too far forward. They collapsed on the sand, Thomas shouting—

"Chill, man!" Thomas said. "What's one more day?"

Griff stood up. A squirrelly part of his mind gauged the distance again—but he didn't know where the tape was.

"I can't wait."

"It's been eight months," Thomas said. "What's one more day?"

"I need to know it's still there," Griff said.

"I promised Charity we'd wait."

Thomas stepped between Griff and the car. Thomas didn't break promises. Griff turned back, picked up his copper pole. Thomas got his. They walked back.

"Did you hear that crowd?" Griff asked. "Last night."

Thomas nodded. "Yeah."

"It sounded big, didn't it?"

Thomas nodded. They put their headphones back on, waded into the dark water. The moon hadn't risen yet—it would be big and bright just shy of full but for now the dark line of water curved beyond the strength of his eyes. Still a big world. He looked at Thomas.

"I want to hear the crowd," Griff said.

Thomas took off his headphones.

"What?"

"As much as the music," Griff said. "I want to hear that crowd again."

Thomas looked at him. He might've been crying.

"We'll make it out of here, Griff," Thomas said. "I promise."

THIRTY-SIX

"WHAT ARE YOU SO WORRIED ABOUT?" THOMAS ASKED CHARITY.

In the Rat's Nest, three of them clustered around the cassette tape player. It sat surrounded by old analog RCA wires snaking into speaker towers stacked so high Griff imagined when they hit PLAY, they'd go catapulting out of the room.

"It's because of Leo," Charity whispered.

"What?" Thomas asked. "Why are you whispering?"

"He said he knew when the Band would play again. Said we'd catch the biggest fish there was. The Great Big One. But we weren't supposed to record it."

"What?" Thomas asked. "Why?"

"No recording, no preserving," Charity said.

"That's spooky, Charity," Thomas said. "What the hell does that mean?"

"Leo said there was a voice on the broadcast before the Band played. It said 'no recording.' That's why he needed me to hear it live."

She eyed the tape.

"Maybe it didn't record anything," Thomas said.

"This whole thing feels cursed," Charity said.

"Are you going to play it?" Griff asked.

Thomas carefully reached forward, pressed the REWIND button. The little knobs jumped to life, white teeth of the cassette blurring. The tape halted so quickly Griff feared the ribbon would snap.

Thomas pressed PLAY.

The current came through the speakers. Like an ocean sound, the wash of the crowd. Griff leaned into it.

"Still there," Thomas whispered.

Their music from the night before. Better than he remembered. Like fingers prying at hidden knots in his shoulders. His body loosened. Something brushed his back and he flinched. Charity. She'd reached out and he'd jerked like a frightened dog. Sometime since October, he'd forgotten how to be touched.

The music soaked into them. They nodded along to the beat. Leaned closer to the speakers, and each other. Five minutes. Six. Griff held his breath. Please. A little more tonight. He gasped when the sound cut out. A dull hiss. Flatline on the equalizer. Over.

"So it's real," Thomas said. He smiled.

"It's amazing," Charity said. "Leo thought they were recording in a hidden studio. He wanted to go find it."

"With you?" Griff asked.

Charity nodded.

Thomas rewound the tape and played back the crowd. Stopped. Played again.

"Wrong," Thomas said.

Thomas flipped on a desk lamp. Went to his mixer. He fuzzied the music, submerged the vocals and strings to a faint burbling, and teased out sharp rat-scratching sounds that softened to—

"Voices," Griff said. Emerging from the crowd like ships in fog.

Hey—sure, wow, wow, omigod—

"No one talks like that in a studio. You can hear the distance between them, I mean—based on these acoustics that's a big crowd. I'm talking stadium."

"Yeah," Charity said.

"That's what it sounds like," Griff said. "Leo wouldn't have missed that."

"Nope."

"Then why would he say that?" Charity asked.

"Because he wanted to find it first," Griff said.

And it made sudden sense. Griff had shared Leo's mental maps and schematics. Ducts and vents. Half of his brother's plan flashed into his mind—and Griff knew where to find the rest.

THIRTY-SEVEN

GRIFF CAME INTO HIS BEDROOM WITH TWO CRESCENT WRENCHES. Unlocking the Unifying Theory of Everything was a challenge. Unlocking the TOE Box was simple. He knelt by the painted mailbox and clutched the wrenches gingerly, like fine-boned birds.

He stood up and double-checked the door. Locked.

When he knelt, his right knee brushed the butcher paper on the closet door. To bust a padlock, you used oppositional force. Pressed heads of twin wrenches together like toothless gears within the narrow window of the hasp.

He took a breath for accuracy, the way Leo claimed to do when shooting.

Griff squeezed. Wrenches slipped. His elbow glanced off the papered mirror with a tearing sound. From the corner of his eye, half a face.

"No," Griff whispered.

He looked again. The eye winked.

Griff gasped. Grabbed the paper, pressed it to the mirror. With his other hand, he probed for tape, something. The only thing he could reach were the wrenches. He tucked the side of the paper beneath the tear and picked up the wrenches.

Lazily, the paper flopped back down. Griff turned to the mirror.

It was Leo.

"Hey, bro," Leo said.

His face in the mirror, cast in a torn paper frame. They blinked at each other. Both breathing. Trembling, Griff reached up and Leo's eye flicked toward his wrist.

"Nice bracelet," Leo said. "Reminds me of something."

"I'm so sorry, Leo," Griff whispered. He could barely find the words.

"Give me a hand here?" Leo blew up at the torn paper, like he had hair in his eyes. Griff extended the tear, revealing his complete face.

Another long stare.

"What could you do?" Leo shrugged. "You screamed my name. Right? Jumped right in? You're a strong swimmer. I imagine you did everything you could."

"I made a line. I tried—"

"Little late, though. Right? Always been a little late, Griff."

Griff looked back at the lock.

"I need to open the box," Griff said. "You'd be fine with it."

"I'm not."

"Yes," Griff said. "You would be. We worked on this together."

"I put a lock on the box, Griff. That's pretty clear. And I'm telling you not to."

"That's questionable."

"Also," he said, looking up, "that shit is cursed. From my watery grave."

Leo did the curse fingers.

"Please stop," Griff said.

"Spiders, too. Crawling. Breeding. It's actually a spider farm."

Leo knew he hated spiders.

"Okay," Griff said.

Griff crawled across the carpet and returned with Scotch tape. Ripped a strip. Leo watched with determined eyes and said nothing as Griff papered over his reflection. He lifted the heavy wrenches from the carpet. His blood felt thick. Arm wobbled.

Griff inserted the wrench heads and made a fist.

The lock shattered. It felt loud as a gunshot. Griff sat, panting, staring at the lock's broken pieces. What had he done?

KNOCK KNOCK

"What!" Griff spun.

"Okay in there?" his father called.

"Jesus, Dad. I'm fine!"

Footsteps plodded off. Griff shut his eyes. When he opened them, the box was listing open, just a crack. The smell of low-tide sulfur. He pulled open the heavy, swinging door.

Griff exhaled.

The TOE Box was packed. Fuller than he'd imagined.

Cassette tapes. Radios. Headphones. Waterproof notebooks. A thick white cardboard tube, deadheaded with tamper-proof tape.

KEEP SEALED

"No recording, huh?" Griff said. He took the cassettes out and stacked them click, clack. Over twenty tapes, labeled with longitude, latitude, times. Coded like the Preppers had taught them, don't make anything easy. Griff split the tube's tamper-proof tape with a soft pop. He reached his fingers inside. A tickle.

Spiders!

No. Two tight rolls of graphing paper. He spread them out on the carpet. Leo's cramped, meticulous handwriting clustered in the corners, slashing across great, wide swaths of geography.

One of the maps was of Oregon. Even with coded labels, Griff recognized how the banks and cays fit together like the loops and sockets of a puzzle. The first map was casually marked.

The second map was much more detailed. Dotted arrows. Interlocking circles, drawn by a compass. Meticulous elevation lines. The markings depicted a vast plateau between crisscrossing mountain ranges. If Griff understood the scale, the landform was too massive to be unknown to him.

Where could it possibly be?

If Leo's map was scaled at 20 miles to an inch—as it appeared—the plateau was hundreds of square miles wide. There couldn't be many such spaces on Earth. Griff went to his computer. He searched California, Idaho, Oregon, Washington, Nevada for an elevated landform that size, between 250 and 300 feet high. The Midwest. Russia. Siberia. Africa. Europe. What was he missing?

He texted Thomas: I NEED YOU TO FIND SOMETHING FOR ME.

ON IT CHIEF, Thomas responded. SHOOT.

Griff sent him the rough dimensions. Hundreds of square miles, a few hundred feet high.

Hours later, Griff lay exhausted on his bed. Lights on. Still dressed.

NADA, Thomas texted. SURE YOU'VE GOT THE MEASUREMENTS RIGHT?

"Where?" he said out loud. He looked at the paper on the mirror. He rolled around in his bed. Punched his pillow. Flipped it.

He looked at Leo's bed, neatly made.

"Whoomp," Griff said.

Griff remembered the first night, when Leo had locked the TOE Box. Griff scooted to the foot of the bed and hung his head upside down, from the bottom. He stared at the box. Looked up at the pebbled ceiling.

The realization struck his body first. Goose bumps up the back of his neck, nipping at his hairline.

"Upside down," Griff whispered.

He sat so suddenly the world jerked, tilted him sideways out of bed, and he stumbled up to his computer. Tapping the screen. Then grabbing the map.

No plateaus of that size 250 feet above sea level.

But Leo's elevation lines were 250 feet below.

"Atlantis," Griff whispered.

Leo had tracked the radio signal to the bottom of the ocean.

THIRTY-EIGHT

GRIFF, THOMAS, AND CHARITY MET THE FOLLOWING AFTERNOON at Spawn Drive Peak. Just within city limits, the park's wide strip of sloping grassland hugged sheer sandstone cliffs. Terraced picnic benches, a few BBQ pits, and the town's best inland ocean view. Wind whipped tall reed grass in great gusts. Tourists often marveled at the vacancy of coastal picnic benches until the moment they tried to eat their club crackers in 40-mile-per-hour winds.

"Sperm Drive Peak," Thomas said, claiming a table with his bag.

Charity looked at him. "What did you call this?"

"Sperm Drive Peak," Thomas said. "This is our classic small-town make-out spot. Do you even live here?"

"I thought they called it Swan Dive Peak" Charity said, looking down. "Because it was the classic small-town suicide spot."

"It's both," Griff said. "Like my mom says—in small towns everyone just has to wear two hats and do more."

Charity laughed.

"Okay. So what else did you learn?" Thomas asked.

Griff removed a handful of cassettes from the backpack and slapped them on the picnic table. Then another. Another. Twenty-two, all told.

"One," Griff said. "Leo had no trouble with recording or preserving."

"Wow," Charity said.

All the late nights with muddy boots—he must've logged almost a hundred hours.

"Hold the corners," Griff said.

He unfurled the map in the wind. Thomas got down close and pulled a ruler from his bag. A flat magnifying sheet. He measured the notches.

"See?" Griff said to Thomas, pointing to the large depression.

A flat-bottomed crater between mountain ranges.

"Atlantis," Thomas said, lifting his hand. The corner of his map beat the table in the wind, *tickatickaticka*, fluttering like cards in spokes. "Looks like it."

"Can you explain?" Charity asked.

"This is all hundreds of feet below sea level. Griff thinks Leo was looking for something underwater."

Tickatickatickata—

"How does that make sense?" Charity asked.

"It doesn't," Thomas said. "It makes no scientific sense. Radio waves can't penetrate water. It's physically impossible. Think about SubWatch. Even those monster receivers can only get a whisper, and that's if the subs are close to surfacing."

A shadow fell across the table. Charity shivered. Zipped up her coat.

"How is this June?" Charity said. "God."

"Oops," Thomas said.

"I'm not cursing, I'm asking the Lord a legitimate question."

"It's June-uary," Griff said. "You know. Just before Ju-lie. And Fog-ust."

In the distance, a low buzzing.

"Look," Thomas said. He plucked a blade of reed grass. With the tip, he traced Leo's hand-drawn elevation lines. "Your brother spent a lot of time on this."

Louder. A vehicle. The group perked up.

Spawn Drive Peak was on the way to nowhere. No one should be here. The engine swelled and a truck overtook the curve—a hard black edge around the corner. Jonesy's truck.

"No way," Griff said.

It slowed. Pulled into the lot.

ticktickticktick

"Is that Jonesy and Slim?" Thomas asked. "What are they doing here?"

"Make out?" Charity said. "Or suicide?"

Jonesy gunned the engine. Whipped the truck around in a quick screeching loop. Low-frequency bass rattled the windows. He gave a quick patter of honks, a signature tire-chirp, and lurched back onto the road toward town.

"Was that a secret message?" Charity said.

"The tire chirp is Morse code for *I'm an asshole*," Griff said.

"I don't know how they found us," Thomas said. "Maybe they're reminding us about the meeting."

"I could never see another pickup truck," Charity said. "I'd be fine."

Thomas divided up the tapes. A stack for him, a stack for Griff, a stack for Charity.

"Listen to everything," Thomas said. "Take notes. We reconvene in two days. Let's go over everything we know."

They stopped abruptly at the sound of the alarm. The 1000T. Warbling, distant.

ooooooooeeeeeebadadadadadadada

"We'd better go," Griff said, rolling up the map. Wind snatched at the corners.

"Why?" Charity asked. "Nuclear strike? Tsunami?"

"City Council meeting," Griff said.

"And you're going?"

"We have to," Griff said. "They're voting on the lighthouse."

THIRTY-NINE

THE CITY COUNCIL MEETING SMELLED LIKE STALE CIGARETTES, gasoline, and low-tide mud. His hometown smell. A little fishy. Griff liked it. There were dockworkers, a crew from the cannery, the downtown shop owners, lumber workers, and a handful of teachers. Jonesy and Slim sat up front. Griff and Thomas stayed near the back beside a bulletin board with tear-off advertisements for house sitters, potential roommates, ads for gutter repair, Ron's Surf Shack, Burrito Chuck, a poster of an anthropomorphized paper document with cartoon legs, eyes, and gloved hands wagging its finger and saying: Remember Information Is Key to Good Decision Making.

The first presentation, from a University of Oregon research fellow, was about the National Oceanic and Atmospheric Association's improvements in navigation systems since the early 1900s. The second presentation, from the Lost Coast Preppers, featured Dunbar and the beefcake Regional Prepper Director Tom Schaloob. They described the advanced tectonic and nuclear submarine monitoring techniques and air-raid alerts that would be available should the lighthouse be dismantled and repurposed. The third presentation was in support of maintaining the lighthouse as a cultural treasure, led by volunteer librarian Mrs. Ciota and retired language arts teacher Mr. Locke, speaking on behalf of the Clade City Culture Keepers.

They discussed the poetic importance of Sense of Place and aesthetic beauty in the built environment.

"Not looking good for the lighthouse," Thomas whispered.

Griff watched the crowd, pressure growing behind his eyes.

Someone, he thought. Say something.

Had anyone in the crowd heard the Band's song on K-NOW? What music could capture their hearts? The surfers, dockworkers, lumberjacks. It couldn't all just be talk toads and Rack Rock and commercials for sleep-number beds. They, too, must dance in their kitchens. Sing in their showers. Surely these people must ache and lie in bed and cry listening to *something*.

After the debate, Griff's father managed to defer the vote on the lighthouse. The crowd was not with him. As the meeting dispersed, the murmur of voices hummed like an alert turned down low:

brrrradadadadadbreeeeeee

His town had become afraid.

Griff had played one brave song. The screaming yellow Thunderbolt had been broadcasting almost a year. It had its own Specific Absorption Rate. Leeching into their cells, blood, and bones. Sowing its message, steady as the tide.

FORTY

After the meeting, Griff visited his piano.

Are you still playing?

He opened the French doors and the room exhaled a stale breath. Pages on the stand waved a limp hello. The room smelled like a vacuum bag that needed changing.

Every piece of music on the stand was written for four hands. Griff touched the laced cord on his wrist. He could not play with it on. He could not take it off.

The bench had been still for months.

Grooves in the carpet recalled the struggle. Small, square dents where Griff preferred the bench. Ahead of them, the brass-capped legs where Leo liked them. Like notches on a belt, Leo Position or Griff Position. No in-between.

The bench remained in Leo Position.

Griff sat down. Stared at the keys. On the music stand, Stravinsky's Symphony in Three Movements. Right where they'd put it. The score had been left on his part, andante.

Griff held his fingers out.

He knew it well enough, but then what? The page turns inevitably ended with the scherzo. The terrifying final act— Italian for "the joke"—which upended the themes introduced in the overture and sped them up, twisting them in startling ways.

How could he do it alone?

Griff settled his hands on the keys. Cool on his fingertips.

Movement at the window. His head jerked up.

His mother stood with her face neatly framed in a pane of glass. A frozen gasp. Crying. She looked caught. Like she shouldn't be looking. Gone.

And that was the reason it would never work.

His mother's face. Horrified to see him in the dark room.

Like she'd just seen a ghost.

FORTY-ONE

WRONG, THOMAS TEXTED THE NEXT DAY. YOU'RE WRONG. FLAT WRONG. COME OVER.

Lately, escape from home had been tricky.

Griff's living room looked like a freshly exploded tourist trap. His mother was doing a shop reorganization and half the contents of Shoreline Gifts had washed up in their living room. Spinning wire greeting card racks. Books about enlightenment, Buddhism, mindfulness, Jewish rituals, Oregon history. Dead sea horses and sand dollars and sea stars lying in drawers like open caskets. Box of agates.

"Geez, Mom!" Griff said. "It's like the beach of the damned in here."

"Where are you going? Thomas's again?" she said. He picked his way through, leaning back to avoid postcards, seeking the door handle—

"Griff, stop," his father said.

Oh no.

"What, Dad?"

"You've been spending a lot of time over there," his dad said. "What are you boys doing?"

"Tutorials," Griff said. "Earning hours for the Gap."

His words spat out ticker-tape robotic. Griff's postmortem autopilot brain occasionally still took the wheel.

The I'm Fine Machine. Sometimes it talked all on its own.

Griff took a step toward the door. His father looked at his phone.

"By my count, SubWatch has you ahead of schedule. You've got all year. We're concerned about how much time you spend in that basement."

Griffin exhaled. His hand curled around the doorknob.

creak

"He's a stoner, Griff," his mom said.

Griff stared at his mother. Didn't know where to start. He let go of the doorknob.

"It's true," his father said. "I've heard things."

"People respond differently to loss," Griff said to his dad. "Some people drink."

"Some smoke copious amounts of marijuana," his father said.

"*Copious*," his mother said. "That's a stoner word. Like *myriad*."

Silence hung in the air.

His mother turned the rack of greeting cards, all ocean-themed. Birthday cards were footprints in sand, lighthouses, sailboats. Sympathy cards: footprints in sand, lighthouses, sailboats. Like Spawn Drive Peak, small-town greeting cards just had to wear two hats and do more.

"Stoner or not," Griff said, "he invented EARS. He does a million other useful projects."

"Myriad projects," his mother said. "Copious projects."

His father sighed.

"Okay," Griff said. "I'll be careful. Love you guys!"

The perfect words for blastoff. Out the door. One more time.

●　●　●

"It's not the ocean," Thomas said. "It's the desert."

He spun his laptop so Griff and Charity could see.

First shot: A vast, prickly wasteland. Another shot, 30,000 feet up. Undulating mountains fell like crooked shadows over a broad palette of beige. Salt deposits pocked the landscape like sores. The next shot—a road straight to nowhere. It began broad and gray. Narrowed to the width of a thumbtack in the blazing blue horizon.

"Death Valley," Thomas said. "Once an ocean, then a lake. Now a desert with the lowest elevation in America at 282 feet below sea level. Same dimensions as Leo's map. Same topography. It maps with all his notes. As far as I can tell, your brother had the broadcast site narrowed to about 200 square miles."

"You think there's a concert in the middle of Death Valley?" Charity said.

"No," Thomas said. "Death Valley has the highest recorded ambient temperature on the planet. It's not a fry-an-egg-on-the-sidewalk place. You could fry an egg in midair. Like, the air—as in, the same place your face occupies—is hot enough to cook food. So no, I don't imagine there is a giant stadium concert happening in Death Valley."

"Then how is this theory better than Atlantis?" Griff asked.

"I didn't say better," Thomas said. "I said more accurate. And I never expected the Band to be playing where they broadcast. This thing is on a repeater somewhere. You know, beaming from this satellite dish to that trailer to that chicken shack—but even finding a repeater would be huge. From there we could track it."

Griff looked at the map mounted on the pegboard.

"If Leo got it down to 200 miles," Griff said, "we can triangulate the signal."

"Sure," Thomas said. "We just need to know when they broadcast next. Last time it took nine months."

"Maybe we just drive out there," Charity said.

They both looked at her.

"I'm serious," she said.

"I can tell," Griff said. Him and Charity in a car—a thrill in the blood, a forgotten feeling, whipped up and stirred inside him.

"If you two idiots want to drive to Death Valley to fall in mine shafts and get your faces melted off, you can. Godspeed."

Thomas's eyes looked dark and heavy on the undersides. He'd not been sleeping.

"Can we analyze the recording?" Griff asked.

"There are no more clues in the tape we've got. We need more material," Thomas said. "How far have you gotten in your stacks?"

"I've listened to four," Griff said. It had been agony. Song fishing was thrilling with some measure of control, but a tape with someone else's choices—where they chose to linger or tried to penetrate ear-shredding static—was torture. The novelty of listening to Leo's Sound Expeditions had worn out halfway through the first tape.

"I'm five in," Charity said. "Should finish tonight."

"And I'm done," Thomas said. "Got anything yet?"

They shook their heads.

"You know what I think is on these tapes?" Thomas said.

CLACK. CLACK. CLACK.

"Nothing," Thomas said. "It's a diversion. A hoax."

Charity and Griff stared at him. Thomas whistled. Got down on all fours, whistled again.

"If there's nothing on the tapes, why keep them?" Griff asked.

"Who knows? He's your crazy brother. He coded his own maps and wrapped them in tamper-proof tape. If he'd gotten a good recording, he would've kept it somewhere special."

Thomas whistled again, knelt down. Neapolitan came bounding into his hands.

"Aww," Charity said.

"The TOE Box was the most special place," Griff said.

"Maybe you didn't know him as well as you thought," Thomas said.

He was being mean. Thomas stroked the rat. Charity walked over. Touched her behind the ears.

"Anything else you remember him saying, Charity?" Griff asked.

"Leo knew exactly when they were going to play. He wouldn't leave me alone about coming that night. I even stayed home sick just to stay away from him."

"I remember," Griff said.

Her eyes went distant, back to October.

"Kept saying—I need you to hear this. After the show, he kept texting and texting and I—"

"It's okay," Griff said.

"I got the texts the morning you went," Charity said, like she couldn't stop. "I got them. I read them all, you know? To please come. To get the coat from your house—"

Griff tried to touch her. Her jaw clamped shut, she shook her head. Wiped her eyes. Stayed still.

"I didn't say anything," she said. "Not a word. Didn't respond—"

"It's okay," Thomas said.

"No! He'd be alive," Charity said. "What I'm trying to tell you is that he'd be alive right now if I'd said yes, or if I'd said anything."

Loss did this. Hid in plain sight, then pounced.

"Or if I'd asked him to stop for coffee," Griff said. "If I'd let him go—"

He hovered on an edge of a deep, dark plunge and Thomas pulled him back, physically by the shoulder.

"Stop, Griff," Thomas said. "Both of you. Not useful. If Leo had a recording, he'd want us to have it."

"You're sure?" Griff asked.

"Yes."

"Okay," Griff said. "I'll look again. Will you two be around tonight?"

"I'm going to be on lockdown," Charity said. "But you can throw a pebble at my window. First floor, second to the left."

Griff smiled. Did she mean it?

"Do people actually do that?" Thomas asked.

"I've always wanted to," she said. She laughed, wiped her eyes.

"For me go ahead and use the phone," Thomas said. "Where are you going?"

"To find the tape."

FORTY-TWO

WHEN GRIFF GOT HOME, THE FRONT DOOR WOULDN'T OPEN. IT snagged on something. He shoved lightly, then pressed his eye to the door crack. One of his mother's wire card racks stood in the way, bare as a winter tree. He shoved the door slowly. The rack skittered with metal-twig feet, then tipped in slow motion. The crash, like a car accident. It echoed in the house. No response.

That haunted feeling. Parents gone.

Lights on. Cards in plastic sleeves swooped out over the floor in a wide arc. An upturned box of agates, glinting like spilled jewels. Another shimmer beneath the kitchen table was green glass. Wine bottle, red liquid. Griff's hand went to the knife in his pocket. He called out:

"Mom?"

Bad move. Not strategic, but the child had gotten ahead of the prepper. He opened the blade on his knife, looked at his father's security system.

The light blinked green.

His training took over. Griff held the knife in a firm fist so it could not be easily taken. He approached the corner to the bedroom hallway, then stepped around in a wide, sweeping fashion, clearing the corridor—empty. The door to his parents' bedroom was shut.

Griff walked slowly. Beyond the whir of the bathroom fan, a familiar sound.

MuGaMuga. MUGAMuga. BadaddadadadadadMUGA-MUGAA.

Muffled by the door. The sound of discontented whales, moaning and chattering. It triggered recent, foggy memories. Griff pinched the silver blade of his knife, slipped it back into the handle. He'd snapped into the wrong survival response. This was not How to Clear a Home Invasion.

Teeektateeek. TsktskadadadaDADADADA.

It was How to Brace for a Fight.

He went to his room and shut the door. His only vessel. A little drywall submarine. Griff jerked open his desk drawer, pawed through binder clips, jump drives, pens—he couldn't find the little blue foam earplugs and could feel it, about to hit. Did not have long. He grabbed his best headphones—which song to ruin this time? Tattoo with parents' voices and make forever unlistenable, and he settled for seventies psychedelia, one of his father's old recommendations—Iron Butterfly's "In-A-Gadda-Da-Vida."

Dun dun dad dad da da

Originally intended as "In the Garden of Eden," misinterpreted due to the drunken slurring of the vocalist. His father had told him in the basement, one of their old song-fishing days—

MY GODDAMN FAULT? WHAT ABOUT YOU? THIS WHOLE FUCKING MESS!!!! DON'T TALK TO ME ABOUT LEO DON'T TALK TO ME ABOUT LEO DON'T YOU TALK TO ME—

He turned it up. Closed his eyes.

THIS HOUSE! LOOK AT ME, DAVID, DAVID, LOOK AT ME—

The I'm Fine Machine whirred to life. Griff went to the

computer, blaring music, and examined the facts. He'd done this many times, relocking his door, securing the window, poring over information like Scripture because it was normal for parents to fight. These links had been clicked, tabs open, but it was gospel and prayer to read the lists, the Five Stages of Loss: denial, anger, bargaining, depression, acceptance, and the nuanced Kübler-Ross model, which took you from hell to acceptance in a gentle sine wave and—

Fact: Parents will find it challenging to bring comfort to their surviving children.

Fact: The Standard Internet Picture of Surviving Child is a boy sitting on a hunk of driftwood on the beach. Like people celebrating birthdays and remembering anniversaries, this boy, too, preferred to be near the ocean with his face buried in his hands. Faceless, the boy is relatable. He could be anyone.

Fact: Surviving Children should expect to be faceless and among driftwood—

Nothing about whale sounds. Nothing about greeting cards, broken wine bottles, or what happens when you share a bedroom with a dead brother whose bed remains forever tidy. The bed didn't know anything. Tucked in corners, neatly centered pillow.

Tidy.

The word needled him. Tidy bed. Tucked in neat, beddy-bye.

Griff bolted across the room. He threw Leo's pillow. Stripped that perfect white line of a sheet backward. Ruined it. Ruined the neatly made bed and the blue-and-white-checkered comforter like wake up! WAKE UP!—he jerked the fitted sheet until elastic crackled and screamed and would never be the same. Good!

Nothing under the mattress.

"Where?" he said.

Across the room, Griff grabbed the black backpack. Reached inside and jerked everything out, dumped it. A candy wrapper—piece of dark chocolate? Great! Griff grabbed it, unfoiled it, shoved it in his mouth. His dead brother's chocolate. Delicious. He spiked the backpack on the ground. Touchdown!

A drawer. He jerked it open. Keeping secrets?

He grabbed the socks out in a giant, pressed-together lump and flung them across the room. Next drawer. Papers, toys, empty, guts spilled all over the floor in the closet, he jerked the shirts from their plastic shoulders and back to the mattress, flipped it over and found nothing underneath, and he kicked the shoes—WAKE UP! Stomped them, kicked them, then tried to squeeze his feet into his favorites, too small now, his feet couldn't fit in the boots and so he tripped, fell on the carpet. He lay breathing. Pretended he was dead. He could be dead.

He looked across the wrecked horizon of the room. Good. There.

Mood-compatible bedroom.

No tape.

"Where?" he asked.

Griff addressed the butcher paper over the mirror.

He listened. No more whales. Maybe his parents had heard him. Maybe huddled over their own computer monitor, looking at facts about faceless boys and driftwood. Griff pinched his wrist. Another survival response kicked in. This one, from his therapist. He needed to get out and see someone. Maybe Thomas. Maybe he'd throw a pebble at a window.

Outside, it was raining.

The floor, a perfect wreckage. He grabbed the black backpack by the top hoop, shook it free. He closed the door. It looked good, shut. Tidy. His parents' door remained good and shut and quiet. When Griff turned the corner to the living room, he was surprised by his parents' own wreckage. He laughed. Tipped-over racks, boxes—it had come at last! The famous disaster! A small, unreported quake on the fault line of their family. He went to the wall mirror and began to pull jackets and fleeces from their hooks, looking for a raincoat.

Griff peeled back through the seasons. His father's sporty waterproof windbreaker and then his soft shell and his mother's bright aqua slicker, dropping them, peeling back to winter's heavier red cycling hard-shell, revealing the first oval mirror his mother had ever covered—

But the glass was exposed, and Leo stared back at him.

"Where you going?" Leo asked.

Griff's breathing caught. He looked around.

"I don't know yet," he said.

"Why did you trash our room?" Leo asked.

"Why did you hide the tape from me?"

"Maybe I didn't," Leo said. "Maybe stop making me the villain for once."

Griff removed the bulky blue winter jacket his mother wore and called the Man Coat, the green fleece from November, and in the end the final coat hanging was his father's camouflage jacket, which Leo had tossed on the kitchen table on Sunday, October 28.

Which Griff had forgotten.

He looked at Leo. Leo looked back at him.

Hand shaking, Griff took the coat from the hook. Closed his eyes. Slipped his hands through the cuffs and snugged it on his body and took a deep, shuddering breath. Tighter than he remembered. It actually fit. He pulled the left cuff over the bulky paracord. When his arms fell to his sides, his elbow rapped something in the jacket's inner pocket.

—tok—

He froze.

Griff's fingers traced the outline. Rectangular, sharp corners. He reached inside and pulled out the cassette. He'd meant to bring it that day. Leo's writing, on the spine:

THE GREAT BIG ONE

FORTY-THREE

ON HIS BIKE.

The tape. He had the tape.

Warm, drizzling air condensed in his front lamp. Droplets blazed red in his wake. The smell of wet leaves, and a flooded campfire. The rain pulled wildfire ash from the air, drowned it in the gutters.

Had Charity meant what she said?

Griff's bike jumped the curb at the Simms home. He downed it in the grass and huddled beneath a stand of well-mulched pines. Breathed warmth into his hands. Aside from this lonely trio of trees, their home was landscaped like a prison yard. Bare grass without a lick of shadow. He'd be lucky to find a pebble to throw. The second window over from the front door shone like golden foil.

That was it.

Griff took a step from beneath the trees.

Ms. Simms—what might she do? What if Charity had been kidding? But the trembling in his stomach said GO! He had the tape, a cassette player, and two sets of headphones in his backpack. He took a step. Damp grass tickled his ankles, pants too high. His heart felt swollen.

This black backpack—way too tight. The straps felt wrong. Too much clattering.

calackalackalack

Griff retreated to the pines. Pulled his pant cuffs down. Socks up. He adjusted the packing of the player, the headphones to reduce noise. Zipped the backpack up. Adjusted the straps, moving the plastic cleats over the nylon ribbon, chewing new dents. Had he gotten stronger? Wider in the chest? He'd never had to adjust anything of Leo's—similar activity levels, identical height measurements, a shared affinity for chocolate. The bite of the cleats in the backpack straps reminded him of what?

The piano bench. Like the carpet. Little divots. Memory markers.

What had he done to those straps?

He'd erased Leo. The straps had remembered the shape of Leo's body and were not the same size because Leo had stopped growing in October and Griff had not. He sat and pulled at the straps, tried to seat them back in the wear marks, but they slipped again—damn things go back, JUST GO BACK—

Leo's coat, Leo's backpack, Leo's tape. He'd trashed Leo's room and was bringing Leo's tape to the girl Leo had loved and god, he was garbage, grave robber, killer, Griff got back on his bike. He rode and when there were no more houses, he screamed into the rain and found himself on the edge of Marine Drive. He dropped his bike and stood and held the tape in the rain. Stared over the guardrail at the waves.

"Is this what you want?" he asked.

He could not play the tape. He could not throw the tape. Could not throw a pebble at a window. He stood until his shivering felt like tremors and the tips of his fingers went white. He rode home, soaking and exhausted. Inside, the wire rack was still toppled, lights still on, wine bottle still there, red droplets on the tile because in a nightmare life nothing healed itself. No one left to reset the pins when the big black ball knocked them down. It all just kept going.

He went into the ruined bedroom and he found the calendar on the wall.

He had circled today in red, because he had seen Charity. But he was also a coward who did not deserve a red circle.

"You failed," he told himself.

He raked his damp thumb across the ink and smudged it. Scratched until the paper frayed. God, he missed her.

He looked back over weeks of no-circle days.

Boxes stuffed with scratch marks and symbols, meaningless, colorless days.

A May without circles, an April, March, February—without, without. Like with any weight, you adjusted to carrying loss. Could not appreciate the crushing bulk of it until you remembered how airy life had felt before. The breezy feeling of a kiss, an autumn dance. He needed to remember. He found the calendar from last year and opened to the final month. No circles in December. Nothing in November.

Finally in October, a feast of red ink. Study hall. Rehearsals. The day she had taken him to the stars in practice room 5, so many days and so few blank. Just that week, before the show.

The day she'd missed school, when Leo had come home singing.

On that day, October 19, a small printed black circle instead of a hand-drawn red one.

Still holding the calendar, Griff approached the coat on foot, slowly. He removed the tape from the pocket. Opened it. Leo's notations, always the same. Latitude and longitude markers they'd been unable to decode. But the date was plain.

October 19.

Griff went back to the new calendar. Went to the day Charity had found him on the front steps of the library. The first red circle of the year. And behind it, another black circle, white center.

The night Griff had woken up. The night they'd played the Band for the whole town.

"Oh my god," Griff whispered. His mouth went dry.

He knew what Leo knew.

The Band would play again on the next full moon.

FORTY-FOUR

"READY?" THOMAS ASKED. GRIFF HANDED HIM THE TAPE.

The three of them sat together in the submarine glow of the ThunderChicken's green elastic dash. A strange view, up front. Old-school speedometer. Numbers rose with the tall authority of epochs and ages, steering wheel the size of the sun. The mouth of the cassette player held the tape loosely—not yet inside.

"You sure the Chicken won't eat it?" Griff said.

"Tapes aren't in the Chicken's diet, man," Thomas said. "I wouldn't roll with a tape eater. Once a vehicle has a taste for musical celluloid, it can't be trusted."

Thomas mimed shooting the dashboard.

"I'm having that cursed feeling again," Charity said, leaning forward.

"Curses can be exciting," Thomas said. "Let's roll."

They drove the long, winding scribble of Marine Drive, barreling north with the windows cracked, past familiar signs, flashing in the headlights. The engine, not chirping tonight. The low hum of adventure.

"Now," Griff said.

Thomas pressed the tape into the player. Windows up. The car crackled.

"Are you sure it's not eating the tape?" Griff asked.

"These speakers," Thomas muttered. "That's the only—"

He turned it up. A voice pounced:

"No recording. No preserving."

Thomas's hand snapped to STOP.

"Was that God talking?" Thomas asked.

"That's exactly what Leo said." Charity leaned up from the back. "No recording. No preserving."

"That wasn't Leo," Thomas said.

"No," Griff said.

Thomas took a long curve and they topped a small hill— mile marker 155, where the road untangled itself from low-hanging switchbacks and rose to a view. Moonlight went liquid on a horizon of cold, silver fire. It looked brand-new. Like the whole world had just been born.

"Okay," Thomas said. "It's time."

Griff pressed PLAY. Charity took his hand.

● ● ●

They descended to the Rat's Nest in a silence that felt sacred. Shirts rain-soaked from rolled-down windows. Voices hoarse. Three hours roaring up and down Highway 101, bending themselves around hairpin turns. Switchbacks and roller-coaster climbs and the music. Better than they remembered. Roof punching, full-throated howling, and head-bobbing silence. Better than anything had a right to be. THE MUSIC.

Griff flexed his right hand, creaky from the cold. His left, warm from Charity's grip.

She smiled at him in the blue light of the basement.

"Water," Thomas said. Raw voice. They could hear him glugging from a bottle like a cartoon character. He sang out:

"Time for some anallllllyyysis!"

He did not come back.

"Hug me, please," Charity said.

Her hair brushed his cheek. The fresh silence whistled in his ears, rang little bells. Her body against his.

Just this, Griff thought. Just this forever.

FORTY-FIVE

AFTER GRIFF WALKED CHARITY TO HER CAR, THOMAS DEMANDED he return to the basement.

Seven missed calls. Texts marked URGENT.

"Hello?" Griff asked, opening the wooden door. "Rats!"

He tried to startle them, watching his feet for furry escapees.

"Finally!" Thomas bellowed.

"It's after midnight," Griff said. He shut the door and moved toward the blue glow of Thomas's workstation.

"Who can sleep?" Thomas said. "What took you idiots so long? You were out there for an hour."

"Just talking," he said.

Curb dancing in a light drizzle. The first time they'd talked in so long. Time slipped. Gotta go, should go, circled and echoed meaningless and maybe they'd been talking ten minutes, or maybe the sun was about to come up. But Thomas just kept calling. And calling.

"Talking," Thomas snorted. "At a time like this."

Thomas sat ensconced in mission control. Three curved monitors, piled-up speakers, stacked sound decks, and his trusty board. Laptops on a table behind him.

"How many computers do you have?"

"Three things to share with you" Thomas said, ignoring him. "First, look at this."

He nudged the computer screens awake. On each of the five screens, a separate musical search engine.

"You found the Band?"

An anxious twist in Griff's throat. Was the mystery solved?

"No," Thomas said. "Much better than that. I didn't find anything."

Thomas played the tape, a great guitar riff—a moment of exceptional vocal clarity—

—sun drenched you and me too, you know the moon's our oldest friend away we go—

He went from engine to engine, pressing GO and START and SEEK. Verdicts came quickly. NO RESULTS. PLEASE TRY AGAIN. NO INITIAL MATCHES.

"Wow," Griff said.

"These programs use a time-frequency spectrogram," Thomas said. "Like a musical fingerprint. Between them, we have access to over twenty million songs, and these don't match any of them."

"Why is that good?"

"Because it's on purpose," Thomas said. He rewound the tape, ejected it, and carefully moved it to the deck near his sound board and monitor.

"They don't exist, on purpose. Listen. Discovery two."

The voice:

"NO RECORDING. NO PRESERVING."

On the analog decibel dial, golden needles did sharp, arcing leaps. On another monitor, horizontal lines like old video game life meters stretched green to yellow to red. Thomas ran it back. Again and again.

"NO RECORDING. NO PRESERVING. NO RECORDING. NO PRESERVING."

"Great," Griff said. "We're cursed. Nightmares for everyone. What am I looking at?"

"The levels," Thomas said. "Aren't you seeing this? Right when the band starts?"

There was a shift. Golden needles pulled back, the life meters stopped pinging into red.

"It's not as loud?"

"Don't just look at the decibels, you student."

Thomas grabbed Griff's chin, turned his head toward a display he hadn't noticed, a digital sound board with sixteen additional monitors—PAN, EQ, BASS, AUX, abbreviations Griff did not know or understand, but the next time the audio shifted between DJ and music, he noticed the change. Colored bars jerked in new configurations. A sudden leap in the levels. A whole different organism.

"See," Thomas said. "He's got his own setup. The DJ. He's not necessarily in the same place as the band."

"Is that good?"

"It means they know what they're doing. It's interesting," Thomas said. "Mostly because—well." He stopped. "I really brought you down here for revelation number three."

He was staring at Griff. Unsteady energy rippled through Thomas. A shaky look, like he was biting down on an electric toothbrush. Griff was just beginning to sense the enormity of this, a slow-building atomic reaction—

"What is it?"

Thomas fast-forwarded the tape, watching a digital counter. Glanced down at his gridded notebook. He stood and tapped the counter backward.

"This tape is full of clues, Griff," Thomas said. "Leo knew that."

He grabbed Griff's shoulders. Bounced on him like a human pogo stick.

"Ready?" Thomas said. "Ready?"

"Yes, get off me."

Griff swatted him and Thomas went back to the board. Hovered his finger over the PLAY button. Licked his lips.

"Everything we need, in five seconds," Thomas said.

He pressed PLAY. A guitar solo tore through the room, wild and dreamy, and the roaring crowd cut off with *click*.

"Hear it?" Thomas said.

"Guitar?"

"Listen again. That sound in the back."

Thomas got on the board. Suppressed guitar. Muddied the crowd. He played the tape back in slow motion. A sound became distinct. Like a slowly torn sheet of paper.

"Airplane?"

"Jet," Thomas said. He swiveled to another computer. Played the sound again. This time, clean. No background noise.

"The same jet," Griffin said.

"Yes," Thomas said. "Exactly the same jet. That, my friend, is the sound of an MQ-4C Triton, flying across the desert."

"And."

"According to what I can dig up—the MQ Triton is currently being tested near Nevada's western border. And it wasn't invented until last year."

"So—"

"Griff," Thomas said. "The show is happening live."

"In the middle of Death Valley."

"And it's happening again," Thomas said. He crossed the room at a gallop, drummed his hands on the pegboard. Tore off one great sheet. Another. The old calendar. With a thick black Sharpie, he mocked up a new calendar, looked at his phone, drew a giant black circle in July.

"Right there!" Thomas said, stabbing Saturday, July 13.

"Two weeks," Griff said.

Thomas inked his familiar Sharpie stick figures, a microphone, faces.

"We've got to find them," Griff said.

"We'll need at least three days in the desert," Thomas said. He nodded to the copper SubWatch poles. "And we'll need those."

"And Charity," Griff said.

"Of course," Thomas said.

"Three days away from home, out of state? Impossible."

"No," Thomas said. "If these assholes can put on a giant live show in the most inhospitable place on the planet, I find it increasingly difficult to believe anything is impossible."

Thomas lifted a bag of chips. Salt and vinegar.

"Oh shit. The S and Vs."

Thomas reserved salt and vinegar chips for only the most massive undertakings. All-night study sessions, project deadlines. He'd been doing this since seventh grade. Thomas tore open the bag and made the same joke—always.

"Crunch time," Thomas said. He ate the first chip.

"We're really doing this?"

"Are you kidding? It's the greatest mystery of our lives— like, the one thing we'll remember as we pass into our shitty adulthood and thankless jobs and sad addictions and broken families. Or maybe we die sooner. The nukes drop, or Juan de Fuca finally drowns this town like a mercy killing—but let's be real. For once—we have the luxury of a real fucking mission. That's a rare and precious gift. You think Fawcett turned back from the Amazon? You think Shackleton said, oh no—no Antarctic for me—I might get *grounded*?"

Thomas shook his head, ate chips.

"Okay," Griff said. "So what's your plan?"

"I've got two." Thomas chewed on his lip. "The first is possibly illegal and requires the people in our life to be slightly dumber than they actually are."

"Okay," Griff said. "How about plan B?"

"Plan B is 100 percent illegal." He smiled. "And—"

"What?"

"Might scare the rats," Thomas said. His smile fled. "And we won't ever come back home."

FORTY-SIX

"WE'RE GOING ON A THREE-DAY TRIP?" CHARITY ASKED. "HOW can this possibly work?"

"I have no idea," Griff said.

Charity and Griff returned to the Rat's Nest three days later. Thomas had virtually disappeared—terse responses to texts. Strange questions coming at 1 AM, 2:30 AM—

HOW MANY HOURS DO YOU STILL NEED FOR THE GAP?

WHEN IS YOUR DAD HOSTING HIS NEXT WORKSHOP?

The last time Thomas had hermetically sealed himself in the Rat's Nest, he was creating the Early Alert Response System. When he was done, they had to bring two giant black garbage bags to clean up the food, soda cans, chips, and plates. A box fan to clear the smell.

Charity wore a sharp yellow sundress that hung perfectly on her shoulders, made every curve look better. Impossibly out of place in the wood-paneled walls of Thomas Mortimer's basement. He continued to wonder how long she'd show up in their lives.

"Should we knock?" she asked.

"Come iiiiiiin," Thomas called.

Griff opened the door.

"Oof," Charity said. "Boys' locker room."

Although Thomas must've slept at some point, the smell of rats, pizza pockets, and body odor exceeded what should've been possible in several days, with one person.

"Thomas?" Griff called. "You okay? It smells like death in here."

"Also Pestilence," Thomas said. "Famine. War. Sorry, sorry."

He appeared in the doorway. Bloodshot eyes. White tongue.

"Wow," Charity said.

"You live in your own stink so long you become it," Thomas said, peering at them. "It becomes you." '

"It does not become you," Charity said.

"Congratulations," Griff said. "You're a creature."

Thomas hauled a box fan into the doorway and plugged it in. Propped open the door. He did not say hello. Thomas spoke as if his train of thought wouldn't stop for the boarding of passengers.

"Packing is critical," Thomas said. "We have to be very well prepared."

He crossed the hallway and flung his shirt off, opening the door to a partial bathroom. Toilet in a slab. Drain in the floor.

"Avert your eyes, villagers!" he said. The shower turned on.

"So you assume I'm going?" Charity shouted. She did not seem concerned about the Naked Thomas Situation.

"You're going," Thomas called over the water. "So every-one listen up. Death Valley, at 3.3 million acres, is just west of America's nuclear test wasteland, home to over 10,000 aban-doned mines, and has the highest documented temperature on planet Earth at 134 degrees."

"I can't conceive of that," Charity said.

Steam billowed from the bathroom.

"Try just 107 degrees. Heated to that level, the human body experiences irreversible organ failure and death. We will need plenty of water, obviously. Salt tablets. Electrolyte supple-ments. Mirrors for signaling, in case. Sunblock, bandannas, shemaghs. Counterintuitive, but remember—most of the heat comes directly from the sun. You don't want it on you. And then, of course, whatever else you'd bring for camp, to throw our parents off the trail."

The water stopped. Shuffling clothes. "Thomas," Charity said. "Could you back up? I can't be gone for three days. Do we really need that much time?"

Thomas emerged wet in a fresh, Sharpied T-shirt and change of jeans. He dropped the bundle of dirty clothes in a black garbage bag and walked directly into the Rat's Nest to the maps on the pegboard.

"Minimum of three days," Thomas said. "It's 765 miles away. Even at top speed, the ThunderChicken will be hard-pressed to chirp its way there in under fourteen hours. Based on Leo's records, there is likely to be some kind of transmission the evening before, but we can't get anything until the sun goes down. So—we need to leave Clade City a day before the full moon. As luck would have it, that's on a Friday."

He tapped the calendar. He'd drawn more pictures around the date.

"So I tell my mom I need three nights away with a couple boys and some salt tablets?"

"No," Thomas said, walking to his largest computer monitor. It was tagged with a canning label—LA GRANDOTA. "You can't possibly come, because you have a major schedule conflict. There is an incredible camp experience happening that very same weekend."

Thomas woke the screen. There it was. A church, tall stained-glass windows, and a group of bright young women energetically talking in modest pastel dresses. Books and Bibles devotedly clasped to their chests.

"Camp Pilgrim," Charity read. "A Holy Space for Bright Young Women."

"Check the log line," Thomas said.

PIETY. DEITIES. ALL THE FEEL-ITIES.

Thomas clicked on the workshop schedule.

"Is this for real?" Charity asked.

Thomas smiled. "The website is."

"Oh my god," she said. She laughed. "Oh. My. God. Thomas—you invented a camp! A giant, big old liars camp to show my mom. That's about the sweetest thing anyone's ever done!"

She gave him a hug.

"I also got you a scholarship," he said.

A printer chugged in the distance. He'd manufactured all the paperwork. Everything she needed to prove she had applied, been accepted, tuition covered. Charity examined the website.

"You missed the *H* in *Christian*," she said. "Also, there's just one deity."

"Maybe vet the workshops," Thomas said, scrolling. Matchsticks for Jesus. The Reluctant Judas. Anatomy of an Apocalyptic Horseman.

"Yeah," Charity said. "I'll go ahead and send you some."

"So you're into it?" Thomas asked. "You'll do it?"

She sighed. "My mom will question everything. She'd ask Saint Peter for ID."

"That's why there's a hotline," Thomas said, pointing. "Go ahead."

"I'm still grounded from my phone," Charity said. Griff handed her his.

"Put it on speaker," Thomas called, disappearing into their band's old practice space.

The phone rang. Three times. Four.

"Thomas!" she said. "Who am I calling?"

"Welcome to Camp Pilgrim," said an older woman with a Minnesota accent.

"Hi," Charity said. "Um. I was just checking on my enrollment status."

"Name?" the woman asked.

"Charity Simms."

"My goodness, Charity Simms!" the strange woman said.

"What is happening?" Charity mouthed.

"She is a chaste young woman," Thomas said, walking into view. Running the call through voice distortion. Disturbing, watching his lips form the words. "So well-behaved. And celibate as the dead!"

Charity hung up, handed Griff his phone.

"I'm supposed to sell this shit to my mom?" she said.

"We have a pact," Griff said.

"A pact!" Thomas shouted.

"Okay," she said. "So how are you two getting out?"

"I've got a plan," Thomas said. "We'll know by tonight."

FORTY-SEVEN

THOMAS AND GRIFF WENT TO THE BUNKER. GRIFF HADN'T BEEN TO a meeting in months. It was incredible how little had changed. Same general-store smell, same stackable chairs, same lights that made his eyes ache. Thomas had brought along the largest speakers he could fit in a backpack, projector, bedsheet for a screen.

"The theatrics," he'd said, "will be important."

"Movie time," Scruggs said, drumming fingers on a blue Rubbermaid labeled POPCORN.

"Those are reserves, Scruggs," Dunbar said.

"I'd put it back," he said. He wandered, over to his seat.

The men poured themselves whisky in paper cups as Thomas set up the video. Slim and Jonesy stayed as distant as you can in a bunker. The whole thing felt like a mix of dream and memory. Griff kept counting chairs. Missing one.

"As you all know," Thomas said, "Griff and I have been very excited about the Gap Academy, and have nearly completed our requisite hours for attendance. What we haven't told you is that we have also applied for an affiliated preview experience, this summer."

"Is this a new program?" Dunbar asked.

"Very new," Thomas said. "The newest."

"What is it?" Jonesy asked.

"A three-day experience, ten days from now. We weren't

going to share this because the odds of acceptance are quite low, but—well. I'll let the video speak for itself."

Griff's dad gave him a curious look.

"Okay," Thomas said. "Kill the lights."

"Got it," Slim said.

The video began.

Black screen. White letters drop with percussive beats.

BEFORE THE END

Heavy drums. *BOOM. BOOM. BOOM.*

LET US BEGIN

BOOM. BOOM. BOOM.

[Camera flare.]

[American flag bandanna.]

[Bootstraps.]

TO TRAIN

Music—hard-rock guitar riffs.

[Person tries to physically pull self up with bootstraps.]

[Servicepeople run tires on obstacle course.]

[Rat threads pencil maze.]

[Slow-motion close-up of a sweaty high five, scattering droplets.]

TO PREPARE

[Person tackled onto wrestling mat, writhes, struggles for help.]

[Guy lift-kicks a gun magazine and it miraculously lands in well of AR-15.]

CLICK

[Zip line.]

[Man voluntarily Tased by other man, buckles and screams.]

[Bald eagle snatches up a rat with spliced red-tailed hawk scream.]

FOR THE TIME OF OUR LIVES

Music—wild, driving surf-style drumbeats.

[Pistols up-close ejecting casings and jerking to the beat as they fire in sexy rhythm.]

[Tsunami wave rears.]

[Men, black masks.]

[Tsunami wave curls.]

[Something spins inside a tornado rising from the sea. Shark?]

[Rapid gunfire.]

[Closing montage: Guns, flags, deer, trucks, six-packs, bald white men, bald white-headed eagle, then a rapid-fire reel of American flags, strobing on-screen to the sound of semi-automatic gunfire. Flags billowing, tattered, brand-new, being folded, at rest, hoisted, half-mast, flag swelling large enough to dwarf a town, the moon, wrapping the whole globe like a Christmas present.]

Off-camera scream: *"Red, white, and blue, baby!"*

Off-camera scream: *"That's how we do!"*

[Eagle feeding the regurgitated rat to raw, pink-headed baby eagles.]

BOOM. BOOM. BOOM.

FRIENDS OF GAP ACADEMY PRESENT: CAMP LONGSHOT

THE SUMMER SESSIONS

Silence.

Griff's face burned.

"And you boys got in?" Dunbar asked.

"Full scholarships," Thomas said, producing the paperwork.

Dunbar started clapping. They were all clapping. Griff flinched at the pat on the back. His father. Kept patting him, like burping a baby. Thomas shared the website, the forms, explained the organization. There was a number to call.

"Looks awesome," Slim said from across the room. "Congratulations."

*   *   *

When Griff and his dad got home, the greeting-card racks were still tipped over.

It had been days.

Their life now flowed around the racks the way a river diverts around boulders. A new tributary around the brown chair, past the couch. The same way their eyes flowed around the wine stain beneath the kitchen table and Leo's unmade bed.

Griff closed his door and sat on his own mattress.

The deception was still so fresh. Atmospheric. Solidifying by the second.

A knock on Griff's door. He jolted.

"It's Dad."

He came into the room. His eyes gracefully flowed around the wreckage and just found him—Griff. His dad entered with a wild rush of energy. When had he last been so excited? For a moment, he resembled the untroubled stranger in family photos hung in the hallway—the man kissing Griff's mother, wearing his hat of red-feathered fishing lures, holding baby boys who'd since grown and evaporated.

This man sat on the side of Griff's bed. *Creak.*

"—just incredible to see how quickly this all came together—"

He tapped Griff's knee as he talked. Looked right at him. Not his ear, not his drink. Griff went back in time with him becoming a shy second grader kicking the carpet. His father's smile went crooked. A little sad.

"Why didn't you tell me, kiddo?"

His father hugged him.

His dad was stronger than Griff remembered. Or maybe they hadn't really touched in a long time. A long hug. Long enough to sting the eyes and unravel a stir of memories like a rush of feeling without images, the reservoir of a thousand shared meals, pushed on swings, hiked with, held and rocked and laughed and played with and the lighthouse winked through the window and—WHOOMP—

Griff shook.

Leo, who got tired of losing. Who worked harder and smarter and faster. Who had Dad's jacket, the keys to Dad's truck—it was all right here. Before the Theory of Everything, before music and maps and Charity Simms—their very first contest, the first treasure hunt.

When his dad held him, he felt like the Most Important Kid in the World.

FORTY-EIGHT

CHARITY COULD GO.

After two calls to the Christian Academy Call Center and Oscar-worthy performances from Thomas Mortimer, Charity was granted clearance for takeoff. The plan had worked.

Two words, little jolts in his mind:

Overnight. Together.

It made him wobbly.

It was July 11. Eighteen hours until launch. Griff, Thomas, and Charity met at the Rat's Nest to account for the orbital thrust of the ThunderChicken's rocket boosters and discuss potential galactic complications. Triple-check the equipment. A moonshot was tricky. Full of careful, orbital calculations. They had to be safe.

Thomas even scanned them with his Bug Detector.

"Your backpack's hot," Thomas said.

"My phone's in there," Griff said.

"Okay," Thomas said. "What are we forgetting?"

He was chewing on a pen cap. So abused, it looked like blue bubble gum.

Packing list:

Copper poles. Mercator grids for radio triangulation. Flares and cones and jumper cables; defibrillator, spare battery, lithium ion charger/jumper, salt tablets, water purification system, generator, air compressor, electrolyte supplements, 20-ton bottle jack, fix-a-flat kit, full medical first aid system, night goggles, Bug Detector, gorp, oatmeal, jerky. Headphones. Borrowed surveillance drone. Dancing shoes.

Judiciously chosen glow sticks.

Thomas would pack everything in the ThunderChicken that night.

"Is that everything?" Charity asked.

"Well," Thomas said, looking sly.

"What?" Griff and Charity both said.

"Don't be nervous," Thomas said. "Just a few more things to share."

"I'm nervous," Charity said.

Thomas walked them back to the rear workshop, dashing aside a blue tarp like a theater curtain. On a workbench, three objects. Each covered with a black utility blanket.

"Oh my," Charity said.

"First," Thomas said, "a little something for the music."

Thomas removed the first blanket. An object the size of a desktop globe. Its pearled surface held the light like an open clamshell.

"Wow," Charity said.

Her voice lanced through the object in a hot, white streak.

"Was that me?"

Her question dropped like a pebble in a pond, sending out aqua ripples. Griff clapped his hands. A yellow shock wave. Thomas did a vocal didgeridoo: *WAABWABAWABAWABAWABA!* Warbling notes passed through like psychedelic smoke rings. Charity laughed—purple bursts.

"The Everlight! The EternoGlow!" Thomas said. "Still working on a name."

"It's amazing!" Charity said.

"You've outdone yourself, friend," Griff said.

He covered the device. Went to the next object.

"Griff? The honors?"

"Hey yes," Griff said. He whipped off the covering.

"Ta-da!" Thomas said.

"It's a sandwich," Griff said.

A blue plate special. White bread. A thin strip of purple jelly.

"Peanut butter and jelly," Charity said. "Your favorite."

"Not jelly," Thomas said. "Jam. A jam sandwich."

Griff touched the sandwich. Hard plastic. Thomas fingered a groove in the back and popped open the bread. Inside, a nest of circuitry.

"Holy shit," Griff said.

"Go ahead," Thomas said, flipping a switch. "Try your phone."

Charity took her phone out. No signal. No Wi-Fi. Nothing.

"Signal jammer?" Griff said. "Sweet."

"Fleeing the state? Out on the lam?" Thomas said, resealing the device. "Perfect for your pic-i-nic basket! It's a Jam Sand-wich. Get it?"

"We get it," Charity said.

"Charity," Thomas said. "Please unveil the Portable Early Alert Response System. I'm calling it—PEARS."

Charity whipped off the blanket.

Eyes and little claws, grabbing mesh.

"Ahh! Damn it, Thomas!"

Charity walked away.

"It's a perfect system," Thomas said. "No batteries or cell service required. Rats are one of the rare mammals that can actually survive in Death Valley. And I can't leave you, little sweetie."

Neapolitan settled in her carrier. Made a quiet humming noise.

"Oh my gosh. Do rats purr?" Charity asked.

"Go on. Touch her."

They did. All three of them, touching a rat.

"How did my life come to this?" Charity asked.

"I keep wondering why you're still here," Griff said.

"Are you kidding? You are the most interesting people I've ever met."

Their smiles evened out, and the silence took on weight.

"Tomorrow," Thomas said. "Five thirty AM. We rendezvous at the Point parking lot."

Charity leapt and danced and then ran in place.

"I'm just too excited," she said. "Can't even control it."

When Charity hugged them goodbye, Thomas took a new, bright blue pen cap, popped it in his mouth.

"You're more nervous than usual," Griff said.

"Just don't want it to happen today," Thomas said.

"What?"

"The earthquake. The nuclear strike. The closer we get, the more impossible it feels. Like something bad is going to happen."

"Don't say that," Griff said.

"Like flipping heads twice in a row," Thomas said.

Thomas took a quarter out of his pocket.

"Don't do it," Griff said.

He flipped, slapped the coin.

"Heads."

"Thomas. Don't."

"Griff. I never had a choice."

Thomas flipped the coin again.

—*slap*—

"Don't look," Griff said. "I'll back away slowly."

Thomas stood with his hand on the quarter. Like holding a grenade with the pin pulled. Griff laughed and sprinted for the stairs. All the way from the front door, he could hear Thomas scream.

FORTY-NINE

WAKING UP FELT LIKE CHRISTMAS IN JULY. THE FLUTTERY-FEET feeling. Griff had barely slept.

His parents were not awake. He left quickly on his bike.

They were going to the desert. Together.

On days like this—birthdays, holidays, travel days—the whole world got fresh corners and a bright new palette of colors. Today, on Marine Drive, the blue-gray sky glowed with pigments borrowed from heaven. The air tasted like sacred water crashing on stone. The whole world had already changed.

Down the last dip in the road, there they were.

The plan, assembling in front of him. Flesh and blood and bags and a blue Thunderbird, all waiting in the Point parking lot. Charity wore a hoodie, her small face peeking out from inside. Curls tousled in the wind.

"C'mon," she said. "Let's go."

They stashed Griff's bike in the trunk of Charity's blue Sonata. They stashed the Sonata in the west end lot by beetle-browned pines and cathedral gorse and packed into the ThunderChicken. Inside, quiet as church. Charity rode in the back with the copper poles, canvas bags, tents, a case of MREs, and two blue 5-gallon water bricks. The trunk was full.

The ThunderChicken's engine came to life:

Cheepcheepcheepcheeep

It was real. The Band was real. They were leaving.

Thomas used his signal, pulled out slowly. Driving the length of Marine Drive, Griff felt the town hang heavy. Molasses pavement. Road shoulders squeezed like pinching fingers. A feeling of urgency. They followed the tsunami evacuation signs. Griff ate his first square of dark chocolate. Chewing too quickly.

"Seven more," Thomas said.

He and Griff had dug the postholes.

"Six," Griff said, another sign flashing past.

"Five," Thomas said.

There were on Highway 2. Home to mudslides, washouts, and falling rocks, but TripCheck had showed nothing but a bright green line and on they went—banking away from the ocean, the long, undulating road toward the redwoods. They counted the last three evacuation signs.

"Three."

"Two."

"One!"

EXITING TSUNAMI EVACUATION ZONE

They passed the pullout, Florida Fork—as Leo had named it—approaching 50 miles per hour. Thomas removed the cassette from his pocket.

"Let's wait," Griff said. "Just a little longer."

He wasn't ready to celebrate yet.

"C'mon," Thomas said. "I'm delirious. It's time for a little levity. Charity, spark that thing up. Clap three times."

Charity did. Thomas cheered and the ball in her hands pulsed bright green. Charity tossed it to Griff, who bobbled it in his hands.

The ball shuddered and glittered. Purple and yellow. Signs hugged the next curve.

WARNING: FALLING ROCKS

WARNING: TIGHT CURVE AHEAD

"Freedom!" Thomas yelled. The lights flashed red, white, and blue.

"Did you program that?" Griff said.

Thomas looked in the rearview mirror.

Lights continued to flash. In his hands, the globe was green.

"Hey," Charity said. "No, no, no."

BWWWOOOP! BWOOOP!

Police siren.

"It's okay," Thomas said. "We're all legal. Seat belts on, hands at the ol' ten and two, click the signal. He'll probably blast right by."

He signaled. Gently, Thomas eased the car over.

Just ahead, the road curved into a shady chute of old growth. The way out of town. They stopped just shy of the deepest part of the canopy.

"Go on," Thomas said, waving. "Go on!"

The police officer stopped.

"He pulled over," Thomas said.

"No. He pulled us over," Charity said. "We've been pulled over."

Charity sat up straight. Put her hands on her lap.

"We have nothing to worry about," Thomas said.

"Don't be ignorant," Charity said. "Put your damn hands out front. Don't mess around."

It didn't sound like her. She was more worried than Griff had ever seen her. In the rearview mirror, more traffic. A familiar black truck—hard to see through the reds and blues. Another squad car.

"It's a whole convention," Thomas said.

"Oh Jesus." Charity pressed her palms against her eyes.

The officer's door opened and clapped shut. Griff squinted

in the mirror. On the front of the squad car, a familiar sticker. Gold letters on matte black:

NOAH WAS A PREPPER

"Dunbarred," Griff whispered.

Thomas chomped down on his bottom lip.

"I need you to listen carefully, Griff," Thomas said. "Charity, listen. No matter what happens—listen to the radio."

"What?"

Thomas had clicked into plan B. Griff could see it, but didn't know the script.

"We meet in the same place," he said.

In the rearview, the officer advanced quickly. Sunglasses and a uniform.

Thomas ejected the tape and gave it to Griff.

"What's this?"

"The music," Thomas said. "You'll need it. Just hold on, buddy. Promise me. Hold on."

"What going to happen?" Charity asked.

The worst thing. The worst possible thing.

Officer Dunbar reached the car. Squatted down. His face, adorned with a calm little smile. Outside, it was already warm. It was going to be a beautiful day.

"Hey, Thomas," Dunbar said. "Just wanted to catch you on the way out of town. See if you and Griff and your special friend are all familiar with State Penal Code 807.620."

"Yes, sir," Thomas said. "I'm intimately familiar with that goddamn code."

"Oops," Dunbar said. "Get out of the dang car. Griff, your father is waiting. What's your name, in back? Could you please remove that hood? Slowly, please."

The door creaked. An aching sound. Griff's shoes touched the pavement.

He could feel the gravity of disappointment from inside his father's truck. His father watched him walk. Didn't get out. Griff wouldn't be able to breathe in that truck. This was the last of the air. The end of the sun. That truck, like a black hole.

Not even light could escape.

FIFTY

A<small>LONE IN HIS ROOM, </small>G<small>RIFF CONSIDERED THE PARACORD.</small>

Over six hundred known uses.

"You're on lockdown until further notice," his father said. "No contact with those two."

"We can get you someone to talk to," his mother said. "We want you to be okay."

There were games. If you had a friend, you could do a cat's cradle.

Hold the paracord in such a way that if you had a partner to play with, you could trap their hand in a rectangle of strings and then let that person go.

They could trap you and let you go.

That week, the fires returned. Creeping up the coast. The air quality meter was so red it turned purple. Particulate matter hung and made the landscape look like charcoal etchings. Griff picked at his paracord. He could make a pulley system to lift water jugs. Dampen their roof to guard against embers. He could tie a mask on his face.

No red circles on the calendar. Empty boxes.

He had one standing appointment on Wednesday at eleven, when the whole town shook with the weekly test.

bbbadabadabadawwwEEEEEEEEEEEEE

Griff was not allowed to work with Thomas. Thomas was out there picking up roadside trash. Doing ocean cleanup.

Cutting gorse. Worse than SubWatch. Winter-thick gloves in summertime, chopping the thick, sticky stems to stumps. Swabbing poison on the blunted ends.

Thomas had been right about the tape. Griff needed it. Every listen, like a quick breath.

But he couldn't keep air in his lungs.

Without weekdays, weekends, or school, or reliable daylight, everything became a slow, dark circling. The sun had burned out in its socket, like a dead bulb. One twilight, his father opened his bedroom door without knocking. Red-rimmed eyes. He said:

"I just don't know who you are, Griff."

He stood a minute longer, shifting his weight. Silence.

"Can you just tell me why? Was it drugs?"

Drugs.

That would've been easier. How could he explain the value of music? That he would give anything to see the Band and meet the people who loved the Band. Explaining this to his father would be like trying to explain a shuttle launch to a golden retriever. The dog might love you, the dog might wish to understand, because it loves you. But the dog could not understand.

When his dad left, Griff sat on his bed swallowing his spit and breathing and trying to survive from one minute until the next.

Hold on, Thomas had said.

Griff listened to the radio, but Thomas was never there.

The coast burned father north. The air was a gray stew and the sky fell in small dandruff flakes on the black truck like God scratching his head. The smoke killed small things. Dead fruit flies in the kitchen. Tiny corpses on a pile of brown bananas. One day, a larger thing died. In the endless twilight, that day emerged like an alligator wandering from the fog to clamp its jaws on your leg and remind you things can still get worse.

Griff did not hear the car accident, but he saw the furry thing at the base of his driveway and thought it was a rat. Large ears. Small face and a golden coat. An Abyssinian cat with a broken leg and internal injuries and it chose their home as the place to die. With a paracord, you could make a cat leash to keep it from running into the road. You could make a tourniquet or hold a splint in place but you could not make it better when it was too late. You could not, with a paracord, tie the cat back to this world.

Music stopped working.

At some point, the Band was intoning the wrong things. Emphasizing words like *dark* and *the end* and *black* and *knotted* and Griff could tie twenty-two different knots so he listened to K-NOW, but Thomas was out cleaving gorse because he had lied to a police officer and no longer had a show:

bbbadabadabadawwwEEEEEEEEEEEEEE

Wednesday again.

Scruggs had taken their shifts on K-NOW but did not say anything mean about them. One afternoon, he played a new PSA for Lost Coast Student Government.

"This is Charity Simms, one of your Lost Coast Student Leaders. We want to tell you students at home, we are here for you. A safe place. You can find us, September in the student union. Just hang on. School will be here before you know it."

GASP!

A red-circle day. A lungful of hope! The air should've lasted for days, but as soon as the red ink dried, he felt like he'd made the whole thing up. Griff listened all day for a few days and the announcement never played again. The lilac bush across the street—Griff's favorite, which dripped with fragrant cones of the deepest purple in the spring—died from the ashfall. The neighbors came outside in N95 masks and lifted drooping branches, shook dead leaves. Griff had never seen that before, with a plant. Limp and brown all at once. Just decided—enough.

That same night, Griff woke in a panic. Breathless, like he'd forgotten something. Slept too long. One word ricocheted in his head:

Terrible, terrible.

He went to his window.

He could not see it. No flash. No glimmer. Could the ash be that thick? He padded out into the hallway. Deactivated security. Laced up his boots, stepped into a still night that smelled like a concrete fireplace. Stinging eyes, closing throat, and a clawing feeling in his lungs saying *run run panic run*. You learn fast that all five of your senses are designed to tell you when something is burning.

"Please," Griff said. "Please."

He rubbed his eyes and screamed.

"Hey! C'mon!"

Screaming at the lighthouse.

This is where you lose your mind, Griffin Tripp. Complex metal alloys such as cadmium, atomized by 800-degree fires, have melted like mercury butter in your brain and driven you batty.

Shhhhh, the ocean said back. *Shhhhhh.*

Paracord use #437 would be to tie it to the guardrail at the edge of Marine Drive and rappel down to the mud flats. He'd make it. Five hundred pounds dead weight, two hundred swinging. Across the mud flats, there was no light. Really. No light. He walked home in the dark. Showered off the campfire smell and lay watching his window. He tried to summon with his voice:

"Whoomp," he whispered. "Whoomp."

No one to hear it, he said it louder.

"Whoomp!"

At breakfast his dad told him:

"They shot up the lighthouse."

Probably two people in a truck, they left tire tracks in the mud. Tired of waiting, they shot out the handmade Fresnel lens with bullets from a semiautomatic gun. Over 370 individually cut panes of glass. They could not replace the shattered lens with any amount of money. They don't even make them anymore.

"It survived the '64 tsunami," his father said. "Couldn't survive Clade City."

Paracord use #137, to choke the ones who did it.

"Who?" Griff said. "Dad, who did it? You know. Tell me who. Tell me. Tell me."

"Please stop, Griff," his mother said. "Please."

Her voice choked off. What was he doing? Grabbing the skin on his forearm. Pulling until it bled.

Ah, he'd done that before. All coming back.

Instead of clothing, he'd grabbed loose skin on his arms and pinched his throat and grabbed fleshy fistfuls from the back of his neck. In the hospital, they'd asked him:

Have you ever slipped something around your neck? Do you have a plan?

"Come to work with me tomorrow?" his mother asked. "It will be fun."

Tomorrow. Too many tomorrows. They stacked up heavy beyond his bedroom door, which he locked. One specific use for a paracord. He tested his desk chair. Five hundred pounds dead weight. His pants hung looser than ever. It would work fine.

He sat on the chair and unclipped the bracelet. The thing was, you had to unlace the paracord and would not be able to lace it back the way it was, resembling the black-and-white piano keys. That would be challenging to explain, if he decided not to. A permanent thing, unlacing the cord. He stood and unlocked his door and went to the piano room.

If he was ready to die, he could at least play it.

Sheets of music, unmoved since October. Like the shoes and hanging clothes, they didn't know Leo was gone. It was time to be honest with the music. He removed sheets labeled duets, piano four hands.

I'm sorry.

He removed more.

I'm so sorry.

He removed more sheets and the piano seemed to spring up a little, like a sagging pine bough, shaken free of snow. Griff sat on the bench. The sheet facing him was familiar.

Andante.

His piece. It was okay for him to play it.

A nervous jolt, placing his fingers. Like a current ran through them. At first, he just let them sit. Felt the weight of the keys and the hammers behind them. The tension of strings. Slowly, he allowed fingers to wander like strange animals across the keys—not too fast, not too far, still tethered by the cord around his wrist. The notes slipped like a key into a lock deep in his chest and he could breathe.

He could breathe.

It came. The flow. He could play.

Crying with gratitude. Head above water. He clung to his piano like a hunk of driftwood. Could not let go, or he would be lost. The keys saved him. They gave his fingers something else to do today and so afterward he hauled in his sleeping bag and a pillow and slept at the instrument's rounded, brass-capped feet. Right where Leo had left them.

Hold on, he remembered. One more day. *Hold on.*

FIFTY-ONE

BBBADABADABADAWWWEEEEEEEEEEEEEE

Griff sat up. Blue light. Piano legs. Dark outside.

Wrong time for the siren.

The sound dipped a moment. He heard his own breathing.

"Griff?"

Doors opened. A slim blade of light.

"Mom?" he said, tongue heavy.

"Griff!" his father shouted. "Griff!"

"I'm in here," he said. "In here!"

Griff went to the window. Peeled back the gauzy curtain.

bbbadabadabadawwwEEEEEEEEEEEEEE

Outside, the neighborhood murmured like an arrhythmic heart. Doors clapping open. Lights flicking on. Dogs.

A dream. Déjà vu.

"What are you doing in here?" his dad asked, flipping on the light. Already dressed.

"I was playing," he said.

"Let's go," his father said. "This one's been verified."

"Earthquake or nuclear?" Griff asked.

"The tsunami," his father said. "Grab your BOB."

Bug Out Bag. So it was real. They were leaving the house. Everything got sharp. The house felt alive. A blast of music came from his parents' bedroom.

Was that—

His mother rushed past him in the hallway. Wild hair. Jeans and a light jacket.

"Hey," she said. She looked a little excited. Maybe she was ready for Florida.

Griff went to his bedroom. It looked like a museum. Set piece from a bygone era. He grabbed his backpack—what else? What did he need, besides the piano? He took the Walkman, the cassette tape. Make sure it's inside. Click, clack. Okay.

The radio.

"Griff!" his father said, filling the doorway. "We've got three minutes.

In the kitchen, a sound like someone dropped a fishbowl of marbles.

"Honey!"

His father left. Griff pressed the radio's orange button.

The riff screamed out of the small speaker.

A thousand electric notes picked like a firestorm. And the unmistakable voice:

THUN-DER. THUN-DER.

K-NOW was playing AC/DC's "Thunderstruck."

He leapt up. Tingling.

"Thomas," Griff said.

He cinched the backpack to his body. Impossible.

"Let's knock those doors," his father said. "Move!"

Griff stepped into the garage. His father's truck running, puttering exhaust.

Griff removed his bicycle from its hook. Tires bounced on the driveway.

"Griff?" His mother said. She stood in the gold light, framed by the door. Backlit as she was, he could not see the details of her face. He leaned his bike and ran to her.

"I'll be okay, Mom. I promise. I'll be back."

"Where are you going? Griff! Griff!"

She screamed. She ran and screamed an awful scream, like her insides were burning out. Like he was being pulled out to sea, and he hummed to drown her out, made noise in his head, bicycle gears clicking, and he pedaled. His father, walking fast down the sidewalk, looked up. Wide-eyed. He mouthed words lost to the hum—

Griff pedaled harder.

Sorry, sorry, sorry—

He passed idling cars and open garages and people rattling out of their homes, moving fast, and maybe he was wrong. And if he was wrong, the shaking would happen any second and it would be over. Griff whipped onto Marine Drive and— the moon! The moon was right. He'd lost track but the moon was just a sliver shy of full and he pedaled faster, all the way to the lot, where dull red reflectors bounced back moonlight and a single figure sitting on the trunk.

"Thomas!" he hissed.

The figure leapt up. Another figure bolted from the shadows.

She ran and Griff flung his bicycle to the pavement with a clatter. She jumped and they collided in a sloppy, wild, swinging way and almost toppled, so fragile and electric and alive, and it was her! Her! He buried his face in her neck, my god—

"You came," she whispered. "Oh my god, you're alive!"

She looked at him, worried. Like something was wrong.

"What now?" Griff asked.

"Evacuation," Thomas said. He was tan. Looked stronger. "Ditch the phones."

They took them out and threw them into the Krummholz. Beneath the crash of waves, they fell soundless. The interior of Thomas's car felt surreal, a moment from another life. Food smells, sagging ceiling, the old clinging odor and every memory of this specific car. Thomas swept a bag of chips onto the floor and started the engine.

The ThunderChicken roared. He swung them out on Marine Drive.

"So this earthquake isn't actually happening?" Griff said.

"Oh, it is," Thomas said, turning the wheel. "Just not tonight. Probably."

Thomas shot into the left lane, blowing past a Mazda. A Ford pickup. Cars honked and he swerved back, blasting past an evacuation sign.

"Seven," Charity said.

"Six," Griff said.

In the rearview mirror, distant police lights.

"Five," they said together. "Four."

Wind whipped through the car. Griff remembered to breathe.

Please be there, he thought. Please let this be real.

"Three," Thomas said.

Griff turned and looked out the back window as they climbed. His hometown, a dim, shrinking light. Like the whole Earth, viewed from heaven.

"Two," Charity said.

"One," they said together.

Blastoff.

SCHERZO

We don't want to be identical, secondhand.
Tell the truth, that we are citizens of the Milky Way
and we can sing. We can make love. We can dance.

—JOHN ENGMAN, *Keeping Still, Mountain*

FIFTY-TWO

THIRTEEN HOURS TO DEATH VALLEY.

Every set of headlights felt like the police. Every small town, a Venus flytrap. The early-morning squeals of the Thunder-Chicken sounded terminal—stretched belts, overworked pistons. The car shook as if whole mechanical systems were about to clunk off, dropping thrusters like a shuttle leaving Earth. They outran clouds and wildfires, eased through towering redwoods and sequoias—those ponderous, gentle giants. They listened to the whip of wind through windows, the tape on repeat.

Doubt crept in.

Some big ideas hold their substance right up until the moment you rush toward them at 70 miles per hour. By now, the town would know it was a false alarm. They would've traced it back to Thomas. The three of them, missing again.

"What if the whole broadcast is coming from some van parked in the desert?" Thomas said around 3 AM.

"Can we wait at least forty-eight hours before we start to regret this?" Charity said.

At 6 AM they slipped into the early-morning traffic of Reno. The air smelled clean.

Griff had imagined Reno like a sad, peeling Las Vegas but there was beauty here, in the way the road snugged against the tumult of a green river canyon. Turbulent water. Mountains sponged up the sunrise in mottled patches of gold, and light ricocheted from high-rise windows in the city center. A radio antenna, like a golden lightning bolt.

"Look!" Griff said. "The Most Important Radio Station in Nevada."

Dawn broke like a slow-motion yolk, cracking over the ThunderChicken's powder-blue hood. They played the tape again.

"I feel like an explorer," Charity said.

"I feel like coffee," Thomas said.

At 9 AM they stopped for iced coffees and ice. They had the Portable Early Alert System, and Neapolitan could overheat. By 2 PM, heat bled into the car, a physical presence.

Landscape shrank to gristle. Pebbles, scree. The sprawling desert floor lay flat and beaten by the sun. A yellow-talcum color, as if dimly lit from beneath.

"Look," Thomas says. "The radio's got the spins."

The dial galloped to the top of the band at 1600, looped back to 550. The gray road rose into the distance like it was pointing straight up. The ThunderChicken shook with the heat, ascending.

"Lean forward, everyone. Wheels, please stay on," Thomas said. Speed to 40, 30.

Cresting the mountains, the landscape changed. More hospitable. Touches of green speckled the valley like the leafy ends of giant vegetables.

"Irradiated carrots," Griff said.

"The size of human legs," Thomas said.

"A Joshua tree!" Charity said. "Can we stop?"

"Sure," Thomas said. "Chicken needs a rest."

Thomas pulled over. Windows down, the heat rolled in.

"It must be 100 degrees," Griff said.

"This car feels like a bag of microwave popcorn," Charity said.

Neapolitan squealed. Skittered in her cage.

"You can cut 20 degrees in the shade," Thomas said.

Although stunning, a Joshua tree is not particularly inviting. A crooked octopus with morning star pom-poms, it threw small bursts of uneven shade. The ground resembled pulverized gravel. They crowded beneath the spiked tree.

Blue shade blunted the heat and cast their skin in bruised light. Things felt late-night wobbly again. Exhaustion. What were they doing? The immensity of the desert made their plan feel small.

"How much farther?" Griff asked.

"We can stop anywhere and wait for dark," Thomas said. "Two hundred square miles is a lot of miles."

They were hungry, tired, and hot.

"I'm going to change," Charity said. "Don't look."

Griff sat very still. He listened to clothes hit the dirt. Skin sounds. Shuffling.

"Ta-da!" Charity said.

She looked strong. Glowing. Red-and-white sarong to her knees.

"You look like a flag for a brave new country," Thomas said.

One dress changed the whole mood.

"We all look epic out here, in the desert," Griff said.

They did! Framed by sand and sky and miles of nothing. They struck poses.

Then it was just hot. Slow time. The mood hovered between joyous and tragic, trembling on the edge of fatigue. They had to keep moving from one spiky patch of shadow to another. Griff couldn't tell if he was angry at the tree or just starving. Thomas unboxed the MREs—Meals Ready to Eat, which came in gray-brown packages with chemical heater packs.

"No need!" Thomas said.

He tossed a sealed packet of Pork Sausage onto the blacktop.

"Thomas's kitchen!" he screamed. "Throw those puppies right in the GODDAMN ROAD!"

The wide-open space felt ripe for cursing.

"Shit yeah!" Griff said. "Middle of the GODDAMN road!"

He tossed Beef Patty, Grilled onto the asphalt.

"Right in the middle of the FUCKING road!" Charity screamed.

She threw Chicken and Dumplings. Griff and Thomas stared.

"Don't look so scandalized," she said.

The packets began to stir, like something inside them was alive.

"Creepy," Griff said.

Thomas retrieved them—*ouch, ouch-eee*—and brought them back. They sat in the plumpest spot of blue shade and Thomas pulled out a silver canteen. Rattled it like a cocktail shaker and poured them each a glass of ice-cold Tang. Charity took a sip and exhaled. Orange, tropical, sweet enough to make Griff's teeth ache.

"Nectar," Charity said. "My god."

"So cold," Griff said. "How did you keep ice?"

"A country boy can survive," Thomas said.

With a full belly and a cold drink, suddenly this was a good decision. Just the flies. Little, black and buzzing. Fast with sticky feet. They landed, seemed to lap the sweat on your skin—Griff slapped them. He thought about his parents. The way his mother had screamed.

"Do you think we'll find the Band?" Charity said.

"We'd better find something," Griff said.

The sun shed its brightest layers—white to yellow and now orange, painting the scrub with long shadows. Thomas came back, hauling the SubWatch receiver. The copper pole cast a long bolt of darkness.

"It's burning me through the gloves!" he said, laying it down.

"How long until sunset?" Charity asked.

Griff held his hand up to the sky, index finger flush with the horizon. Sun balanced on his pinky.

"One hour," Griff said. Charity watched him. "Fifteen minutes a finger."

"How do you know so much?"

"I'm a prepper, Charity," he said. She smiled, and it felt good. Thomas beckoned them over—the sun an orange ball in his sunglasses.

"Let's get started," Thomas said. "We need at least one live reading."

They prepared the hot copper. Set the frequencies. The sun smeared itself on the tops of the mountains and dimmed. Thomas put his headphones on. The light extinguished in his sunglasses.

"Surf's up."

FIFTY-THREE

THE MOON ROSE BOLD AND ORANGE. IT GAVE THE DESERT THE SOFT glow of a Halloween pumpkin.

The static out here was different.

Back home, near the heaving mirror of the sea, signals swarmed in a constant, refractive buzz. In the desert, even the Skip was quiet. Static bricked up tight and hard between your ears, like an invisible wall. The roar of emptiness only grew louder as light bled from the sky. Time passed. Griff's eyes fluttered. He felt conscious of every breath.

"We are a night early," Griff said, an hour later.

"We just need something," Thomas said. "Any little peep, and we can track them."

Deep nothing. Like the spins on the car's AM dial. They held the giant copper receivers like sightless periscopes. Twisting them. Listening. Taking turns.

Then it got cold.

In the desert, light and heat turned out to be the same thing.

They put on jackets. Sarong turned back into a hoodie. Charity's eyes fluttered and she stumbled forward with her pole. Griff took a turn while she lay on a blue blanket in the sand. The cartilage of his ears ached beneath the headphones. White noise began to whisper:

Griff. Grrriiiiiffin.

He flung off his headphones.

"Where are you going?" Thomas asked.

"I'm going to give the drone a shot."

"Over 100,000 acres," Thomas said.

"I'll just try."

Thomas shook his head. Griffin walked past the Joshua tree to the ThunderChicken. Removed the hard case from the trunk, and the drone from the hard case. Surveillance model. Roughly the size and shape of a football. Top speed of 70 miles per hour.

The best model the Preppers had.

Griff took out Leo's map and spread it out over the blue steel hood. He placed the drone on the scrub. Activated, it rose into the air.

Whhhhhhheeeeeee

Red light blinking.

Charity and Thomas looked up. The drone paused, then shot through the sky. Fast. Griff watched the viewfinder, racing over scrub. Thickening vegetation blurred to green waves. He got higher. The mountains ahead reared up in a loose, swirling formation. From the sky, they resembled a nautilus shell.

"Strange," Griff whispered.

A faint glow. Maybe a reflection of the moon. He pushed toward it. Silver light limned the mountains. A touch brighter than the surrounding cliffs. He pushed forward. Over the next rise. Something.

"Guys—" Griff said.

The screen went black.

"Shit!" Griff said.

"What did you do?" Thomas asked.

"It died," Griff said.

"That's impossible," Thomas said.

Griff banged the handset. It had been fully charged. Thomas

and Charity went back to listening. Then Charity froze. The way she had in the ocean, the first time they'd caught a song.

"Oh," she said.

She put a hand to her headphones. Thomas's eyes opened wide.

"What?" Griff asked.

"The radio," Thomas said. He took off his headphones. "It's for you."

FIFTY-FOUR

"You know the rules," the man said.

The voice. He'd heard it hundreds of times, repeating the same stern mantra. In the ThunderChicken. In the Rat's Nest. Lying in his bed at home, and again right now. Live, in Thomas's headphones.

"No recording," the voice said. "No preserving."

"I copy," Griff said. "Hello?"

"He can't hear you," Thomas said.

SHHHHHHHH—a blast of static.

Griff jumped. Flipped off the headphones.

"It's real," Griff whispered. "There's someone out here."

"We found it?" Charity said. "What did we find?"

"We'll know soon," Thomas said, grid paper out. "I got our first reading. Let's roll."

● ● ●

They drove toward the mountains. The ThunderChicken fought the pavement grade, squealing—

EeehehehheheeeeEEEEEEEEEE!

"Turn up the radio," Thomas said.

The radio had the spins. Nothing. Landscape stacked around them. Spires of rocks, dimpled like thick-stemmed mushrooms. Narrow canyons vanished into clefts of stone.

Numbers looped on the radio.

Then stopped. Dial frozen at 1550 AM.

"Got something," Griff said.

"What?" Thomas said, slowing.

Thomas stomped the brakes. They lurched forward.

"Great," the voice boomed in the car's speakers. "Stop right there. We'll come get you."

"Get a reading," Thomas said, scrambling for the headset.

Laughter in the background.

"We'll come running!" Another voice. More than one!

"Here we come! Here, here we come!" voices sang.

The signal cut loose, running the loops.

"That's a bit haunting," Griff said.

"Damn it!" Thomas threw the headphones. They clattered against the windshield.

"I guess we wait," Charity said. She smiled. "This just got fun."

"Wait?" Thomas said. "No, no, no. You don't wait for someone in the desert. That's like going to the basement in a horror movie. Who knows what kind of people these are?"

"Well," Griff said. "I'm assuming they're the ones we came here to find."

"Oh my god, Tripp," Thomas said. "Really? You want to hang out and let the target identify us? Haven't you learned anything?"

He reached into the backseat. Grabbed his backpack. The rat carrier.

"What's happening?" Charity asked.

"Protocol," Thomas said. He shouldered open his door. Got out. Slammed it shut.

"Where's he going?" Charity asked.

"Carrying a pet rat," Griff said. "Talking about protocol."

Thomas made a signal with his hands. The number four. A plunging fist.

"What are we doing?"

"We're supposed to hide," Griff said. He looked back at her. "How do you feel about camouflage?"

FIFTY-FIVE

THE SCRUB, THICK IN THE VALLEY, SOAKED UP THE MOONLIGHT and cast deep pockets of shadow. They tucked themselves into a thick, spiny hedge behind a gray boulder. Thomas scanned the perimeter with a thermal monocular. The Thunderbird sat like a polished blue robin's egg that had dropped from its nest.

"See anything?" Griff asked Thomas.

"Snakes and despair," Thomas said. "Nothing but snakes and despair."

"Hilarious," Charity said from nowhere.

"Geez! I forgot you were there," he said. "You're so good at being still."

"Church is all waiting," she said, still nearly invisible. "Can I?"

She sat up and looked through the monocular.

"Oh look," she said.

"You see someone?" Thomas asked.

She pointed to a spot in the distance, on the ground. Movement. Griff sharpened the focus on his own eyepiece. A small white creature stared back with pink eyes.

Leapt toward him.

"Yikes!" Griff said.

"Like tarantulas," Charity said.

"Kangaroo rats," Thomas said. "They're everywhere."

Headlight pricked the distance.

"Them," Thomas said. "Target confirmed."

Far away. The white blots looked painted on the still glass of night.

Gradually, the headlights gathered the roar of distant engines, multiplied to four. Swelled to terrible brightness and became vehicles. Griff's hands shook, breath ticklish in his chest. A small, unmarked buggy. The other, a jeep. About half a dozen people.

Thomas withdrew his Bug Detector.

"No phones," Thomas whispered.

The group looked rougher than Griff had imagined. Dusty and pierced. A brown-skinned woman in leather with long braids piled up on her head. A man—also brown-skinned, probably ten years older, had countless facial piercings, a long ragged coat. He cocked a foot on a small boulder, like a pirate. One small white guy with close-shorn hair. A Black man with camo pants. Others.

"Should we say something?" Charity asked.

Thomas mashed his finger to his lips. Shook his head.

"Hello, friends!" the pirate man said, his voice as booming and textured as an opera singer's. "Come out, come out, wherever you are!"

Charity mimed saying hello.

"Oooooowwowowowwwwww!"

The small guy howled.

The group surrounded their vehicle. Conferred and laughed. At one point, they all hopped up and down together, arms around each other's shoulders, singing—

Where did you go, draw me a map, where did you go!

"That's the Band," Griff said.

"That's not the Band," Thomas hissed.

"I mean the music," Griff said. "It's the Band's music."

"I have a bad feeling," Thomas said.

Charity stared at Thomas, like she was reading something in his eyes.

"So what do we do?" Griff asked.

"We wait," Thomas said. "Then we follow them. Oh my god. Look. They're going through our car!"

Someone with a long, heavy rope. The small guy howled again.

OWOWOWOWWWOoooooowwwwww!!!

They huddled around the jeep and the ThunderChicken. Arms around one another. Swaying. Humming too soft to hear.

"Thomas," she said.

When they broke apart, the ThunderChicken was tied to the jeep.

"Thomas," Charity said. "Why are we hiding? They are taking the car."

Engines roared. Door clapped shut.

The cars drove away. Pinprick taillights. Gone. Just the three of them. Together and breathing. Getting colder. Griff and Charity stared at Thomas.

"Okay," Thomas said. "I think we're safe. We can start walking."

"Safe?" Charity said. "They just took our gear. All our food. Our car."

"My car," Thomas said. "Yeah. Why would they do that? Right?"

"Why would we hide from the people we were trying to find?" Charity asked.

"My gut told me," Thomas said to Griff. "I don't know. Something was off."

"Off," Charity said.

"They looked rough."

"Rough?!" Charity said. "Thomas. They were singing our songs! Sing-ing! A band of violent, singing criminals? What was this? A Broadway Musical Situation?"

"They just didn't look like the type—"

"Ah!" Charity said "Not the type. You mean piercings. Long coats."

Thomas looked at Griff. And Griff looked at Charity.

"You mean not white enough," Charity said.

They stood in silence.

"They just didn't look like—I'm not saying, like, it's just, the Band sounded like—"

"A white band?" Charity said. "Tell me what a white band sounds like?"

"I just expected—"

"White," she said.

"Yeah! Fine!" Thomas said. "They looked rough, and also, they were not white. Except for maybe one who might've been a baby wolf. I wasn't trying to—"

"Where are you with this?" Charity asked Griff.

"Me?"

"Just look at you! Two white guys in camo. The living profile of every mass shooter in America terrified of the singing brown people. It's just unbelievable."

Something hot prickled in Griff's gut.

"Then why didn't you say something?" he asked.

The words, when they hit the air, grew blades and landed wrong. She stared back at him.

"I trusted you! Because this is what you do!" She grabbed his camo vest, shook it. "For a split second, all the way out here, I forgot about racism."

She sighed.

"Well, I'm doing my best," Thomas said.

"Great," Charity said. "Because it's always such a relief when white people are doing their best."

"Oh, so now we're the white people," Thomas said.

"You've always been the white people!" Charity said.

She walked away, took a long loop back toward them. Stopped herself.

"You know—" she started. "All the way out here."

She walked toward the mountains. The same direction they'd dragged the car. Thomas looked at the map.

"She's going the right way," he said.

They followed Charity.

FIFTY-SIX

WHEN THEY CAUGHT UP, THEY DIDN'T SAY MUCH.

Charity's reaction had jabbed at something bone-deep. Griff had pictured the group white, like most of his town. Like most people he knew. And he'd been afraid like Thomas, probably for the same reasons. Griff had thought he'd be better, but somehow the poison had gotten into his deep tissues. Just breathing the air. Like cadmium in the lungs.

The Specific Absorption Rate of Clade City racism.

"Charity," he told her. "I'm sorry."

He placed the small words into the new space between them. To say *I'm sorry* was to toss two hopeful coins in the well and wish for forgiveness. Quiet lingered. Scratchy footfalls. Breathing. They should've been thrilled. The mood was prickly.

They walked toward an impassibly steep mountainside and eventually dead-ended at a wide, flat face of stone. A narrow fissure penetrated the rock's interior. Inside, the light changed from silver to blue to black.

"What now, survivors?" Charity asked.

They scanned the maps again. Thomas was fairly certain—

"I think it's through here."

He pointed to the crack. Barely big enough for a person. Thomas set down the rat carrier, then stripped off his backpack, put a flashlight in his teeth.

"What are you doing?" Charity asked.

"I'm going first," Thomas said. "Penance for latent racism and transgressions unbecoming of a redneck."

"Seriously?" Charity asked.

"Yes," Thomas said. He crammed himself into the narrow crevasse.

Griff went next. He hoisted the green backpack over his head. Five steps in, rock nipped at both shoulders, so he twisted sideways. Thomas shuffled inward. Upward. Griff drew a breath and coughed out powder. Talcum.

His arms wobbled, holding his pack. He walked duck-footed.

The density of the rock was palpable. Air stacked heavy around them. Above, the wedge of navy sky shrank to a ribbon. Floss.

"Can you breathe?" Charity whispered.

"Kind of," he whispered.

Tighter. He could no longer turn his head to see her. The rock would scrape his nose flat. When he inhaled, the stone resisted his expanding ribs.

"Thomas?" Griff asked.

Breath condensed to a curl in front of him, bumped stone and swirled. Thomas shoved himself around a corner. Griff's knees wobbled.

"You okay?" Charity asked.

Griff tried to turn. Stuck. Backpack, pinched in the rocks. Couldn't move.

A sneeze could crack a rib.

"Where are you?" Thomas asked, voice hollow.

He reached around the elbow of the corridor, found Griff's hand. Griff exhaled and buckled his body around the corner. Scraping his cheeks. Ahead, Thomas wiggled and kicked through a hole in the stone—out!

His moonstruck face. His jaw hung open.

Thomas wiped his cheeks. He was crying.

"Thomas?"

He stared ahead.

"Thomas!"

"Let the air out of your lungs. Don't breathe."

Griff exhaled. His heart fluttered.

No air. Little razor blades of panic, slashing his lungs. This was how it was to drown.

Thomas jerked him out to his chest. Griff exhaled, kicked, ground his way out into the light and lay heaving on the slab. Sucking air. Oxygen didn't stick. His breath had scampered into the desert like a lost white rabbit and he had to catch it. Behind him, Charity escaped the stone.

"My god," she said.

Griff recovered and stood on wobbly legs. What they'd found was impossible.

A man-made tower. At its tip, a blinking green light.

And below it, all around it—Thomas exhaled:

"Atlantis."

FIFTY-SEVEN

ATLANTIS.

A hidden city. Encircled by a jagged ring of mountains, a vast plateau spread out before them like a flat-bottomed bowl. On the plateau stood two towers—one near, one far. Between the towers, a smattering of tents, vehicles, various high-ground encampments.

More thrilling still, what lay below.

Carved deep into the desert floor—a full story or two beneath the high camps, a series of broad habitable canyons. Accessible by ladders and ramps, channels that looked carved by industrious, human-sized ants. Wide as city streets in some places, narrow as alleys in others. Lit, ramshackle structures flashed like jewels inlaid in stone channels. The paths branched through the expansive landscape like the roots of a wild tree, recessed walkways glowing for miles, stretching dreamily toward the pall of mountains like a flickering fuse.

Movement. People down there.

"It's a whole other world," Charity said.

"Is this all for the Band?" Thomas asked. "Where do they play?"

The stage could be anywhere.

"Where to?" Thomas asked.

"That giant blinking tower seems like a logical choice," Griff said.

They walked. With proximity, the structures in the sub-terranean walkways gained details. Kitchens, yurts, lean-tos. Handmade and strung with lights, colorful flags, carvings. Some thatched and primitive, others filigreed and ornamented like medieval art that had tumbled off the dirigible of a time-traveling pirate. Together, the tapestries, lights, and makeshift structures came together with the bright and balanced inco-herence of a patchwork quilt.

They stepped into the moon-shadow space beneath the tower. The structure looked as if it had rocket-shipped to Death Valley from the nineteenth century and taken a few whacks from each decade. Crooked eaves, slanted windows. A wooden-slat rope ladder stretched from the ground to a green spot in the tower's belly. A door?

Above, a low hum of voices.

Griff grabbed the first wooden rung. Warm. Like it had drunk a million desert suns.

"You're going up?" Thomas asked.

The ladder made him want to climb.

Griff watched his hands move rung over rung. The air cooled. With each step, the ladder swayed farther. Another moment—What am I doing? Griff stopped. Above, a flash of eyeballs. Bright white. The eyes had been painted on the trap-door. Small, stenciled letters read: BELLY OF THE BEAST. Griff took a deep, full breath. The air! It smelled like an old leather suit-case. Like skin, after a full day in the sun. He'd never smelled anything like it.

Griff knocked on the trapdoor.

Below, Thomas and Charity looked very small, as if viewed through a telescope. The trapdoor's hinges screeched.

breeeeechecheeee

A square of light washed over him. A face eclipsed the glow.

Light danced on eyebrow hooks, nose barbs. The pirate man. He smiled silver-capped teeth and spoke with a honeyed voice:

"The Thunderbirds have arrived!" he said. "Welcome home."

The man grabbed Griff's hand and vacuumed him up into the room.

"Rumblefish!" he said. His name?

Dozens of them inside, talking and singing in little clusters, they clapped and stomped and laughed and howled—

Oooooowoowowoowowow!!!!

"Welcome home!"

They were thrilled to see him. So many faces, white and dark black and brown and sunburned, but what he would remember were the eyes, mostly, shot through with light and clarity—the unclouded, singular possession of joy you find once in every hundred good dreams. No fist bumps, or elbow taps, a full embrace to go along with each name—

Alea, Moondog, Malachi, Stitch, Semele—

Another explosion of joy as Charity entered. Then Thomas. Then a full song. No one started the song. It just started, and it sounded like the Band:

Turning over rock and stone,
Out here we know we're not alone,
We seek we find,
Out here remind,
That the sometimes are still worth looking for

Was this the Band? Guitars, banjos, tom-toms adorned the walls. Monitors, too. Powerful broadcast equipment attended by an older couple—maybe their grandparents' age.

"Drinks!" Rumblefish said. "We must drink. How serious do you like them?"

"I'm a serious man," Thomas said.

They were introduced to Stitch—messy-haired, broad-shouldered. Her patchwork coat interlocked like pieces from a thousand ragged tapestries, eyes blazing with confidence.

"C'mere," she said, voice like a teacher. "Allow me to show you our selection of wild juices, tonics, and teas, such as this chocolate maté, which will blow your goddamn mind, rum optional—"

They were given drinks. Little Punch for Griff and Big Punch for Thomas and tea for Charity and before he could give thanks, another hand on his arm—no shyness about touching—a warm hand guiding him away. A guy his age, Black, with a leather vest, torn jeans. Single earring shaped like a UFO.

"Malachi," he said. "I took your drone down. I'm on security."

He flashed Griff a black fabric wristband.

"I'm Griff. Nice shot on the drone. What did you use? EMP?"

"Naw," Malachi said. "Not this time. Went with a rifle mount. Drone defense."

"You run on 1575?"

"You know it," Malachi said. He smiled. "You could be helpful."

"Yeah?"

"You should talk to Marilyn and the Mole," Malachi said, pointing to the older couple. "They help run the crews and do sound for the shows."

"For the Band?" Griff said.

"You did come for the music, then," Malachi said.

"Why else?"

He laughed. "Good, good. Go on and talk to them. They're easy. Don't let his handshake fool you."

The older pair looked like they'd tumbled off a Harley-Davidson a few years ago and never got back on. The woman, full of energy. Leaning on one foot, then the next. A shock of bright purple hair. Her necklace of small shells clacked together as she moved. The man had light brown skin and a body structure like how a snowman might look if you built him out of boulders. His face looked like it should hold a chest-length beard and was somehow more terrifying without one.

Griff twined his way through the crowd, then was shaking the stone man's hand. He gripped Griff's bones like a sleeve of crackers. Crunch.

"I'm the Mole," he said. The voice!

No recording. No preserving.

"Wow," Griff said. "So nice to meet you."

Like meeting a celebrity. Or a terrifying Greek god.

"What did you have in those receivers?" the Mole asked. "Copper coil?"

When the Mole talked, his face opened like a straight hinge. A rock puppet.

"Yes, sir."

"Hey there, Thunderbird," the woman said. "Marilyn." Older than his mother, but she drawled her words and slung her hips like a surly teenager. Every wrinkle looked as if it had landed by mistake.

"That wardrobe! Thought you might be here to shut this place down," Marilyn said.

"I don't even know what this place is," Griff said.

She laughed, touched his arm.

"First thing," she said, "we ought to get you to Mirror, Mirror. Get you outfitted, get you to Simon. I assume y'all are going to stick around."

"I'm—"

Marilyn's Mirror, Mirror comment landed like a spark in a pile of dry leaves, the whole room crackling with it—

Mirror, Mirror! Mirror, Mirror!

"Can I touch you?" someone asked in his ear.

"Uh," Griff said. "Sure."

Stitch had him by the hand. A small and powerful engine and something lovely about it, being dragged with firm affection toward—who knows?

Mirror, Mirror.

The crew was packing up, downing drinks, pouring new ones. Malachi, with the UFO earring, found Neapolitan a cozy place to be under a worktable—all climate-controlled to keep equipment safe—and Stitch pulled him with her vortex energy through a purple tapestry into a small dark space.

"You the adventurous type?" she asked.

"Yes," he said.

They were standing very close. He could smell maté and liquor on her breath.

Her right hand reached toward him, then grabbed a latch. She pushed a portion of the tower wall swinging out into the night. A cool breeze tickled his cheeks. Moonlight. Griff was laughing. The whole desert, spread out in front of him.

A small steel catwalk, a railing he gripped tightly—*go on*. Griff stepped outside. He could see for miles. Mountains looked stemmy and cratered as coral. Below, people moved in productive clusters—tents, sun sails, glittering paths, an anomalous grove of distant trees and yet—where was the stage?

"Where does the Band play?" Griff asked.

"The shows?" Stitch asked. She pointed to a cluster of peaks. "Through there. Pocket canyon. Oh no. Oh no."

"What?" he asked.

Her face went slack and solemn. So fast, it sent goose bumps bolting up his arms.

"I shouldn't have told you. I'm not supposed to tell."

He knew what would happen before it happened, and it was already too late. Stitch leapt from the edge of the catwalk and screamed the whole way down.

FIFTY-EIGHT

A FIRE POLE. THE PREPPERS WOULD'VE LOVED IT.

The whole crew watched from the sand, hooting and clapping.

"His face!"

Did he really think Stitch would kill herself? He knew only one thing—he was going down this fire pole.

"Griff! Griff! Griff! Griff!"

He grabbed the cool steel and leapt. A giddy, stomach-dropping feeling and he touched down feather-light. They shook his shoulders, slapped his back, and there was Charity, smiling.

"Was that as fun as it looked?" she asked.

"Better," Griff said, rubbing his hands together. "I don't think I've ever felt so light."

"You've never been so light," Charity said. "I was so worried about you."

She hugged him. Good, long squeeze.

"Is this happening?" Griff asked.

"It appears so," she said.

"I'm—" he began.

"I know," she said.

The group walked from the base of the tower to the top of a wooden ladder.

"We get to go down into The Paths," Thomas said, clapping his hands. He said "The Paths" with capital letters, as if he'd already learned so much. His breath smelled like rubbing alcohol and Kool-Aid.

One by one, they descended into the Paths. A dozen rungs down, the air in the canyons felt different. Cooler. The smell of sawed wood and burnt sage. The effect was incredible. Like parachuting into the heart of a city. Booths and tents clung to tall dirt walls like wild mushrooms cleave to a log. Benches and tents. Caves and squirrelly little dens.

"Ooooh," Thomas said, pointing. "Sneaky coves."

"Your lips are blue," Griff said.

"I drank the Truth Juice," he said.

Moments later, Thomas was holding hands with a girl with long, braided green hair. Thomas looked at Griff, then down at his handholding situation, as if he was carrying a suitcase of large, unmarked bills.

Already holding hands? How did this happen?

Someone sidled up next to Griff.

"Can I hold your hand?" Moondog asked.

Moondog held Griff's hand. Strange. He wore a blue bracelet, like Malachi's black one. Moondog looked to be about their age, but small. All of him seemed like it could fold up and fit in a tiny suitcase. Griff took a deep breath. Charity was arm in arm with the tall girl with braids, Alea.

"Look," Moondog said.

A brilliant peach made of blown glass—one bite missing. It rested precariously on a wooden crate. Art, everywhere. Slabs of driftwood with mosaicked spawning salmon. Handmade water spigots. Crooked benches looked worn and knotted in the right places, slanting and tucking into each space just so. To Griff's left, a path carved wide switchbacks back up to the plateau. A ramp for cars?

Who'd built this place?

Ahead, wild decorations hung across the steep canyon walls, a makeshift roof of ribbons, flags—or clothing. Underwear clipped and knotted to look like birds, shirt cuffs holding hands, skirts and dresses pinned as if twirling. As they walked, disembodied clothing slowly consumed the sky. A carnival of potential identities.

Hats heaped on crooked tables. Clothes spilled from whisky barrels. Wooden boxes of jewelry. A wire racks of masks. Smiling tigers and expressionless mimes. Hook-nosed vultures. The group broke apart, tried on new faces.

Ahead, the path dead-ended in a wall of sky-high purple curtains.

"Time to change," Stitch said. She whipped off her shirt. Bra! Griff spun around. What was happening? Now they were pilling things into his arms—

Oh, here—you'd look smashing, this is just your color—

Somehow, almost immediately, Thomas was wearing a pink cowboy hat and mirrored sunglasses. Sleeveless white shirt, leather chaps.

"Ride 'em, cowboy!"

Thomas whooped and rode an invisible horse, swatted it with his hand. People loved him. Charity went next, vanishing through a fold in the elevated curtains that must've been the changing room. Did Griff imagine it—all of them glancing in that direction, the trailing off of side conversations as suspense mounted? Were they all waiting to see her, too?

Moments later, she exited to whistles, wild applause.

Like when he'd first seen her on stage—dazzling. Brand-new again. The dress was blue and white and lacy like she'd slipped through a hole in the sky and come out wearing a piece of it. He wanted to tell her how good she looked. Wanted to hold her—

"That's my girl," Stitch said. Then she grabbed Griff by the wrist. "Your turn, handsome. Watch your step!"

Behind the curtains, a small wooden stage. Griff stepped up, grabbed for an opening. He followed the folds until he was nestled into the fabric. Straight ahead, a full-length mirror. Leo stared back at him.

"I know you found it first," Griff said. "What do you want? Should I leave?"

Leo shook his head. He looked worried.

"What?" Griff asked.

A pained, familiar expression. The last look Leo had ever given him. Again, Griff saw the wave pounce. Saw the emptied ledge and churning water and tasted the spray and could not breathe. He shoved through the curtains, couldn't escape, dropped his clothing, tripped down the wooden stage onto the grit and—*hey, you okay*—they were pulling him up but something else was happening.

A set of headlights, gliding toward them down the Paths.

Light washed their faces. Doors opened.

"All right, boys," said the familiar voice. "Get in the car."

FIFTY-NINE

THE CAR WAS A JEEP—THE MOLEMOBILE.

Charity was already inside.

"Hey," she said. She scooted next to Griff in her heavenly dress. She looked unbelievably happy. Like she'd peeled off a whole hard layer he'd never even known was there. She leaned her head against his shoulder. Solid. Still her.

"Do you know where we're going?" Griff asked.

He suddenly didn't care.

"To see Simon," Charity said. "I guess he decides if we can stay."

"Stay?" he said. The Band hadn't even played yet. What did they have to do?

"Where's Thomas?" the Mole asked from the driver's seat.

"Gettin' froggy," Marilyn said.

The Mole flashed his brights.

"Oh gosh," Charity said.

Griff had never known Thomas to kiss anyone—yet there he was. Tucked into a pillowed little enclosure made up to look like a frog's mouth, doing some serious, face-tilted, advanced-level tongue business.

"C'mon, lover!" Marilyn screamed. She reached over and honked.

Thomas tumbled out of the cove and wobbled into the jeep.

He straightened his cowboy hat. Put his sunglasses in his front pocket.

"What was that about?" Griff said.

"I don't know exactly," Thomas said, settling in beside them. "But I'll tell you this. I, for one, am loving the desert."

The jeep inched through the narrow corridor, advancing toward the curtained wall. To the right of the central mirror, Rumblefish and Malachi pulled a rope, lifting the curtain. Beyond the fabric, another network of vast alleys and avenues. Charity pointed to the right. A statue of a white rabbit, holding a stopwatch.

The Mole accelerated, bumping them farther into the Paths.

"Make-out coves," Thomas said matter-of-factly. "I mean—that person just asked me to make out. And then we were making out in a proper cove. I mean—"

Charity laughed.

"Why not more make-out coves? For the benefit of civilization, why are we not making out at all times?"

"Kissing is more than a hobby," Charity said.

"It's my hobby now," Thomas said. "Seventeen years of nothing. A wasteland of missed opportunities! Out here, you just have to ask the question."

Thomas looked at her closely.

"Charity," Thomas said.

"Not a chance," Charity said. "I've barely forgiven you. And kissing is not a hobby for me."

But what if Charity changed her mind out here in the breezy desert? Clade City had an entire physical and psychological infrastructure and enforcement system designed to keep teenage bodies apart. Expectations, reputations, prying eyes, doors that were meant to remain open, parking restrictions, curfews, but here—you were one *yes* away from anything. Griff suspected from the the way he'd winced at Moondog's platonic handhold, he was not yet worldly enough for casual desert polyamory.

"You have a stunning voice," Marilyn told Charity. "You know that?"

"Oh, thank you," Charity said.

"You should hear her perform," Griff said.

"Tomorrow, my son," Marilyn said. "Girl can find her light."

"Is that when the Band plays?" Griff asked.

"You know I'm a sound guy," Thomas cut in.

"Sound guy!" the Mole boomed. "You seasoned?"

"Seasoned and salty as fuck," Thomas said.

"No wonder you were getting lucky," Marilyn said. "Forget the musicians. They play for themselves. You want a guy who gets paid to read the signals and respond. Nab a sound guy for a lover and you'll never go back."

They laughed and the jeep tilted upward, a ramp leading out from the Paths and up to the plateau. Straight ahead stood the second tower.

"Who is Simon?" Griff asked.

"The first builder," the Mole said.

An older tower. Planks and driftwood. A hermit's cabin on knobby stilts. To the left, a long boat rope stretched up to a golden bell. They climbed out.

"Just be honest with him," Marilyn said.

She walked to the rope and shook it.

Dingdadingdingding

Thomas and the Mole were debating:

"—what I'm saying is, that level of amplification with a stone backdrop—"

"Good instinct," the Mole said, "but have you considered—"

A trapdoor swung open from the bottom of the tower.

WHUMP

"Goodbye, then," Marilyn said. She spread her arms in a hug. Her shells pushed into his chest.

"You're leaving?" Griff asked.

"You'll see us soon," the Mole said. "Probably."

They climbed into the car. Waved and called *bye-bye* like they'd dropped their kids off at school. Dust plumed up from their wheels. Taillights receded. Griff walked to the ladder.

The rungs were splintered and uneven. He tested them with half weight, the way you check branches on a rotten tree. He climbed toward the golden square of light. Reaching the top, he poked his head through a neatly trimmed hole in plush carpeting. Inside, a familiar smell. Like his grandparents' home.

Could this be real?

He rose into the lofted cabin. The space was stunning. A cobbled-together gallery in the desert. Small glass cases. Shadow boxes. Fabric-draped lumps of furniture. The walls, adorned with hung art. A painting of snowy footprints on a windswept peak. A snowcapped range, jagged against dark clouds. Crampons.

Art depicting mountains. And whales.

The exploded diagram of a blue whale's bone structure. A painting of a great rising tail—two flukes split by a neat notch. A ship in a bottle. A small case of knives. On the farthest wall, rows of iridescent what—jewels?

When Griff stepped forward, a figure emerged.

He seemed to shake himself loose from the surroundings. Plaid skirt, not quite a kilt, girded by a leather tool belt. Frilly pirate shirt and a plaid scarf. Reddish moustache like a swatch of rough fabric with neatly pointed ends, and eyebrows that leapt up in a constant state of surprise.

Beautiful eyes. Wide and clear and bright as a child's. An accented voice—though it was unclear from where.

"Simon," he said. "And you must be Griffin. Welcome home."

SIXTY

SIMON SHOOK THEIR HANDS AND KISSED CHARITY'S, THEN SAID:

"Oh, my. Sorry. May I?"

He grabbed Griff's hand, kissed it. Thomas's.

"Always working," he said. "Always improving. You kids keep me young. Never expected so many kids. Shouldn't be a surprise, I suppose. Sit down, will you? Would you like some tea or something?"

The cabin's furniture was largely shapeless, backless lumps. Everything layered over with cloth and tapestry so you couldn't tell precisely what you were sitting on, or what posture might make it tip. Griff contented himself on a purple hump in the shape of a toadstool. Simon brought him tea that smelled like anise and something else—grass after it rains.

"You're one day early," Simon said. "How did you discover us?"

"The radio," Griff said.

"Oh. Wonderful. Wonderful!" He set the teacup down. "Quite an effort, the radio. Of course, people disagreed about the broadcast. Thought we'd be overrun. But it's just right, isn't it? The right people find their way."

Griff nodded. Silence. Simon watched them, and Griff's eyes were again drawn to the glinting glass case on the far wall—

"Go on," Simon said. "Have a look."

They stood and crossed the carpet. It wasn't jewels. The case held butterflies. Pinned wings. Some shone with the pearly glow of a mollusk's nacre. Others looked velvet, like the rumpled nap of rose petals. Simon remained seated.

"I used to see the wings," Simon said. "Now I only see the bodies. Little reminder."

Shriveled bodies between. Black, pinhead, staring eyes.

"Reminder for what?" Thomas asked.

"No recording," he said. "No preserving."

Charity exhaled. Her face clenched.

"Why not?" Thomas asked, turning from the case. "Why keep it so secret?"

"Pardon my language but—you must understand, being young, what would happen. We'd be Facefucked. Instafucked. Permafucked. Like the rest of everything. Like floods! Like locusts! There'd be nothing left. And here you came without phones for us to take away. Maybe a first. Please, indulge an old man with a story."

They did. Simon echoed certain parts, energetic refrains—

Song fishing! You broadcast us! Police! False alarm!

"Can you imagine?" Simon said. "Learning it was just a false alarm. They must've been so relieved."

Griff looked down, recalling the Walk of Shame.

"They'll be mad," Griff said.

"Think they'll come looking?" Simon said.

"They won't find us," Thomas said.

"They will or they won't, I suppose," Simon said.

"Did you start this whole thing?" Griff said.

"I did," Simon said. "I always liked the undertaking of big imaginings. Great big things, you know. Accomplishment!" He knocked his teacup into the saucer, stared with ferocious eyes. He laughcd. But the ferocity was real.

"You climbed mountains," Griff said.

"Plenty," he said. "Mountains worked for a while. I tried to get a mountain. But you can't get a mountain, is the problem. Can't put it in your sack and carry it down with you. You climb a mountain a million times but the mountain is still the mountain and not much different from the climbing. And neither was I, at the end of the day. Adventure becomes routine. Chapters to check-boxes, you understand? So then—I chased the next great big imagining."

"The sea?" Thomas asked.

"Whales," Simon said. "I was fascinated. Worked fishing boats. Killed my way through thousands of fish. Literally thousands of little souls, you know? Working up to a whale."

Charity's face was drawn. Simon's, too.

"So then you do," his words even. "You kill a whale. You learn your hands can kill a thing so much bigger and more beautiful than you. It can be done. You can simmer it down. Steal its bones. You can reduce it to something small enough to smear on toast. That's power, isn't it? Then you're sitting there eating your toast with a bit of blubber. And how different are you then? You can climb the biggest mountain. Swallow a whale on your toast. What is it, then, you're seeking out there?"

In silence, Griff considered the TOE Box. Diagrams and theories, files and maps.

"Music?" Griff said.

"Yes," Simon said. "Maybe that."

"Will we get to see the Band?" Griff asked.

"The Band," Simon said, his voice deep. "Well. I have a secret."

"What?"

He leaned forward. They leaned forward.

"I'm in the Band," Simon said.

Thomas leapt out of his seat.

"Oh my god," he said. Griff and Charity exchanged looks—what now? Kneel? Request an autograph?

"You're, well, you're amazing, I mean you, thank you—" Thomas stuttered.

"No, no," Simon said. "You'll see it all tomorrow. Thank me then. For now, why don't we find you a crew."

"So, we get to stay?" Griff asked.

"Yes," Simon said. "As long as you like."

Thomas slapped Griff's back, hard, and the three of them pulled into a reflexive hug. Simon laughed and went to a map stuck with colorful pins and fabric swatches, dotted with names—the Springboard, the Velvet Den, Rapture Palace, the Slitherhound, Naughty Noodle, BrindleBurner, and every crew had their own campsite—the SandDogs, the Hydras, PooperScoopers, ReFuel, the Electrolytes, WeedWhackers, TrundleBunnies—

Charity got a blue band for the Hydras, in charge of water/hydration, a red wristband for Thomas in Soundscaping, and Griff got a black one.

"A crew so secret we can scarcely say its name," Simon said. "Shhhh-curity."

He placed it on the opposite wrist from the paracord.

Outside, an approaching engine. Lights flared through the window and Simon was suddenly rushing, gathering up glasses. They knocked together like gentle chimes—

"Your ride! Almost forgot," he said. "We must drink!"

He poured four small golden goblets of a greenish, grassy-smelling liquid. They touched glasses and drank. It tasted like mowed lawns and dandelions and turpentine. He hugged each of them in turn, the same way he shook hands—strong, grace-ful. The moment of their embrace, it was there again—

—the smell!

It struck Griff that he'd been wrong. It was not his grand-parents' home. Just the way it had smelled one particular morning.

Griff remembered him and Leo, eight years old and in pajamas, stepping onto the back patio with their father. Griff had been holding his dad's warm hand, his dad, whispering— *perfect timing. Perfect timing.* Bracing air. Their breath, swirling vapor.

Overnight, their grandparents' lawn had become a fairy tale. A fence transformed to cloud-castle ramparts, lawn furniture to marshmallow sculptures. Hills glazed in sheets of twinkling stillness. An impossible scent, all the way out in the desert.

Simon smelled like snow.

SIXTY-ONE

MALACHI DROVE THEM IN THE JEEP THEY'D SEEN EARLIER. DUST behind them caught the moonlight—a sturdy vapor trail in the sky. Thomas was in the backseat with Charity. Not kissing. Griff turned back. Still not kissing. Behind them, Simon's tower pulsed a faint red.

"What's with the light?" Griff asked Malachi.

"Didn't Simon tell you?" Malachi said. He laughed. "He's the Weatherman."

"What's red mean?" Griff asked.

"Means it's gonna be hot," Malachi said.

In the distance, dreamy blue light rippled on the horizon. Umbrellas, tents, sunshades.

"Is that the lagoon?" Charity asked.

"Hydra Camp," Malachi said. "Lagoon's farther out."

Music, on the breeze. Gusts of guitar and fiddle.

"Hear that?" Charity asked Griff.

She squeezed his shoulder. A hot bolt raced through his blood and—YES—they could play again. But what kind of keyboard would they have, if any? No chance of a piano.

"Your drone's under the seat," Malachi said.

Griff tapped the body with his foot. "Oh great!" He took it out, examined the propellers. It would fly again.

"Just make sure it's not transmitting," Malachi said.

"No worries on transmissions, brother," Thomas said. He reached into his own pack and pulled out the Jam Sandwich.

"No thanks," Malachi said. "I ate."

Thomas removed the top slice of bread. Circuitry.

"Whoa hey," Malachi said, slowing to a stop. He took a palm-sized device from his vest. Similar to the Bug Detector, but better. "How'd I miss that? This thing's scared of its own reflection."

"Not a transmitter," Thomas said. "It's a jammer."

"Jam sandwich," Malachi said. "Ha! Lithium-ion?"

"Replaceable," Thomas said. "Check it."

Thomas worked his fingers in, popped out a silver disk.

Malachi's detector squealed. A bright green spot leapt on-screen.

BrreeeeeEEEEE!

Griff froze.

"Transmission!" Malachi said. He shifted to park. Yanked out the keys.

"It's off!" Thomas said, fumbling. "I turned it off, I can— let me—"

Malachi leapt out of the jeep, trained the device on Thomas. Charity.

"You."

Malachi pointed at Griff.

"Me?"

"Gimme that bag."

Griff handed over his green backpack. Malachi probed the underside and frowned. Retrieved needle-nose pliers from the jeep. He opened the metal jaws and plucked something from the fabric. A green hunk of metal, the size of a cocklebur.

Griff's skin went cold.

"One of ours," Thomas said. "Maybe you picked it up at the Rat's Nest."

"Crush it," Griff said.

Malachi squeezed the pliers. Crunch.

"Hope that's not bad," Malachi said.

"It's fine," Thomas said.

Maybe it was fine. A tiny green twinkle of data in the vastness of sky and stars. And a moon they somehow shared with Clade City. The blue light from Hydra Camp suddenly reminded him of the sea, and a long walk home. He could almost glimpse the distant figures of Slim and Jonesy.

Griff squeezed Charity's hand.

But this was real, right now. Fingers in his, willing to squeeze back, warm, perfect fingers. He shut his eyes and smelled the air, felt the wind—remembered the most important lesson from the Skip. Sing when you can sing. Dance when you can dance.

You never know how long the song is going to last.

SIXTY-TWO

THE GROUP STOPPED PLAYING MUSIC WHEN THEIR CREW ARRIVED at Hydra Camp—just to greet them.

"Thunderbirds!"

No one had ever been so happy to see him. Hugs, everywhere. The joy felt real. Natural. Less and less hard to believe. Like the messages of love and welcome were part of a much older story, had been twisted deep in their DNA, inscribed in their bones. If joy was so natural—why not all the time? Like—why no make-out coves?

Everyone seemed to play music.

They went for their instruments. Rumblefish with a resonator guitar, Alea with a fiddle, Moondog with a little wooden cajón that looked hand-carved for his small butt. Thomas tested the acoustics and Charity carried her glowing gift in her chest but—nothing here with black and white keys. Not a Casio. Not even an accordion. Griff got a drink from a hand-mosaicked bar, relaxed into a beautiful plush sofa, and watched them play.

The group covered some of the Band's songs and played originals and Charity opened up her sweetest, deepest voice. As they played, the whole place felt buoyant. Rocking him back and forth. A smooth, hypnotic glide, and Rumblefish sidled up beside him like a wild pirate boarding his sweet, sleepy ship—

"What do you play?" he asked.

Griff sat up straight. "What?"

"Instrument."

The music had stopped. They were looking at him. Smiling.

"Piano," Griff said.

"Is that it?"

"Yeah," Griff said. "That's really it."

"Piano," Rumblefish told the group.

The vibe changed. A tightening.

"It's okay," Griff said. "I'm sure there's not a piano in the desert."

"No," Rumblefish said. "There's one."

Rumblefish stood. Cinched up his backpack. "Are you prepared?"

"Prepared?" Griff asked.

"Like, how far are you willing to go?"

"Wait, wait," Stitch said. "I implore you, Rumble of the Fish, to apply reason. We are deep in the night. Our friends have traveled far and wide for tomorrow night's show and could be in need of some rest. I'm pretty sure Charity was just sleeping with her eyes open."

Charity laughed.

"So what then?" Rumblefish asked.

"We Cuddlenap," Stitch said. The idea seemed to take hold.

"Pianooooo," Rumblefish protested through a yawn.

"Get your nighty-night drinks, people," Stitch said. "Let's rally."

Curtains opened, people vanished, and others clustered near the bar.

Griff and Charity stood, staring at each other. Charity smiled.

"What?" Charity asked.

Griff beckoned her closer.

"Did she say Cuddlenap?"

Charity raised her eyebrows and grabbed his hand.

SIXTY-THREE

THE GROUP MADE A PILGRIMAGE TO THE BIG TENT.

There were dunes in this distant spread of desert. Blue, still waves that sloped up slow and slippery. You lost your steps. Lost time. Like you'd been climbing this dune your whole life. Charity was beside him, sky dress, bright eyes. Her hand brushed his and locked with his fingers and—every time, her skin was a surprise. Every other hand stopped at flesh and bone. To hold hers was to somehow walk in the grasp of the whole sacred world.

"You're really here," he said.

"You too," she said.

How could they be alive here—the facts of their bodies in this place: swinging arms, moving legs, watching eyes, a million strands of hair, skin, teeth in mouths, fingers interlocked in the desert? It was true. His whole life could orbit this moment; a moment worth living a whole life to arrive at and worth living beyond to remember. Charity and the desert.

The music had been here. Strangers who already felt like old friends. All this had been alive and out in the world the same day he'd considered knots and the strength of a cord to snap his neck.

Out here, it felt foolish. And small.

He squeezed her hand.

"It's a big world out there," he said.

"Even bigger than I thought," Charity said. "I can't imagine where this tent might be."

No one knew the exact route. Out here, it seemed, everything shifted in the sand, month to month. Night to night. Never the same place twice. Griff's eyes got heavy. The group talked in a low, soft drone—he learned stories in scraps, pieces.

Rumblefish claimed to have worked in grease pits from Cincinnati to San Louis Obispo with every breed of the Great North American Asshole. Stitch had run away from home two years ago. Indiana to California. Moondog lived in a trailer in Utah. Alea, San Francisco. They'd all climbed and scraped and fought their way to the desert. Some traveled back and forth, others stayed somehow—then Moondog howled at the top of the next dune.

There it was.

A big-top tent with twin white peaks.

A wooden sign hung near the long, dark slit of an entrance:

SNOOZEYLOVE

At just the thought of sleep, the drag of the week settled into Griff's bones and begged for some soft, quiet collapse. Charity was warm and close against him. Arm around his waist. The word *nap* drew him toward collapse, then the word *cuddle* woke him with little electric jolts, bringing him back. The words danced this way, in his brain.

Cuddle cuddle, nap nap

"Best part of the desert," Rumblefish said. He yawned.

They descended, then passed through the slit of the tent. The smell of straw and sunbaked wood. Lavender. Center poles tall as masts. The canvas turned the light a perfect, liquid blue. Blankets, pillow piles, people. Chests rose and fell. So many.

The crew removed their shoes.

Griff looked at the sleeping, breathing bodies. How would he join?

"Follow me," Stitch whispered.

Again, she took him by the hand.

Charity walked behind him. They worked their way into a gap on a wide, soft cushion. They all nuzzled in, Stitch and Moondog on one side of him, Charity on his other side. When his body found a place to rest, fatigue accumulated like droplets. A steady drip of images. Twirling Charity in the parking lot. His mother's face. Sunrise in Reno, beside the wild river. The Joshua tree.

Bodies shifted, making room. Faces softened by moonlight through canvas.

Stitch moved a cushion beneath Griff's head. Nuzzling his neck. Charity laid her left hand on his chest. He almost laughed, and didn't know why. Were they doing this? Sleeping together? He stared at Charity's hand. Beautiful fingers somehow wanted to touch him. Her leg hooked around his. His eyes, wide open. He'd never lain with another person this way.

But it was not strange. It was normal and good.

Like the most human thing he'd ever done.

It struck him suddenly—that same feeling from the tent. As if they'd unlocked a great secret they'd carried quietly in their hearts since birth. All the minds and all the bodies. They fit together like a puzzle.

Charity's eyes closed. Moondog and Rumblefish. They looked young and perfect, like nothing had ever been bad for them. A sharp pang. Griff already missed this. Already not enough. It had just started and was already over too soon.

He didn't expect to cry. Or the words that came:

This Aching Life.

How to do this again? In his real life—always alone in the

hallway, alone at a desk, the on and off buses, a lonely bed, the trapped behind glass, the side by side in cars, the bunker, the glass tower. In Clade City, the world of touch was so small. He could slap backs, fist bump, or fight; he could grab or grope, try something, but here and now—a whole brilliant cosmos of touch, where touch was its own goal. Where did this exist in his life?

This Aching Life!

Please don't let this be over. Please don't let this be done. He was trembling. So thirsty for this. Wanting, the way cracked earth aches for rain. Could he still accept it? His body was shy, the way soil dry for too long becomes hydrophobic, forgets the taste of water and cannot drink—

The tent hummed.

Of course. Because the heart beats electric. The mind thinks electric. The whole body sings. We, the transmitters. We, the receivers.

The reason a parent holds their child close. The head on the chest. The beat of the heart. The oldest poetry our bodies still remember. The song we all ache for:

You are loved. You belong.

SIXTY-FOUR

HAMMERS.

The ticktock woodpecker sound of nails being driven into wood. When Griff woke in the tent, the carnival was going up all around him. Charity was gone. Thomas was gone.

Ticktock, ticktock, ticktock.

Clusters of people under blankets. Tangles of threesomes and foursomes and twelvesomes but plenty of space to walk now. He found his shoes near the door. He pulled back the canvas flap to a sliver of sunlight. It fell across his face like a gentle thump.

Hot.

Griff stepped out to a rush of sound and dust. Bold blue sky, stark white ground. Tents speckled the alkali. Red, green, blue, orange, yellow. A motorcycle raced by, dragging dust. The driver in plumage, like a green parakeet. A shirtless team hauled an old, desiccated tree across the sand. A man on a tiny collapsible bicycle with massive tan legs. A small team in space suits. Everywhere, people were building. Knocking, drilling, stitching things together.

He wanted to find Charity, Thomas, join in somehow—

A fleet of dune buggies!

Massive engines and shifters in steel skeletons, mechanical little cockroaches. Piloted by muscle-bound men with little clothing. Out front, a man in a cowboy hat hauling a flatbed trailer and on the flatbed, pouncing from the world of dust—

"No," Griff whispered.

A grand piano. Red. Was that a Steinway? He squinted. Mashed his eyes and it was still there—traveling fast. He watched. Walked. Ran after it. The buggies were heading toward what looked like the Paths, hard to tell. He raced through people, sculptures. A two-story hourglass with a ladder and a bucket, a lion with the head of an eagle, and—fleeing piano! The white grit seemed to ignite in his lungs but he had to track the dust, the great, crushing wave pluming out behind the buggies—it looked like—

Two topless, splatter-painted girls smiled at him. One had a brush dripping green paint.

"Good morning, beautiful," the other girl said.

Incredible breasts, really stunning, and smiles and hair falling along their shoulders—geez, what just happened? It was as if the entire landscape conspired to pull him off-mission. He smiled but his tongue couldn't lift a single *good morning* and then he was running and somehow the Paths had gotten between him and the piano. The buggies must've turned off, or gone down a ramp, so much activity boiling on the horizon he couldn't see anymore and there, across the way—a pink cowboy hat!

"Thomas!" Griff shouted.

Him, with a crew. Building something. Long steel poles and stretched fabric. To reach him, Griff would have to climb down into the Paths and back up to the plateau.

He climbed the long ladder down.

Focus, he told himself.

Like a city street on market day. High walls packed in the energy and made it hum. Hammering in booths, unfurling banners, flags, hauling, everyone hauling in wheelbarrows and buckets and stacks, piles, heaps, cloth, dirt, mulch, tools, fans, banners, paint, and a great steaming carafe of coffee being pumped by a pink Elvis. A stoneware mug with BORN TO RUN pressed into his hand—yes, thank you!—everywhere this great, quivering energy of YES!

Griff tucked into a spot of shade beneath a lofted, curtained space—damn good coffee.

"Holy shit," he said. It was the best thing he'd ever tasted. Roasty, hint of caramel.

He stood in the shade and drank his coffee and watched the singing, dancing human parade because it was the most important thing he could be doing in his life. Then—other needs. He took on the universal look of urgent confusion and was led by a woman with green hair and a peacock feather to a shaded little hut with a squat silver device that flushed with a rumble and fire—incineration, imagine that—and not the loveliest smell but then a purple sink and foamy soap dispenser and his hands smelled like peppermint oil and back into the sun, 5 degrees hotter. Had to find Thomas but—

—cinnamon and frosting?

Starving. Must eat. Griff chased breakfast down a line of happy chewing, fine-smelling people to a woman in a rainbow coat with a vendor box full of cinnamon rolls. Each big as a fist and dripping with goodness. My god!

"How much?—just give me a smile you wonderful creature!"

A smile! For this cinnamon-and-frosting heaven—and where did he put that coffee? Found it! Still hot of course and that plus a cinnamon roll in the desert was surely a miracle! But—Thomas, Thomas, focus!

Griff took a steaming, gooey bite—so much cinnamon it crunched a little, almost spicy and life improved as he turned back into the crowd, trying to find the right ladder.

A girl with hair full of ribbons shouted and flung past him into a crowd of five others, all screaming, clutching one

another like lifeboats, and it was happening everywhere—
airport hellos—screams of greeting and joy popping off like
firecrackers and always singing, because the songbooks were
embedded in the landscape—lyrics bright, hand-painted on
earthen walls in slim calligraphy, etched into wood. One song
took hold, then another, endless:

We see the sun with different eyes

Want to hear it like you saw it, want to taste it on the
breeze

Songs held the whole thing together. Music made pulleys
lift, paint splatter, bodies move—and there he was! Thomas!
Griff found a painted green-and-yellow bin—LOVE 'EM & LEAVE
'EM—and dropped his dishes in clattering—now buzzing
from sugar, frosting, and caffeine, he had an alarming smile
stretched across his face. So foreign-feeling he actually raised
his finger to touch it and a squat man stood staring at him.

Strong, with close-cut hair. A number 1.

Griff froze, a familiar prickling. The man would ask him
what he was smiling about, what he thought he was looking at.
Might shove him backward. The man said:

"You have kind eyes."

A sweet, long hug.

"Want to get tea?" he asked.

Griff sure did. Sounded great but—no, really, thank you
so much—he had to reach Thomas. Had to just get. Up. This.
Ladder.

"Thomas!"

Thomas's crew had expanded, standing in an assemblage of
reflective fabric, rope, tent poles.

Set the clips, right there. Yep—

"Hey, K.T.," someone shouted. "Are we ready?"

K.T.?

"Let's put this together, people!" Thomas said.

The team crawled out from beneath the material. Poles clicked together and it took shape, pulling taut, expanding in height—maybe 10 feet tall. Dozens of facets. Like the EARS sensor Thomas had built, but twenty times bigger.

"Griff!" he said, finally spotting him. "Great to see you!"

"When did you build this?"

"I had a lot of time in July," he said. "Okay, now. Hoist!"

Two guys scaled the rock, free-climbing. They had muscles like knotted shipping rope, crimping, shoving their hands like trowels into tiny mouths in the stone. Thomas fumbled a knot on the metal housing at the sculpture's crown.

"Hey, Griff," Thomas said. "Give it a shot? You're good with your hands."

Griff worked his fingers into the knot. Complex, because of the housing and slip of the rope through sweaty hands, and there was a dull, electric pounding between his temples now that made it hard to focus.

"The Band plays right through there," Thomas said. He pointed to a wide fissure in the rock wall. "This is a prime spot. I can't believe they're letting me hang it."

Griff finally secured the line. Thomas tossed one end to a climber. Then, magically, his sculpture lifted like a giant chandelier into the top of the stone entryway.

"I give you," Thomas said, "the Eternal Encore."

Thomas clapped three times. Light flashed across the facets. A white-hot glowing miracle. Even in the sun, Griff could see traces of color—green, lemon yellow, blazing-hot red. The louder the crew screamed, the brighter it became! An incredible green shimmer and Griff remembered what he wanted to tell Thomas.

"Thomas," Griff said.

"Beautiful, isn't it?"

"I meant to tell you something last night. About the transmitter. I think Jonesy put it on my backpack."

"What?" Thomas asked, distracted.

A pair brought in congas, to see the light they'd make. Red
and orange. People collecting in a great, dancing swirl. Thomas
danced and then—c'mon, Griff—he danced too. Shouted, but
now the soft electric hammer between his temples was a small
train, a thing with density, and he was still shouting and dancing when he suddenly felt made of water, like a tall glass tipping
backward, falling down the stairs—

The Earth jerked, tilted to the side and—

Okay, brother?

Easy to forget the heat, the crush of heat, but he was fine,
fine—

Let's rest, brother. We'll get you to Shady Lane.

Do we need to call an OMG—no, just his first day, just
bring him down—

They helped Griff down the ladder, into the Paths. Led him
to a thatch-hooded avenue of shade. Lean-tos. Tents. They
pushed aside hanging blue draperies, entered a dark structure
with fans spinning out mist. An open cot. He lay down. Above
him, a sign laced with white lights.

REMEMBER: YOU ARE MADE OF WATER

"Take this," Thomas said, handing him a silver bottle.

He drank. Water sat in his stomach, an unmoving puddle.

"Eat," Thomas said, handing him a sticky, tan-colored bar.

"I'm fine," Griff said. "Did you hear what I said, about
Jonesy?"

"Just rest," Thomas said. "Get something in your stomach."

K.T., a girl was saying. Her voice choppy in the fan blades.

"Yes, yes—" Thomas said.

Thomas was gone again. Griff tried to sit with a head full of cement. He lay down and let his eyes flutter, listening to the fan. White noise, softer than the radio. All frequencies of sound. A million voices at once. And the voices came together on—

Griff-griff-griff-griff-griff—

"Griff."

He stared at the fan.

"Griff!"

"Yeah? Yeah?" His head, wobbly.

A man in a shemagh entered the tent. Military facial covering.

They'd come for him. He knew that walk anywhere. Jonesy. They'd take him away—Griff bolted up and the man unwrapped his facial covering. Malachi.

"Oh my god," Griff said. "I thought I was getting abducted."

"Sorry, brother," Malachi said. "K.T. told me to find you here."

"K.T.?"

"Kissing Thomas," Malachi said. "Take it easy. Eat the bar and we'll go for a walk."

"Where?"

Malachi's eyes slipped off to the side.

"We've got a visitor," Malachi said. "I think someone's looking for you."

SIXTY-FIVE

IN THE HEAT, A TWENTY-MINUTE WALK TOOK FORTY-FIVE.

The sun wrapped every inch of bare skin like hot cellophane. Hair curling. Smelled like toast. There were three patches of shade on the way, and they stopped at all of them. Breathing in the deep blue spaces. Drinking cool air.

"That sun can add 40 degrees," Malachi said. "Let's be wise."

At the mountain's edge, bouldering left them breathless. Scree, slippery. Griff turned his body into a machine. *Move*, he demanded of his legs. *Keep moving.* They paused partway. Griff leaned against the silver sandstone and heard his flesh sizzle. He dribbled water on the burn.

"Don't waste water," Malachi said.

Near the top, a crack in the mountain's flank gaped like a half smile. A decorative silver fish had been painted near the opening. Bright eyes. Sad lips.

"The Snookout," Malachi said. "This is where I nailed your drone."

They pressed into the cool wash of shade. He could breathe. In the deepest pit of shadow, a cache of equipment. Malachi cleared a space for Griff to sit, and the two of them tucked into the viewing area.

"Pretty sweet," Griff said.

"Yes it is. Want a look?" Malachi asked, offering the binoculars.

"Got my own," Griff said. He took out his monocular.

"You military?" Malachi asked.

"Prepper," Griff said.

"What's a prepper?"

"Like a Doomsday Boy Scout," Griff said.

"Ah, doomsday preppers," Malachi said. "Wow. Never met one in the wild. Take a gander. This is what's got Simon worried."

The car was immediately obvious. Regardless of its markings, it moved the way every cop drives everywhere. Like a breezy little shark with the biggest teeth in the ocean. Griff turned the dial, crisping up his focus. No sticker on the front bumper. Not a car from Clade City.

"Prepper, huh?" Malachi said. "What finally gets us, you think? Nuclear attack? Bigger, badder pandemic? Natural disaster?"

"Hopefully not this asshole," Griff said.

"Shoot," Malachi laughed. "He's getting close. See those shrubs? That's our access road. We don't want him there."

"What can we do?"

"Well. I got the jammer from yesterday. And the Imp Cannon."

"What?"

"Electromagnetic pulse," he said. "Everything out here gets a new name."

From the elevated position, Griff could just make out the white trail snaking through shrubs around a shoulder of stone. Malachi took out the device. Telescoping pieces and two battery packs. He had quick, practiced hands. On the barrel's tip, someone had affixed little felt ears. Hand-painted: IMP CANNON.

"Do you know how to work it?" Griff asked.

"I do," Malachi said. "But that's an officer of the law. I'll go ahead and let you do the honors, Captain Tripp. Not going to stop him unless he's a robot."

"It might stop the car," Griff said.

Maybe, this far from civilization, it would be enough to scare him off. The police car stopped a moment. Griff adjusted his monocular. The officer was pulling out a pair of binoculars, twin glasses flashing.

"Down," Griff said.

They ducked into the dark, breathing hard. A soft rumble in the air. The squad car was moving again. Griff adjusted his grip on the EMP. Braced it against his shoulder.

"Is it warmed up?" he asked.

"Not quite." Malachi tapped Griff's paracord. He flinched. "What's that?"

"Nylon paracord. A prepper thing."

"You play piano, right?"

"Yeah," Griff said. "I actually saw one earlier today. I'd love to find it."

Malachi raised his eyebrows.

"The piano?" Malachi said. "Talk about scary."

"What?"

"You're armed."

The battery pack felt warm against his burn. Griff reminded himself the EMP would not hurt the officer. Just a pause button. Buy a little time. Griff squinted the monocular into his left eye. The car beetled along. Griff led his target by a few yards and pressed the button. *Zwoop*, like an old arcade game, vaporizing an alien.

The car shuddered, stopped.

"Oh dang! That's the business right there," Malachi said. "Ha!"

High five, and the car grunted.

NNnnnn Nnnnnn

The door banged open. The officer was wiry, broad shoulders. He looked around. Took his phone out. Shook his phone. Threw his phone in the sand.

"Oooo he's pissed," Malachi said. "You know that guy?"

"No," Griff said. "Thank god."

The officer tried his car again. Malachi and Griff slipped down into the shadows, giggling. It felt fun. Like they'd just toilet-papered a house together.

Eventually, the car's engine fired. A roaring sound.

The cruiser only got a few miles away. Stopped again. A small blot in the landscape.

"Car trouble, Officer?" Malachi said.

"I hope he can get out okay," Griff said.

"I'll radio Simon," Malachi said. "He'll send someone to check on him."

"What time's the show tonight?" Griff asked.

"After sundown," Malachi said.

Malachi put the call into Simon, who told them to stay put and out of sight. They waited another hour. Using Malachi's Bug Detector, they got only one ping. A drone, 3 miles away.

"See?" he said. "Too sensitive for its own good."

They stayed in the shade, talking music, survival gear, discussing the potential fate of the officer, debating tonight's playlist.

"They'll never play that one," Malachi said. "You're dreaming."

"Damn. Can you tell me what the shows are like?" Griff asked.

"Your first night," he said. "You've got to see for yourself."

The alarm cheeped and Malachi grinned.

"Five fifteen. Quittin' time!"

Slipping out of the cavern, Griff anticipated the slap of sun-light, but shadows of the narrow enclosure stretched like gray taffy. The sky had grown hazy and dimmed to slate.

"That's a relief," Griff said, looking through his monocular. "The cop's gone."

"Hmmm," Malachi said. "Never seen that before."

"Clouds?" Griff asked.

"No," he said. "That."

On top of Simon's tower, the light was blinking blue.

SIXTY-SIX

IN THE PATHS, FINDING FRIENDS WAS LIKE CATCHING A SONG.

Without phones or reliable plans, you listen to the crowd's white-noise buzz, adjust focus like a radio dial. Griff twisted hard at a pizza place called the Boondoggle, right at a counter labeled Liquid Sunshine. Closer. He could almost feel her. Then her heard his own name in the noise:

"Griff!"

Charity.

She tore loose from the group and came barreling into him like they'd been shipwrecked—lost for generations. He spun her three full times. Could spin her forever. She tucked herself against his neck. Her lips brushed his ear.

"Where have you been?" she asked.

"Shhhh-curity," Malachi said. He popped his collar. "We're classy-fied."

"What about you?" Griff asked.

"Keeping the water flowing," Charity said. She turned her palm to the sky. "Which may not be a problem."

The group caught up, clustered around them.

"Is it actually going to rain?" Griff asked.

"Fifty-fifty," Thomas said. "Let's flip a coin."

"Let's not," Griff said. "You brought the rat?"

"Neapolitan wanted a night out!" Thomas said, lifting the carrier. "Everyone loves a guy with a pet."

"Rat pets?" Charity said.

"There are some straight-up weirdos out here, Charity," Thomas said. "Just like me."

He put on the mirrored sunglasses, and they walked.

Lights blazed in booths and lean-tos. The show-night party mood was revving up with drinks and hoots and laughter. Charity held his arm, his whole arm, miraculous to have her holding a whole arm—

"How long are you all going to stay?" Stitch asked.

"Forever," Thomas said.

Griff looked at Thomas. Was he serious? Griff assumed they'd head back sometime tomorrow after the show. But this was Thomas. He had the car. And where would they head back to?

They rounded a wide corner. Lanterns gilded the sunken avenues in amber. A guitar and a fiddle tuned up in a wooden loft above. In front of them, a man stopped his bicycle. He was towing a small coffin. Inside the coffin, a stand-up bass. A person wearing bunny ears and a rodent mask stopped to help him. Everywhere, suddenly, people were wearing masks.

"How long do you want to stay?" Griff whispered to Charity.

"At least until the show," Charity said. "And the lagoon."

Griff looked at the sky, afraid to ask: What if they postponed the show? Would the Band play tomorrow? Or would they hide out another month? Should they have a plan?

"Hey, Rumblefish," Griff asked. "What time is the show?"

"Noodles!" Rumblefish screamed.

The plan was noodles.

Nobody was talking about the show. All off-ramping to the Naughty Noodle, which smelled great. Fresh, steaming odors of crushed basil and pine nuts, juicy green olives popping in the pan oil, cackling at the names: The Devil's Got Angel Hair,

F-U-Silly Pesto, Curry Some Flavor—and when Griff picked up his plate of bright green corkscrew pasta, Charity had vanished in the crowd.

Griff found a small wooden stump and sat to eat. Noodles, slippery with butter and fresh pesto. Small nuggets of hard cheese, garlic, my god. Griff ate and watched a guy in a fedora sweeping the back kitchen of the Naughty Noodle. A lady with a tight, short mohawk approached and watched him. She unslung her guitar and played a magic lick along to the beat of the broomcorn.

Griff knew the song. A perfect song. It played to the memory of his parents pulling the car over to dance, him and Leo rolling their eyes from the backseat. They'd really done that!

"'Harvest Moon'!" Rumblefish screamed. He came rushing in with his dobro. More musicians arrived on the scene like EMTs trained to make sure the moment kept its pulse.

And there was Charity. Across a sea of arms, legs, heads, elbows in a red dress, and would she dance?

The whole crowd loved her. The whole world.

He should ask her to dance. They'd come to the desert together. Cuddlenapped. And when he pictured the person walking confidently through the crowd and taking her hand, he still could not see himself. He saw Leo.

Griff forced himself to move. Like when he tried to go to her window. Moving forward, retreating—maybe she wanted a moment alone—maybe she wanted to dance with someone else—and finally when the song was two verses deep he was close enough.

"What took you so long?" she said.

She stood and her body came against his. Electric awareness. Breasts against his chest. She moved his hand to the place where waist became hip. It felt obscene, remarkable. They were here with hundreds, kicking up the same dirt, and they were alone.

"I never once expect you to say yes," he said.

"I don't know how else to show you," she said.

"I know," he said. "I—"

"What else?" she said. "Whatever poem you've got rattling in your head—say it."

"Oh," he said.

"No one else can hear you," she sang softly, imitating his warm-up song. "Charity loves your voice."

He bit his lip. Breathing.

"Sing it, boy," she whispered in his ear.

"I don't love anything like I love you," he said.

She hummed. "Mmm. What else?"

"I feel like we've been singing together since before we were born."

She hummed more, along with his words.

"I miss the music," she said. "I miss your ear."

She took his earlobe between her teeth, tugged gently. He jerked upright, laughed.

"There's a piano in the desert," he said.

"Mmm," she said. "Let's get it."

The song was almost over.

"One more time!" Rumblefish told the band. Ah! Sweet miracle! And Rumblefish deserved every good thing and any sum of money, the best possible life forever for playing "Harvest Moon" one more time.

She pressed her body against him. His hand pulled the small of her back, harder. A soft grind. He wanted her so badly he laughed—didn't know what to do. The laughter just shook out.

"Good, huh?" she whispered. She kissed his neck. Then the song was over, maybe had been over. She was laughing too.

"Okay," she said. "The Band."

"Right," Griff said. "The Band."

Thomas, Stitch, and Alea plowed into their group like a rudderless boat, well sloshed. Stitch was drinking from what looked like a giant tin can.

"Where's the party?" Stitch asked.

"Shouldn't we get to the stage?" Griff asked.

"Don't worry," Malachi said. "There will be an announcement."

"They chirp, right?" Thomas said. "Like—*Che-che-chirrup!*"

Thomas made a strange, squirrelly sound in his throat and people looked in their direction.

Others took up the call:

Che-che-chirrup!

Che-che-chirrup!

"Nope!" Malachi said, waving his arms. "K.T.! No false alarms!"

"Sorry," Thomas said.

"We've got an hour," Malachi said. "Maybe two."

"We drink!" Stitch said.

"What about the piano?" Griff said.

"Well," Stitch said.

"Yes," Charity said.

"Piano!" Rumblefish screamed. "Exactly, fucking exactly perfect what we need to do right now. Find the Bagman. It's written in the sky—"

Hooting, Rumblefish led them to the ladder.

Bagman?

"Maybe he won't be there," Stitch said.

They kept talking—he's always there—as Griff climbed the rungs to the top of the plateau. Thomas followed. As the first to the top, they were the first to see it. Beyond the blinking blue light of Simon's tower. A dark boil of clouds, churning over mountains. The rest of the group collected around them.

"You know what they call that in Australia?" Thomas said. "The black layer of sky that rolls out like a fuck-you pirate flag at the front of a storm?"

"Don't ask him," Griff said.

"What?" Rumblefish asked.

"The Razor's Edge," Thomas said, looking them over. Raising an eyebrow.

"Oh god," Griff said.

"Not coincidentally, the name of AC/DC's twelfth studio album. The opening track has played at every single live show since its release."

As they walked, thunder clapped. A flash of light scribbled through clouds.

"Turn back?" Charity asked.

"No," Griff said. "Walk faster."

SIXTY-SEVEN

THE NIGHT HAD A NEW, WILD FLAVOR.

As if the flash of light had cut a slit in the sky's dark curtain. A thrown-open door to somewhere new. Fresh gusts carried the gratifying tang of ozone, the muddy breath of a river.

"That storm smell!" Charity said.

"Water," Griff said.

A long crackle of thunder like a log broken over a giant's knee. They howled back at it.

"OwwwowwwOOOWWWW!"

The ancient song tore out through their chests and the group went spinning out across the dunes, whirling like autumn leaves. At the next thunderclap, Griff counted the seconds. *One, two, three* . . . Wet his finger in his mouth and checked the direction of the wind. *Thirteen, fourteen—*

Lightning. A hot pop of broken tungsten.

The flash glazed the mountains in silver and clutched the clouds with sudden light. Dark and scalloped, overfull bellies scraping mountaintops about 3 miles away. Gusts blowing hard in a favorable direction. Maybe they'd be okay. Thomas predicted otherwise:

"It was their last night on Earth!" he declared, throwing his arms up in a V.

KABOOM!

"Stop," Stitch said. "You're scaring your rat."

In the swinging carrier, Neapolitan was pacing, sniffing at the window. Hairless paws clutching the door.

"This way!" Rumblefish shouted, windmilling his arms.

"Hear that?" Charity asked.

The wind heaved itself across the sand and carried the soft chime of scattered notes.

"Piano," Griff said.

A modern-sounding composition. He couldn't quite pick it out. Their scattered group coalesced into a steady line. Like a march. A forever climb up the dune and so Griff started jogging, lifting his knees. It felt suddenly urgent. The wind might catch the piano's lid like a sail, carry it over the horizon.

"You're fast when you're nervous," Charity said.

"Just want to get there," Griff said.

The piano was louder now, discernible notes. It had the warmth of a grand. Perfect string tension. Very close. Just over this dune.

Griff and Charity were in the lead.

"They're good," Griff said.

Maybe one player. Maybe two. The playing was that fast.

The last slippery footsteps—Griff considered how awful it would be, to finally reach the instrument and find two players at the bench. How it would, in a sense, be the worst thing he could imagine.

Cresting the top of the dune, he saw it.

"Impossible," he whispered.

A nine-foot Steinway concert grand. The most beautiful instrument conjured by the patient hand of mankind. And a big crowd. The small basin between dunes had been arranged like a plush living room. Lanterns hung from hunks of driftwood, dangled from uprooted trees. Red knots of fabric tied like raspberry drupelets, throwing red splotches on the sand.

The player sounded skilled. But too fast. He played like he was running out of time.

Griff looked more closely and froze.

The player was clothed and masked with burlap. Ripped holes for eyes. Where a mouth should be, crude stitching. Pinkish hands fluttered from ragged cuffs.

"What's that?" Griff breathed.

"Bagman," Rumblefish said, catching his breath.

A hand clutched Griff's shoulder and he jumped. Turned to see Thomas, his lips outlined in purple.

"Griff," Thomas said softly. "Do you see that? A man in burlap playing piano like Maserati?"

"You mean Mozart?" Griff asked. "Or Liberace?"

"I mean a fucking burlap suit with eyeholes," Thomas said. "Yes."

"We'll never get him off the bench," Stitch said.

"We need to hear Griff play," Rumblefish said, holding Griff's shoulder.

"This guy doesn't take turns," Stitch said.

Bagman finished the piece with a one-handed flourish. The crowd applauded.

"This is a concert," Griff said. "I can't interrupt."

"No," Rumblefish said. "There's only one piano in the desert. It belongs to all of us."

The Bagman started a new piece. He stood. Put a knee on the piano bench. Lengthening his arm, he reached into the guts of the piano. Mashed the wires.

"Is that legal?" Stitch said.

"It's 'Black Earth,'" Griff exhaled. "That's how you play the piece."

Together, the group moved down the dune. The piece sounded like a hollow, ticktock jangle interrupted by brief, percussive bursts. The crowd noticed them. Turning heads and chatter. When they reached the low, flat center of the performance space, Bagman was hunched over the piano, hands on exposed wires, elbow jerking.

"We'll come with you," Charity said.

A small contingent of them inched forward—Thomas, Stitch, Charity, Rumblefish, and Griff. The rest of the group hung back. Griff took a few more steps, standing separate from the audience now. Hanging in the liminal space between spectator and performer. As if slowly approaching a nonexistent tip jar.

"One step at a time," Rumblefish said.

"I'll just ask him for one song," Griff said. "That's it."

Bagman played harder. The closer they got, the more he pounded. Hammers crashing, rent edges of fabric fluttering at his wrists, Griff wondered how that felt, and touched his own wrists. When the Bagman stopped, the great instrument's soundboard shuddered. Applause.

"Do you want me to come?" Charity asked.

"I got it," Griff said.

Bagman suddenly looked up.

Ragged eyeholes. Griff half expected buttons for pupils. Dark mirrors. But the Bagman's eyes were very much alive in their cloth caves. The crowd held the silence.

Griff stepped forward. Suddenly he and the Bagman were quite close. The man's arms hung loose at his sides. Long fingers trailing shredded cuffs. Bare feet.

Griff's hands were itchy.

"Can I play one?" Griff asked.

The Bagman stared back at him. He breathed beneath burlap. Lungs, a heart, and all the parts of a human. Why couldn't he respond? He tilted his shoulders a bit, moved over on the bench. Making room.

"I meant," Griff said, "could I play my own piece?"

He was still. Griff turned back toward his friends, far away. Thomas signed to him:

Want to leave?

DA DUN!

Griff's knees shook. He turned back to face the Bagman.

The crowd hooted and clapped. Seeming to feed on the applause, Bagman raised a hand. Again, his finger pounced on C-sharp.

DA DUN!

Sharp, clean notes rang out.

For Griff, the paracord was just instinct.

A snap calculation of the body. He could not play his best with it on, and he could afford nothing less than his best. He unclasped the piece of durable plastic that held the bracelet halves in place and turned to his friends. He chose Stitch. Standing out front, beaming confidence. She had no idea what it meant. He removed it. Removed his black security band. He threw both to Stitch and rubbed his plain, smooth wrists.

DA DUN!

"You know this one!" Thomas shouted.

Yes. First at camp. Then low through the drywall. Rattling panes in French doors. The unmistakable shave-and-a-haircut summons of the four-hands duet. Griff knew exactly what it meant.

The Bagman slid over.

Showtime.

SIXTY-EIGHT

THE CROWD LOST THEIR MIND. UNGLUED FROM THE DUNE, THEY sprang up clapping. The world narrowed to the remaining steps to the instrument. Griff paid attention to his own breath. Hushed the audience into static.

Tune the dial. Focus.

Griff stood beside the bench and the man in burlap.

There are certain things you know about a player before they touch the keys. Bench position, hand position, the way they turn toward the audience. Set of their shoulders. Griff had seen the Bagman play two pieces. He was aggressive. Impatient. Trying to prove something.

DA DUN!

How would they proceed? There were three major varieties of four-hands literature for Hungarian Rhapsody No. 2, but Bagman was only playing the two Cs, which meant the next set of notes belonged to Griff. This ruled out the Ricordi, or the simplified Bendel composition—no, this would be the Hand Smasher—the Potestani—the version he and Leo had chosen, with full-fingered pyrotechnics and unfettered dynamism—

DA DUN!

Griff exhaled his wild, fluttering panic. Inhaled—

Potestani.

Inflexible and mathematical in the portioning. The piano

split straight down middle C, which meant the players must sit very close.

Bagman left Griff less than half the bench. Too far forward. He sat. The crowd howled. Wooden legs creaked in the sand.

Bagman looked at him with damp brown eyes. Not pools. Not pits. Eyes. Pounding blood flexed fists in Griff's temples. Did he know him? Heart valves and flaps, open and shut:

Boom boom

Thunder. Wind carried the Bagman's scent. Sweet and sour like spoiled milk. Burlap brushed Griff's arm. Itchy. Wanted to scratch—

DA DUN!

And this time—*DUN! DUN!*

Griff answered with his own two chords.

The audience erupted, and the piece began. Griff and Bagman played together. Slipped into the opening bars sloppy, Griff dropping notes. One. Another. He tried to stomp a pedal and the Bagman's bare foot mashed his ankle—

Griff jerked to the side.

Bagman played impatiently. Snapped at the keys.

From the top of the dune he'd looked like a perfect devil, but up close—he made mistakes. Staccato when the piece called for legato. Hammering notes like nails into wood. Never a miss, exactly, but it was not exquisite piano, merely perfect piano. More Morse code than music.

They danced their way through the first half of the piece. The gentle *lassan*. Building toward the next chapter—the turbulent, cavorting, finger-blasting *friska*, which could crush any pianist on a bad night—their hands leapt and sprawled and pressed toward the piece's second half, rumbling like a waterfall in the near distance—

Coming—it's coming, then—

Griff!

Friends shouting his name as he and Bagman tumble over the cliffside in a barrel together—the *friska*! Bagman leaps middle C, steals a note. An entire arpeggio!

The crowd screams and Griff hammers an octave on Bagman's side of the keys they are moving 40,000 miles per hour and the cheering grows and it's messy and wild, Bagman's fingers knock his knuckles and the tempo snaps at their heels, metronome cleaving too close, they must KEEP PLAYING feet mashing pedals and the piano bench tips—

Backward, hits the sand and they're standing now, side by side, this wild burlap creature, and he makes the mistake of glancing over, seeing him with eyes, no mouth—

Griff drops a chord.

Bagman is going too fast now, taking the wheel, hijacking the piece, of course Griff is behind, of course he loses, of course he's LATE, hands are tired and Bagman knows Griff cannot win—

Then it's coming.

He's come this far and it's coming like a highway on the downslope of an axle-breaking mountain road, no brakes and still coming—the off-ramp to improvisation, the exit to As You Desire, At Your Pleasure—

CADENZA—

As You Wish.

And as Bagman grips the piece to steer it safely to The End, Griff pulls the whole shaking, wild thing off the page. He will not stop. Will not quit. Must speak and his hands this time say YES and Bagman cannot stop him because the song belongs to whoever has the courage to take it and Griff leaves Liszt's elegant notes with all the grace of tires trading asphalt for gravel—

THUD—

His own cadenza—never done, but allowed by the music, and Griff hears himself in need of a lifetime of work, but the Bagman cannot know the notes because the song now belongs to Griff and the Bagman is standing. Stepping back and my god, Griff is playing! Bare wrists light and soaring over all eighty-eight keys, playing, playing, playing and it's over—

Cheers. They come to him, his new friends.

And Charity. Mostly, Charity. Charity says I'm so proud of you, and has anyone ever been proud? The way she holds him, the crowd, the eyes and hands and bodies around him, telling him again, like they've told him from the start:

You are loved. You belong.

For a weightless moment, he believes them.

SIXTY-NINE

THE BUGGIES CAME QUICKLY, IN A STORM OF PALE DUST.

Griff was only halfway through his first solo piece—Charity had not yet sung. The vehicles overtopped the dune in a blaze of lamplight, disturbing the crowd. A man walked from the haze, ahead of the others. He wore a broken-in cowboy hat adorned with a red feather. The man he'd seen leading the charge that morning.

"So sorry," he said with a slight bow. "We're going to need that piano."

"What?" Griff asked. "I just started."

"I can tell you," the Cowboy said, pursing his lips, "I would love nothing more than to see you with this piano. Right, boys?"

The tone reminded Griff of his father, about to give a consequence. Two men in his crew nodded supportively.

"Can we just do one song?" Charity asked.

"Breaking my heart," the Cowboy said. "This Steinway here is a damn fine instrument, but not at all waterproof. Orders from Simon."

Other men fanned around the instrument with tools. One with a double-braid rope hung in the crook of his arm.

"So no show tonight?" Griff asked.

The cowboy shrugged. This wasn't right. He'd won the piano.

Two men gently closed the lid. They unfurled a large blue tarp. It sheeted out to the wind. Charity shook her head.

"The storm is moving the other way," Thomas said. "The piano will be fine."

"Can't we say no?" Charity asked.

"We say yes," Stitch said. "We say yes and we go to the lagoon."

Lagoon! Lagoon!

Like Mirror, Mirror, like the mention of noodles, another desert spell had been cast.

The idea seized hold of the crowd and they were moving again—their whole existence, shifting like the dunes. Moments bloomed with firecracker suddenness, just as quickly gone to ash. The crowd dispersed. Many came with them, toward the lagoon. Charity grabbed his hand. Strangers gave compliments like gifts:

You did it, blew me away, you're amazing, man, are you in a band, want a drink?

Griff didn't know how to respond, but he took the drinks.

Time slipped. Maybe 2 miles later, the distant roar of the buggies rumbled behind them. He couldn't tell where the piano was headed. The drinks tasted good. The dunes smoothed down to flat earth. The brush softened to shrubs and desert trees reached for the moon with their bent, pineapple logic. Air thickened with the pulp of clay.

Ahead, dancing in the tops of trees with leaves, the refractive glint of water.

"Almost there," Stitch said.

This idea of swimming, Griff hadn't fully considered. What underwear did he have on?

"What about the show?" Griff asked.

"Don't worry," Stitch said. "It'll happen or it won't."

Won't?

Thomas ran by in his underwear. His feet made wet little slaps.

"That's one eager beaver," Stitch said.

Would there be magic communal swimsuits, like the clothing at Mirror, Mirror? Did he remember how to swim? Griff looked at his wrist.

"The bracelet," Griff said. "Stitch, can I have it back?"

Stitch looked at him blankly.

"The black-and-white paracord I threw you? Before I played?"

"Ri-ight," Stitch said. "I gave that to—Alea?"

"Is that a question?"

"I gave that to Alea because, you see, it seemed important. And I am hammered. I was ready to hit on that cowboy for godsakes. That's like, Stockholm or some kind of syndrome—"

"Moon rising!" Rumblefish yelled.

From behind him, a half dozen naked bodies. Running. Parts moving in ways Griff had never seen parts move. Bouncing, swaying, and seven naked butts in the moonlight looking very cute and entirely spectacular and he laughed again.

"This can't be real," Griff said.

He came from a clothed family. This did not happen.

"Just remember," Stitch said, "This is as real as anything else."

Stitch pulled off her shirt. A white bra with sunflowers, and this time Griff did not whip his head to look elsewhere—and he saw her scar. Jagged, puckered skin from spine to hip bone. A deep cut.

Griff drew a sharp breath.

"That's real too," Stitch said. She touched it. "I'm not shy about it here. I walk around with that thing all day."

Griff took off his jacket. His shirt. In solidarity, he felt like he should. Boots. He stuffed his socks inside. Bare feet on mush. Soft and quaggy. Now this was real—him walking publicly in gray underwear. Wearing the backpack felt strange, so he carried it.

They approached a low-slung canopy of trees.

Another herd of naked runners. Bobbing away like white-tailed deer. All singing a song from the Band:

Rush away, the water here gets thirsty too—

"Surreal," Griff said.

"Shouldn't be," Stitch said. "There are only two sure reasons we're all here. To sing and get naked."

They parted dangling willows and stepped onto sun-warmed stone, contoured like an elephant's back. Griff followed Stitch's dim form through the trees. Water. Laughter. Griff clutched his clothing to his chest.

Through gaps in green, he saw the lagoon.

Moonlight blazed in a half dozen emerald pools clustered around a massive central crater. Sprawling, spectacular. Everyone naked. In the water, splashing, laughing—so naked. Plain to see. A full moon is subtle as a spotlight.

Thomas tripped, removing his underwear.

"Whoopsie doodles!"

Dozens of bodies, all kinds—more bodies than Griff had imagined seeing in a lifetime and—my god, gorgeous humanity! The bodies, surprisingly beautiful. So many shapes and shades and sizes and ages and it should've been terrifying, mortifying—but it wasn't. It was a complete thrill.

A giggly, campfire feeling. Like everyone telling the same secret at the same time.

Charity in underwear.

"Hey," she said, walking toward him. Very slim blue bra, blue underwear. This was different. Every cell at attention.

Griff remembered the clay underfoot, soft, squishy, keep calm. His gray underwear would not tolerate any display of excitement. He tried to distract himself. Azure bra. Cerulean bra.

"Glad you waited," she said, standing close.

Careful.

He had not been swimming since October. His wrist was bare, which was wrong but a burning engine of YES in his chest and Charity in underwear, reflected in the lagoon. His own mirrored face settled in the water—mouth, nose, eyes—stop!

Griff shoved his foot in the reflection, disrupting the image.

"How's the temperature?" Charity asked.

"Amazing," Griff said.

"Going all the way?" Charity asked.

This wildness. The part of Charity he'd glimpsed in practice room 5, coming out to play. Like the moment just before he'd felt her teeth, nipping the lobe of his ear.

"Ready?" she asked, reaching behind her back. Bra strap.

He'd never even seen Charity in her bra. Light blue bands scooping just above her nipples and the thinnest straps holding the fabric between her thighs, red alert, blood rush—

"Let's a play a game," she said.

"Okay," he said.

"The game is: Maintain eye contact."

She removed her bra. Let it drop.

Impressions of color and curves. Unfair. My god.

"Good job," she said.

She bent, looking up at him, and pulled off her underwear.

She stood. Her eyes held his eyes like two chained dogs.

"Okay," she said. "Your turn."

Now he needed to move. How does one gracefully expose a penis? Sad turtle or angry missile—so rarely just right, he couldn't tell what was happening down there. She would not look anyway, then—*whoopsie doodles*—stomping his under-wear into wet stone and standing. The air felt strange over his whole body. Tingling.

Charity looked down. She smiled.

"Well."

"Hey!" Griff said.

"I lose," Charity said.

She turned and leapt into the water. A glimpse of her—a hot flash of a vision he'd keep forever and he leapt in naked and the fresh water grabbed hold of him.

His whole body woke up alive.

A scissor kick, limbs gliding through water tickly smooth graceful and the sudden revelation we are not primates, reptiles—WE ARE FISH! Ha! Death Valley was once a salty sea, and we are fish! Bare in the water, like being unzipped from more than clothing—you could escape the whole trap of humanity. An erasure of self. He followed Charity's bare body through the blue. They dipped beneath a stone bridge and sur-faced in a wider pool, dozens of swimmers. A group, singing—

Where we go, we go together—

We can't stop the race—

And Griff knew the words. Could feel them tingling in his skin. The water felt conductive, carrying the refrain.

You belong, you belong—

"How can a swimsuit make such a difference?" Charity asked.

It was true. A tiny piece of cloth, blocking out so much—worse than a blindfold. We are fish trapped in tiny bowls and stuffed into clothes and ah, This Aching Life!

Someone called his name. He followed Charity.

Pulled his body through the water, as far and fast as he could go—then gone!

Charity vanished.

Feet flashing, she dipped beneath a curve in the stone. More calling:

Griff!

No! He laughed. He'd hide! Treading water, he brushed the stone with his toes. He held his breath, went down, probed the rock, and—there! A hole! The mouth of a tunnel!

You could get trapped. Suffocate.

Big yellow signs with stick figures—

Griff filled his lungs with air and went under.

Chest tightening, he pulled himself against the rock, felt for the opening. Two hard downstrokes and he was inside, moving headfirst through darkness. Stone ceiling. He swallowed hard, pawed his way toward trembling light. He kicked, pulled at the water, looked up. A blue oval wobbled and within it, a body. Charity pedaling water. Blood rushed. He kicked hard, broke the surface, and her eyes were wild, hair wet and plastered to cheeks, and they were alone in a small stone room. Moonlight spilled through cracks in the stone.

"You made it," Charity said.

"Had to," he said.

She hummed a bar of the first melody they ever played together. They were inside of a song. She reached out, touched his bare shoulders.

He touched her shoulders and water stirred when she got close. She pulled him close. He pulled her closer. His hands, alive in a new way. Her skin pressed against his, the fullness of her body and her lips, a trembling universe.

Kissing like breathing.

Music without words.

SEVENTY

SOMEHOW, ALL THAT TIME LATER—THEY WERE STILL CALLING Griff's name.

The words came to him faintly, drifting through thick air.

Griff pulled away from Charity like he was nudging backward into the world—they'd been wrapped in each other, a top spinning slow and fast on the dark glass of time, tilting, sparking, and the dizzy hum of it shook deep in his chattering bones. Her eyes, full of awe and wonder and him, brimming with the question HOW?—how could there be so much pleasure, just narrowing the space between bodies?

Every droplet of water was alive.

He laughed. Laughter fit here. The sound ricocheted and Charity laughed and he dipped beneath the water, passed through the blackout tunnel, back to the world. He gave a kick and exploded to the surface.

"Griff!"

How long had they been gone? The sky was clear. No sign of the storm.

Thomas was out of the water, prowling around naked.

"There he is," Malachi said.

"Thought we lost you," Stitch said. They smiled, treading water.

"Is the show starting?" Griff asked.

"No, no," Malachi said. "Simon wants you to check in. I put the radio with your clothes."

"Okay," Griff said.

His stomach churned. What was Thomas doing? Griff swam closer.

"Thomas!"

Thomas was shaking his head. Picking up pants, putting them down. Griff swam until his toes touched and he could stand. Water hugged his waistline. Thomas pattered over, biting his lip. Looking embarrassed.

"Just need to find—" Thomas began.

Wait.

"Did Stitch give you my bracelet?"

"What? No." Thomas shook his head. Whispered. "It's Neapolitan."

"You lost your rat?" Griff asked.

"Shhhh," Thomas said. "Let's not incite panic. It's not like her. She chewed through her case."

Griff pulled himself onto shore. His clothing and the backpack were right over there, actually. Just below those palm fronds that sloped like a pair of mad eyebrows and—

No clothes. But that was the place.

"Missing something?" Rumblefish asked.

A whole group had paddled over.

"Oh my," Alea said. "It's almost as if your clothes are no longer in the place you so carefully put them."

Charity laughed.

"Look at that bod, though!" Stitch said.

Griff turned toward them and reared back with a howl.

Did he do that? He did. They howled back. It was wonderful.

"We'll give you hints," Stitch said. "Brrrr. Chilly."

Griff continued walking left.

"Freezer, bro," Rumblefish said. "Ice truck."

He turned right.

"Warmer," they said. "Oooh, smoking."

Laughter felt so good, the steady purr of it.

He ran his tongue along the backs of his lips, which felt thin and pleasantly raw from kissing. Would they kiss again? He felt gently held by the air. Warm desert wind, happy exhausted body. Smells of stone and desert mud.

Griff stepped up and pushed through a brittle curtain of shrubs. Farther up, a small clearing. And his clothes! Neatly folded. On top of his pack, someone had placed a little white flower. He took a deep breath—held it in his chest until it throbbed like a breath he'd been holding since October. His eyes found the moon.

"Ooooooooooowwwww!!"

Release. In the distance, new friends howled back. Like they'd always be there.

Please don't end, he thought. Please never end. Still a show. Still Charity. Still a thousand paths to explore and brilliant strangers to meet. Griff felt his toes curling around the edge of the next big something. The whole runway of the night and the rest of his life spread out in front of him, naked in the moonlight and there, just a flickering rustle in the undergrowth and damp bristles brushed his ankle—

—tickling things from the bushes, small, writhing, darting. Thin tails whipping over toes flashing eyes rippling from the brush, dozens, hordes, a living carpet over the bare skin of his feet JUMP RUN LEAP—a skittering tide of fur claws tails teeth and rats rats rats.

SEVENTY-ONE

HIS FOOT CAME DOWN ON ONE—

—crunch, pop—

Bone-splitting and still naked, greasy-footed, leaping on a prickled stump gasping—sucking air to scream:

"Rats!"

Flooding the stump, a swarming, leaping river. Sunbaked desert kangaroo rats with black button eyes tumbling down the embankment toward the nude lagoon, little splashes *plip-pliplip* paddling bodies because rats can swim, hold their breath—

Screaming.

Rats pouring in *thupathupathupa* and Griff's inner stopwatch clicked START. Instinct activated. Underwear on, pants, shirt. Boots laced, mind tracking time, sniffing the air, accounting for wind speed. A deep part of him, waking up. Griff grabbed his backpack—a rat hopped with flashing eyes. He screamed. From the lagoon—more screaming, but the rats were not the thing to worry about.

A lumbering creature crashed at him through the thicket, bearing down. Griff leapt and twisted toward Naked Thomas.

"Shit, Thomas. I thought you were Sasquatch."

"See all those rats?" Thomas raised his eyebrows. "Something's up."

"You're a genius," Griff said. "Please put your pants on."

Charity appeared, clothed. A branch brushed against her neck. She shrieked and slapped it. Ripped it off. Shuddered.

"What's happening?" she said.

"Let's get out of the trees," Griff said.

The three of them slipped through the brush, descended the stone slope onto the white desert floor. Griff pressed his palms to the dust. To feel the earth shake, one sometimes needed to be still. He closed his eyes. Nothing. Above, a clear sky stretched all the way to the mountains. A distant, dark boil of clouds.

Griff's thoughts fumbled for the answer. The answer was a word. Too slippery to grab with all the drinks and adrenaline. He knelt to his backpack and removed the drone, began to unfold the wings.

A burly voice screamed *Rat!* but the rats had mostly gone and left them with a riddle.

He snapped on the propellers.

Where's the emergency?

The drone hovered with a needling buzz. A small crowd gathered. Looked up as the drone gained altitude, beacon blinking red. Griff drove it straight toward the mountains, in the direction the rats had come from.

"What is it?" Malachi asked, squatting beside him.

They watched the landscape reel past in the viewfinder.

"I hope nothing," Griff said.

The prickling in his skin knew better.

"Oh shoot," Malachi said.

He noticed the lights first. On a road a dozen or so miles away, a cluster of cars. Griff zoomed in.

"Police," he said.

A half dozen vehicles. Two marked cars, black-and-white with lights up top. The rest were trucks, SUVs. They were turning, moving out.

"They're coming," Griff said. He slowed the drone to a hover.

"Not that way, they aren't," Malachi said.

He was right. The cars were moving away from them. Retreating. Like the rats.

Griff adjusted the camera.

"Why are they leaving?" Griff asked.

He banked the drone left and descended into the farthest reaches of the Paths.

He flew 30, 40, 50 miles per hour. The presence of humans slowly vanished, like a time-lapse video. Man-made structures grew sparse, then decomposed, rotting down to driftwood bones, scrub, vast leagues of decay stretching mountainward. The drone's glass eye raced closer. Ahead, a pall of gray clouds smeared like charcoal.

Rain.

"Careful," Malachi said. "That wind will grab you."

Turbulence. The drone shook, up-down jerks. The mono-lithic black smudge sharpened to rainfall. Clarified droplets in torrents—sheeting out like square sails. Clouds' open throats pouring hard into natural grooves, worn by centuries. Water fell like a river from the sky and the word emerged with its slippery vowels:

"Arroyo," Griff said.

Because the desert had once been underwater. And it would be again.

"Shitballs," Thomas exhaled. "The Paths."

"What's an arroyo?" Malachi asked.

"A dry river," Charity said.

"Not for long," Griff said.

Clouds trembled with light. Griff amplified the camera's volume. A new signal, thrumming under the rain. Through the viewfinder, shadows leapt on low walls.

HhhhhssSKKKRRAKKKKSSSHHH

The sound of a waterfall, chewing.

"Pull up," Thomas said.

It rounded the corner with the shape of water, but it was not water.

"Pull up!"

A dead forest, tipped on its size. Crackling logs. Trunks. And the galloping wave swallowed everything. Behind wooden jaws, a muddy tail rushed and lashed. Overtook a boulder. It tumbled in the current like a buoy.

"How much time?" Thomas asked.

Griff lifted the drone. Pulled it even with the leading edge of debris.

It moved at 5 miles an hour, 10.3 miles away.

And they finally knew what the rats knew.

In two hours, everyone in the Paths would be dead.

SEVENTY-TWO

THEY HAD NO PHONES, NO SIRENS, NO MAPS, NO SIGNS, NO DRILLS, no flares, no protocol.

They only had two hours.

People gathered around Griff. Maybe because of what he was wearing. In a disaster, camouflage had the opposite of its intended effect. Everyone found you right away.

"Crisis statement," Thomas said, prompting him.

"Thousands die if we can't get them to higher ground," Griff said.

"Communication assets?"

"None," Griff said.

"We got walkie-talkies," Malachi said. "Simon. And the SandDogs. The ones in the buggies."

"You tell Simon what's up," Griff said. "Let me know what he says."

"Gotcha."

"So it's a flood?" Rumblefish said. "Can people swim it?"

"It's barely water," Griff said.

"We've got crews," Alea said. "They're organized. Hydras, SandDogs, Electrolytes—they'll take orders. We can use the lodestar routes for our gear—"

"I got Simon," Malachi said, handing him the walkie-talkie.

"Hey, team," Simon said, crackling through. "We've got to evacuate the Paths."

"Right," Griff said. "How?"

"Just tell them," Rumblefish said. "We just spread the word, right? Like with the shows."

Thomas grabbed his forehead, squeezed.

How could Griff explain? Clade City had a siren. Dozens of posted evacuation signs, wall-sized calling trees, portable shortwave radio cupboards, scores of volunteers, a Knock-for-a-Neighbor Program, and Mandatory Evacuation Squads, all because human beings could not, in any scenario, be trusted to move with the simple efficiency of rats.

"Maybe we offer them something," Malachi said. "An incentive."

"Food?" Rumblefish said. "Drugs?"

"Could that work?" Simon asked, crackling over the speaker.

"Pizza?" someone said. "Sex?"

They giggled. Losing seconds. Entire minutes. Griff froze, staring ahead.

A boy with dark hair wandered off, threw a green light-up toy in the air. These people had no idea. They would die. Screaming. Drowned. Bludgeoned to death by wood and stone. There would be funerals and heartbreak and lifetimes of aching and they could not conceive of it. A siren would sound like a party favor. Shouting *Flood!* under clear desert skies would get you a protein bar and a cot in the chillout tent.

"We need the SandDogs," Griff said. "Can we get them here?"

"Got it," Malachi said.

"What's the plan?" Thomas asked.

Two plans. Only one would work. An awful thought:

You won't save them all.

Griff pinched the skin on his wrist. Plan one: Scare them

into survival. Post guards at all ladders. Use headlights and horns and water if you need to. Do a sweep. Link arms, check every nook, every table, every corner and crevasse, and the ones who don't come, you drag out. Beat them out. Because to scare them is the way to save them.

"Captain Tripp?" Simon asked on the walkie-talkie.

The SandDogs came quickly, screaming engines and dust and diesel. They clambered out of their buggies in a plume of alkali. The crowd covered their mouths, coughing, and Cowboy arrived with his crew.

"Didja see all those rats?" Cowboy asked.

Plan two: Something Rumblefish said. Find something everyone in the desert wanted.

"Simon," Griff asked. He took the walkie-talkie. "Can you gather up the Band?"

"The Band?" Cowboy asked.

"The theater is on high enough ground," Griff said.

"Theater's cleared out for the night," Simon said.

"Can you just gather up a few members?"

He had no idea how many people were in the Band. No one would even tell Griff their name. Simon's voice hissed in the walkie-talkie—a sigh like, how do I explain?

"A show," Thomas said. "That could work."

"The shows take a while to get going," Malachi said.

"What if we play?" Charity said, grabbing Griff's arm. "You and me."

Others stepped back. They looked at her. Looked at Griff.

"I'll run sound," Thomas said.

"Everyone out here loves a show," Rumblefish said.

"Captain, my captain," Simon barked through the walkie-talkie. "Do we have a plan?"

No waiting.

"We need every crew leader to the lagoon," Griff said. "This will be Crisis Command. We stage assignments from here."

"Rock and roll," Simon said. "Let's follow Griff's lead."

One hour and forty minutes.

"What can I do?" Cowboy asked.

"I need you to bring the piano to Main Stage. Right now."

"Giddyup."

SEVENTY-THREE

THE VENUE WAS STUNNING. A NATURAL STONE-WALLED AMPHI-
theater in an elevated pocket canyon. The only way in was a
stone access tunnel no wider than 10 feet across. Delicate work
to trailer the piano through, and it took seven of them to lift
the Steinway onto the stage. The audience capacity was in the
thousands, but only a few dozen milled beneath the stars in
loose groups, talking, laughing.

Another engine boomed from the tunnel.

Headlights flickered, then emerged. The MoleMobile. It
rolled in fast, stopped sharp just short of the stage. Marilyn
flung herself out, cables crisscrossing her shoulders like bando-
liers. She lit up the sound boards, shoved cables into jacks. The
Mole dropped his stone feet onto dust and said:

"Thomas, we got your speaker rigged up."

"Great," Thomas said from the stage. "Marilyn, could you
light up microphone one?"

"It's hot," she said, thumbs up.

Thomas clapped his hands three times.

Beyond the tunnel, green light blazed.

The Eternal Encore. The cheer in the Paths was immediate—
a full-throated roar. It rolled around the amphitheater walls
like a wild boulder.

"People might come," Thomas said softly.

Toward the back of the stage, Marilyn yanked coverings from
racks of instruments: guitars, mandolins, banjos, a corner of

cajónes, bongos, bata drums, a towering fiddle shelf on wheels, rows of brass, woodwinds—how many of them were there?

Would the Band come?

Griff desperately hoped they would.

● ● ●

The Mole said it right before they started:

"No recording. No preserving."

His voice bounced around them. The crowd did not come suddenly, in a single great wave. They came steadily. Persistently. Poured into the amphitheater the way they described the flooding of Clade City in '64. Like a bathtub, slowly filling up with water.

Playing music with Charity, it felt like it was still their dance.

Their sacred place in the stone cave. Charity had never stopped singing. Never stopped building her gift bigger and brighter. Her voice rang clear against the tall stone walls of the amphitheater like it belonged there, mingling with the steady chirp of the incoming crowd:

Chi-chi-chirrup! Chi-chi-chirrup!

Griff let her drive the songs. She could hold the whole space. A giddy, nauseous adrenaline, trying to keep up. He punched through the false floor of how deep he could go. He talked out the last ten months of anguish through the keys and pedals of this glorious instrument—such power, like it might buck him off. He sounded better than he was.

The audience came running. Then someone leapt on stage. Griff froze and two more came—bolting for the instruments. Adrenaline made his legs shake. What to do? Charity just kept singing. More came up! Marilyn was not rushing them off.

When the song concluded, he hissed:

"Is that the Band?"

She shrugged.

"What do we do?" Griff asked.

They kept playing. The song they'd played at the Urchin, in which Charity sang like the wind. A prickling in his guts when they started, but her voice smoothed it all out. Beautiful. Better than before. Whole and rolling through the space, held aloft by the crowd's eyes and upturned faces and then a small group rushed the stage. Griff would not let this be ruined— he stood to defend the space but Thomas was on it. Leaping up. Going for—what? Their feet? Gently? He was setting up footer mics. Marilyn plowed up with a silver condenser mic on a stand and the couple peeled hair back from their faces. The group joined Charity's song.

Their song.

Their voices slipped in, a haunting counterpoint to the gale in Charity's voice, and Griff found himself bending along to the new voices. The sound of strings slipped in along with the soft brass of a horn, a cello. Charity carried them all, lifting her voice like wings, and the audience stopped chirping and began to roar. Their gathering had become a crowd and the song did not stop. It grew. Swelled around them until they were playing with ten or more. Maybe a dozen, and when Charity gave him the right look, Griff brought them to a thundering climax and the crowd made his ears ring.

"Amazing," Griff said to Charity. He was breathless. "We'd better go."

"Why?" she asked.

He looked around. Real musicians. Cocked hats and swagger. Their experience written firmly in their posture and the flash of their eyes.

"To make room for the Band," Griff said.

"Griff," she said. "We are the Band."

The crowd applauded. A Black man with a peacock-feathered hat winked at him, played a lick like—*c'mon then*. A girl with a shaved head rapped on her tom-toms, waiting for his cue. The sudden explanation for rotating singers and impossible ensembles. Every work song in the Paths had been a rehearsal. Lyrics painted on lean-tos and lofts, their sheet music. Like the piano, the stage here belonged to everyone. But beneath the audience, Griff heard the old song echo:

You don't belong.

He'd just wanted it so badly.

He looked at his hands on the keys. Bare wrist. His dim reflection in the fall board.

He'd rushed ahead again. Who would have to die this time, so he could be first?

Griff stood, and dropped down the front of the stage.

Still time to fix it. He kicked his way out, shouldering through the crowd. What had he gotten wrong this time? He'd put Rumblefish at the ladders, Moondog patrolling the Paths, Simon wrangling crews—PooperScoopers to guard bathrooms and Electrolytes to keep the Encore fed with energy, Malachi on the final sweep. So what had he missed?

The access tunnel was packed. Air thick, like breathing through a washcloth. The Encore pulsed color from singing voices—a psychedelic chapel of song and bodies—then he was back in the air, sweat cooling to a prickle on his skin.

The edges of the plateau were mobbed.

A buggy boomed down in the Paths, sound pulsing up the canyon's sides. A final few clambered up from ladders. The *chi-chi-chirrup* had given way to a low murmur, like they knew what was coming. Malachi stood at his post near the tallest ladder, as promised.

On the surface, it all looked good.

But Griff had trained eyes. He knew better. Strangers tried to stop him.

"Hey, brother, Paths are closed—"

"Yo, bro—"

"Bro!"

Griff shoved and twisted his way to Malachi, who looked surprised.

"Hey," Griff said. "What's the status?"

"Handled," Malachi said. "Just did a final sweep."

Malachi looked confident. Like nothing could go wrong. Griff tapped his monocular in his pocket. He twisted past Malachi and grabbed the ladder.

"Whoa, what are you doing?"

"Making sure." Griff knew. He could feel it.

"Bro," Malachi said. "I can't let you go down."

"There's still time," Griff said. "It's not too late."

Malachi gave him a strange, steady look.

"Can I see your scanner?" Griff asked.

"We did what you said. We've gone down there with six full crews," Malachi said, pulling out his Bug Detector. "I've run this thing three times. I'm telling you. There's no one down there."

Griff took the scanner from Malachi. He pointed it down one dark corridor of the Paths. Another. A slight flutter. An underwater shiver. Because it took a practiced hand to find it. A well-trained eye to see. To tune in, you had to live every day knowing you should've been down there. It should've been you.

A tiny light.

The signal he'd chased all the way to the desert.

"No—" Malachi began.

Malachi got in his way. Shouted, and tried to stop him, but Griff moved fast. Stumbled and leapt, and threw himself down into the Paths.

SEVENTY-FOUR

GRIFF KNOCKED AGAINST THE GULLY WALL. LANDED WITH A screaming, aching twist deep in the meat of his foot. But this had been the deal all along. It had to hurt. He had to know he'd done everything he could.

"Move," he told his throbbing foot.

Malachi, shouting. On his transmitter, the green light remained faint. When Griff turned the transmitter left, it vanished. He ran to the right. Hard to focus, with the crowd roaring at him to get out, GET OUT but—

You've got to find them.

Who would leave themselves down here to die?

"Hello!" Griff screamed.

Empty booths, lofts, nooks. Griff turned down the right fork of a path, the beacon in his hand glowed green—the right way. He ran toward a dark enclosure in the Paths. Something flashed inside. The sky blocked with ragged tenting.

Griff ran. Not tenting. Clothing.

Gossamer lines strung with armless shirts, legless pants, faceless masks. Lidless barrels and tables jammed the space and he leapt, tripping over a heap of discarded pants, shirts—his injured foot screamed, pulsed in his ankle.

On the table to his left, a flat burlap face.

A crouching figure, straight ahead.

He raced toward it, and the figure sprang and came running.

The detector screamed green and Griff dropped his shoulder into a charge. He would fight. Drag them out. Force them to live. The crowd screamed at a new pitch—like the moment a band takes the stage.

Behind him, the Encore blazed white light.

WHOOMP

The figure he was chasing was Leo.

WHOOMP

The figure was faceless.

WHOOMP

Griff met a stranger in the glass. A boy who had outgrown his camouflage clothing. Pants, short. Shirt, tight. Skin tanned and budding stubble on his cheeks. Intensity in the eyes. Too skinny. And Leo was gone.

"Bro?" Griff asked.

And Leo was gone.

"Leo?" Griff said.

Bring him back. God, please bring him back.

Leo was gone and sound drummed in his ears. Snapping wood. Tearing canvas. Explosive, like a car being dropped from a bridge. Griff's held breath burst into a wet, ragged sob as water reached the curtains. The glass-and-thatch overstory caved with a buckling roar. The expression in the mirror changed. Panicked. And a familiar voice said:

Run, brother. RUN.

SEVENTY-FIVE

TOO LATE TO MAKE IT OUT ALONE.

The enclosure collapsed around the mirror. Curtains jerked from supports, clotheslines whip-snapping like power cables. Avalanche of clothing, stumbling, tripping and pedaling dirt—he could not fall.

Over his shoulder, the Paths were gone.

With jaws of water and wood, the wave had claimed the horizon. Ahead of itself, it pushed a cool breeze of decay—mud, clay, rot. The pain in Griff's foot ballooned. He twisted, grabbed a clot of earth to climb—dust in his fist. Handholds evaporated like mouths snapping shut.

He couldn't climb out.

Ladders, all pulled. Part of his plan. Paths branched left and right, forked again, confusing. He made a curve and remembered the switchback for vehicles. He banked right and crashed into a booth's sharp corner, but the wave had forked with the paths—muddy freshet churning toward him, snapping, swallowing. It tumbled closer and the crowd shrieked.

WHOOMP!

He set his eyes to the Encore.

Sprinting, he stumbled on something sharp and his foot screamed—these strange new objects on the ground—paper, coins, and fabric coming down like snowfall. People tossing objects into the Paths. A giant wishing well. A big goodbye. They were burying him.

A blast of rotten air on his neck.

Colors rippled on the Encore's surface.

He could hear their voices before he heard the words, or recognized his name in the noise. His friends, calling for him. A signal. And slender cords dangling like spider silk, the black only visible when it brushed against the white, and although they looked delicate, Griff knew they held 500 pounds dead weight and 200 swinging.

He could not make out their faces. He tangled his hands in the lines. He used his knees. He pulled and kicked and climbed and fought through hot streaks of pain and sound. They pulled him onto higher ground and he rolled himself over. Shut his eyes, curled on his side. His lungs rose. Fell.

Breathing. Alive.

His friends saved his life with the lines he gave them.

SEVENTY-SIX

THE LOST COAST PREPPERS HAD TRACKED THEM TO DEATH VALLEY. They'd contacted the Nevada authorities, then showed up in person. Dunbar, Scruggs, and Griff's dad. Ultimately, the Clade City team took the lead on crisis response and flood mitigation.

They were pretty proud about it.

By dawn the next morning a low, sad feeling hung thick in the camps, but the air tasted clean. Dust tamped down to clay for hundreds of miles. Without the low mist of loose alkali, blue sky met the desert floor in a bright line.

The Paths were destroyed.

Canvas and poles, lean-tos and huts, shanties and so many small fine things all smashed. But a stir of wonder hung in the air. All across the plateau, above the Paths in every camp—a sweet and unexpected melody. Zippering zippers, clapping car doors. The cadence of planning, seeking.

That hopeful song—*Where to? What next?*

No one knew, except maybe Simon.

He played the disaster site and its visitors like a perfect ring-master. His whole face changing, depending on the audience. With police, a very straight-backed, dour-eyed look. With the old hippie couple in expensive sandals, he leapt around, wild-eyed, shaking his hair and making them laugh. To the cleanup crew, he employed a bashful *aw-shucks, y'all*, and when he spotted Griff his eyes were wide and boyish and full of wonder, the way they'd been the night they met.

"You, my friend," Simon said, "are the best security captain this festival ever had."

They hugged. Griff let the words sink in.

"Thank you," Griff said. "Do you plan to rebuild?"

Simon gave a wild peal of laughter that struck the mountains and ricocheted around them.

"Ah, this whole thing was a wash," he said. "No, no. It's time for some other bit of foolishness. I can feel the wings sprouting from my back. What about you?"

"I don't know," Griff said. "We might get arrested."

"Always a possibility."

"Otherwise—back to the real world, I guess," Griff said.

"Same world as the rest of us," Simon said. "Pick the real you want."

● ● ●

"Zero casualties," Dunbar said in Recovery Hut #2. He looked disappointed.

Griff's dad did not have much to say. He'd lost weight. Dry skin and something with his lips. Thin and gray, like he'd chewed all the color out of them. So Griff had to try. He had to sit down with his father on a crooked bench in the desert and try to explain a shuttle launch to a golden retriever.

"I don't know," Griff said, at the end. "It felt like life or death."

"To be out here?" his father asked.

Griff nodded. His father stared back.

"Was it worth it?" he asked.

"I got to play a Steinway grand," Griff said. "Twice."

"Oh," his father said, perking up. "How was that?"

"Well," Griff said. "It's a damn fine instrument."

His dad smiled and nodded. Griff wiped his eyes. His father held him and it was good to be held. They didn't say much more. He didn't even mention the false alarm.

After the Hydras packed up their site, the crew gathered at Rendezvous Point #5—the Far Side Parking Lot where they'd stashed the ThunderChicken. Rumblefish, Moondog, Alea, Stitch, Charity, and Thomas. The Shady Lane crew set up mist tents for the afternoon heat. Police and travelers and media huddled, everyone wondering—*what's next?*

Rumblefish started playing first.

Just a sweet, low slide guitar desert hymn that sounded like goodbye. Moondog hopped on his cajón and Alea took up the fiddle. Even Stitch picked up a pair of shakers. Charity hummed and sang low, sweet sounds.

Friends drifted away. Dandelion seeds, out to the wind.

The core held. The Cuddlenappers and piano seekers. They played as the sky bled out its last colors, giving up day to dusk. Civil, marine, astronomical. A first shiver.

"Time to go," his dad said.

The words like a cold gust through a crack in the door. What waited for him, out there?

This Aching Life.

Was this all you could hope for? A couple of perfect days in the desert? Griff walked quickly. He approached the song circle. They stopped playing.

Malachi, Alea, Rumblefish, Moondog. His friends.

"It doesn't have to end," Griff said. "We can keep it going."

They looked at him.

"What's your plan, prepper?" Malachi asked.

Rumblefish stopped, put his guitar away. Snapped it into its case.

"You don't have to stop playing," Griff said. "I just—"

"I do, though," Rumblefish said. He wiped his eyes. "That was the best time of my life."

The rest of them held their instruments, not sure what to do. Rumblefish looked them over and walked back to his truck. Griff had to stop him. It was key, somehow, to keeping the whole thing alive. Rumblefish had been the first to welcome them in. He'd brought them to the piano, led the charge to the lagoon—he was the engine!

"Rumblefish!" Griff shouted.

His friend climbed into his truck. Rolled down the window.

"We have a radio station," Griff said. "Where I live. Maybe we can work something out. You could come up and stay with friends, probably Thomas—"

Rumblefish shook his head.

"Don't bother with all that, brother." He smiled, put a key in the ignition. "No recording. No preserving."

His truck started up. A low, rumbling chug. He drove the length of the parking lot. Turning onto the road, he reached his hand out the window. A gentle wave.

The song was over.

SEVENTY-SEVEN

IN THE CAB OF HIS FATHER'S TRUCK, THE PRESSURE WAS ATMO-
spheric. The crushing old smells of upholstery and WD-40.
Same songs on the radio. Same profile of sad dad. The truck's
interior insisting:

It never happened.

Griff grabbed the passenger-side sunshade and flipped
down the mirror.

Just him. His own eyes. Own nose. Lips that had kissed Charity's lips. Sand in his hair. Grit, clotted under his fingernails.

He'd carry the desert home with him. A flash of light in the
mirror and Griff gasped.

Flickering red and blue.

"Dunbar?" his dad said. "Jesus Christ."

"Oops," Griff said.

They pulled over.

The lights weren't quite right. Red, blue, gold, purple, green.
Wild surges and flickers.

Griff's father rolled down the window, leaned out.

"Hey there!" called a familiar man in a wide-brimmed hat.

"Can I help you?" his dad asked.

"Yes, sir," Cowboy said. "We've got a problem. A big, one-
thousand-pound problem."

His father sighed. "We've had a really long day—"

"See," Cowboy interrupted. "We've got a 1924 Steinway

grand piano. Little dusty. But a nice little instrument. It's packed up on a trailer, currently homeless. Simon advised you've got a hitch and plenty of horsepower."

His father stared back.

"We'd love to give it to you," Cowboy said. Big, toothy smile.

"A Steinway grand?" his father asked.

"The whole thing?" Griff said. "I—"

"Absolutely," his father said.

"Well, good," Cowboy said. "Y'all sit tight. We got this."

Cowboy gave a loud whistle. Feet crushed onto the grit.

Griff smiled. "We get to keep the piano?"

"Well," his dad said. "It is a damn fine instrument."

CLADE CITY FINALLY HAD ENOUGH. THEY CAME FOR THE SIREN.

It went down the night after the second false alarm, right after Dunbar left town. First one man tried to shoot it, the way they'd gotten the lighthouse, but the bullets just ricocheted all over. Broke every window in the K-NOW studio, one window at the Drift Inn, and went through Scruggs's favorite leather jacket. The siren didn't flinch. Plan B—as captured on security camera—required teamwork. Four people showed up with a cherry-picking ladder, a pickup, and a chain saw. When the siren dropped, it left an impact crater. Like ripples fanning out from a stone dropped in a dark pond.

The group loaded up the siren in the bed of a pickup with a duct-taped license plate and drove away. Conventional wisdom says the siren took a trip to Swan Dive Peak that night and ended up in the ocean. They'd find it when the Great Big One finally hit. Eventually, it would wash right back up on Main Street.

"Will probably still work," Scruggs said. "Can't kill them things."

"Sons of bitches," Dunbar said.

Like most crimes in Clade City, everyone knew who did it. They also knew two false alarms was one too many, and the lighthouse had been a step too far. When the city council voted on funding to restore K-NOW's windows, Griff's father introduced a measure to repair what could be fixed in the lighthouse and restore the half-shell amphitheater for a summer concert series. The Tripp family contributed the piano, as an in-kind donation. It was worth over 80,000 dollars.

That spring, Mr. Tripp gained back some weight. Bizarre projects slowly resurfaced in the basement—grinding lenses for his own telescope, befriending a Tsunami Sister City in Japan. The most shocking moment happened in the kitchen, and began with a mechanical roar so loud it pulled Griff from piano practice, through the French doors, down the hall.

His parents were wearing giant parrot hats.

"Why are you blending margaritas?" he said.

"You wouldn't understand," his dad said. "Music is a big part of our lives."

His mother cackled. Turned up the radio.

"Jimmy Buffett?"

"I hope we're not late," his mom said, looking at her phone.

"Are you going to a show?" Griff asked. He couldn't imagine a venue within 200 miles.

"Oh, shoot. It's in Vegas," she said. "I don't think we'll make it."

They nuzzled their parrot hats in a disquieting manner.

"We never make the show," Griff's dad said, being sly.

His father was supposed to be done drinking. Now they were drinking together. Griff didn't know. They seemed happy right now.

"You'd better make at least one show this year," Griff said.

This May they were finally going to give Leo the show they'd promised him.

Over the last six months, he, Thomas, and Charity had worked off the bulk of their community service in the Ruins. Their concert was the first in the summer series. Scruggs had agreed to broadcast the full show on K-NOW, and was helping with promotion:

"This Saturday, folks. Circle your calendars. A local trio. Survivors of the Great Desert Rescue and our first summer show at the restored half shell. You can catch them there and right here at the end of the dial at the end of the world—"

They'd struggled with a band name. Thunderbirds, Touchdown Jesus.

They settled on the False Alarms.

By late April, the school hallways were buzzing the way they had about the Urchin, and Griff was increasingly uneasy. There hadn't been a show in the Ruins in decades. People might not even know how to find them. Griff expected about fifty friends and family. Thomas estimated between one and three thousand.

On the morning of the show, Griff peeled down through the layers of coats in the hallway and found his dad's camo jacket. Tight in the shoulders. Riding too far up on the wrists, but it was the only thing to wear today. And it looked all right in the mirror.

Three hours before showtime, Griff drove his dad's truck to the venue for sound check. Overcast. Mid-fifties. Maybe no one would come, but there was a police officer stationed at the floodgates. Griff had never seen them open before. The officer grinned and waved him through. When Griff arrived at the half shell, their designated city employee had come early, waiting in his white truck.

"This is happening," Griff told himself.

On stage, the Steinway. Even the grand piano looked small in the heart of the wide arched structure they'd cleaned and swept and scrubbed and scraped and painted. One microphone. A sound board. Set like a banquet. Griff's hands ached to play.

First—he left the parking lot and walked toward the ocean. Crossed the grass they'd weeded and replanted. Went to the ribbon of beach where breakers pounded sand flat and foam popped and whipped around like flimsy kites.

"Thank you," Griff said.

He'd been saying thank you since the desert. Thank you to his lungs for breathing, his heart for beating. The sun and moon. This time, who was he thankful for? Leo? The ocean? The whole world? He looked back at the piano.

"I wish you could see it, bro."

A muffled sound drew his eyes. Charity, closing her car door.

She walked toward him. Windblown hair, long skirt. He hadn't seen her outside of practices in weeks. The desert hadn't changed anyone as much as Charity Simms. New friends in Portland. She'd been to LA three times this year. Two bands. Side projects. Every time she left, she came back stronger in herself. Like she'd slowly turned from straw to wood to steel. She still called late at night. Texted short bursts, like Morse code. He felt like he still saw Charity through the small, shrinking window of Clade City, and she was an expanding universe.

He wondered how long she'd stay in his orbit once school got out.

He was grateful for however long he had.

"Making peace with the sea gods?" Charity asked. She hugged him. A good, long hug.

"Gotta buy this town one more night," he said.

"What did you offer?" Charity asked.

"Stale chocolate? What do we got?" He thrust his hands into the pockets of the coat, reaching deep. In the low fold of the right pocket, something jabbed his finger.

"Ah!"

"What's wrong?" Charity asked.

He wrapped his fingers around it. Stopped breathing. Wind blew damp on his cheeks.

He pulled it out slowly.

A puzzle piece.

Cardboard backing. On the other side, water, and a white glimmer.

Griff held it up to the sea.

"Leo, you motherfucker," he said. It felt good to say it. Leo could be a motherfucker. It was so precisely him. Clever and bold and a little mean. Something like *she's mine.* Something like *I love you.*

Charity gasped. "Unreal," she said.

It was an artifact from another life.

"His, I guess." Griff moved to throw it. Charity grabbed his wrist.

"You keep that," she said. "That's yours."

They held hands, walking back across the grass toward the stage. He walked as slow as she'd let him.

"Look what we made," Griff said. "Aren't you so glad you live here?"

"I'm glad right now," Charity said.

cchhirChirChirChhheeeeeeepCHEEEP!

The ThunderChicken careened into the parking lot— Thomas double-parked beside the stage. Removed large orange cones from his trunk, labeled VIP PARKING.

"Seriously," Griff said.

He unspooled yellow caution tape. Put on his sunglasses. Pink cowboy hat.

"Hello, Clade City!"

The city employee, who had been lingering beside his truck, climbed back inside. Thomas unsnapped a card table. Set a box on top.

"C'mon. Check it out. Merch. Get a whiff."

He opened the box to the benzine tang of permanent maker—it smelled just like Thomas Mortimer. Thomas pulled out T-shirts—stick figures playing under the shadow of a crushing tidal wave, wild-haired punk rockers straddling a fault-line fissure, a three-part harmony sung within the stem of a mushroom-cloud explosion. Each T-shirt with giant, hand-drawn letters:

THE FALSE ALARMS

"My god," Charity said. "How many did you make?"

"A hundred?" he said.

Charity looked across the empty parking lot.

"There are a few more boxes, in back."

"Is this your big mystery project with my dad?" Griff asked. "T-shirts?"

"No," Thomas said. "You insult me, Tripp. Get on stage."

Thomas rigged up the microphones. Griff sat at the piano. Stood and adjusted the bench. Sat again. The view from the stage was stunning. Right there ahead of him, the ocean slipped off the horizon and wrapped around the whole wide world. Could they make it beautiful enough? He looked at his fingers. Nervous. Excited.

"Sound check!" Thomas said.

"Don't we need that guy?" Charity asked, pointing to the man in the truck.

"Forget about that guy," Thomas said. "This is for us. And for Leo. This is critically important. This is everything."

"Okay," Griff said.

"Okay," Charity said.

"Listen carefully. Now, Griff," Thomas said, miming his instructions. "I clap three times. Then you send one giant, mother-loving chord out there. A big one. Way out past the breakers. All the way to Atlantis."

"Happy to," Griff said.

"Right after the claps," Thomas said. "No waiting."

"I got it," Griff said.

Griff raised his hands over the keys. Thomas raised his hands to the microphone, looking nervous. He clapped once.

The sound boomed over land and sea. A large wave labored toward shore.

Thomas clapped a second time. A third.

Before Griff's fingers could drop, the wave crashed—*HOOM!*

The lighthouse exploded with color. A flash of white, swallowed by blazing blues and purples, greens and golds. Their faces glowed.

"Ah, Griff," Thomas said. "I think he beat you to it."

The man in the vest got out. He clapped. Colors danced over his face and the white truck. He reached inside and honked, clapping again.

The three friends drifted together on stage. They held each other. Swayed the way a bridge sways so it doesn't break. The song came to them just as it had that night in the ocean, growing stronger with touch. Their energy turned to music and their music reached for words they'd all heard once before and still remembered:

Out here on the water—I sing the ocean song—
Out here on the water—we know we won't be long—

The final lines of the chorus came just in time. Maybe they'd heard the lyrics in the Paths, or out on the Skip. A whisper from the ocean, or a ghost. Later, they decided the end had been there all along, just waiting for them to find the words:

Be the lighthouse.
Be the lighthouse.

ACKNOWLEDGMENTS

A WRITER MIGHT CHOOSE TO LIVE AND WRESTLE WITH A CHALLENGING project for years, which means innocent bystanders must then live and wrestle with a challenging writer. As Rachel Carson wrote—"In nature, nothing exists alone." If you have helped me to become a better writer or a better person, you've effectively done both. I am grateful for you all. To name just a few:

Endless gratitude to Emily—teacher, mother, wife, and fearless first reader. She'd make a hell of a Pacific lighthouse keeper, but prefers Midwestern lakes. Thank you, Tobias and Sahalie, for your story-themed LEGO creations, enthusiastic applause of finished drafts, and for lending your dad to this story.

Thank you, Mom and Dad, for instilling the foundational love and support that gives me the confidence to make questionable choices, such as being a full-time writer and living near a fault line.

Thanks to Teacher Deb and Teacher Chris, who quietly live their lessons every day, but will pause to clarify and make large signs for those of us who need assistance.

Thank you, George and Paula Saunders and Mary Karr, for giving me what felt like an MFA in life, love, and writing on Patmos. You were so brilliant I threw my book away and started over. A special, full-throated howl at the moon for Flaminia, Katie, Sofie, Karl, Alina, Thaddeus, and Teresa, who will read poetry and sing and dance and swim without ever once being asked. I love you always.

Thank you, Jenny, Dan, Satchel, and Weezie for giving us

a safe harbor to howl from. And the Oregon Arts Commission and Oregon Community Foundation for the Career Opportunity Grant, which helped me find my way to the island.

Thank you, Charlie Ruff and Robin Bernardi—you are living, breathing doors to magic, and introduced me to the Oregon Country Fair and Culture Jam. I'm grateful to have never recovered. Thank you, Andy, for housing the bookmobile, and building a people-powered engine for turning dreams into reality. Thank you, Simon, for finding us on the Paths.

Thanks to David Wimbish and The Collection, who caused me (twice) to travel thousands of miles just to see them perform, and Matt Hopper for writing "False Alarm" and playing the finest "Harvest Moon" I've ever heard. Thanks to Blind Pilot for stirring my first imaginings of this book, and to Israel Nebeker for leaving the window open to synchronicity.

Thank you to the wonderful Rotem Moscovich for cutting the dock lines and dropping the sails on this project and Heather Crowley for helping it along. Great Big Thanks to Abby Ranger, who blazed through piles of supposed eloquence to the bones of a real, living story. Your editorial letters should be framed and bowed to. Thank you, Alvina Ling, Ruqayyah Daud, Victoria Stapleton, Liz Kossnar, and Hannah Milton for welcoming me with kindness and grace to my new home at Little, Brown as if I'd been here all along.

Agent Sara Crowe—let it be said—has struck a mythic balance between kindness and efficiency which could be studied and turned into a spiritual philosophy. Big thanks to you and all the Pips!

Thank you to SCBWI, who helped open the door to publication, and the Mudflat Heathens of Western Washington—one of the finest, dirtiest, most eloquent and profane groups I've ever run across. You're writers to the bone.

Thanks to Hunter Noack for saying "yes" when I asked him to wear a burlap suit and play his Steinway in the desert, and to Thomas Lauderdale for his irrepressible brilliance and contagious generosity. You both stretch the world wider than it would otherwise be.

Thank you, Bob Malmquist, for gathering a lifetime of radio knowledge and sharing it with me one sunny afternoon in Nebraska. SubWatch wouldn't be the same without you.

Thank you, Tamathy, for reading piles of manuscripts and treating each one like something special. You are a true master of art and story, and I learn from you always.

Thank you, Anna, for doing a late read and giving wonderful advice and feeling everything that was there.

Much gratitude to pianist and composer Alexander Schwarzkopf, whose mind could set a piano on fire just by thinking about it. Thank you for your insight on musical semantics, Liszt lore, and helping me strike the right tone.

Thanks to the friends and family of the Kesey Farm Project—Shannon, Jay, Sunshine, Sheryl, Kate & Kate—for your endless generosity and willingness to plow toward dreams with spark and grit—it's lovely to know you.

Thank you to the ALA, the ABA, and PNWBA for your support of the road trip and everything after, and to the many friends I met along the way. Thanks to Bruce Springsteen and AC/DC, who taught me it's a long way to the top if you want to rock and roll.

Thanks to the vibrant communities of the Pacific Coast and the kindnesses you've shown me over the years, including my friends in Crescent City and SeaQuake Brewing for some great pints and a tour of your emergency response facilities. What a blast! Thanks to everyone who ever dug a posthole for a tsunami evacuation sign, recorded a PSA, braided a paracord, tested a siren, or handed out a pamphlet on disaster preparedness. The science is real.

To any writer who has stolen my breath or made me leap up and curse aloud at the quality of their prose—Tobias Wolff, Toni Morrison, Rachel Carson, Mary Karr, L. Lamar Wilson, George Saunders, Robin Wall Kimmerer, Laini Taylor, Ray Bradbury, Hanif Abdurraqib, Tim O'Brien, John Steinbeck, Natalie Babbit—thank you for showing me how it's done.

And, finally, I wish to thank John Engman for giving the profound gift of his poetry to the world, whether or not he knew anyone was listening. We were listening. Someone is always listening. Thank you, artists, for trusting this is true.

Shine the light. Bring the noise. The world needs you always.

J. C. GEIGER

(jcgeiger.com) survived an earthquake on the Mouth of Hell volcano in Nicaragua, learned to drive stick shift on a bookmobile, and once fell asleep while running. He also writes fiction. He is a GrandSLAM Story Champion at The Moth, and his work has appeared on stage at The Second City and No Shame Theatre. His debut novel, *Wildman*, was named by Bank Street as a Best YA Book of the Year. J. C. lives about 60 miles from the Oregon coast and makes the trip as often as he can.